SKELME

D0854359

AUTHOR	CLASS
PEARCE, MARY E.	F

TITLE	
Jack Mercybright	

Mary E. Pearce, a Londoner by birth, now lives in the relative peace of Gloucestershire. She tackled various jobs – shop assistant, filing clerk, waitress, usherette – before settling down to write seriously in the 1960s. Her career began with the appearance of short stories in magazines and has led to the publication of nine highly successful novels.

Praise for Mary E. Pearce:

"A keen eye for beauty in everyday things"
Sunday Telegraph

"Warm and vivid" *Publishers Weekly*

"About the human nature of people which is Mary Pearce's secret . . . The dialogue both convinces and entertains" *Manchester Evening News*

"All the characters are drawn with warm understanding and humour"   *Eastern Daily Press*

MARY E. PEARCE OMNIBUS

Jack Mercybright and *The Sorrowing Wind*

Books Two and Three
of The Apple Tree Saga

WARNER BOOKS

08383099 6

A *Warner* Book

This omnibus edition published by Warner Books in 2000

Omnibus edition © Mary E. Pearce 2000

Jack Mercybright first published in Great Britain in 1974
by Macdonald and Jane's Publishers.
First published in paperback by Warner Books in 1993.
The Sorrowing Wind first published in Great Britain in 1975
by Macdonald & Jane's Publishers.
First published in paperback by Warner Books in 1993.

Jack Mercybright copyright © Mary E. Pearce 1974
The Sorrowing Wind copyright © Mary E. Pearce 1975

A CIP catalogue record for this book
is available from the British Library.

ISBN 0 7515 3130 8

Printed and bound in Great Britain by
Mackays of Chatham plc, Chatham, Kent

Warner Books
A Division of
Little, Brown and Company (UK)
Brettenham House
Lancaster Place
London WC2E 7EN

No, I'm a man, I'm full a man;
You beat my manhood, if you can.
You'll be a man if you can take
All states that household life do make:
The love-tossed child, a croodlèn loud,
The boy a-screamèn wild in play,
The tall grown youth a-steppèn proud,
The father staid, the house's stay.
   No; I can boast, if others can,
   I'm full a man.

William Barnes

JACK MERCYBRIGHT

On cold wet mornings his knee still gave him trouble, and climbing the ladder to cut hay from the stack was a slow, painful business. He was half way down, with the heavy truss balanced on his head, when he saw that the farmer was watching from below. But he took no notice, sensing from past experience that Dennery was in a bad temper.

"What's wrong with you – creeping paralysis?" Dennery asked, following Jack as he limped across the yard to the cow-pens. "You're supposed to be loading mangolds in the clamp-yard."

"I shall get there, don't you worry."

"Your old war-wound playing you up? Is that your excuse for swinging the lead? By God, I've seen old women move faster than you do!"

Jack said nothing, but moved from crib to crib, shedding the hay out as he went.

"Mercybright? – I'm talking to *you*!" Dennery shouted. "You don't mean to tell me that leg's still dicky after all these years 'cos I don't believe it!"

"Then don't," Jack said. "It's no odds to me."

"Not exactly a hero's wound, neither, was it, eh? The way you got hit? Breaking into your own stores?"

"Did I tell you that?" Jack said, surprised, and remembered an evening spent with Dennery at The Drum and

Monkey in Aston Charmer. "I must've had more than a few that night, if I told you that story."

"It'll teach you a lesson not to get drunk, won't it?"

"It'll teach me to be a lot more fussy who I get drunk with, more likely."

"Not a *Boer* bullet!" Dennery said. "Oh, no! An English bullet, that's what gave you that crooked leg, warnt it, eh? That's what you told me. Ent that so?"

"Boer or English, a bullet has pretty much the same effect on a man's knee, all in all. Except that the Boers would've got me in the guts, I reckon, 'cos the way they shoot, they can pick the pip from a cherry without even stopping to take aim."

"The hero of Majuba!" Dennery said. "Something to be proud of evermore! I bet they gave you a medal for that, didn't they? I bet they gave you the bloody V.C.!"

"No, they gave me a month in the cells," Jack said, and returned to the stack for more hay.

While he was up on the ladder, Dennery was called away into the house by his wife, and Bob Franks, the cowman, having been listening in the milking-sheds, came out to the yard to speak to Jack.

"What makes men behave like pigs, I wonder?"

"I dunno. Worry, perhaps. The times is pretty bad for farmers."

"Hah! *He* don't go short of nothing, does he? Nor his missus neither. It's the likes of you and me that suffers. Dud Dennery don't go short of nothing. Oh, no, not he! Yet he don't even fork out to pay for his pleasures."

"What does that mean?"

"My cousin Peggy, skivvy to the Dennerys this twelve-month past, that's what I mean. Don't tell me you hadn't heard?"

"I know the Dennerys turned her out, and I know

Peggy's got a baby, but are you telling me Dennery's its father?"

"Bible oath!" Bob said. "Cross my heart and hope to die! And although Peggy Smith is no better than she should be, I reckon a man ought to pay for the trouble he brings on a woman, don't you?"

"Why don't her father see about it?"

"What, my uncle Sydney? He wouldn't ask you to tell him the time! And what'd Dennery likely do? He'd laugh in Syd's face just as surely as pigs see wind."

"Ah, he's a mean bastard," Jack agreed. "There's no better side to *his* nature."

And he walked away, wondering why a young girl like Peggy, pretty enough to take her pick among the young men of Aston Charmer, should have let a middle-aged sot like Dennery get near her.

When he got to the clamp-yard he found that the farm-boy, Noah Dingle, had already filled the cart with mangolds and was trying to urge the old horse, Shiner, up the steep track towards the pasture.

"Can't budge him!" he said. "I been trying a good ten minutes but he won't budge no more'n a fraction!"

"Your load's too heavy," Jack said. "Poor old Shiner will never pull that." He climbed onto the load of mangolds high in the tip-cart and began pushing at them with the pitchfork, so that they rumbled out onto the cobble-stones below. "How would *you* like to have to pull a load the size of this lot here?" he asked.

"Mr Dennery said pile 'em up well. He said to save on too many journeys."

"You don't save much if you kill the horse."

Jack had the cart about half emptied when the farmer came into the yard from the dairy and began shouting at the top of his voice.

"What in hell's name do you think you're doing? I told that boy to fill to the cratches and when I give an order I want it obeying!"

Jack took no notice, but went on forking out the mangolds. A few of them rolled to Dennery's feet and he had to skip smartly out of the way.

"Do you hear me, blast you, or are you deaf as well as idle?"

"I hear you," Jack said, "but I only listen when you talk some sense and you ent talking much sense this morning, master. Shiner's too old to pull big cartloads. He ent got the strength nor the breath neither so why break his heart?"

"Christ Almighty!" Dennery said. "We'll see if he's got the strength or not! I shall soon shift him – just you watch me!"

He went to the horse, took hold of its tail with both hands, and twisted it sideways. Shiner gave a loud whinny of pain and danced a little on the cobbles, but, being a prisoner between the shafts, could not escape his tormentor's hands.

"Another bit more?" Dennery shouted. "Will another twist shift you, you lazy brute, 'cos there's plenty more if that's how you want it!"

Jack got down from the back of the tip-cart and caught hold of Dennery by the arm, swinging him round in a wide circle. Then he hit him full in the face and sent him sprawling against the cart.

"If you want to twist someone's tail," he said, "go ahead with twisting mine – I've got used to it these past two years."

"By God, that does it!" Dennery said, wiping a smear of blood from his nostrils. "That flaming well does it, believe you me! You've done for yourself this time, I can tell you, and no two bloody ways about it!"

"I was thinking the same thing myself," Jack said, "almost to the very words."

"You're sacked off this farm! As from this minute! You can drop what you're doing and get moving without delay!"

"Suits me. I dunno why I ent gone sooner."

"Then get off my land, you useless limping swine, you!"

"I'm going, don't worry."

"Then what are you standing gawping for?"

"I was wondering if I'd fetch you another clout, that's all, before I got moving."

"You touch me again and I'll have you up for assault, man, and Dingle here shall be my witness."

"It's all right. You can breathe easy. It ent worth scraping the skin off my knuckles for. But ent you got a sleeve to wipe your nose on? You're getting blood all over your waistcoat."

Jack went to the cart and began unharnessing the horse, Shiner. He undid the traces and let the cart-shafts fall to the ground. Then he took off collar, pad, and mullen, and gave them to the boy Noah Dingle, who stood with eyes and mouth wide open.

"What do you think you're doing with that there horse?" Dennery demanded.

"I'm taking him with me," Jack said.

"Oh no you're not! I'll see you burning in hell first!"

"Oh yes I am. I'm buying him off you for ten pounds."

"Ten pounds? Don't make me laugh! Where would *you* get ten pounds?"

"I've got it right enough and it's money just as good as the next man's."

"I should want to see it, though, before I let you take that horse off this farm."

"You won't never see it 'cos I'm paying it over to Peggy Smith. You know the whys and wherefores, so don't ask awkward questions or the boy here will learn a bit about your private business. If he don't know all about it already."

"I'll have the law on you, Mercybright, for stealing that horse from off my farm!"

"Do," Jack said, "and maybe the law'll be interested to know about Peggy's misfortunes at the same time."

Dennery glared. He was swearing quietly under his breath.

"What's your interest in her?" he asked, sneering. "The same as most men's?"

"No," Jack said. "I've got enough weaknesses one way and another but women ent one of 'em, thank God."

He took a hold of Shiner's halter and led him round towards the gateway.

"You're not going to get away with this!" Dennery shouted, following half way across the yard. "I'll fix you good and proper, you lopsided swine, you, and you'll be sorry for today's doings, believe you me! I'm pretty well known in these parts, remember, and I'll see to it you never get work on none of the other farms around here, not if you try from now till Domesday!"

Jack did not stop. He merely glanced back over his shoulder.

"Then I'll have to try farther afield, shan't I?" he said, shrugging.

He went to his lodgings at Jim Lowell's cottage, put his few clothes into his old canvas satchel, and took his savings from under the mattress. Mattie Lowell saw him off at the door.

"Off again, wandering?" she said to him. "It's time you

was settled, a man your age, instead of always on the move. – Settled and married to a sensible wife."

"I shall have to keep my eyes open," he said, and kissed her fat cheek. "If I find one like you, I'll snap her up straight away."

When he called at the Smiths' cottage, Peggy was alone there, except for the big ungainly lurcher bitch, Moll, and the month-old baby boy, Martin, asleep in a clothes-basket on the settle. The kitchen was steamy and smelt of hot bread.

"Ten pounds?" Peggy said, suspiciously. "How come Dennery sends me ten pounds?"

"I've walked off with Shiner," Jack said, "and I'm paying for him by paying you." He dropped the money into her pocket. "It's all quite genuine, every coin."

"I don't want Dud Dennery's money! Nor yours neither!"

"It ent a question of what you want. You think of your baby for a change. That's money put by for him when you need it."

"Him!" Peggy said. "Little mullocking nuisance!" But her sullenness melted as she looked at the baby in its cot. "Money for him, the trouble he's brought me!"

"You've brought him as much. More, maybe."

"Oh, is that so? And what does he know of trouble, I wonder? All he ever does is eat and sleep!"

"He'll know it soon enough, the start you've given him."

"And what about me? Who'll marry me now, saddled with Sonny there all my days?"

"Some chap will marry you, sooner or later."

"Not you, I don't suppose?"

"I've just bought a horse. I can't afford a wife as well. Besides which, I'm on the move."

"And where are you heading for, looking for work?"

"I dunno. Wherever the fancy happens to lead me. Then it just depends what offers."

"That won't be much at this time of year, but I wish you luck of it all the same. Is there anything I can do for you before you go, Jack Mercybright?"

"Yes," he said. "You can give me one of them hot new loaves and a tidy hunk of cheese to go with it. I shall be fammelled by the time I've walked a mile or two."

"Why walk, for goodness' sake? Can't you ride Shiner?"

"Ah. So I can. That's a good idea."

People stared at him, sitting up on the old grey's back, going at a walking pace through the village, and one or two even nodded a greeting. But nobody spoke to him. Aston Charmer was that sort of place. He had come to it only two years before and now, leaving it, he was still a stranger.

At Charmer's Cross he had a choice of six roads. He took the one going due southwards. And as he went he turned up his collar against the cold rain blowing behind him.

A dozen times during the day he stopped at farms to ask for work, but it was a bad time of year and he met with refusals everywhere. So he travelled on, along the narrow winding lanes, between dripping hedgerows, looking out over the wintry landscape, featureless under the wet hanging greyness.

At about dusk, he came to an old derelict cottage, lonely beside a bend in the road, and decided to shelter there for the night. The garden was a wilderness and beyond it, through a little rickety gate, was an old orchard of perry pear trees, planted on steeply rising ground. He let Shiner into the orchard, then he entered the cottage and lit a fire on the open hearth-place.

There was plenty of wood about the place and he built a good blaze, sitting before it, on the floor, eating a portion of Peggy Smith's bread and cheese and drinking beer he had bought along the way. And gradually, as his clothes dried, the heat of the fire worked through his body, thawing him out and easing his cold, stiff, aching muscles. Once warm, he buttoned himself into his jacket and lay down full length on a bed of straw, heaped against the driest wall. He fell asleep in a matter of minutes.

Some small sound awoke him: light footsteps crossing the threshold; hands fumbling against the door-post. He raised his head and saw, dark against the open doorway, the shape of a girl dressed in a long hooded cape.

"Bevil?" she whispered, and then, a little louder: "Bevil? Are you there?"

Lying perfectly still, Jack heard her soft exclamation of anger, with a little sob of disappointment in it that told him she was very young. For a moment she stood there, peering all round into the darkness, and tapping her foot on the stone step. Then, with another angry exclamation, she turned and swept out again, her cape brushing the briars at the doorway.

Jack turned over and went back to sleep, only to waken a little later as another step crossed the threshold. This time a youth stood framed in the doorway: small, slim, with a shock of untidy light-coloured hair.

"Nenna?" he said, and even at a distance of ten feet or so, Jack caught a strong smell of drink on the air. "Nenna, are you there?"

And, receiving no answer, he also departed from the cottage. But whereas the girl had gone away angry and disappointed, the young man went out with his hands in his pockets, singing aloud as he sauntered down the lane.

"Oh, Mary had her hair down;
It reached her knee below;
For she was afraid, this pure young maid,
Her nakedness to show . . ."

The voice faded and died in the distance; silence came back to the ruined cottage; and Jack settled down again as before.

"Perhaps now," he said to himself, "a man may be able to get some sleep!"

In the morning, while his can of water was boiling, he walked about inspecting the cottage. It was very old, built with a sturdy timber framework and clay infilling, now mostly fallen out, so that only the criss-cross beams remained. The thatch was almost all gone from the roof; so were the floorboards of the upper storey; but the brick-built chimney stood intact and the oak framework was perfectly sound, and in his mind's eye he saw it as it must once have been: its timbers well tarred, its panels whitewashed, its casements gleaming in summer sunlight: all trim and neat among its fruit trees.

Across the garden, there were two brick-built sheds and a lean-to, with tools and a ramshackle cart inside. So the cottage, it seemed, had once been the farmhouse, displaced, probably, by some larger, more modern building elsewhere. He could not see where, because grey wet mist still curtained the landscape.

While he walked about, trying the timbers with his shut-knife, a peremptory voice called out to him, and two women came down the orchard. One, very young, dressed in a dark red hooded cape, was the girl Nenna of the night before. The other was a woman of perhaps thirty, with strong features and a high colour in her cheeks, and dark hair severely braided over her ears. They came through the gate into the garden, and the older woman spoke sharply.

"You're trespassing here. Do you realize that?"

"I do now you've told me," Jack said.

"This land is mine. This cottage is mine. I don't like tramps lighting fires in my buildings. You might very easily have burnt the place down."

"I ent, though, have I, as you see for yourself?"

"Is that your horse up there in my orchard? What right have you to make free with my grazing?"

Jack took his hand from his trousers pocket and offered her twopence.

"D'you think that'll pay for the thistles he's eaten?"

The younger girl smiled but the older one looked more haughty than ever.

"What is your name? Where have you come from all of a sudden? What are you doing hanging about in my cottage?"

"My name is Jack Mercybright. I've come from Aston Charmer, up Woeborough way, and I'm travelling about in search of work. Is there anything else you'd like to know?"

"There's no work here. I'm laying men off at this time of the year, not taking them on. And you'll get the same answer everywhere else about here, especially as –"

"As what?"

"Especially as you seem to be lame."

"That don't stop me working."

"Well, I'm sorry," she said, "but I can't help you."

For a moment she looked at him, hesitating, almost as though she might change her mind. But suddenly her glance fell away and she pushed past him into the cottage. He was left with the girl, who made a wry face at him, repudiating her sister's behaviour. Then she came closer.

"Were you here last night?" she asked in a whisper.

"Yes," he said. "I didn't speak – I thought it'd scare you."

"I knew I smelt woodsmoke, but I thought perhaps Bevil had been here before me."

"He came a bit later. I reckon he must've mistook the time."

"Don't say anything to my sister. She doesn't approve of Bevil, you see. At least, she wouldn't approve of my slipping out at night to meet him."

"Why don't you tell her to go to the devil?"

"I couldn't do that."

"Why not?"

"Well, I'm under age, and she's my guardian. We're not really sisters, properly speaking – Philippa's father married my mother – and I'd have no home if it weren't for her. The whole of the property is hers, you see."

"Aye, I heard her say so," Jack said, "two or three times."

The older woman came out of the cottage, shaking the dust from the hem of her skirt.

"Been checking?" he said. "Been making sure I haven't damaged the straw or sacks or the few old hurdles you've got stored in there?"

"I suppose I'm entitled to safeguard my own property?"

"Since you value your property so much," he said, "why let it fall to rack and ruin?"

Again she gave him a long hard look, and it was some time before she answered.

"Let me give you a word of advice!" she said then. "If you're looking for work, as you say you are, you'd be wise to keep a curb on your tongue. No employer will stand for impertinence and a man of your age ought to realize that. As for me, I'll thank you to get out of my cottage and on your way as soon as possible."

"All right. Just as you say. I'll move on when I've had my breakfast."

And he watched them walking away up the orchard, where the younger girl paused to pat Shiner's neck in passing.

When he was gathering his things together, packing his satchel, he found a bracelet on the floor, which the woman had dropped while searching the cottage. It was solid silver, in hinged halves, and, among some delicate tracery, was engraved with her name: Agnes Philippa Mary Guff. Jack hung it up on a nail in the wall, where it was bound to be seen at once, but then, on second thoughts, he took it down and put it into his pocket instead, deciding to take it to the farm.

On his way up he saw how neglected the fields were: pastureland rank with reeds and mare's tail; hedges and headlands so overgrown with briar and bramble that they measured fifteen feet across; and, in the few poor acres sown with winter corn, the sparse blades were labouring up, sickly and yellow, choked by weeds and poisoned by the rabbits infesting the hedgerows.

The farmhouse was a big square building of grey roughcast walls and brown paint-work, its windows much curtained with lace and velvet, giving it a look of closeness and darkness. He made his way through the back yard, between tumbledown barns, cowstalls, sheds, and arrived at the back door of the house. But as he put up his hand to the knocker, a white bull terrier sprang growling from its kennel under the mounting-block and hurled itself at his outstretched arm.

The dog's big teeth went right through his sleeve and

sank into the flesh of his forearm, penetrating as far as the bone. Jack hit out with his left fist, but the dog only growled more ferociously, closing his eyes and laying back his ears, impervious to the blows on his flat hard skull. The brute was tugging with all his strength, growling and snorting, his jaws clenched as he tried to bring his teeth together through flesh, muscle, sinew, bone.

Jack looked round and saw an old riding-crop hanging up on a hook on the wall. He took it down, thrust it under the dog's collar, and twisted it till the collar tightened. The dog snarled, trying to shake Jack's arm as he would a rabbit, but the collar was now pressing his windpipe. He was gasping and choking; his eyes were rolling, showing their whites; and another twist made him lose his senses. The flat head lolled, the jaws relaxed, and he gave a cough deep in his throat. Jack took out the crop and threw it aside. He took the dog's upper jaw and eased its teeth out of his flesh. The animal slumped down onto the cobbles and lay on its side, its legs rigid.

Jack took off his jacket and rolled up his shirt-sleeve. He was walking across to the cattle-trough when the house door opened and the older sister came out on the step.

"What have you done to my dog?"

"What's he done to me, more like!"

"You shall pay for this, I promise!" she said, and then saw his arm, where the blood was welling up from the punctures. "You'd better come in," she said quickly, and led him into a kind of wash-house.

"Your dog's unconscious, that's all, though he's lucky I didn't choke him to death. I was in the mood for a moment or two."

"You must have taken him unawares. We don't get a lot of visitors here."

"With him as a pet, I'm not surprised."

"Roy's a good house-dog. It's what he's there for. But I'm sorry you've been hurt, all the same." She ran a tap into the sink and held his arm under the icy cold water. "Stay like that. I'll get some ointment."

She went through into the house. He heard her voice in the passage. The girl Nenna came into the wash-house but stood a little way away, white-faced and wincing. Seeing her without her hood, he realized she was young indeed, probably not more than sixteen.

"What's up with you? Don't you like the sight of blood?"

"No. I hate it. It makes me feel sick."

"I ent all that keen, neither, specially when it's my own," he said, "and I'm making a fair old mess of your nice clean slopstone."

The older woman came back again. She turned off the tap and dried his arm. She was quick and efficient, smearing the wounds with carbolic ointment, binding them round with a thick cotton bandage, tying the ends in a neat knot about his wrist.

"Why did you come here, anyway? I thought I told you to take yourself off?"

"I found this," he said, and gave her the bracelet. "You dropped it on the floor of the cottage."

"Did I? How extraordinary! I'd no idea. The catch must be faulty. I shall have to take it to be repaired."

She put the bracelet into her pinafore pocket and became preoccupied, rolling up the spare strip of bandage, replacing the lid of the ointment jar, swilling the last of the blood from the sink. Her manner amused him. He could read her thoughts. He was not surprised by her next words.

"I believe you mentioned you were looking for work?"

"Ah. That's right. But you said you had nothing to offer me."

"Well . . . there's not much to do at this time of year."

"There is on this farm," he said bluntly. "The state it's in, you certainly shouldn't be laying men off. – You ought to be getting them out stirring. Your ditches want cleaning and your hedges want laying and that's nothing more than a bit of a start-off."

"I can't afford to employ a lot of men."

"You can't afford not to, the way things are. Another two or three years of neglect and this here farm will be useless to you."

"Yes! Yes! It's just what I tell them!" she said, in a little burst of passion. "But the labourers here all take advantage, knowing they're dealing with a mere woman."

"Even when that woman is you?"

"I can't *force* them to do things, can I? I can't stand over them with a whip! And, anyway, I don't know enough to decide what's best."

"I know enough," Jack said. "Take me on and I'll set things to rights."

"You're very persuasive."

"I need to be – I'm down to my last eighteen pence," he said.

"I can't afford to pay a bailiff's wages."

"A labourer's wages will suit me."

"Perhaps I do owe you something," she said, "seeing my dog has done you such damage."

"You owe me nothing!" Jack said. "Let's get that straight before we start. You'll be paying me my wages for the work I do, not as compensation for a dog-bite."

"Very well. I'll take you on for a trial period and think again in a month from now. At least I can be fairly sure you're honest, since you brought my bracelet back to me."

"Aye, that's why you left it there, warnt it?" he said. "To see if I was an honest fellow?"

"Rubbish!" she said, the colour flaring even more redly on her cheekbones. "You flatter yourself, I do assure you! Do you think I would risk losing a solid silver bracelet just to test a labourer's honesty?"

"Not much risk, considering how easy it would be to trace me . . . a limping man with an old grey horse . . . travelling about in search of work. You'd have had your bracelet back in no time."

"Utter rubbish, I do assure you!"

"Just as you say," he said, shrugging. "Have it your own way. You're the gaffer."

"Yes," she said, and looked at him with hostile eyes. "Exactly so, Mercybright, and I counsel you to remember it always!"

His arm was so swollen that it stretched the sleeve of his jacket tight. He could scarcely move it. It was stiff to the shoulder and the slightest touch was agony. For three days he could do no work, and spent the time tramping about all over the farm, till he knew every acre from boundary to boundary.

One afternoon, while inspecting the lower fletchers, he met a man named Joe Stretton. It was getting dark, and Jack was prodding the flooded ditch with a long pole, when he sensed someone watching from the opposite side of the hedgerow. The man stood perfectly still, a grey shape in the grey dusk, his head seeming to rest on his shoulders, so short and thick was his huge neck.

"Who're you?" he asked, as Jack stood up and looked straight at him, in between the tall thorns. "You the chap that's been strolling about, poking your nose in everywhere, acting as if you was God Almighty?"

"Ah, that's me," Jack agreed. "And who might you be?"

"My name's Joe Stretton. I work on this farm and have done for nigh on forty years. Except I've been laid off this past two fortnights."

"Are those your snares I seen about the fields?"

"Yes. What of it?" And Stretton raised both his arms up high, above the level of the overgrown hedge, showing the rabbits dangling in bunches from each hand.

"You got something to say about it, have you?"

"No. Nothing. There's too many rabbits about the place so you go ahead and keep them down."

"Who are you to have such a say-so? You a foreman or bailiff or what?"

"I'm just a labourer, same as yourself."

"But why've you been took on here at all, that's what I should like to know? You! – A stranger! – When I've been laid off and others like me?"

"That's just my good luck, I suppose," Jack said.

"And how long d'you reckon your luck'll hold? – From Christmas to Easter, if I know the missus who runs this farm, and then you'll be out on your ear like us others. God Almighty! It makes me spew! I've got a sick wife, did you know that? I've got four children still at school and I've been on this farm since I was a tadpole yet *you* come along and take my job! So what's that Miss Philippa think she's doing?"

"I dunno," Jack said. "You'd better ask her."

Later that day, returning along the edge of Hew Meadow, he caught his foot in one of Stretton's snares and measured his length in the wet mud, falling on his swollen arm. The snare was the usual kind set for rabbits: a running noose of copper wire fixed to a peg stuck in the ground; but the noose was twice the size used for rabbits, the wooden peg twice as strong, and Jack felt sure that the snare had been set on purpose for him: a warning to him that he was not wanted at Brown Elms Farm.

He had set himself to clean out the big main watercourse known as the Runkle, but although he got the waters moving, running clear over the pebbles, the field-ditches remained choked, for the drains and outlets had all fallen in. So he set to work to clean out the ditches, starting in the big Bottom Meadow, working from the bank with the long-handled graffer.

"Still puddling about, making mud pies?" Miss Philippa said, coming to see what he was doing. "When will you start doing something useful?"

"First things first," Jack said, "and that means drainage."

"I hear you're still sleeping at Perry Cottage. You don't need to do that, you know. I could get you lodgings with one of the cowmen."

"Thanks," he said, "but I'd just as soon stay as I am."

"What, sleeping rough like that, in this sort of weather?"

"I'm all right. It don't worry me."

"I might even have a cottage for you, if you prefer to be alone. Up at Far Fetch, beside the wood. You may have seen it."

Jack stood up straight, his legs straddling the wide ditch, his feet wedged in the mud at the sides. He looked up at her, standing above him, among the alders.

"I know the cottage. It's Joe Stretton's. What would you do about him and his family?"

"Stretton would have to go, of course."

"You'd give him the push?" Jack said. "Turn him out to make room for me? Now why is that? Because you think I'm better value?"

"Stretton is a surly malcontent. He's a trouble-maker and always will be. He's been here so long he thinks he ought to be in charge of the farm."

"Then why not *put* him in charge as a proper bailiff? If he's an old hand, he deserves it, surely? A farm runs better if the men have someone to look to for orders, and each one knows exactly where he stands."

"*I* give the orders on this farm."

"Ah. I know. That's why it's gone back the way it has done."

"I warned you before, Mercybright! — I won't be spoken to in that manner by you or by any any other men I employ!"

"And I warn *you*!" Jack said, growing impatient. "If you sack Joe Stretton, you lose both him and me together, 'cos I don't want your blasted cottage nor any lodgings with your cowmen neither! I'm fine and dandy as I am so leave me alone and let me get on with what I'm doing."

He stooped again over the ditch and began shovelling sludge from the bottom, flinging it up to the top of the bank, careless whether it splashed the woman's skirts as she stood above him among the alders. He was tired and wet. His knee was giving him a lot of pain. His arm still ached where the dog had bitten him. And he was suddenly so out of patience that one more word would have set him on his travels again. But the next time he glanced upwards, Miss Philippa was no longer there.

Sitting at his fire in the ruined cottage, he ate his supper of bread and boiled bacon and drank a mugful of strong milkless tea. The night was a wet one. Rain dripped through the floorboards above and squeezed through the walls to trickle down, glistening darkly, inside the crumbling plasterwork. His bedding of straw and sacks was soaked, because there was now no dry place to put it, and as he sat eating, two rats crept out of the deeper shadows to drink from the puddle in the central floor.

He got up suddenly, and the rats vanished. He heard them scampering overhead. He shovelled ashes over the fire and pushed the heap to the back of the hearth-place. Then he put on his oilskin, pulled his cap over his forehead, and went out into the rain, making for Niddup, a mile away down the lane.

The Bay Tree was a small public house, no more than a cottage, standing a hundred and fifty yards or so up on the bank of the River Ennen. Inside, there was light and warmth and tobacco-smoke, a smell of beer and spiced rum, and the sound of a group of bargemen singing, accompanied by one who played the taproom squeezebox.

Jack ordered a rum and a pint of Chepsworth. He drank the rum in one go and carried his beer to the fireside. He sat in a corner of the big settle. The group of bargemen had stopped singing. Their audience broke up and a fair-haired youth of about eighteen came, glass in hand, to sit in the arm-chair opposite Jack.

"I see you drink wisely," he remarked, and, pointing to Jack's mug: "Rum after ale makes a man pale, but ale after rum is good for his tum."

"All men drink wisely when they first begin. It's later on they run into trouble."

"You speak like a man of some experience."

"Seeing I'm probably twice your age, you may well be right, young fellaboy."

"Is your name Mercybright by any chance? I thought it must be! Then you're the new bailiff up at Brown Elms. Allow me to make myself known also. My name is Bevil Ames."

"I'm no bailiff," Jack said. "I'm a plain labourer and get a labourer's plain wages."

"And you skulk in Perry Cottage, eavesdropping slyly on Nenna and me . . . It's a good thing I was late for my assignation that night or you might have been party to a lovers' meeting."

"That girl Nenna is only a child. D'you think it's right to lure her out of doors after dark?"

"Nenna is the one that does the luring. She thinks it's romantic. My own feelings run more with yours. That's why I'm often late for the meetings."

"If you don't care for the girl," Jack said, "why the hell don't you leave her alone?"

"But I *do* care! Heart and soul! She's the one person in all the world who tries to understand me. Besides which, it's only right and proper that a man like me should have an attachment."

"A man like you? And what sort is that when it's at home?"

"Oh, when it's at home it's a dull dog indeed, for it has a father who insists that the law must be its profession. But the truth is – at heart I am a poet!" And the young man, making mock of himself, bowed gravely, one hand pressed against his breast, the slender fingers delicately stretched. "Yes, a poet!" he said. "A man endowed with much sensitivity and refinement of spirit. And yet, as you see, fate constantly thrusts me among the barbarians!"

"Aye," Jack said, glancing at the company gathered in the taproom, "yet they seem to bear it cheerfully enough."

The young man laughed, head thrown back, shaggy fair hair rippling over his collar.

"Drink up, Mr Mercybright, and I'll join you in another. You look as though you could do with a really thorough warming and I know just the thing to do the trick. Come with me and we'll get Sylvanus to make us a jug of his hot rum flip."

While they stood at the counter, waiting, Joe Stretton came in and flung down five or six brace of rabbits. Sylvanus Knarr whipped them away and passed a few coins across instead. No word was exchanged throughout the transaction, but Stretton, finding Jack standing beside him, gave a loud grunt and spat in the sawdust on the floor.

"This used to be a pretty good place for company," he said to Sylvanus, "but it's going off sadly by the look of things."

"If you two chaps've got a quarrel, take it elsewhere," Sylvanus said, and reached for the malt-shovel hanging from one of the beams above. "Otherwise, a fight occurring, both parties get batted with this and my missus here follows it up with a pail of cold water."

"No quarrel," Jack said. "I'd even buy the man a drink if that'd wipe the sneer off his face."

"I'm taking no drinks with *you*!" Stretton said, and walked out.

"Seems you've made an enemy," Bevil said.

"It's a knack I've got," Jack said, shrugging.

When he left The Bay Tree late that night, the rain was falling as hard as ever, but, hunched inside his oilskin cape, he was almost indifferent to it, warmed by the spirit in his veins. And when he lay down on the straw in the cottage, sleep came to him in an instant.

After Christmas, there were two or three weeks of dry, open weather. Jack felt better when the weather was dry; his knee scarcely troubled him at all; and the sight of the teams out ploughing the slopes above the Runkle made the farm seem alive and meaningful for the very first time since his coming there.

When the frosts came, ploughing was halted. Jack had the fields to himself again. He was working on the overgrown hedges in the Home Field now; cutting them back to the very bone; laying the thorns and pleaching them; burning the brushwood in heaps on the stubble. Miss Philippa came there twice a day, stamping the ground with booted feet, fretting because the frosts persisted.

"You see what I mean about the men here?" she said once, warming herself at Jack's fire. "There were four ploughs out at the beginning of the month. – Fourteen days' work done altogether. – Yet all they managed was about forty acres!"

"It's not their fault. It's the state of the ground. And that won't improve till you've got your drains all running again."

"How many years will it take," she asked tartly, "before you've got them cleaned and dug out?"

"How many years did *you* take," he asked, "getting them all choked up as they are?"

She was silent a while, watching him as he forked more brushwood onto the fire.

"You're perfectly free to offer advice, you know, if it's worth hearing."

"Advice is easy. When the frosts ease off you should set more men to work ditching. Joe Stretton, for one, who's been laid off for God knows how long."

"I shall take Stretton back when I see good reason."

"There's work crying out to be done all around. Ent that a good reason? Then I hear his wife's took a turn for the worse. Ent that a good enough reason for you? Not to mention he's got four children!"

"That wife of his is sick in the mind. She ought to be put away in a home. I told Stretton that two years ago and he chose to ignore me. It's his own fault he has no work. Still, I'll think over what you've said, and I'll see what other men I can spare for ditching."

And she went away.

Stretton was often about the fields, going the rounds of his rabbit-snares, helping himself to turnip-tops and spring cabbage, and openly raiding the clamps for potatoes.

Sometimes, too, he was at the cottage, bent on mischief. Jack never caught him, but once when the pump in the yard failed to work, he found clods and pebbles stuffed up the spout, and once he came home to find his tea-kettle hammered flat, nailed to the lintel above the back doorway.

There was an old two-wheeled cart in one of the sheds behind the cottage, and a set of old harness, and one Saturday afternoon, Jack put Shiner into the shafts and drove the six miles into Egham-on-Ennen. He returned with a load of thatching-straw, three balls of twine and a pot of tar, shears, a rake, and a new billhook. He spent the evening splitting hazel spars and withies. He had made up his mind to repair the cottage.

By the end of a week, he had cleared the last of the old rotten thatch, brushed the beams and rafters clean, and replaced those laths that were riddled with worm. On Sunday morning he started thatching and in the afternoon he had a visitor.

"What are you doing?" a voice asked, and, looking down, he saw the girl Nenna standing below at the foot of the ladder.

"What's it look like I'm doing?" he said. "I'm putting a new roof on this cottage, ent I?"

"Do you mind if I watch you?"

"Suit yourself. It's all as one to me."

"You seem to be good at this work," she said.

"Well, I worked with a thatcher at one time of day, years ago when I was a boy."

"Does Philippa know you're repairing the cottage?"

"I daresay she does. She don't miss much of what goes on around her property."

"You'll have to watch out or she'll soon be asking you for rent."

"She can ask. She won't get it."

"She might even sell it."

"She might so. I couldn't stop her."

He came down from his ladder to fetch more straw, and the girl watched him as he wet it and combed it into yelms. She sat on the staddle-stone nearby, her hood thrown back, her hair a bright red-gold in the sunlight. Her face was rather beautiful, the features small and neatly made, the skin very pure and honey-coloured, the eyes and lashes unexpectedly brown. Although so young, she had a direct way of looking at people, and the set of her chin suggested a strong and resolute will.

"Doesn't it worry you," she asked, "that you might have all this work for nothing?"

"I like having something to do," he said. "It keeps me from moping."

"Why should you mope?"

"Don't you, ever?"

"Yes. Sometimes."

"Then don't ask silly questions."

"But it's different for a man. You can do what you like. You're independent."

"Doing as you like always costs you something."

"Does it?" she said. "Yes, perhaps it does. But aren't you willing to pay the price?"

"Maybe. Maybe not. The trouble is, we never know what the price is until afterwards, and then it's too late to change our minds."

"I must go," she said, moving suddenly. "I'm meeting Bevil down by the river. He's taking me on a barge to Yelland."

"And is he bringing you back again?"

"Of course," she said, laughing. "More's the pity!"

When she had gone, he climbed the ladder with the yelms of straw in a piece of sacking, and set to work on the "eyebrow" arching over the second dormer. He had worked since first light, and, looking along the stretch of shaggy yellow thatch, now almost covering this side of the roof, he was well pleased.

About mid-afternoon, from his perch on the roof, he saw Joe Stretton going home across the orchard with a bundle of firewood on his shoulder. Jack was suspicious, for Stretton had woods at the back of his own cottage, and he watched till the man went out of sight among the bushes behind the cartshed. He was still looking out, wondering what mischief Stretton was up to, when something came hurtling through the air and flashed past him. It was a blazing bundle of birch twigs, with a four-pronged hook at one end, and, the hook catching in the dried-out thatch, the whole roof was ablaze in an instant, the flames whoomphing out to scorch Jack's face and set his shirt and waistcoat burning. The heat was such that even the newly wetted straw was set alight between his hands.

He slid down the ladder and ran to the cartshed, but although it contained a great variety of tools, there was no swat-pole or thatch-lifter to be found among them. All he had was an old pitch-fork and already, when he returned, the new thatch was shrunk to a mat of black ashes, burning through the thick oaken laths, which were dropping in flaming charcoal fragments into the inner part of the cottage. Sparks had fallen in the loose straw strewn about the yard, and now this went up, licking high about the ladder, scorching his boots and the legs of his trousers.

It took two hours and twenty buckets of pump water before he felt sure that every last spark was douted. He sat on the edge of the water-trough, with the stinking wet straw smoking blackly all around him, and rested himself, counting the damage. The cottage was now in worse case than ever. The laths were gone. The rafters were blackened. He had wasted eighteen hours' work, lost a week's wages in thatching materials, and been badly burnt into the bargain. He rose and took a drink of water. Then he set out for Stretton's cottage.

As soon as he knocked, heavy footsteps clattered down the stairs inside, and the door was wrenched open by Stretton himself. Jack took hold of him by his waistcoat. He thrust him against the passage wall.

"I've had about enough of you, Stretton! The time has come to sort things out! So how would it be if I took you and broke your thick ugly neck?"

"Leave go of me!" Stretton bellowed, and shook himself in Jack's grasp, his face contorted. "Leave go and help me for pity's sake!"

Jack stared, appalled at the tears splashing off the man's face. He relinquished his hold and saw that Stretton was smothered in blood. Upstairs, a woman was sobbing.

"It's my wife!" Stretton moaned. "She's in one of her fits and she's cut her wrists open with my razor. God! Oh, God! What next, what next?"

There was a scream and a loud crash. Stretton ran back along the passage and Jack followed him, up the steep stairs, into the bedroom, where the sick, demented woman knelt on the bed, plucking at the rags tied round her wrists.

"Lucy, no!" Stretton groaned, and leant across her, holding her arms and trying to tighten the knotted rags. "Leave them alone, will you! Will you leave them alone, for Christ's sake!"

The woman's face was a terrible colour. There were black circles about her eyes, like terrible bruises, and her lips bore the red raw marks of her teeth, where she had bitten herself in her frenzy. The shift she wore was brown with blood. Her throat and chest were lacerated. Staring at Jack, she wrenched herself free of Stretton's grasp and moved on her knees across the bed, reaching out with her nails as though she would claw at Jack's face.

"I don't want *you!* I know who you are, you cunning devil! You've come to have me put away!"

Jack took hold of her by the arms, forcing her backwards until she lay down. He kept her there while Stretton re-tied the rags on her wrists.

"Have you got any laudanum in the house?"

"I've got some, yes, but she's had a few drops and I'm too damned scared to give her more."

"Get it," Jack said. "She's more danger to herself like this than the laudanum will be."

Stretton went away and returned with a cup. Together they forced her to drink the contents, and gradually she became quiet. The fierce tension went out of her body, and her eyes, from being stretched unnaturally wide, became heavy-lidded.

"Have I been naughty again, Joe? Have I been giving a lot of trouble?"

"You had one of your turns," Stretton said, gently stroking her arm with his fingers. "You was sick again, warnt you, my girl, like you was the last time?"

"I had that pain again in my head. I didn't mean to cause no trouble. I sent the children over to Ivy's. *She* don't mind their screaming and yelling but it hurts me, Joe, when I get this dothering in my head."

"Never mind, old girl," Stretton said. "You're a lot better now and Joe is here to see you get your proper rest."

"Who's this man here? It ent the relieving officer, is it, Joe?"

"No, no. This here's a friend. He called in to see how you was faring."

"That's nice," she said. "We ent got a great many friends, like, have we? I suppose it's because I get so fractious."

"Have you sent for the doctor?" Jack asked Stretton.

"There was no one to send. She seen to it the kids was gone and out of the way before she started. When I got home—"

"I'll go," Jack said. "You stay with her and keep her quiet."

He hurried out and took the short cut across the fields to Niddup. He delivered the message to Dr Spray and waited to see him set out on his pony. Then he went home and began clearing away the mess he had left there.

There was a small coppice of oak about half a mile down the lane from the cottage; he went in the evenings and cut what he wanted; carried the poles home in bundles and split them into laths. Sometimes, up on the roof late at night, working by lamplight, nailing the laths into place, he disturbed the rooks in the hedgerow elms nearby, and they floated above him in the darkness, quietly cawing their disapproval.

On Saturday, when he got home after work, he found a new load of straw in the cartshed, together with twine, spars, withies, and nabhooks. He was washing himself under the pump, still wondering where they had come from, when Joe Stretton walked into the yard-place.

"I sent 'em," he said, "in place of what I burnt last Sunday."

"It's twice the amount of straw that got burnt."

"Is it? So what? I've got a cousin in the trade." He did not try to meet Jack's glance. He stared instead at the roof of the cottage, where the new laths were now all in place. "I'd offer to give you a hand," he said, "only I ent much of a mucher at thatching."

"How's your missus?" Jack asked.

"She's dead," Stretton said. "Yesterday morning, about nine. I thought you'd have heard about it by now."

"I've heard nothing. The men don't speak if they can avoid it. But I'm sorry about it all the same."

"She warnt a bad old girl, really. There was lots worse than my old Lucy. It was only since she got knocked down by that horse and dray in Rainborough that time. She was always a good wife to me before that." He stood for a moment, kicking at the cobbles with the toe of his boot. "The burial's on Tuesday morning," he said. "Niddup church, eleven o'clock. I thought maybe you'd come along."

"Ah," Jack said. "All right. I'll be there."

When Stretton had gone, he went to the shed and brought out the trusses of new straw. He set about combing it into yelms. It was good wheaten straw, grown on heavy land: tough and even: the best to be had. It would last twenty or thirty years. He brought out the rest of the new tackle and climbed the ladder. He was ready to begin thatching again.

Towards the end of March he was out with the other men, ploughing the end field below the Runkle. They watched him with interest, for, being a newcomer, he had the worst plough on the farm: an old-fashioned breast-plough, heavy, cumbersome, badly balanced, that seemed to possess a will of its own. Joe Stretton was also at work and so was his eldest boy, Harvey, a cheeky sprig just twelve years old, helping to lead his father's team.

"How d'you like your plough, then, Jack?" Harvey asked. "Or ent you properly acquainted yet?"

"Well, I've ploughed with some funny things in my time, but I never did come across the likes of this here. It must've been made for a man with three hands and wrists like tree-trunks."

"Out of the Ark!" Stretton said. "Like most of the tackle on this farm. And *she* expects us to work with such rubbish."

"Why not ask for a new plough, Jack?" Harvey suggested, winking and nodding. "Seeing you and Miss Philippa seem such good friends? Ah, and while you're at it, ask if I can have a half day's holiday into the bargain, to go to the sale at Darry Cross."

"I'll ask if you can ride along with her in the trap if you like. I believe she means going to look at some heifers."

"Oh, no!" Harvey said. "I reckon that's your place, Jack, not mine."

Later that day, when Jack knocked off ploughing and led his team home into the stable yard, he found Harvey Stretton giving an imitation of him, watched by Eddie Burston and the two Luppitt brothers. The boy was limping along grotesquely, jerking his body this way and that, pretending to wrestle with an imaginary plough. Jack took no notice. He walked past with Diamond and Darky. But Joe Stretton, coming out of the stables, cuffed the boy and sent him reeling.

"That's enough of that, Clever Dick! Get back to work before I tan you." And to Jack he said, "You've got to watch these youngsters nowadays. Give 'em an inch and they'll take from here to Constantinople!"

Now that the evenings were drawing out, Jack was able to spend more time repairing the cottage. He had finished thatching the main roof. He had made a start on the little wing containing scullery and wash-house. But sometimes he had to wait a while, until he had money to buy materials, and in these between times he worked on the walls: knocking out the old clay and wattle and putting in new, dealing with two or three panels at one time.

He had cut down the hemlock and nettles and tall dead grasses in the garden, and now had two pigs there, cleaning the ground. He also had a goose and a gander keeping Shiner company in the orchard.

One evening in May Miss Philippa drove up the lane from Niddup and stopped the trap outside the cottage. She had often driven that way before; she had seen him working on the cottage; but never once had she mentioned the matter. This evening, however, she was plainly in a difficult mood. She sat in the trap and called out to him in a loud voice.

"Did it never occur to you to ask my permission before interfering with my property?"

"I took it you would've told me pretty damn smartish if you didn't like it. You've seen me at it often enough."

"Perhaps you'd be civil enough to ask me now."

"No, not me, 'cos I hardly know what civil means."

He was up on the ladder, his bucket of moist clay in one hand, his trowel in the other. He turned a little and looked at her fully.

"If you tell me to stop, I shall stop," he said. "If you don't tell me, I shall carry on."

"Where did you get those two weaners?" she asked suddenly, changing tack.

"I bought 'em," he said. "Three shillings the two, from Mr Ellenton up at Spouts Hall. And I got the geese from the same place. Why do you ask?"

"*Bought* them?" she said. "The same way you bought that old grey horse you've got in my orchard?"

"So that's it!" he said. "You've been hearing stories, ent you?"

"I was over at Woeborough market this morning and I met a Mr Dennery, whose farm you were on at Aston Charmer. His story was that you took that horse without so much as a by-your-leave, to spite him when he dismissed you for idling."

"Dennery's a liar. I paid ten pounds for that old horse, but I gave the money to a girl by the name of Peggy Smith, that Dennery had got into trouble. Did he happen to mention them little details?"

"No. He didn't. And it's only your word against his."

"That's right," Jack said. "It's up to you to choose, ent it?"

"I shall ask Mr Ellenton when I see him, whether he sold you those pigs or not, for I'm not at all sure I can trust you, Mercybright."

"You don't trust nobody," Jack said. "But you go ahead and check by all means. It'll give you something to pass the time."

She flipped at the pony and drove away. Jack turned back to his work on the cottage. When he saw her again the next morning, and in the days following, the matter of the pigs was not mentioned. She had no doubt checked the truth of his story: she was that sort of woman; but she never troubled herself to say so.

All through that summer, the young girl Nenna came to the cottage two or three evenings every week to meet the boy, Bevil Ames, and often they stayed a while, sitting together on a makeshift bench, watching Jack as he pounded wet clay in a wooden bucket, or split green hazel-rods with his billhook.

"I've put you out a bit, squatting here in your meeting-place, I reckon. But no doubt there's barns and such you could meet in together if you had a mind to be really private."

"Tut-tut!" Bevil said. "What are you suggesting, Mr Mercybright? Barns indeed, for a well-brought-up girl like Nenna, here? Whatever next!"

"You are my chaperon," Nenna said to Jack.

"Am I indeed? Who would've thought it!"

"You never finished telling us about the Battle of Majuba Hill," Bevil said. "About your Irish friend in the Army."

"Ah. Well. He fell in front of a shunting engine. Lost both his legs and got scalded all over in a rush of steam. He was lying in the hospital, screaming for something to stop the pain, but the M.O. said he had nothing to give him."

"Wasn't it true?" Bevil asked.

"Of course it wasn't bloody well true! They expected Paddy to die any minute. They warnt going to waste their drugs on him."

"So you broke into the medical stores?"

"I tried to break in, but the sentry shot me in the knee."

"What happened to Paddy?"

"He died three days later, still in pain."

"Were you with him?"

"No, not me. I was laid up and behind bars."

"What made you join the Army in the first place?"

"I couldn't find work, that's why. Not once I'd finished my bout of navvying on the new canal at Borridge. Then Paddy said to me, 'Let's join the Army' and the next thing I knew we was on our way out to South Africa."

"So you never actually saw any fighting?"

"Not a stitch," Jack said. "It was all over by the time they let me out of gaol."

"I would never let Bevil join the Army," Nenna said. "I think it's all wrong for people to go and fight in wars."

"There, now!" said Bevil, slapping his knee. "The very thing I had in mind!"

"No! I won't let you! You'd be sure to get hurt!" And she sat with his hand held tight between her own, as though she feared he would go that minute. "I shall never let you go away from me. Never! Never!"

Bevil leant forward and kissed her lightly on the mouth. He drew his hand away from hers and got up from the bench, taking his watch from his waistcoat pocket and looking at it with a frown.

"I must go, Nen," he said, sighing. "I promised my father a game of chess and the poor old man does depend on me so. But I'll walk with you as far as the farm."

They went off together, arm in arm, and Jack stood watching them, thinking what strange young lovers they were: like two sedate children, moving through courtship as though through the steps of some slow, formal, old-fashioned dance.

Later that evening, when he went to The Bay Tree for a drink, Bevil was there, standing on his head on the taproom floor, singing a song with ten long verses, encouraged by the usual Friday evening crowd of villagers and bargemen. Jack took his drink out to the garden and sat on the seat beside the bay tree, looking across the quiet river to the Ludden Hills strung out in the distance, charcoal-coloured against the yellow sunset glow. After a while, Bevil came out and sat beside him.

"Be sure your sins will find you out!"

"Playing chess with your father, I think you said? Why do you tell that girl such lies?"

"Ah!" Bevil said, "Why do we ever lie to women?"

"You tell *me*. I know nothing at all about it."

"To spare their feelings, of course, what else? Would it be kinder, do you think, if I told her straight out that I better prefer coming down here to spending the rest of the evening with her? A man must be free! He's a lapdog, else. And women, God bless them, however lovable and loving they may be, do stifle a man most dreadfully, don't they? But perhaps it's not the same for other men? Perhaps it's merely because I'm a poet!"

"D'you feel more free in a village public? And does it make you more of a poet?"

"Why, yes, I compose my best lines when I'm drunk!" Bevil said. "The trouble is, I forget them all by the time I'm sober."

He became silent, sitting perfectly still on the seat, his

brandy glass between his hands. The night was a warm one. Gnats were flying and the smell of the river was strong on the air. Behind the distant hills the sky was still a lemon yellow, but overhead it was already a deep night-blue, with a few stars throbbing in it.

"Do you ever wonder," Bevil said, lounging backwards until he was staring directly upwards into the sky: "do you ever wonder what lies beyond the most distant stars?"

"Sometimes I do," Jack said.

"And what do you see?" Bevil asked. "In your imagination, I mean?"

"I dunno. More stars again, I suppose, and maybe another moon here and there."

"More stars and moons . . ." Bevil murmured, and then, declaiming:

> "Stars unknown, a universe undreamed of,
> And gods, perhaps, that out-create our own!"

He sat up suddenly and turned to look into Jack's face.

"But what beyond that? – Even the stars must finish somewhere! What do you see, beyond it all, at the very last ultimate finish, when you're lying in bed in the small hours, just you and the sky outside your window?"

"If you was a labourer on a farm, always on the go from dawn to dusk and out in all weathers, you'd have more sense than to ask that question. It's sitting all day dozing on your clerk's high stool in that stuffy lawyer's office of yours that keeps you awake in the small hours, my lad."

"But aren't you afraid?" Bevil asked. "Of whatever worlds might lie beyond?"

"I'm more concerned with what happens in this one."

"Oh, yes, that too," Bevil said, shivering. "All the terrible things that happen on earth . . . birth and pain and sickness and dying . . . don't all those things make you afraid?"

"Everybody's afraid of dying."

"And are you afraid of living too?"

"I can see why you drink!" Jack said. "You've got a problem and no mistake!"

But the laugh Bevil gave was not his usual cheerful laugh. It sounded sickly. And Jack, looking closely in the dim, fading light, did not attempt to tease him further, for the fair face had an unnatural pallor and the eyes were like those of a small boy awaking from a nightmare.

"Sometimes I feel myself changing in texture. I feel myself growing thick all over and my lips feel numb and warm together, as though my flesh were made of clay. Then a cool light rain starts falling and passes right through me, and I have a feeling of immense relief, as if everything is now all right and the worst is over."

Bevil paused, tilting his glass and peering in at the drop of brandy, rolling like an amber bead at the bottom.

"Do you think death is like that?" he asked.

"If it is," Jack said, "it don't sound all that bad, does it? I shouldn't mind the rain going through me, not once my bones had stopped aching."

"Sometimes I wish it would come and he done with, because then I need never be afraid again. No more fear or pain or disgust . . . or self-pity because of other people's disgust . . ." Bevil emptied his glass and leant towards Jack. "I shall never be able to marry Nenna. It's as much as I can do to face up to life, myself, let alone look after a wife and family."

"A good wife would look after *you*."

"Oh, my God! Nenna's as much a babe as I am!"

"Together you'd be strong, like a bundle of sticks,"

Jack said. "Women've got more faith in life than us men, somehow, I often think."

"I'm getting cold!" Bevil said, and jumped up quickly, putting on gaiety as though it were a coat. "Let's go in and join the party. I can hear Angelina playing her squeezebox." And then, going in, he said suddenly: "I'm not a thorough liar, you know. – I *did* go home and play chess with my father."

The two cowmen at Brown Elms were brothers named Peter and Paul Luppitt. One morning when Jack arrived, they were in the farmyard, looking at two new cows in the paddock.

"Where did they drop from?" Peter asked Jack.

"I dunno. They're both strangers to me."

"They must've arrived late last night, then, that's all. Miss Philippa must've bought 'em at Hotcham."

"She's off her hinges," Paul said. "I've seen more milk on a three-legged stool than we'll ever see on them eight legs there."

"Watch yourself," Peter muttered. "The missus is with us."

Miss Philippa came out of the house, and the two cowmen went off to the cowshed.

"Well, Mercybright, what do you think of my two new purchases?" she asked.

"Why not ask Peter and Paul? They're your cowmen."

"I prefer to ask you. Can't you give me a straight answer?"

"Well, the roan has got a withered quarter, and I'd say the black will go the same way. But, of course, if you got the two for next to nothing . . ."

"I paid eighteen guineas! Surely you don't call that next to nothing?"

"No," he said, "cheap always comes dear in the end, I reckon."

"They looked all right when I saw them at Hotcham."

"You was dazzled by the notion of getting a bargain."

"So you think they're useless?" she said crossly.

"Not useless exactly," he said, shrugging. "They're pretty to look at, the pair of them, and they'll make the shed look a bit more fuller!"

A week later, when she was going to a sale at Ludden, she took Jack with her in the trap. And again in June to another sale at Darry Cross. And then again to a sale of sheep at a farm near Boscott. It was his duty to look at the animals in their pens, mark those he favoured in the catalogue, and nudge her unobtrusively if he thought the bidding went too high. Afterwards, when the sale was over, she would go off to take tea and seedcake with her neighbours, leaving Jack to settle with the agent and find a drover.

"Mercybright will see to it!" she would say, in a voice always just a little louder than was needed. "Mercybright is acting on my behalf!"

"You should take Peter Luppitt by rights," he said once, driving home from Darry Cross. "And Will Gauntlet when you go to Boscott on Friday."

"Don't you like attending the sales?"

"I like it all right, but Peter Luppitt's your senior cowman, and surely the shepherd should choose his own ewes!"

"I don't trust them. I've known them longer than you have, remember, and I'm sure they would cheat me at every turn."

She drove a little way in silence, sitting erect, her back very straight, looking too hot in her thick black skirt and jacket, for the day was a close one.

"I trust *you*," she said abruptly, and, as though seized by embarrassment, she cut with her whip at the brambles growing out from the hedgerow. "Whose hedges are these? They're a rank disgrace! My new varnishwork is quite scratched to ruins!"

For two weeks in June, the cornfields became a bright acid yellow as the wild mustard bloomed in the sun, the flowers growing up very tall, overshadowing the sickly corn just as the ears were breaking out of their papery sheaths. Then the mustard flowers died and the mauve dog-thistles bloomed in their place, swaying with the corn in the hot July winds, and spreading their strong, sweet, almondlike scent.

"It breaks my heart," said Joe Stretton, working alongside Jack in the hay-fields. "Every year the place gets worser. In old Guff's time this farm was a winner, every acre as clean as a bean-row. But what do women know about farming? All they know is eggs and poultry!"

The hay, too, was poor stuff, thin and sour, with a great deal of sorrel and rattle in it, for the meadows were all sadly neglected.

"She grazes heavy all the year round and still expects to make good hay!" said Jonathan Kirby, coming to a halt, and he spat contemptuously, holding up a pitiful wisp on the tines of his hay-fork. "Look at it!" he said. "I've seen better stuff poking out of a scarecrow!"

"Have you ever told her?" Jack asked. "About grazing, I mean?"

"Hah!" Stretton said. "What good is that? It's like blowing on mustard to make it cool. She don't choose to listen to the likes of us. A farm this size needs twenty men and it had 'em, too, in her father's time, with every man in his proper place and proud to say he came from Brown Elms."

At the end of August, when the first twenty acres of corn was cut, Miss Philippa herself was there in the field, binding and stooking in the wake of the reaper. Sometimes Nenna was there too. The two sisters worked together. But there was always a clear space around them, for the labourers' womenfolk and children liked to keep their distance if they could.

The thistles in the sheaves were now dry and deadly. The women and children sometimes cried out in pain, stopping to remove the sharp spines from palms and fingers. But Miss Philippa always worked in silence, without even wincing, and frowned severely at Nenna if she grumbled. She thought it beneath her dignity to betray any sign of suffering, and she wished to convey, too, that the thistles were nowhere near so bad as the labourers pretended.

All through harvest, she was about from first light to last, eager and watchful, quick to pounce if the reaping machine missed so much as an inch between swaths, quick to scold if she caught the children nibbling the grains. She would walk the same field again and again, her gaze going hungrily over the corn-cocks, almost as though she were counting the sheaves.

"But it won't make the crop any bigger or better, will it, now?" Oliver Lacey said to Jack. "However much she gawples at it!"

And as soon as the last load of barley was carted, safely under thatch in the stackyard, she wanted the first lot of wheat threshed and measured, so that she could take a sample to market at Yelland on Wednesday.

"Aye, that's what she likes!" said Joe Stretton. "Gadding to market, playing the grand lady farmer! And the way she watches her precious stacks! You'd think she had the bestest corn crops this side of the Luddens!"

But Jack, coming into the barn after the threshing, found Miss Philippa there alone, counting the sacks and biting her lip in open vexation.

"Which field is this from and what is the yield per acre?" she asked him.

"This lot came off the South Wood Field, so it's just about thirteen or fourteen bushels."

"That's poor, isn't it?"

"It's worse than poor. It's tragical. And, what is more, a lot of that seed is probably mustard. Land like you've got in the South Wood Field would likely give you as much as forty bushels to the acre if only that was in good heart. But you've took too many corn crops off it and you've let the mustard get too strong a hold. Not to mention the docks and thistles."

"*I* let the mustard get a hold? And what do I pay the men for, I wonder, if not to see the fields are weeded?"

"Did you give orders to hoe the corn?"

"I don't know. I don't remember. Do I have to tell them every single thing? Surely they know when a field wants weeding!"

But the long, hot, anxious days of harvest had tired her, and there was no strength in the angry outburst. Tiredness and disappointment together had brought a hint of tears to her eyes. She looked worn and defeated.

"What must I do, to put the land into good heart?" And she stood over one of the sacks of wheatseed, running the grain through fingers roughened, swollen, torn, after her weeks of labour in the fields. "When my father took samples of corn to market, the dealers welcomed him with open arms. But now, when I go, I see them sniggering up their sleeves."

She closed the sack and brushed the chaff-dust from her fingers. She turned to Jack with a look of appeal.

"Tell me what to do and I'll do it," she said.

*

"I don't like it!" Stretton shouted. "I'm the one that ought to be top man here by rights. I've been here the longest. And if I warnt your friend, Jack Mercybright, I'd knock you into that there furrow!"

"Here, Dad, are you going to fight?" Harvey asked. "Shall I hold your jacket?"

"I ent fighting, you silly fellah. I'm holding a friendly confabulation. So get back to them hosses before I belt you."

"I get the same wages as you do," Jack said, "so how come you call me a top man?"

"More fool you, then, that's what I say. You wouldn't catch *me* working as bailiff just for the buttons. Oh, I know it's *her* that shouts the orders, but they're coming from you in the first place, ent they? They wouldn't make sense the way they do if they was all her own idea. Well, I don't like it, and I'm telling you outright so's we know where we stand. Now how would you like a chew of tobacco?"

"No, thanks. I'm a smoker, not a chewer."

"All right," Stretton said. "When I've finished chewing you can have my quid to smoke in your pipe."

By late September most of the stubble grounds were ploughed, and a week or so later the soil was a gentle green all over, where the mustard seed, shed in the harvest, grew apace in the soft moist weather. The ground was then ploughed again and the mustard turned in, a green manure, and then a little later on, the tangled couch-grass was harrowed out, to be burnt at the foot of each field, filling the air with sweet-smelling smoke.

"This is all very fine!" Miss Philippa said, coming to inspect the work in progress. "I can't afford to bare-fallow so many precious acres all at one and the same time! And all this labour! – Ploughing the same land over and over while other work gets left undone – "

"Get more men. That's the answer."

"Is that what you're up to? Creating more work for the benefit of your own kind?"

"God creates the work, not me." Jack said. "I'm only the go-between. But have a look at this bit of paper. I've wrote down some notes for a cropping rota. I ent much of a hand at writing but I daresay you'll make out what I mean well enough."

"Rye?" she said, scanning the paper. "My father never grew rye in his life! And fifty acres of new grass ley! Have you any idea what you're suggesting?"

"Right you are," Jack said, shrugging. "You tell me what to do instead and we'll go on the same old way you have done for years, raising rattle and thistle and mustard!"

Miss Philippa turned and walked away, taking the piece of paper with her. She was shut in her office for three mornings running. But the following week there were two new men employed on the farm, and a month later, on entering the barn one afternoon, Jack saw that the grass and clover-seed had come, as well as the turnip-seed and rye-seed. And Miss Philippa was there, checking the items against her list.

"The clover is all Dutch White," she said. "It's what my father always preferred. The grass is mixed as you recommended. As to the artificials you asked for – they are being sent over from Stamley on Monday."

Now that the evenings were drawing in again, Sunday was a precious day indeed, and he divided it evenly in two, spending the morning on the garden, the afternoon on the cottage. He had turned the pigs into the orchard, to feed on the fallen pears and apples, and the old horse Shiner, disliking pigs, had gone to graze in the Long Meadow.

He had dug all his ground and planted a couple of rows of cabbage. He had cut the hedges and pruned the fruit trees. Now he was re-laying the old flagstones that paved the yard between the two wings of the cottage.

Nenna had brought him an apricot tree, grown from a stone planted in a pot on her fourteenth birthday. It was now three years old and twenty-seven inches tall, and she had planted it under the south wall of the cottage. He did not really want it. He cared nothing for apricots, and there were too many trees in the garden already. But Nenna would not take no for an answer, so there the tree was, and whenever she came she watered it carefully and removed any weeds that grew around it.

"I thought you'd feel you really lived here, if you had a new tree planted in your garden."

"I *know* I live here," Jack said. "I live nowhere else!"

"Jack has no soul," Bevil said, watching Nenna as she tied the tree to a stake for support. "At least . . . he hasn't got my poet's soul."

"No, well, it wouldn't look right on me," Jack said.

Nenna was kneeling on the grass path, and Bevil put out his hand to help her, smiling at her as he pulled her up. There was great sweetness in the boy's smile sometimes, and today he seemed to be treating the girl with especially tender gallantry.

"A man who jeers at apricot jam is not worth troubling about," he said, and Nenna laughed, suddenly flinging her arms around him and laying her head against his chest.

"Oh, Bevil! I do love you so! I shall miss you most dreadfully while you're away!"

"Away?" Jack said, "Why, where you off to?"

"I'm going to London, to spend six months in my uncle's office. He's in law, too, and my father thinks it will be good experience for me." Bevil touched the girl's hair, smiling at Jack over her head. "Nenna and I have never been very far apart in our lives before. I rely on you to look after her for me."

"All right. I shall do my best."

"Wouldn't it be terrible," Nenna said, drawing away from Bevil's arms, "if you met some beautiful woman there and never came back to me at all?"

"Or fell among thieves and was murdered," he said. "London is a place for terrible murders, you know."

"When do you go?" Jack asked.

"Next Saturday. Ten in the morning. I get a train from Kevelport."

"I shall come and see you off," Nenna said, "whether your father likes it or not!"

There followed a week of north-westerly gales, with four dark days when the rain lashed down without pause, turning the ditches into torrents, the fields into marshes. On Friday evening, though the rain had eased off, the gale blew harder than ever, going round a little till it blew straight from the westerly quarter.

Nenna and Bevil were with Jack. They had nowhere else to go, it seemed, for the girl was not welcome at the boy's home, and the boy was not welcome at Brown Elms. So they spent the evening in the cottage, sitting in front of a fire that blazed ferociously, drawn by the wind whirling and thumping in the big chimney.

"I hate this weather!" Nenna said. "We had an apple tree down in the garden last night. It fell and crushed the old summer-house. It frightens me, when the wind is this fierce."

"But it's wonderful!" Bevil said. "It makes me feel very wide awake. It fills me with power and energy. I fancy I must have been born on a night of storm and tempest like this. Just hark at it roaring out there in the orchard! Doesn't it fill you with excitement?

"What a noise of wind in the trees on the hill
In the wild, wild land of Never-Go-Back!
What moonlight and starlight and swift-flying
 clouds!
And, in the day-time, what suns, what suns!

"I shall remember tonight's clean gale when I'm stuck in smoky Cheapside, listening to some old Moneybags discussing how best to do down his partners. I shall write you poems full of nostalgia and send them to you tied up in lawyers' green silk ribbon."

"I hope you will write me letters too."

"Of course I shall! Every day, I promise."

At nine o'clock, Bevil took Nenna home. At half-past nine he was back at the cottage.

"I'm going to The Bay Tree. Are you coming with me?"

"At this time of night? And in this weather?"

"Sylvanus expects me. Angelina, too. It's by way of being a farewell party. Oh, come on, Jack, don't be a spoilsport!"

So Jack went with him, leaning forward against the wind, under a sky where moon and stars looked down now and then between the frayed black clouds rushing eastwards.

Down at Niddup the gale was worse. It screamed up-river for a mile and a half with nothing much to break its force. The inn on the bank got the full blast. The tiny place shuddered repeatedly, and all the pewter tankards, hanging in rows along the rafters, swung very gently on their hooks.

"It's a good thing we've got a full house tonight," said Sylvanus, "or The Bay Tree would likely get uprooted!"

"I'm the one that's being uprooted," Bevil said. "At this same time tomorrow night I shall be in London."

"Try The Dolphin at Deptford," Sylvanus said. "I used to go there when I had a spell on the Thames lighters. It's a good house, The Dolphin. – Poets and painters and all sorts go there."

"Poets and painters and singers of songs! – I must keep in practice!" Bevil said, and, borrowing the squeezebox from Angelina, the landlord's wife, he played and sang his favourite song:

> "Oh, who will grieve for Jimmy Catkin,
> Buried with his seven wives?
> How many more would lie there with him
> If Jimmy had had a cat's nine lives?
>
> "What if each wife had had ten children
> And each of them had had ten more?

> The Catkin family tree would number
> Six thousand, nine hundred, and ninety-four!"

The crowd in the taproom sang the chorus: "Oh, iddle-me, tiddle-me, riddle-me-ree! – The Catkins hang thick on the crack-willow tree!"; and the noise they made singing together even drowned the noise of the gale.

Towards midnight, two drovers came in, bringing with them such a gust of wind that the smoke came puffing out of the fire-place.

"Ennen's rising fast," one of the men said to Sylvanus. "There's folk in the Dip will have two or three inches in their kitchens by morning."

"Ah, that's rising like yeast," said the second man. "I ent seen such waters in a month of Sundays. And there's folk upriver that ent been very clever about it, neither, for there's dead sheep and hen-coops and privvies and all sorts getting washed down from Dudnall or somewhere. We seen 'em as we come across the bridge."

"Let's go and see!" Bevil suggested, and Stanley Knarr, the landlord's son, turned at once towards the door, his pint-pot held high as he pushed his way through the crowd.

"Who else is coming?" Bevil shouted. "Reuben? Jim? Henry Taylor?" He drank the last of the flip from his mug so that Angelina could fill it again. "Up to the brim, if you please, Angelina, for this is the bard's farewell to Ennen! Are you coming, Jack?"

"Might as well, I suppose," Jack said. He was feeling just a little drunk. "I ent seen much of this Ennen of yours when it's running in one of its famous spates."

The noise of the water was as loud as though it came off a weir. Ennen was in full spate indeed, and, rushing round the circular sweep known locally as the Dudnall Loop, it hurled itself into the narrow channel at Niddup with such force that it broke its banks there and flooded out over the meadows. And the gale coming up the straight stretch from Egham whipped at the waters as though trying to hurl them back.

There were twenty men crowded together on the bridge. The young ones were singing bawdy songs, but broke off now and then to cheer some dark object as it came rushing down on the foaming torrent.

"What is it, what is it? A Kevelport dumpling, do you think?"

"Maybe it's Dudnall's big bass drum!"

"Here's somebody's dinghy! Whatever's the matter with the folk upriver? Didn't they see this flood a-coming?"

"Watch out, here's an elm! That'll give us a bit of a knock, I reckon."

There were quite a few tree-trunks coming downriver, and often they got caught up at the bridge, pounding against the cutwater walls until at last, released by a sudden swirl in the water, they found their way through one of the arches.

"Plenty of firewood there!" shouted Stanley. "Enough to warm The Bay Tree forever!"

"The Bambridge folk'll get most of that," said an old man standing next to Jack. "It'll fetch up against the lock at Mastford."

The water was rising all the time, flowing over the banks at either side and looking, Jack thought, like a great tide of fermenting beer, frothing creamily at the edges as it washed out shallowly over the grass of the big flat meadow known as the ham.

"We ought to start back!" Jack said, shouting into Bevil's ear. "Otherwise we shall have a wet walk!"

"Not me! Not me!" Bevil answered, waving the tankard in his hand. "What will the Thames be to me after Ennen?"

"Well, *I'm* going," Jack said. "I don't care for getting my feet wet."

He was in the act of turning away when another tree-trunk came downriver and hit the central buttress like a battering-ram. The whole bridge shuddered and the tremor lasted a long time. He could feel it in the brick-work underfoot; he could feel it in the parapet under his hand: a kind of thrumming that passed right through him. So he turned back again and looked down over the side, and where the cutwater should have been there was now nothing but foaming water.

"Get off!" he shouted, shoving at Stanley Knarr, beside him. "For God's sake get off! – The bridge is going!"

But Bevil and Stanley, still singing at the tops of their voices, merely caught hold of him by the arms and danced him round a pace or two, trying to lift him onto the wall.

"We're used to these floods!" Stanley shouted. "We're Ennen men born and bred – there's freshets in our very marrow!"

"Get off the bridge! The water's breached us! Can't you feel it, you stupid fools?"

There came a loud crack and another shock ran through the brickwork, which opened in fissures at their feet. And then the bridge was falling away from under-neath them, the stone-built pillars heeling over, the huge stones toppling one from another as though they were nothing but great cubes of sugar crumbling and melting away in the foam. And the noise of it all – the stone bridge collapsing, the voices screaming – was lost in the noise of wind and water.

The moment the river closed above him, Jack was sure it meant his death, for he was half drunk and no swimmer. But the torrent tossed him about like a cork and once, by a lucky accident, almost, his left hand caught hold of a slim willow branch and he was able to hang on, dinked up and down, up and down, every moment, sucking in air and water by turns.

Another man's body was swept against him and he caught it up over his shoulder, his right arm around it, his fingers entwined in a fold of clothing. He had no way of telling who it was. He did not even know if the man was dead or merely unconscious. He could only hang on, with the extra weight gradually bearing him down, so that grey moonlit water kept breaking in splinters over his head.

Then the willow bough began to bend, letting him down deeper and deeper, until it snapped from its root altogether. His burden was wrenched clean out of his arms and he himself was swept a hundred yards further downstream, to fetch up again among the arched roots of an elm tree, still on the Niddup side of the river.

His rescuers took him back to The Bay Tree. Sylvanus was out, looking for Stanley. Angelina was there alone. She stripped off Jack's clothes, wrapped him in a thick brown blanket, and put him to sit inside the big fireplace. She brought him hot tea with brandy in it and when he had drunk it he sat, half dozing, still with the sick sensation of water washing coldly through him, as though the river had got into his blood.

Once he got up to peer out of the window, and could see the lanterns flickering small and blurred in the distance, all along the course of the river, where rescuers searched for those still lost in the swollen waters. He returned to the fire and after a while fell asleep, sweating inside his thick blanket.

When he awoke grey daylight had come, and three other men sat like himself, hunched in blankets around the inside wall of the fire-place, their heads in their hands. Angelina was sweeping the floor of the taproom. Sylvanus was bringing more logs for the fire.

"What's the news?" Jack asked.

"They're all accounted for now," said Sylvanus. "There's sixteen left alive all told. Twelve of them are at home in their beds. Then there's four of them dead, lying out there on the grass in the garden." He stood back from the fire and jerked his head towards the window. "Including our Stanley," he said in a flat, calm voice, and went to Angelina, who had stopped sweeping and was bent double over her broom.

Jack put on his clothes and went outside. He was met by a cold pale glare of light, for the whole of the ham was flooded now, out as far as the eye could see, and the big sheet of water reflected the cold grey morning sky. The wind still blew strong, and the tarpaulin stack-cloth that covered the bodies was weighted at the edges with big stones. He removed three of these and turned back the stack-cloth, looking at the four dead faces revealed. Stanley Knarr. Jim Fennel. Peter Wyatt. Bevil Ames. The youngest ones. The children of promise. Each one less than half Jack's age.

He covered them up and put back the stones.

"Why?" Miss Philippa said harshly. "Why should Nenna want to see you? What comfort can you possibly offer?" But, changing her mind, she stepped back further into the passage. "Very well," she said. "You'd better come in. Wipe your feet – the maid has only just swept the carpet."

She showed him into the front parlour, a room not much used, evidently, for the heat of the fire had drawn out the damp from furniture and curtains, and it hung on the air like winter fog, filling the air with a strong smell of mildew. Nenna sat on the edge of the couch, her hands folded over a letter, her face towards the fire, though quite unwarmed by it, and still as a statue.

"Mercybright has come to see you," Miss Philippa said, ushering him in. "He means well, I'm sure, so I hardly liked to turn him away." She remained standing close by the door.

"I was there when it happened," Jack said to Nenna. "I was on the bridge with Bevil and the others. I thought I ought to tell you about it."

"Why did you let him?" Nenna asked. "Why did you take him to The Bay Tree at all?" She spoke without moving. She was still staring into the fire. "Why did you let him go on the bridge?"

Jack was silent, not knowing how to answer. He stood with his fists in the pockets of his jackets, holding it tight around his loins. His clothes were still damp. He shivered inside them.

"Look at that clock!" Nenna said. "I would just be seeing him onto his train . . . We'd still be talking, Bevil and his father and his aunt and me, if you hadn't taken him to The Bay Tree."

"I didn't take him. Going there was his own idea. The Knarrs was giving a sort of a party."

"Couldn't you have stopped him going on the bridge?"

"It wasn't just him. There was lots of men on it. Twenty of us altogether. How could we know it'd get washed away? Bevil was drunk. He'd been drinking pretty well all the evening. He might've stood a chance, otherwise."

"Who got him drunk?" Nenna demanded, and turned

to him for the first time, her eyes overflowing. "Who got him drunk if it wasn't you?"

"Don't you blame *me!*" Jack said fiercely. "Don't you blame *me* for them four boys dead! I ent having that! Oh, no, not me!"

"I *do* blame you!" Nenna said, sobbing. "Why should all the young ones die and all the old ones be left alive? It's all wrong and I *do* blame you! I *do*! I *do*!"

Jack turned and walked out of the house. Miss Philippa followed him to the back door.

"I told you!" she said. "I told you it wouldn't do any good – "

But he was walking quickly away, determined to put the farm well behind him. He was chilled to the bone and walked without pause till he came to The Pen and Cob at Bittery, six miles upriver, where nobody knew him.

He awoke with a smirr of small rain tickling his face, and opened his eyes to a sky that moved. He was lying on his back on an old barge, chugging along a narrow canal, with scrub willow trees at either side and yellow leaves drifting into the water.

He got to his feet with some difficulty and limped along the deck to the stern. The bargeman and his wife were strangers to him, but seemed friendly and knew his name.

"What damned canal is this?" he asked them.

"Well, it ent exactly the Grand Union, but it ent all that bad as canals go. This here's known as the Billerton and Nazel and it links old Ennen up with the Awn."

"How did I get here?"

"We picked you up at The Burraport Special. Day before yesterday. Half past noonday."

"What day is it now?"

"Thursday, November the twenty-second," the barge-man said, filling his pipe, "in the Year of Grace, eighteen hundred and ninety four, though what bloody grace there might be in it I'd be hard put to say." He lit his pipe and flicked the match into the water. "You've been on a blinder, ent you?" he said. "You don't hardly know if it's Christmas or Easter. You said you wanted to go to Stopford but maybe you've gone and changed your mind?"

"I reckon I have," Jack said. "I reckon I ought to get back to Niddup."

"It'll take you more'n a day or two, butty, but Owner George'll see you right."

They put him onto the next passing barge, which carried him back to The Burraport Special. From there he travelled on a Kevelport snaker all the way to Hunsey Lock. By Friday night he was back in Niddup, and on Saturday morning he was out in the eighteen acre field at Brown Elms, singling mangolds.

"So you're back, are you, without so much as a word of explanation?" And Miss Philippa stood on the headland behind him, her arms full of teazles and dead ferns, gathered from the banks of the Runkle Brook. "Did you hear me, man? I asked you a question!"

"Yes, I'm back," he said. "Or someone like me."

"And what explanation have you got to offer?"

"No explanation. I'm just back, that's all." And he worked on without stopping. "Seems I've got a lot to catch up on."

"Do you realize how long you've been away? You've been missing from work for a whole week! And then you come sneaking back here without a word, hoping, I suppose, that your absence hadn't even been noticed."

"I surely ent as daft as that."

"And what makes you think your job is still open? Doesn't it occur to you that you may very likely have been replaced?"

"If I'd been replaced, these here roots should ought to've been singled, but they ent been, have they, so just leave me be to get on with the job."

"Just look at you!" she said, disgusted. "Dirty! Unshaven! Your clothes all covered in alehouse filth – "

"Do I smell?" he asked.

"Yes, you smell like a pig in its muck!" she said.

"Keep away from me, then, and that way you won't suffer nothing."

He went on steadily down the row, aware of the field stretching below him, so many steep wet muddy acres still to be hoed.

"Our young Miss Nenna's gone away," Oliver Lacey said to Jack. "She's gone to stay with a school-friend of hers somewhere up near Brummagem. She went straight after the young man's funeral."

"It's a pity Miss Philippa don't go too," Peter Luppitt said, swearing, "instead of always treading on our tails the way she does."

"Who'd pay our wages then?" said his brother.

"Yes, it's nice to be Jack, coming and going as cool as you please, taking a holiday when he's a mind to and nobody saying so much as an echo. How do you manage it, Jack, old butty? How does it come that you and Miss Philippa's such close friends?"

Jack made no answer. He walked away. He was still in a mood when too much talk made him impatient. All he wanted was to be left alone.

Although he would not allow Nenna to blame him for Bevil's death, he did blame himself, because now, whenever he remembered the man he had held in his arms in the water, it seemed to him it must have been Bevil.

He saw the boy's face all too plainly: the eyes closed and the pale lashes glistening wetly; the short upper lip drawn back a little, as though in a cry; the fair hair streaming out in the water. And as he remembered, his muscles would clench throughout his body as though now, if only he were given the chance again, he could find the strength to hold on, to bear the man up with him out of the torrent. As though *now* his determination would never fail.

At other times he faced the matter with more common sense; knew he could never have saved the man in his arms; felt sure, even, that the man had been dead already. But Bevil haunted him nevertheless. It was something he had to wrestle with. He kept himself busy to drive away the phantoms.

He was working now on the south wall of the cottage. He had taken the old filling out of the panels, tarred the inner sides of the timbers, and was now putting in the new wattlework; four round hazel rods slotting upright into each panel, then the split rods in a close weave across. It was work he enjoyed. He was almost happy. The old cottage was gradually taking its proper shape again.

The day was a mild one at the end of November, and the yellow leaves quitting the plum trees in the hedgerow behind him, were drifting down to brighten the ground throughout the garden. Two or three blackbirds were busy there, turning the leaves in search of grubs, and under the hedge a thrush was hammering a snail on a stone.

"Poor snail," a voice said sadly, and Jack, looking round, found Nenna behind him. "How they must wish there were no such things as stones!"

For a moment her face remained averted. She was watching the thrush. But then she looked at him directly, studying him with thought-filled eyes, as though seeking something in his expression, or reminding herself of something forgotten.

Jack turned back to his work on the panel. He inserted a round rod into its hole in the beam above and bent it until it slotted into the groove below. He stopped and picked up a handful of split rods.

"What do you want with me?" he asked. "I'd have thought you'd said all you had to say to me when I saw you the last time."

"I said too much. I didn't mean it. I'm sorry if I hurt you."

"Aye? So you're sorry. And now you've got that off your conscience nicely perhaps you'll go away and leave me alone."

"Is that what you want? Just to be left alone always?"

"Yes," he said. "I like it that way. It means less trouble."

"But you must want company sometimes."

"When I do, I go out and look for it, don't I?"

"At The Bay Tree, you mean, or some other village public?"

"That's right. Why not? You walk in . . . you meet a few folk and chat with them . . . and when you've had enough you walk out again with no offence on either side."

"And is that all you ever want from life?"

"It's quite enough, just to keep me going. I'm past the age of worrying overmuch about anything."

"You talk as though you were an old man."

"I *am* an old man! You said so yourself." And he rounded on her. "It's what you called me, don't you remember? – The young ones all drowned. The old ones left alive. – That's what you said if I ent much mistaken."

Meeting his gaze, her eyes were suddenly filled with tears, and he relented. She was too much a child to be punished for words spoken at such a time.

"Ah, never mind!" he said roughly. "Never mind what you said! It was true, anyway, every word." He took a split rod out of the bundle and went on working, weaving it in between the uprights. "I'm a man of thirty-seven with a gammy leg and more than half his life behind him. Of course you'd gladly swap me for Bevil, just as the Knarrs would swap me for Stanley. The trouble is, life ent arranged so's we can make bargains over this and that, and I can't pretend I wish myself dead, poor specimen though I may be."

There was no answer, and when he turned round he found he was talking to himself. Nenna had gone. His only companion was a cock blackbird still pecking about among the yellowing leaves.

She was back, however, the following Sunday, feeding crusts of bread to Shiner and hanging a necklace of bryony berries round his rough neck.

Jack was at the top of his ladder, up against the south wall, and saw her making a fuss of the horse in the orchard. He felt impatient, wishing she would keep away. He had nothing against her – she was just a child – but her presence there was an irritation; he felt she was making some claim upon him; asking for comfort he could not give. He dipped his trowel into his bucket and slapped the wet clay onto the wattle.

A little while later, going to the pump for more water, he found her looking at the old stone trough, where Bevil had scratched her initials and his own.

"Why do you come," he asked, wearily, "when everything here is bound to make you sad?"

"I don't know . . . I can't help it, somehow . . . I suppose, when sadness is all you've got left in the world, it becomes almost precious in a way."

"That's morbid," he said. "It ent healthy."

"I get lonely at home. I get so tired of listening to Philippa grumbling all the time. And I can't go to The Bay Tree, can I?"

"You ought to have friends. Young folk of your own age. Your own sort, not people like me. Miss Philippa ought to see about it."

"We never have company up at the house, except John Tuller of Maryhope, and the old Barton ladies now and then. Philippa doesn't much care for having people visit the house. Anyway, I like coming here, because I can talk to you about Bevil."

"What is there to say?"

"I don't know – just things," she said. "I think of those evenings we had round your fire and all the talk we had together . . . Bevil liked you. It makes a link. And then I don't feel quite so lonely."

"I don't think it's right, all the same. You're a lot too young to dwell on the past."

"I shall never marry, if that's what you're thinking."

"Yes, you will," he said, gently. "One day you will. You mark my words. You'll meet some young chap and learn to love him and then you'll get married and raise a few children. All in good time. You'll see."

"No," she said, shaking her head. "I shall never marry."

"All right, have it your own way, but I must get a move on before my clay dries out again."

"Do you mind if I stay and watch you?"

"Please yourself. It's no odds to me. After all, you used to come to this old cottage long before I happened along, so what right have I to turn you off?"

"Is there anything I can do?"

"Ah. Maybe there is. You can chop up that straw on the block there. Little bits, about half an inch long. But mind you don't go chopping your fingers. I sharpened that hatchet only this morning."

She came often after that, and one Sunday she brought him the deeds of the cottage to look at, having taken them secretly out of the safe in Miss Philippa's office. Jack had difficulty in reading the old, faded, elaborate writing. Nenna had to read it to him.

"It was built in sixteen hundred and one, by a man named Thomas Benjamin Hayward, and was known in those days as New Farm, Upper Runkle, near the township of Niddup-on-Ennen. The farm was then about two hundred acres. Mr Thomas Hayward is described as a yeoman, and the house is described as a 'handsome new dwelling house of two bays with a fifteen foot outshot standing at the south western boundary of the holding.' "

"So it is handsome," Jack said. "It's a lot more handsome than the big new house you live in up there."

"Three hundred years," Nenna said, looking up at the cottage. "I wonder what people were like then."

"Not all that different, I shouldn't think. What's three

hundred years under the sun? – Nothing much more than a snap of your fingers. And if you picture six old grannies, hand in hand across the years, it brings it all up pretty well as close as close, I reckon."

"Why grannies? What about all the grandfathers?"

"Oh, they will have played their part I daresay. But in my particular bit of experience, it was always the grannies that mattered most. My parents died when I was a babby. She was only a little hob of a woman, and us five boys was great big slummocking ruffians nearly twice her size, but if we done wrong, which happened often one way and another, she would put on a pair of heavy hobnailed boots and kick us round the kitchen till we howled for mercy."

"Rough measures," Nenna said.

"They worked well enough. We had great respect for my grannie's boots, specially when her feet was in them."

"But wasn't there any tenderness at all?"

"No. None. Just a feeling that we mattered, that's all. And I never had the feeling again, not after she'd gone."

"What happened to her?"

"She died when I was about eleven. My brothers went off – emigrated – and I was put in an orphanage. I didn't care for it over much. I ran away after three months or so."

"And you've been on the move ever since?"

"I suppose I have. It must've got to be a habit."

"Do you like the life of a wanderer?"

"I dunno that I like it exactly. I'm always hoping for a good place to settle. The trouble is, I seem to fall out with folk, somehow, after I've been with them for a while."

"You're quarrelsome, then?"

"No, not me," he said, straight-faced. "It's the other folk that are quarrelsome. Never me."

*

Just before Christmas, Jack was sent to Maryhope Farm to fetch a number of dressed geese, and when he returned to Brown Elms, Nenna came out to help him carry them into the dairy, where Miss Philippa received them, pinching each one and weighing it carefully before laying it out on the slab. It was the custom at Brown Elms that each man employed there should be given a goose for Christmas.

"But why buy from Maryhope?" Jack asked. "Why not raise your own here?"

"I don't have much luck with geese," Miss Philippa said, "not since my father died, that is."

"Then why not give them a good fat chicken instead? You've enough of *them* about the place."

"In my father's time, it was always a goose," Miss Philippa said, rather stiffly. "The men would not like it if the custom were changed after all these years."

Jack turned away with a little smile. He knew how the men regarded the custom. "A Maryhope goose," he had heard them say, "is a loud cackle with feathers on it!" John Tuller's produce was poor stuff always.

"Well, no goose for me if you please," he said. "It would be a waste, me being alone."

Miss Philippa, in spectacles, was frowning at the figures on the spring balance. She made a note on the list in her hand.

"I didn't order a goose for you, Mercybright, as it so happens. You couldn't easily cook it on your open fire, could you? You will therefore have your Christmas dinner here with us this year."

"Here?" he repeated, stopping dead on his way to the door.

"That's right. At twelve o'clock precisely. I've spoken to Cook and it's all arranged."

Jack was astonished. He hardly knew how to answer. And, looking at Nenna, he saw that she was just as astonished as he was.

"Well, I dunno," he said, awkwardly. "Joe Stretton has asked me up to his place – "

"Oh, do come to us!" Nenna said. "Joe Stretton won't mind. He's got his children *and* his sister's family, whereas Philippa and I are all alone. Do come to us, Jack, I beg of you!"

Nenna's tone was warm and excited, and Miss Philippa, turning, treated her to a long, hard, considering stare, over the rims of her spectacles. She seemed to be thinking very deeply. It was fully a minute before she spoke.

"Twelve o'clock sharp," she said to Jack. "We have it early so that Cook can get home to her own dinner."

"Ah," Jack said. "Right you are, then. Twelve o'clock, like you say."

But outside the dairy, fetching more geese from the cart in the yard, he wished he had voiced his refusal more firmly. He was not happy about the invitation. He would just as soon have gone to Joe Stretton's.

"At the farm?" Joe said. "With the Missus and young Miss Nenna? Hell's bells, whatever next! You'll soon be wearing little kid gloves and walking about with a smart Malacca!"

"I'll punch your head in a minute," Jack said.

"At least you'll put on your grey frock coat? I shall take it amiss if you let the side down by not dressing proper."

"Shut your rattle and pass that besom."

"You must mind and take all the condiments with your meat, you know, and not make a noise when you blow on your pudding. Ah, and be sure to say 'Pardon!' after belching or they'll likely think you ent got no manners."

"Are you mucking out here or resting your shovel?"

"I'm giving you a word of advice."

"It's a hell of a long word, ent it?"

"Knaves on the raight and forks on the left, unless you happen to be left-handed, of course, in which event the case is altered. Then there's the matter of saying grace . . . always speak through your nose and make it snappy or the apple sauce gets tired of waiting."

Still leaning on his shovel, Stretton watched Jack sweeping out the piggery.

"I wonder what it is you've got about you that makes the two misses single you out from all us other manly chaps?"

"Whatever it is, I'd just as soon I hadn't got it."

"And shall you be here to milk a cow or two on Christmas morning, the same as us more common mortals?"

"I needn't do much to do a whole lot more than you," Jack said, "if your labours here is anything to go by."

Just before twelve on Christmas Day, in his best cap and suit of black serge, with a collar and neck-tie bought on purpose in the village shop, he walked up the orchard and fields to the farmhouse. His boots were polished; his face clean-shaven; his hair was slicked down with a little of Shiner's embrocation; and he had a white handkerchief in his pocket. But otherwise, he said to himself, he was Jack Mercybright just the same.

The house looked as dark and gloomy as ever, the blinds pulled down in the upper windows, the curtains half drawn in the lower ones. The only brightness showed at the back: a red glow in the window of the kitchen, where the cook, Mrs Miggs, was busy at her stove.

He was crossing the yard when Nenna darted out of

one of the buildings and hurried to meet him. She looked distressed and very angry.

"What's up?" he asked. "Didn't Father Christmas fill your stocking?"

"Come with me and I'll show you!" she said.

He followed her past the house door, into the long open passage that ran between wash-house and dairy, and along to the room that was known as the office. There, the desk was covered with a chequered cloth, and a dinner-place was laid for one, with knife, fork, and spoon, a mug and a beer-jug, and a white linen napkin in a ring.

"This is where you're to have your dinner!" Nenna said, striking the desk with both her fists. "Mrs Miggs has just laid it under Philippa's orders. And *I* thought she meant you to have it with us!"

Jack stood staring at the blue and white cloth, crisply starched and beautifully ironed, and the silver salt-cellar, beautifully polished.

"At least she ent put me to eat with the pigs!"

"I wouldn't stay if I were you," Nenna said. "I'd just walk out and leave it be! You needn't think I shouldn't understand. I should feel exactly the same as you do."

Jack considered doing just that. Then he shook his head. Underneath, he was very angry. It was just the kind of position he hated. But it was too late for withdrawal now, and he blamed himself for his own unwisdom.

"I reckon maybe I'd better stay."

"Then I'll eat here too. Oh, yes, I shall! I've made up my mind! I'll get my things and ask Cook to serve mine out here with you."

"No," he said. "It'll only make trouble all around. I don't want trouble. I only want to be left in peace."

Nenna's face was a bright scarlet, her dark eyes blazing, looking into his. He had never before seen her so angry.

"Very well," she said. "If that's how you want it. But I don't know how I shall get through dinner with Philippa now. I'm sure I shall never be able to speak to her from start to finish!"

"She means well enough. It was you and me that got things wrong. Now get back indoors in the warm before you catch your death of cold. Tell Mrs Miggs I'm ready and waiting."

When Nenna had gone he hung up his cap and sat down, and a moment later Mrs Miggs came in with his dinner.

"Smells good," he said, as she put the plate in front of him. "And I see it's done nice and crisp and brown on the outside. I like a bit of nice crisp brown skin." He spoke up loudly, for Mrs Miggs was very deaf.

"I've gave you a leg, Mr Mercybright, and the first tasty bits off the breast, too."

"Shall I be able to eat all this great lot here, d'you suppose?"

"Of course you will!" And she set another dish on one side, covered over to keep it warm. "That's your plum-pudden, Mr Mercybright. – Go easy as you eat it 'cos most of the silver threepenny bits is in that portion I cut for you."

Left alone, he tucked his napkin into his waistcoat and began eating his Christmas dinner, staring at the old, faded, mould-freckled field-map hanging up on the wall before him. He ate quickly, so that he should be done with it and gone from the place as soon as might be, and when he had finished his plum-pudding, he left the four silver threepenny bits shining along the edge of his plate.

On leaving the farm he went for a long brisk walk

across country, to settle his stomach, unaccustomed to the rich food. There was a touch of frost that day; the ground was crusty underfoot; the air faintly foggy, blurring the landscape; and, walking about for two hours, he had this grey, unlit world to himself entirely.

He went home to the cottage and stirred his fire to life on the hearth. He set up a rough trestle work-bench before it and began making frames and casements for the windows.

His work on the cottage was now a quiet passion. Every penny saved from his wages went to buy lime and tar and lead sheeting; carpenter's tools, nails, and oak planking. He was always on the alert for bargains. When an old barn was pulled down at Hotcham, he got the beams and boards and tiles for a few shillings. When a greenhouse fell down at the vicarage in Niddup, he got the glass for a few pence.

The tiles went to roof the cartshed and toolshed and the lean-to. The glass he cut into small panes and joined together with strips of lead for his casements. And the old oaken beams and boards were just what he needed for rebuilding the steep staircase, rising in a curve behind the fire-place.

"You're good at carpentry," Nenna said, watching one day as he screwed a casement into place.

"Not bad, I suppose . . . I worked for a year or two with a carpenter, once, a long time ago, when I was a youngster."

"Is there anything you have *not* done?"

"Well, I've never sailed the Arctic in search of whales . . . Nor I never played in a brass band . . ."

"But you've been a thatcher . . . soldier . . . a blacksmith, once, I remember you told me . . . and a miner in the Forest of Dean . . ."

"Jack of all trades and master of none, that's me to a shaving, ent it?" he said.

"Didn't you ever have any ambition?"

"Ambition? Yes. When I was a boy I wanted to drive the Royal Mail from Brummagem to London."

"I was being serious," Nenna said.

"So was I serious. I saw myself in a curly-brimmed hat and a coat with five or six shoulder-capes on it, sitting up on the box as large as life, flipping away at six black horses. It grieved me sorely, I can tell you, when they took that there mail coach off the road."

"But didn't you ever want to *do* something with your life?"

"Just live it, that's all."

He was trying the casement, swinging it to and fro on its hinges. He glanced at her and saw exasperation in her face.

"You vex me!" she said. "You're too good a man to be just a labourer on the land."

"The land needs good men. Where should we be if they was all bad ones?"

"You could be a farm bailiff if you wanted to be."

"I was one, once, on a big estate farm up near Kitchinghampton, but I didn't care for it over much. I was either sitting at a desk all day long or riding about on the back of a horse, and I'm too bony about the rump to spend so much time in a chair or a saddle."

"You ought to be bailiff here by rights, with Philippa using you as she does. You could be, I'm sure, if you wanted it."

"I *don't* want it," he said firmly. "I better prefer to stop as I am. So don't go putting no hints about on my behalf, or there'll be ructions, just you mark me!"

Sometimes in the evenings, especially as the days

lengthened and spring was in the offing, the other men would stroll down to Jack's cottage to see how the work was going on. They were interested in it. They were always offering their advice. And one April evening he had three of them there at one time: Joe Stretton, Percy Rugg, and the shepherd, William Gauntlet, whose flock was in the Low End pasture, just a field away to the east of the cottage.

"If I was you," said Percy Rugg, watching Jack as he mixed his whitewash in a bucket: "if I was you I'd give it a couple of dips of the blue-bag."

"I shall when I get to the last coat or two, but that won't be for a long while yet."

"How many coats do you aim putting on, then, Jack?"

"As many as I've got time for, I reckon, and maybe a few more extra, too, on those walls that get the worst of the weather."

"I'd say you was doing a good job," said William Gauntlet, "though I wouldn't have done them panels with clay, myself. I'd have filled 'em up with good brick nogging."

"I ent got the money for bricks," Jack said. "The clay costs me nothing but the labour of digging it out of the ground."

"It's a nice little cottage now you're getting it patched up a bit," said Joe Stretton. "You wouldn't care to swap with me for mine, would you? No? Ah, well! I always knew you was a mean sort of bastard the moment I clapped eyes on you down the fletchers."

"This here chimney," said William Gauntlet, prodding it with his long stick, "ent you going to whitewash that?"

"No, I judge it's better left as it is. The bricks is a nice warm shade of red, and the fire would be sure to discolour it if it was whitewashed."

"Ah. Well. If you say so, of course. But I wouldn't have left it bare, myself."

"I see you got your taters heled in already, Jack," said Percy. "A bit early for that, ent it?"

"A lot too early," Gauntlet said. "Taters go in on Good Friday. Anyone will tell you that. I wouldn't never dream of putting them in no earlier, myself."

A pony and trap came up the road from Niddup, with Miss Philippa driving and Nenna sitting up beside her. At sight of the men gathered together outside the cottage, Miss Philippa stopped and spoke to them in her loud clear voice.

"I see you're admiring Mercybright's labours. I think you'll agree that it's really very commendable indeed. It might even inspire you other men to make more effort in keeping your own cottages in better order."

The three men said nothing. They put on the blank, absent-minded expression they habitually wore in Miss Philippa's presence. Stretton chewed his quid of tobacco. Gauntlet picked at the mud on his sleeve.

"If there's anything you want, Mercybright, you know you have only to ask," she said. "I always believe in helping those that are obviously willing to help themselves."

She drove off, and Nenna, looking back over her shoulder, gave Jack a friendly salute, secretly, while her sister looked elsewhere. The men watched the trap for a little while as it drove round the bend embracing the Low End pasture. It was half visible above the hedgerow. Then it vanished over the rise.

"Lumme!" said Percy. "It's well to be Jack, ent it, eh?" And, doing his best to mimic Miss Philippa's ringing tones: "Anything you fancy, Mercybright, and I'll have it brung you on a silver platter!"

"She says things different," Jack said, "when she ent got an audience listening in."

"There's only your word for that, though, ent there?"

"It's up to *her* to keep the farm cottages in repair, not up to us!" said Joe Stretton. "And it's people like Jack here that makes it more harder for the rest of us, ent it? It's all right for him! He's got nothing else to do but slave his guts out all the time but if she thinks I'm going to do the same for that rotten pig-sty me and my kids've got to live in she's got another think coming!"

"All the same, I reckon he's done a good job on this cottage, give him his due," said Percy Rugg. "But it don't seem all that likely to me, somehow, that a man should go to all this trouble just for hisself alone, like, does it? So when are you thinking of getting married, Jack?"

"I'm not thinking about it at all," Jack said.

"What, not ever?" Stretton asked.

"No. Not ever. Neither now nor never after."

"Laws, somebody's in for a disappointment, then, poor soul, ent she?"

"Is she?" Jack said. "And who's that?"

"Laws!" Percy said, opening his eyes very wide. "D'you mean there's more than one likely hopeful dangling for you?"

"The trouble with you two," Jack said, "you both talk too much damned blasted rubbish."

"That's right, so they do!" said William Gauntlet. "I wouldn't listen to them, myself. They need a few knots tying in their tongues."

One afternoon when the men had just come in from the fields and were unyoking their teams in the yard, Nenna came to the door of the cheeseroom and called for someone to go and raise the old heavy press, which had fallen over on its side. Jack pretended not to hear her; he was busy removing Spangler's harness; Martin Mossmore answered the call.

A day or two later, Nenna wanted help in the wash-house, where a jackdaw's nest was blocking the chimney. Jack ignored her yet again and Charlie Foster went instead.

"Are you avoiding me?" Nenna asked seeking him out when he was alone in the office one morning. "You always used to be so helpful. What have I done that you should turn your back on me whenever there's something wanting doing?"

"You ent done nothing. It's just that I reckon it's wiser, that's all. You know what the men are like here – always ready with their smart remarks."

"What remarks? Because you and I are friends, you mean?"

"That's right. They've got runaway tongues, the lot of them, and they're deadly clever at ferreting out things that ent even there."

"What do I care for their stupid gossip?" she said, scoffing. "It's nothing to me! Not so much as a split pea!"

And, as though to prove it, she called on him at home that evening.

He was in the garden, earthing up his early potatoes, and when he took a rest at the end of the row, he saw her coming slowly down the orchard, carrying something in her arms. He went to meet her and found she was bringing an old Windsor chair.

"It's for you," she said. "Philippa threw it out weeks ago, just because two slats are broken. I thought you might mend it."

"I could, I daresay. But I don't want you bringing me things from out of the farmhouse. I'd just as soon not be beholden."

"This chair has been out in all weathers. It would only rot away in the end. Just look at the state it's in already – there's scarcely a scrap of varnish left on it."

"All right," he said, and took it from her. "But no more presents after this, remember."

He repaired the chair a day or two later and rubbed it down with glass-paper. He stained it dark with permanganate of potash and polished it with best brown boot-polish warmed at the fire. It was now a fine old handsome chair, and Nenna made him a flat cushion, with tapes for tying it to the slats at the back.

"There!" she said, setting the chair at a little angle beside the fire-place. "Now you'll have somewhere comfortable to sit when you want to smoke your pipe in the evenings."

"Yes. The place is getting to look quite homely."

"With just one chair?" she said, laughing, and glanced about at the brick floor, which, although scrubbed and reddled, was still quite bare. "You need a few mats about the place to make it warmer. You need a table and cupboards and then some pegs to hang your coats on – "

"Yes, well, all in good time, I dare say. Rome warnt built in a day, you know. And don't go bringing me things from the house or your sister will say I'm preying on you to my own advantage."

"You don't like Philippa, do you?"

"Not much," he said, "though I sometimes feel sorry for her, in a way."

"She wouldn't care for that, your feeling sorry for her. That would be a blow to her pride indeed."

"I shan't tell her. Nor will you. So she ent likely ever to know it."

Every evening now, while the daylight lasted, he worked on the outside walls of the house, adding coat upon coat of lime wash to the clay-filled panels. Then, after dark, he worked indoors by firelight and lamplight: plastering the inner sides of the panels; renewing pegs in the beams where needed; laying new floorboards in the upper rooms. And sometimes, as a change, he made furniture for the kitchen.

"I suppose you were once a joiner, too, as well as a carpenter?" Nenna said, holding the lamp for him one evening.

"No, I'm no joiner, and anyone looking at this here table would pretty soon know it, too," he said.

"Why, what's wrong with it, I'd like to know?"

"Well, the timber's good, so it looks a lot better than the work that's in it, and a bit of polish will do the rest. Anyway, it's good enough for the likes of me to eat his dinner off of, ent it?"

While he was working, a rat ran across the kitchen floor and passed right over Nenna's foot. She gave a loud scream and almost dropped the lamp she was holding. It made Jack jump, and his chisel slipped, cutting the palm of his left hand. The rat ran out through the open doorway; Jack gave chase and cornered it as it tried to run up the side of the cottage; he killed it with his hammer and threw it over into the pig-run.

By the time he returned, the cut in his hand was bleeding badly, and Nenna turned away from it with a shudder. The sight of blood always made her feel faint. But still she insisted on washing it for him and tying it up with a handkerchief.

"You're always in the wars," she said to him. "You're always doing yourself some kind of damage."

"I must be clumsy, then, I suppose."

"I'm sorry I screamed, but I hate rats."

"There were dozens here when I first came. They used

to run over me while I slept. But they've mostly disappeared since I started cleaning the old place up and generally creating a big disturbance. That one tonight was the first I've seen in more'n a twelvemonth."

He cleaned the rat's blood from the head of his hammer, and took the chisel in his bandaged hand. He looked across at Nenna, who was casting around with the lamp before her, still nervously scanning the floor.

"I never used to trouble about the rats before," he said, "but they're going to notice a big difference now I'm a chap with a chair and a table."

Spring that year was soft, warm, and damp. The new leys grew apace, and the meadows, under improved management, were lush with broadbladed grass and clover. Summer came in full of promise and mowing started earlier than usual, but the year turned out to be one of exceptional thunderstorms, so that in the end haymaking durdled on and on until long after the cuckoo had flown.

"Is it wise to cut?" Miss Philippa would ask, waylaying Jack as he entered a meadow. "There's another storm threatening, I'm almost sure."

"I think cut, storm or no storm. Better to have it in the swath, getting wet, than beaten down so's we can't cut it."

"I suppose so," she would say, frowning. "Yes. Yes. I suppose so."

She was on the go all through haymaking, out at all hours, working in a fever; fretting at every slightest delay; scolding Nenna if she came late into the hay-field.

"The way she goes on," Joe Stretton muttered to Jack, "you'd think she ate hay for every meal."

"Maybe she does," said Peter Luppitt, overhearing. "A nag always likes a fat hay-bag."

The three of them were in Longsides Meadow, at work with their scythes, cutting a pathway from the gateway round, so that Jack could get in with the reaping machine. In the parallel meadow, known as Horner's, the hay was already cut and made and the rest of the men, with their wives and children, were hurrying to get it safely cocked before the next storm broke and descended. Miss Philippa was with them and her voice could be heard even at that distance, berating little Archie Gauntlet because he had broken a tooth in his hay-rake.

In the middle of the afternoon, the reaping machine seized up, for the toughest grasses had wound themselves round the end of the axle that drove the blades. Jack got down, took a few tools out of the tool-box, and went to put the matter right. He was bending over the old machine when lightning flashed in the dark southern sky, followed at once by a crack of thunder, and big raindrops came slopping down. Stretton and Luppitt went at once to push their scythes in under the hedgerow. Then they ran for shelter in the old milking-shed at the top end of Horner's.

"Come on, Jack!" Stretton called in his great bull-like voice. "It's going to be a real drencher!"

Jack dropped his spanners and hammer on the ground and followed Stretton to the shed, where all the haymakers were already gathered, packed close together at one end to avoid a leak in the roof at the other.

"We've finished our lot," Archie Gauntlet said to Jack, and pointed out at the rows of haycocks ranged along Horner's Meadow. "Just about in the nick of time, warnt it?"

"My bonnet's out there," said his sister, Phoebe, with great sadness. "It fell off when I started running."

And she hid her face in her mother's apron as lightning again lit the sky and thunder splintered overhead. As the thunder quietened, the white rain fell faster, blanching across the green landscape and filling the air with a loud angry swish that seemed to foretell the end of the world.

It was all over in a few minutes. Then the sun came out again. Phoebe was running to retrieve her wet bonnet and the rest of the haymakers were trooping through the open gateway into Longsides Meadow. And the smell of drenched hay, steaming hotly, was now so sweet that it made a man giddy, Peter Luppitt said.

Jack went back to the reaping machine. He saw that all was not as it should be. Three of the blades were badly buckled; twisted into crazy curves until they were almost touching each other. The tools he had left in a heap were now scattered, the two spanners quite three yards apart, the hammer under the machine itself. He smelt burning and then became aware that the ground was smoking all around him, where the lightning had gone through the wet grass.

"Christ!" said Joe Stretton, just behind him. "It's a lucky thing you came when I called you or you'd be a goner by now, sure as fate!"

"Ah," Jack said, and stooped to pick up the long-handled hammer, the head of which was still warm. "Would you believe it! It's a lucky thing, like you say."

He went to the mare to comfort her, for her ears were back and her eyes rolling, and she was covered in a froth of sweat. She would not be fit for more work that day. She was scouring badly and her legs would only just support her.

The haymakers were gathering round the reaper, some of them bravely touching the blades, others keeping their hands in their pockets, safely. There was a buzz of excitement among them. They looked at Jack as though he had suddenly sprouted wings.

"You should've covered the machine over," said Joe Stretton. "That's asking for trouble, that is, with them blades there shining so silver bright."

"I reckon I should've," Jack agreed, "but I never brought no canvas with me."

He undid the traces and let the swingletree fall to the ground. He went again to Dinkymay's head. He was still trying to comfort her, speaking to her in a quiet voice, when Miss Philippa came along with Nenna and pushed a way through the little crowd. Nenna looked at the twisted blades of the reaper and touched one gingerly with the tips of her fingers. She looked at Jack with incredulous eyes.

"You might have been killed," she said, shocked.

"He would've been, too," Stretton said, "if it hadn't been for me calling him to come away when I did."

"Oh, really, this is too bad!" Miss Philippa said, seeing the damage done to the reaper. "Everything seems to be against us this summer. We shall never be done with hay-making at this rate. How long will it take to repair, do you think?"

"I dunno," Jack said. "If we get it down to the forge right away, Tom Andrews might have it done by morning. It all depends how busy he is."

"See to it, then, will you?" she said. "Get Andrews to hurry. Tell him we're desperate."

"That's the penalty," Stretton said, "of only having one old reaper!"

Miss Philippa pretended not to hear him.

"Meanwhile, Mercybright, set the men to mow here by hand."

"Right," Jack said, but he made no immediate move to obey, and Miss Philippa, in the act of walking away, stopped and looked back.

"Well, man, where's the point in delaying the matter? Why are you making a fuss of that mare?"

"I'm getting her home in a minute or two. She's in a pretty bad state of nerves. But it's no good trying to chivvy her up."

"Don't talk such nonsense! We've wasted enough time here already. You can use that mare for getting the reaper down to the village."

"Not Dinkymay. She needs rest and quiet. She needs a bit of coddling up. She came a lot nearer to death than I did."

Miss Philippa's lips were pressed tight together, and her eyes glittered, but, knowing he would not give way before her, she thought it best to argue no further. Instead, she gave vent to her temper by sneering at him.

"You're making a great deal of capital out of this, I must say! You and all your fellows here! Perhaps you would like me to declare a half holiday all round? But surely there's nothing so very extraordinary about a bolt of lightning, is there?"

She walked away, and Joe Stretton, in huge delight, treated Jack to a powerful shove.

"So that's put you in your proper place for once and no error! It's no good you thinking you're something special just 'cos you had such a near miss. Oh dear me no! No lections of that! It's as common as pass-the-jug-round-and-find-it-empty. Now if you'd been *struck*, that'd be different. The parson would've preached a special sermon over your poor dead remains and the details would all've been put on your tombstone."

"I'd sooner be a live Nobody than a dead Somebody." Jack said, and led the quivering Dinkymay slowly homewards.

*

They were playing catch with the weather right on to the end of July, but the hay was all got in at last and was all well made. Only one stack, up in the meadow at Far Fetch, had to be opened and dried out because of heating.

"Well, we shan't have to buy hay from Spouts next winter, shall we?" Peter Luppitt said to his brother, making sure Miss Philippa heard him. "Nor shall we have our cattle turning up their noses at the home-grown stuff as they have done in years gone by, poor souls."

The storms continued into August, and some of the corn in the upper fields was laid low under the onslaught. Miss Philippa fretted worse than ever. She was always calling Jack's attention to some new example of the weather's depredations. She behaved almost as if he were to blame.

"Just look at this!" she said, taking him into a field of twenty-seven acres known as Long Pitch, under Tootle Barrow. "Just look what has happened here overnight!"

For the hot boisterous wind, blowing in at the south east corner, had carved a long corridor through the oats, all the way down beside the hedgerow.

"Yes, I noticed it this morning, first thing. It looks for all the world as if someone had left the gate open up there, don't it, and let the wind in?"

"It's even worse in the Round Wood Field. The barley is lodged in great patches all over. And the Home Field too."

"Ah," Jack said. "It's these here hot squalls."

"You don't seem very worried about it."

"What can I do? Stand it all up again, is that what you want?" He plucked a few grains from a ripening oatspray and rubbed the husks off in his palm. "Worrying won't make matters better. It'll only turn your hair grey, that's all."

"It's easy enough for you to say that! You get your wages whatever the weather does to the crops! It's no odds to you one way or the other!"

"You'll still get a good enough harvest," he said, nibbling the oatseed. "Better than you've had these many years past."

The thunderstorms ended eventually, and when harvest began in the middle of August, they were visited only by short light showers falling out of a pale sky. The workers were glad of these little showers. They would turn up their faces to receive the cool drops.

As Jack had predicted, the harvest that year, although not good, was better than the farm had yielded for a long, long time. Miss Philippa was pleased. She was in great spirits. For once she welcomed all the itinerants who came to Brown Elms in quest of work, though she afterwards worried about the gypsies camping in the birchwoods close behind the farmhouse.

"So long as they're close, you're all right," Jack told her. "Gypsies never steal near home. It's your neighbour John Tuller at Maryhope that'll likely lose his eggs and poultry."

"Well, they'll grow no fatter on *that*!" she said, and he glanced at her in some surprise. He had never known her make a joke before. A smile wrought wonders in her rather severe and hard-boned features.

Towards the end of August, the weather turned exceptionally hot, and the harvesters, pledged as they were for every ounce of their strength and endurance, became more silent day by day. The sun's passion was already a burden upon them. Now its demands were cruel indeed.

A man with sweat in his eyes is blind to everything but the need to keep going. He sees only the corn not yet cut, and his blade going through it. He is deaf to everything but the sound of his own blood pounding in his head. He waits for the short night's sleep that stills it. Such a man has nothing to say. His tongue is swollen in his mouth. His lips are burning. He has mortgaged every bit of strength and survives on a budget. Speech is one of the first things to go and no one resents it. They are all as one in this at least.

But the day comes when the silence is broken. A man with a scythe makes one last wide embracing sweep, and the last of the corn goes down before him. Another takes it in his hands; a third steps forward to tie it round; and up it goes for all to see: the last sheaf.

"That's the one! The best of the lot! The one we've been looking for all through harvest!"

The silence is broken. The dumb men find their tongues. The sheaf is held aloft and goes round the field to the sound of cheering and rough laughter. And because the custom has come down from the very earliest ages, the words the harvesters use are old.

"The neck! The neck! Make way for the neck! Here come we, fine chaps one and all! – Make way for us! We bring the neck!"

Ten days later, with the weather still scorching hot, the last load was ready for carting from the Hole Hill Field at Far Fetch. It stood on the brow, with a couple of ropes tied over it for safety, and with Minta, the big roan mare, between the shafts.

The younger lads were gathered in a little circle, making up a special sheaf of barley and oats and wheat together, with scarlet popaies entwined in the bond. When they were done they went to Joe Stretton, the Lord of the Harvest, and put the sheaf into his hands. There was much nodding and winking among them; much whispered argument and banter; and they kept glancing towards Nenna, who stood waving a branch of elder to keep the flies out of Minta's eyes.

"Right you are!" Stretton said. "We'll go and ask her."

With the others behind him, he walked up to Nenna and touched his cap.

"The lads would like you to ride on the load, miss. Bringing in the luck, as you might say. And they've made up a special harvest sheaf for you to carry in your arms."

"Up there?" Nenna said, looking at the load rising above her. "It's very high."

"You'll be all right, miss. It's well roped down, don't you worry, and we shall see to it that you get a smooth ride."

"Very well," Nenna said. "I wouldn't want to spoil the luck."

She stuck the elder branch into the hames of Minta's collar, took the sheaf presented to her by Joe Stretton, and climbed the ladder onto the load. She settled herself comfortably, spreading her blue skirts out around her, and slipped one hand in under the cross-rope.

"All right, Miss Nenna?" Stretton asked. "Feel nice and comfy and safe, do you, and ready to go?"

"Yes, I'm ready. I'm holding on."

"Right you are, then! We're just about off. No need to be frightened. You're as safe as houses with us, I promise."

Stretton went and took the mare's bridle, and Percy Rugg got up on the runner, where he could reach the brake when needed. The ladder was removed; the chocks kicked away; and the word given. The waggon started with a little jolt and moved off slowly down the slope, with Nenna sitting up aloft, the harvest sheaf cradled in her arm.

The harvesters walked at either side of the load, and Jack, coming down the field with Joybell and Spangler, stood for a while to watch it go past. Nenna smiled down at him, inclining her head in a regal manner, playing the part expected of her. She even let go of the rope for an instant to give him a wave, but quickly took hold of it again as the load seemed to surge and sway beneath her. She was wearing a big straw hat with a brim, and pinned to the ribbon there was a bunch of artificial cherries, gleaming redly in the sun.

"Make way! Make way!" Paul Luppitt shouted, and all the others took up the call:

> "Make way, make way,
> And let us pass!
> We sowed it!
> We growed it!
> We hoed it and mowed it!
> Now come we home –
> Pray let us pass!"

As they were moving down the field, the harvesters repeating their rhyme for the third of fourth time, more loudly than ever, Miss Philippa appeared in the open gateway. She stood staring, putting up a hand to shade her eyes. Then she hurried forward and stepped directly into Joe Stretton's path. The mare stopped dead; Percy Rugg put the brake on sharply; and Nenna, sitting up high on the load, received such a jolt that the bunch of cherries fell from her hat. It plopped down into the stubble and Harvey Stretton snatched it up.

"Nenna, come down!" Miss Philippa commanded in a loud voice. "I will not have you making a spectacle of yourself like this, behaving like any cottager's hoyden!

Have you no sense of what is fitting? Don't you think it's time you conducted yourself like a grown woman?"

"It's only our fun, ma'am," said Percy Rugg. "It was us lot that put Miss Nenna up to ride, so's we could shout the last load home in proper style. We meant no disrespect, ma'am, I assure you truly."

"Aye, what's wrong with keeping up the old-fashioned customs?" Joe Stretton asked, his chin out-thrust. "We always *did* used to shout the harvest home in the old days. – Going back, that is, to when the harvests was *worth* shouting!"

Miss Philippa's face was a mottled red. The hot weather disagreed with her, so that she was more than usually peevish today, and Stretton's remark put paid to her temper. She pushed past him and went close to the load.

"Nenna!" she said. "Come down at once!"

"We can't get Miss Nenna down now," said Bob Chapman, " 'cos somebody's gone and took away the ladder."

"Not unless she was to jump, of course, and we was to catch her," said Percy Rugg.

"D'you reckon that's wise?" Peter Luppitt asked gravely. "It's a pretty long way from up aloft there to down here below with us, I would say."

"Well, I dunno, I'm sure, it's a bit of a pickle, ent it?" said his brother Paul, scratching the side of his sunburnt nose.

"We sowed it! We growed it!" shouted Harvey Stretton, peeping round from the back of the waggon. "We hoed it and mowed it so why can't we pass?"

"I reckon my boy's got a point," Stretton said, swaggering up to Miss Philippa. "The way I see it, we've all got a right to insist upon it that this here procession be allowed to continue."

"I'm warning you, Stretton! If you don't quickly get out of my way – "

"Yes?" Stretton said. "And what then, if?"

Miss Philippa was glaring at him. She found it hard to meet his ugly, insolent gaze and was using all her will-power to do so. The air was highly charged between them and Jack was about to interfere when Nenna leant over the side of the load.

"I think I'd like to come down now, Stretton. Would someone please go and fetch the ladder?"

The danger, if any, passed away. Somebody went and fetched the ladder and Nenna came down it, cautiously, bestowing her corn-sheaf on Harvey Stretton, who mounted and took her place on the load, with her crimson cherries pinned in his cap.

"Well, you ent so pretty as Miss Nenna, boy, but I reckon you'll just have to do!" said Joe Stretton, and pulled at Minta's bridle.

As the load moved off, Miss Philippa was already railing at Nenna, and her words could be heard by every man and boy in the field.

"How dare you behave in such a fashion? Don't you realize the consequences of being so familiar with the men? They take advantage enough already without any undue encouragement from you! You're not a child any longer, you know, and it's time you learnt a little decorum!"

She then went off up the field in a hurry, making for the brow, where a few women and children were gleaning, without having first obtained her permission. In another moment, she was venting the rest of her temper on them.

Nenna turned and looked at Jack. He was still standing with the two horses. He saw the trembling of her lip and made a face at her, showing that he was sympathetic. Then, leading the horses, he started after the loaded waggon, and Nenna went with him.

"That's not the first time she's made me look foolish in front of the men. Sometimes I feel as though I could kill her!"

"You didn't look foolish. It's only her own-self she makes look foolish."

"I felt it all the same! Being scolded like a naughty child! Having to come down off the waggon! In front of them all! In front of *you!*"

"She won't change," Jack said, "so the best thing is to take no notice."

"That's easy for you! You don't have to live with her!"

On the following Saturday, the men stopped work at two o'clock in the afternoon, in spite of dark looks from Miss Philippa.

"We've always finished early on the Saturday after harvest," Joe Stretton said to her, "and I reckon we've earned it this year, surely?"

Jack went home and ate a quick dinner of bread and cold bacon. He stripped to the waist and scrubbed himself clean at the pump in the yard. He was shaving the thick growth of stubble from his chin, with his piece of mirror propped up on the spout, when Nenna came in by the orchard gate, wearing gardening gloves and a rough hessian apron.

"I passed here this morning and saw what a mess the garden was in. Your onion patch is a proper disgrace."

"I've had no spare time all through harvest."

"I know that," she said. "That's why I've come to give you a hand. Your potatoes want lifting. So do your carrots. I thought I'd help you to make a start."

"I'm doing no work today," he said. "I'm going to the fair at Kevelport."

"Oh!" she exclaimed. "Can I come with you and see them roasting the great ox?"

With his razor in his hand, poised close to his white-lathered jaw, he turned towards her. Her face was as eager as a child's.

"Well, I dunno . . ."

"Oh, do let me come! I haven't been since I was a child, when my step-father took me and bought me a monkey on a stick."

"The other men'll be going, remember. There's bound to be talk if they see us together. You know what loose-hinged tongues they've got."

"What does that matter? I don't care!"

"We should have to tell your sister first . . ."

"We can call and tell her on the way."

"All right," he said. "So long as you're sure, come by all means."

Nenna pulled off her gardening gloves and threw them down onto the flagstones. She took off her apron and whirled herself round and round on her toes, letting her skirts billow out around her.

"Oh, do hurry up and get yourself ready!"

"That's a risky thing, trying to hurry a man when he's shaving, and if you go on spinning about like that I shall very likely cut myself from ear to ear."

"Then I'll stop," she said, and sat down primly on the staddle-stone, watching him as he finished shaving. "You're a handsome man when you're properly shaved. You ought to do it every day."

"Then I'd look no different on special occasions."

"You ought to do it all the same."

"Ah, well, there's lots of things I ought to do, I daresay, if I did but know it."

"Yes. There are. You should take more pride in yourself altogether. You could be somebody if you wished it. You could cut a fine figure and win respect."

"You're buttering me up a bit today, ent you? I reckon you must have an eye on my harvest money! You want me to buy you another monkey on a stick!"

"No, I want to have my fortune told, and I want to see the dancing bear."

"D'you think he'll be there after all these years? He might have died since you was there last."

"Oh, no!" she said, stricken. "Surely not!"

"We shall have to see, then, shan't we?" he said.

He went indoors and changed into his best clothes. He put on his only collar and tie. When he emerged, he handed Nenna his old clothes-brush and she brushed him down, removing cobwebs and bits of straw.

"I was thinking what fun it would be if we could go in the pony and trap."

"Crying off?" he said. "Because you've remembered it's five miles to walk?"

"Oh, no! Certainly not!" And she gave his arm a sudden squeeze. "I'd still want to go if it was twenty!"

"I'm not so sure that *I* would."

"This jacket of yours! It looks as though you've slept in it!"

"It isn't me that's slept in it. It's that tabby cat of yours from the barn. She had her kittens on this jacket!"

They were standing thus, with Nenna brushing hard at his shoulders, when the orchard gate opened and shut and Miss Philippa appeared before them.

"So this is where you've got to?" she said to Nenna. "I might have known it! Do you realize that I have been

searching all over the farm for you, my girl? Do you realize you left the tap in the dairy running and flooded the
place right out to the door?"

"I'm sure I didn't," Nenna said. "I'm sure I remember
turning it off."

"Do you also remember leaving the milk-pans filthy
dirty? And yesterday's cheese-cloths still in soak? Not to
mention letting the chickens get into the granary?"

"I said I was sorry for that, Philippa. I thought it was all
over and done with. As for the milk-pans —"

"Am I supposed to do everything myself while you gad
about like a giddy school-girl? Don't I deserve some con-
sideration? Surely it's not too much to expect that you
should do something towards your keep!"

She was goading herself into a fury. The blood burnt
in red spots on her cheekbones, and her eyes were glit-
tering. She was careful not to meet Jack's gaze directly,
but her glance kept flickering contemptuously over him,
noting that he wore his Sunday blacks and his best boots
with polished toe-caps. Suddenly she snatched the
clothes-brush from her sister's hands and thrust it savagely into his.

"Surely he can brush his own clothes, can't he? Do you
have to wait on him hand and foot? It's a fine thing, I
must say, when my sister runs after one of the farm hands
and makes herself cheap by skivvying for him! Do you
think I can't guess where you are whenever you're missing from the house? Oh, I know well enough! You've
always been bone idle at home yet you come down here
and work in his garden – '

"Go away," Jack said, in a quiet voice. "Go away, Miss
Philippa, you've said enough."

"How dare you speak to me like that? What right have
you to interfere between Nenna and me in the first

place? Sometimes, Mercybright, I regret that I ever took you into my employ at all and one of these days will very surely be your last!"

"Why not today? Why not send me packing this instant? Or ent I outworn my usefulness to you, trying to set this farm on its feet?"

"I wonder that a grown man like you doesn't feel the awkwardness of such a situation," she said. "I wonder you aren't embarrassed by it!"

She swung away and left them. The gate slammed, and they watched her walking quickly up the orchard, vanishing among the perry pear trees. Nenna was pale. But she had in a way become hardened against her sister's outbursts.

"It's not true that I never do any work at home, but I don't see why I should work all the time and never have any pleasure at all. What do I care for her precious dairy? I hate it and every single thing about it! It's nothing but slavery all day long."

"I know," he said. "I've been in that dairy. I'd say it ent altered since the year dot. She likes to do everything the hard way, that sister of yours."

"Well, I don't and won't!" Nenna said. "Whatever I do is never right. If I'm slow she grumbles, but if I'm quick and get finished early, she makes me do everything over again. And she's *not* my sister!"

"I know," he said. "I know all that. Still, I think there's something in what she says, and I think perhaps you ought to go."

"Go?" she said, staring. "Back home, do you mean?"

"Ah. That's right. To get things sorted out between you. There'll only be trouble otherwise."

"Right now this minute? And not go with you to the fair at all?"

"Better not," he said, and looked away, busy plucking the fluff and hairs and straw from the clothes-brush. "She's right, really. You shouldn't ought to be here with me. It ent seemly."

"Don't you want me?" Nenna asked.

"It's not that. Don't be silly."

"But you're sending me away."

"No, I ent. Well, not exactly."

"Yes," she said. "Oh, yes, you are. You're sending me away." And there was a child's flat dismay in her voice, coupled with a woman's dignity. "I suppose I embarrass you, as Philippa suggested. Well, I won't hang around you any longer, I promise, or cause you embarrassment ever again."

She picked up her gardening gloves and apron, and walked away without another word. She did not look back, nor did she stop to pat old Shiner as she went back home across the orchard.

On his way to the fair he got a ride with two of the gypsies who had come to Brown Elms in time for the harvest. They were still camping in the birchwoods. They had permission to stay there till winter. The two in the cart were a middle-aged couple named Boswell and as they drove along the wife remarked that "the gentleman a'got a lucky face."

Jack gave a shrug. This was the gypsies' stock-in-trade. They thought every gaujo liked to hear it.

"I ent aware," he said, "that my luck is anything much to write home about."

The gypsy man turned and looked him over. Then he looked back at his pony's ears. He was chewing tobacco.

"There's a lot of folk in this world that always chooses to step aside and let good luck go past 'em," he said. "It's a funny thing, that, but I seen it often."

*

Sometimes, when he was out ploughing, he would see Nenna a long way off, coming out of the woods with the dog Roy or throwing a stick for him up on the slopes at Far Fetch. Once he saw her out with a basket, picking mushrooms in the lower meadows, and once he saw her running with a message to Will Gauntlet, ruddling his tups in the yard at Low End. But she never came to the cottage now. Never sought him out while he was working. Never popped out of the barn or dairy to speak to him when he came in from the fields with the horses. She had cut herself off from him completely.

There were many days of cold white mist that autumn: days when, especially in the low-lying fields, he could see no further than Joybell's ears as she plodded ahead in front of Spangler. He had to use the swap-plough. There was nothing else for it. He and the horses went by instinct, ploughing a path through the dense whiteness, which then closed in again, swirling behind them, shutting them off from the rest of the world. And somewhere out in the white darkness were the small voices of the peewits crying.

The mists seemed immovable. They hung about all through September. There was no wind to blow them away.

One Sunday morning, working in his garden, he heard a sound at the orchard gate. He turned around expecting Nenna, but it was only the old horse, Shiner, disliking the loneliness of the mist and coming to the gate for company. Jack pulled up a couple of fat, bolted carrots and took them over, and Shiner munched them noisily, awkwardly, having few good teeth left to chew with.

About the middle of September, Miss Philippa took a few samples of corn to market. Jack was with her and saw the look of surprise on the dealers' faces as they weighed the samples in their little pocket balances. Miss Philippa pretended not to notice. She engaged the clerk in conversation. But afterwards, driving home with Jack, she was flushed with satisfaction.

"Did you see their faces? Did you see Harry Swallow look down his nose and then look again with a bit more interest? Oh, they saw that Brown Elms Farm is far from finished, today, surely!"

"That corn wasn't all that special. It was only one up from the bottom grade."

"But we shall go on doing better! Next year and the year after – there'll be an improvement every harvest. I shall see to it! Mark my words!"

"Aye, if you say so . . ." he said dryly.

"I know a lot of it is due to you, Mercybright, and I'm very grateful, I do assure you. Indeed, if there's anything you want, I shall be pleased to think it over."

"Thanks, but there's nothing."

"Nothing new in the way of tools?"

"There's a long list of the things that are needed on the farm and it's hanging up on your office wall. It's been hanging there for a good long while now but nothing much is ever forthcoming."

"I meant something more in the personal way. Some help with the cottage, possibly, or some plants for your garden."

"No, there's nothing. Except that you might give Nenna a message."

"Oh? What is it?"

"Tell her the bear *was* still dancing when I went to Kevelport Fair that day. Spry as a two-year-old he was, tell her, and the old chap with him in pretty good shape too."

"Yes," she said. "All right. I'll tell her."

"Ah, and tell her there's six or seven apricots on that little tree she planted. – They ought to be eaten. They've been ripe a good while now. Tell her she ought to come and pick 'em."

"Yes. Very well. I'll give her your message, certainly."

The apricots, however, fell to the ground and were eaten by birds, and no Nenna came to the cottage. The sweet williams and wallflowers she had planted in the border under the windows had withered now and gone to seed. Jack pulled them up and burnt them on the bonfire, and dug in the seedlings that had sprung up like mustard-and-cress all around. Nenna, he thought, had probably never been given his message.

On wet evenings now, he sat in his chair beside the fire, his feet on a log inside the hearth. The dresser he was making in the far recess remained half-finished, and his tools lay about there, thrown down anyhow among the shavings.

His injured knee was badly swollen. It was always at its worst when the cold wet weather first set in. So he did nothing; only sat and smoked, enclosed in a kind of obstinate stillness; alone with the pain, as if listening to it.

He got up one evening and hurled his clay pipe into the fire-place. He made the fire safe in a mound of ashes and walked out, putting on his cap and jacket as he went and drawing his collar up to his ears. He told himself he was going to The Bay Tree. He wanted the cheerfulness and the company and he needed to buy a few new pipes. But somehow his feet took him up through the orchard and across the fields towards the farmhouse.

The rain had turned to sleet. It struck hard and cold out of the east. The house was in darkness on every side, no flicker of life even in the kitchen window. So he trudged on into Felpy Lane, and met the trap coming

up from Niddup. Miss Philippa was driving and Nenna
was with her, the two of them huddled beneath an
umbrella. Jack stepped back into the hedgerow, leaning
against the trunk of an oak tree, and watched the trap go
slowly past him. A little while later a light went on in the
kitchen window and glimmered wetly through the night.
Then the curtains were drawn and the place became dark
again, as before.

He began walking towards Niddup. He got as far as
Maryhope Farm. Then he changed his mind and
returned to the cottage, and there he found Nenna, sitting on the staddle-stone, waiting for him.

"I saw you," she said. "I saw you up in Felpy Lane,
skulking under the old oak tree."

He led the way indoors and blew the fire to life with
the bellows. He put on more wood and got it burning.
Nenna wandered about the room, noting the work he
had done in her absence: the two oak stools beside the
table; the tall corner cupboard; the basketwork chair; the
unfinished dresser. She shed her wet cloak and came to
the fire-place, shivering a little as she spread her hands
before the blaze.

"I feel I've come home when I come here," she said,
and looked up at him with the fire reflected in her eyes,
her face and throat warmly lit by the flames. "Don't ever
send me away again, will you?" she said to him in a quiet
voice.

He moved towards her clumsily, and she came to him
without any fuss, giving herself up to him, small in his
arms.

"Nenna, are you mad?" Miss Philippa demanded. "A man twice your age! One of the labourers off the farm! A tramp who came here from God knows where, with nothing but the clothes he wore on his back!"

Nenna was silent, standing with her hand inside Jack's arm. She was smiling to herself as if nothing her sister said could hurt her.

"Have you no pride, girl, with your upbringing? You could marry any one of a dozen gentleman farmers' sons in the district or into one of the professional families—"

"How could I, when I've never met them?"

"Is that the trouble? You never said so. That's quite easily remedied, I assure you."

"It's a bit late now," Jack said. "She's settled for me."

"You! Oh, yes! You've wormed your way in very cleverly, haven't you, winning my trust and enticing Nenna away from me? A girl of eighteen! Scarcely more than an ignorant child! But if you hope to get your hands on this property you're going to be very disappointed, for it's all mine, – every stick and stone on every acre – and Nenna hasn't got so much as a penny piece to call her own!"

"Good. You'll know I'm not marrying her for gain, then, won't you?"

"What *are* you marrying her for, pray?"

"I love her, that's why. What other reason would there be?"

His simple answer seemed to take Miss Philippa by surprise. She stood looking at him for a long time, with frowning eyes, her anger apparently melting away, and when she spoke it was with a tired sigh, as though she admitted herself defeated.

"I was afraid something like this would happen," she said. "I ought to have done something more about it."

She did not ask if Nenna loved *him*. She merely approached the girl and kissed her, rather formally, sorrowfully, as one who believed in doing her duty. Then she shook Jack's hand.

"You mustn't mind the harsh things I said. It's only because I'm anxious for Nenna. I stand in place of both her parents."

"That's all right. I'd just as soon you spoke your mind."

"You'll be married from here, of course. I will make the arrangements."

"Well,—"

"This is Nenna's home, you must remember."

"Right you are. Just as you say."

He left the house feeling rather suspicious. He had expected more difficulties. But Miss Philippa, it seemed, having resigned herself to the situation, was determined to improve it as best she could. She had him drive her to market every week and on errands to neighbouring farms, and she made a great point of treating him with marked respect.

"This is Mr Mercybright, my bailiff," she would say. "He runs things for me at Brown Elms. He is shortly to be married to my half-sister."

And she told him, in private, that after the wedding he would receive an increase in wages.

"I've been promoted!" he told Nenna. "I'm *Mister* Mercybright now, mark you, and going to get a bailiff's wages."

"I should think so too!"

"Is it your doing? You been speaking on my behalf?"

"No. Not a word. But now that you're marrying me, you see, family pride requires that she raise you to an acceptable level."

"Ah. That's it. She's making the best of a bad bargain."

"She's letting us have a bed, did I tell you? And giving us a brand new kitchen range as a wedding present. Oh, and Mrs Ellenton of Spouts is giving us a lamp with a pretty frosted globe on it, and flowers engraved all over the glass."

Nenna was at the cottage every day now, bringing in oddments of china and glass and cutlery unwanted at the farmhouse; screwing cup-hooks into the shelves of the dresser almost before the varnish was dry; measuring for curtains and making thick warm mats for the floors. Miss Philippa talked in vain of the pans standing dirty in the dairy and cheeses that needed turning in the cheese-room. – Nenna had time only for the work that had to be done in the cottage, and when Jack was free, they worked there together. The wedding was set for January the fourth. Sometimes it seemed all too close.

"Shall we be done in time?" Nenna asked. "Shall we? Shall we?"

"Done?" Jack said. "The rate we're going, we could just as well have been married by Christmas!"

There came a day when the last window was in and painted, and he stood back to admire his work. He put aside his paint-pot and brush and walked all round outside the cottage. It looked very trim and smart, he thought: the claywork panels a dazzling white; the beams and windowframes painted black; the thatch now thoroughly darkened by weather and the big redbrick chimney neatly re-pointed from top to bottom; and he called Nenna to come and look.

"When the paint on that window is dry," he announced, "the house is finished!"

"Finished?" she exclaimed. "When there isn't a door on it, front or back?"

Jack was speechless. He felt himself gaping. He had grown so used to the curtain of sacks hanging up in the porch that it seemed the most natural thing in the world.

"If you think," Nenna said, laughing, "that I'm going to live in a house without doors you're much mistaken, Jack Mercybright!"

"H'mm, some folks is fussy," he said, recovering, "but I suppose I shall have to do something about it."

And he went off to see what timber there was left in the out-house.

The two doors were made by the end of December; hung and painted on New Year's Day; and furnished with snecks, locks, and bolts on the morning of the fourth, the day of the wedding.

"A near thing," Jack said to Nenna. "I reckon I came pretty near being jilted!"

They were married in Niddup, in the big old church above the river. There was snow on the ground that afternoon and more fell as they drove in the trap to Brown Elms.

"A white wedding," Nenna said, and squeezed his arm against her body, looking at him through snow-flecked lashes. She seemed warm enough and very happy, enchanted with everything, especially the snow.

The wedding party took place at the farmhouse, in the

best front parlour, where a huge fire burnt for once in the fire-place, drawing the mustiness out of the furnishings and bringing the perspiration out on the red faces of the wedding guests crowded close together there.

"By golly, ent it hot in here?" Jack said, in Nenna's ear. "Don't your sister ever open the windows?"

"Our house will never smell musty," she murmured back. "I shall see to that!"

"Now, then, you two!" said Joe Stretton. "You'll have plenty of time for whispering together in the years to come. It's your guests that ought to be getting your attention now, poor beggars!"

"You know what you are, don't you, bailiff?" said John Tuller of Maryhope Farm, pushing Jack and Nenna together. "You're a cradlesnatcher, that's what you are, marrying this babe beside you here!"

"Ah, you'll have to watch out with a bride as young as that, Jack," said George Ellenton of Spouts Hall. "They're full of mettle when they're under twenty and pretty soon put years on a man if he doesn't take good care about it."

"I hope he knows, that's all," Paul Luppitt remarked to Peter.

"Knows what?"

"How many beans make five."

"I can tell him that — it's six!" said the young boy, Harvey Stretton.

"Drink up, drink up!" said James Trigg of Goodlands. "The nights are long at this time of year."

"I *would* drink up," said Percy Rugg, "if it warnt that my glass didn't seem to be empty."

"I daresay Miss Philippa will have gave Miss Nenna some advice worth hearing."

"She can't have took it, though, can she, or how come we've got a wedding on our hands like this?"

"Lock and key," said James Trigg of Goodlands. "Lock and key was the sound advice my father gave me when I got married. Keep things under lock and key."

"How come our wives warnt invited, I wonder?"

"I reckon Miss Philippa better prefers keeping all us big manly chaps to herself, that's why."

"And who can blame her?" Ellenton said.

Miss Philippa, going about with the jug of ale, turned a deaf ear to these remarks, though the redness in her cheeks showed that she heard them all too plainly, and the way she glared when Peter Luppitt tipped her elbow showed exactly where she laid the blame. The neighbouring farmers from Maryhope and Goodlands and Spouts Hall were respectful enough in the ordinary way, but now, finding themselves in the company of her labourers, they allowed their own coarseness a loose rein and talked as they would in field or cowshed.

"What about you, Miss Philippa?" George Ellenton said to her. "The nights will be long for you, too, now you'll be all alone in the house, eh?"

"Miss Philippa can call me in," said John Tuller, offering his glass for her to fill. "I'd have married her years ago, and well she knows it, if I didn't have a wife already."

"Maybe Miss P. will follow Miss Nenna's example," said Joe Stretton, "and choose a husband from off her own farm."

"Well, Joe," said William Gauntlet, "you're the only single bachelor chap now left here unmarried."

"I know that. I ent simple nor tenpence short!" And Stretton, leaning forward in a familiar way, thrust his thick face as close to Miss Philippa's as he could. "How about it, Miss P? You've always had rather a soft spot for me, ent you?"

Miss Philippa bore it all in silence, with the air of one

who, though her sufferings were due to others, would always do right by them, come what might. Her sister Nenna had brought this upon her, but she did her duty nevertheless and kept the labourers' glasses brimming.

"Why don't you leave her alone?" Jack said. "Instead of baiting her all the time?"

"I'm making the most of things," Stretton said. "Tomorrow morning she'll be back in the saddle again and I shall be trampled underfoot!" He drank his beer and wiped his mouth on the sleeve of his jacket. He was looking at Jack with wicked eyes. "It makes me laugh. It does, honest. I'm as bucked as a doe about the whole thing. You! One of us! Brother-in-law to Miss High-and-Mighty! And her there, looking as if she's swallowed a beetle!"

"You can have a lie-in tomorrow, Jack, seeing it's Sunday," said Peter Luppitt. "Paul and me will do your share of the early milking."

"No need," Jack said. "I shall be there, the same as always."

When he and Nenna were ready to leave, there was talk of the party going with them, "to see them tucked up" as Lacey said, but the joints of cold mutton and beef not yet eaten and the second beer-cask not yet broached were a stronger attraction and kept the wedding guests behind. So Jack and Nenna were allowed to leave peacefully and went arm in arm, treading carefully over the crisp bright sparkling snow to the cottage at the laneside.

The fire was laid in the brand-new shiny kitchen range and while Jack got it going, Nenna went about her wifely duties, filling the kettle ready for the morning and setting the breakfast things out on the table. Then, while he was outside pumping more water, she made porridge and left it in its pan beside the hob.

A little while later, bringing in an armful of logs for the basket, he found the place empty. His working-boots stood on the hearth; his working-shirt was hung up to air; the candle in its holder was burning ready to light the way upstairs to bed. But Nenna was out in the cold night. He followed her foot-prints in the snow and found her standing out in the lane, looking at the cottage with the firelight flickering in its leaded windows and the smoke rising against the stars.

"I wanted to see what it looked like," she said, "to anyone passing up the lane."

She came closer, and her face in the starlight was a child's face, the skin clear and pale, the eyes enormous, the cheekbones delicate and frail-looking. He was suddenly frightened, and she sensed it in him.

"Jack? What's the matter?"

"God, what have I done, marrying such a child!" he said.

She was very small, leaning against him, but she reached up with strong, wilful arms until he submitted and bent his head. The wind blew cold. Light snow began falling again. She shivered a little and he took her indoors.

During the fierce gales that winter, he would sometimes take the lamp from the table and go about inspecting the walls, to see if the rain was driving through them. But the work he had done on the cottage was good. It was proof against every kind of weather.

"Seems the old methods ent so bad after all. That there dobwork is quite as hard as any bricks and a lot more wet-proof into the bargain."

"Come back with that lamp," Nenna said, waiting at the table with her scissors poised above a length of shirting, "or I'll end by cutting your collar crooked."

"Like you done with the last one? And the one before that?"

"You!" she said. "I've half a mind to give you a hair cut!" And as he set the lamp on the table, she made a threatening move with the scissors, going snip-snip-snip close beside his ear. "And your eyebrows too! Great bristly things! I've half a mind to trim *them!*"

"You just get on with making my shirt, so's I look smart in church next Sunday."

"Then you are coming after all?"

"I might," he said. "It all depends what hymns they're having."

"You ought to go to church sometimes," Nenna said. "A man in your position . . . it's only seemly." She finished cutting out the second collar and placed it carefully aside. "Just this once, anyway."

"Why this once?" he asked, amused.

"Well . . . now we know there's a baby coming . . . it seems to me it's only right."

"Why? Doesn't the Lord know we're married? He damned well ought to! We was joined together in his sight, according to what the parson said."

"Shush!" Nenna said. "That's blasphemy." But she laughed all the same. "What would Philippa say if she heard you?"

"If I go to church," he said, watching her as he lit his pipe, "shall I wear my new worsted suit and my soft boots and my smart new wide-awake hat?"

"Of course! Of course!"

"And the spotted silk stock you got for me, too, and the handsome stick-pin?"

"Yes, of course! Where else would you wear them if not to church?"

"Aye," he said, waving away a cloud of smoke, "that's

why you want me to go, ent it, just to show me off in my smart new clothes?"

"Well, what's wrong with that? Oughtn't a wife to be proud of her husband?"

"I could go in corduroys and still be your husband."

"Now you're just being awkward, aren't you?"

"Or send my new clothes along by theirselves."

"You could go to please *me*," Nenna said crossly, and her scissors moved at a great rate, cutting along a black stripe in the shirting.

"Here, steady on, or that there shirt'll end up an apron!"

"Well, will you, then? Go to church to please me?"

"I daresay I shall. Anything for a quiet life. And there's no fool like an old fool, as the saying goes."

"You are *not* old."

"Oh yes I am. I've got bristly eyebrows. Not to mention a gammy leg . . ."

Nenna threw down her scissors and rushed at him in a little passion. She snatched his pipe from between his fingers and threw it in under the stove, where it broke in fragments on the hearthstone. She beat at his chest with clenched fists.

"Another tantrum?" he said, laughing, and put his arms around her waist, drawing her close until she was helpless. "That's the third clay pipe you've smashed for me in a fortnight, woman."

"Serves you right!" she said, clicking her teeth at him, like a puppy. "You ought not to smoke so many pipes. Tobacco is weakening, Dr Spray says."

"Who's weak, I'd like to know?" And he lifted her up against his chest, till her feet were some distance from the floor. "Am I weak, woman? You answer me that!"

"Don't squeeze me so hard!" she said, gasping. "You must think of the baby!"

But when, alarmed, he set her gently on her feet again, she clung to him with her arms round his neck.

"No, don't let me go, Jack! Just hold me and love me. I want you to touch me . . . I want you to carry me up to bed . . . like you did the first time, the night we were married."

This was the time of year he hated: the wet and cold coming together: endless weeks of it, turning the farm into a quagmire; when every steep track became a rillet, and the tumbrils got stuck in mud that reached to the very axles; when the ditches, overflowing, stank of rotting vegetation; and still the rain fell, day in, day out. And in this weather his leg gave much trouble.

He disliked the idea of Nenna seeing his swollen knee; he tried to keep its condition a secret; but one evening when he got home, after a day spent sweeping the floodwater out of the cowsheds, he was limping so badly that Nenna was anxious. She made him sit in his chair by the fire and she knelt before him, turning his trouser leg up to his thigh. The knee was ugly and misshapen, the flesh puffed up, darkly discoloured, like an over-ripe damson, the pus discharged from it drying in a scab.

Nenna sat back on her heels and wept. She looked at him with anguished eyes, and the tears trickled slowly down her cheeks.

"Poor leg, poor leg!" she kept saying, and she wanted to go at once for the doctor. "There must be something he could do!"

"No, there's nothing," Jack said. "I've had this here wound about fifteen years now and any number of doctors've seen it, but nothing they do is ever any good. They all say the same – it can't be mended."

"There must be something!" Nenna said. "Surely? Surely? There must be something!"

"It's the wet and cold that does the damage. It seems to get in between the bones. The rest of the time it ent too bad. I can even forget it when summer comes round."

"But surely there's something? Some ointment, perhaps, or some kind of lotion? Didn't the doctors ever suggest anything at all?"

"Nothing they did ever made any difference."

"But there must be something! No one should have to suffer like that. I can't bear it for you!"

Her distress was such that Jack began casting about in his mind.

"Well, I dunno . . . unless we should try out some sort of poultice . . ."

"Was that something a doctor suggested?"

"Not a doctor, no. It was some old dame I talked to once when I was up at Aston Charmer."

"Did you ever try it?"

"Why, no, I didn't. I forgot all about it until this minute."

"What kind of poultice?" Nenna asked.

"I dunno that I remember. It was two or three years ago. Maybe more." But at sight of her bitter disappointment, he gave the matter further thought. "Bread!" he exclaimed. That's what the old dame recommended. – Bread boiled to a sort of pulp, with a lot of linseed oil in it, and a good pinch of soda. Then you spread it out on a piece of cloth and tie it round the bad place. But I dunno if it really works – "

"It must!" Nenna said, and got up at once to set a saucepan on the hob. "You sit and watch me and tell if

I'm doing it right."

When the poultice was made and wrapped round his knee, held in place by a cotton bandage, Nenna began preparing his supper. But all the time as she moved about the kitchen she watched him closely.

"Is it better?" she asked. "Is the poultice working?"

"I reckon it is . . . I reckon it's taking some of the heat out . . ."

"Are you sure?" she asked. "Do you really mean it?"

"Cross my heart!" he said, getting up and taking a few trial paces. "That's a marvel, that is! I ought to've tried it a long time ago, only I was too lazy to take the trouble. Why, that's very nearly as good as new!"

He said it to please her. The poultice made no difference at all. And yet there was something, as she ministered to him every evening thereafter, that made the pain more easy to bear. It was her tenderness when she touched him; the way she suffered at sight of the wound; the way she cared for him, tireless in doing whatever seemed best. But the poultice itself was nothing much. It was her touch that brought relief.

The doubts he had had in marrying Nenna were now removed. Only a kind of wonder remained. Because of his leg, he had expected her revulsion. Instead, he was cherished all the more. Because he was so much older than she and because he had known a great many years of self-denial, he had thought the roughness of his man's desire might frighten her. But Nenna's passion was as rough as his own. She was eager for him. She wanted him always.

Often during those winter nights, when the rain rattled like grapeshot at the windows, she would draw up the bed-clothes until he and she were covered completely and there in the close warm darkness underneath they would lie on their sides, face to face, two naked children enjoying each other. They had secrets to share. There was laughter between them. They would talk over the happenings of the day together. Until, soft word and soft touch leading at last to hot words and urgent caresses, they would call on each other for the wild union that shut out the black wet winter nights completely; obliterated pain; eased away weariness and brought the deepest sleep.

To please Nenna, he now went to church once a month or so, wore the fine clothes she had bought for him, and lingered with her after the service, exchanging gossip with their neighbours. To please Nenna he now shaved every day of the week; had his hair cut regularly; kept his fingernails neat and clean.

"By God!" said Joe Stretton, waiting in the farmyard one afternoon when Jack returned from Kevelport. "You're that smart it hurts! I suppose you'll be having the mayor to tea before very long? Or the Lord Lieutenant?"

"What, riff-raff like them?" Jack retorted. "Here, give me a hand with this, will you?"

"What the hell is it, for God's sake?"

"It's a butter-making machine, that's what. Miss Philippa ordered it from John Jackson's."

"I daresay she needs it, too, now lately, seeing Miss Nenna is so busy mollying after you that she's got no time to spare for the dairy."

Stretton helped to unload the machine and then walked round it, looking under its canvas cover, tilting the table this way and that, and kicking at the framework.

"I don't hold with machines," he said, "putting poor people out of work the way they do."

"If you want a job as dairymaid, you've only to ask,"

Jack said. "But you might as well get used to the notion of machinery on this here farm 'cos there's going to be a whole lot more of it in the future days to come."

"And that's your doing, I suppose?"

"What if it is? You're always saying yourself that this place is right behind the times so why grumble if we start catching up?"

"Where's the Missus get the money, that's what I should like to know?"

"That's none of my business. Nor yours neither."

"Oh yes it is!" Stretton exclaimed. "If she's got money to spend on machines, why ent she got it to pay our wages instead of laying us off work?"

"But you're not laid off."

"Oh yes I am! She told me so this afternoon. — While you was out doing her shopping! She's got four wheat-stacks there wanting threshing but will she give 'em to me to do? Oh, no, not she! She better prefers to hang on and hoard 'em, hoping she'll get a top price in the summer. Ah, and then she'll likely have the traction, seeing she's so smutten on machinery all of a sudden. But it's all wrong, you know, and you as bailiff should ought to tell her."

"Yes, I'll tell her," Jack said, and went in search of her straight away.

At first she refused even to listen. She liked to see her yard full of corn-stacks. Her pride in them was beyond belief. She was always sorry to see them go.

"But if you hang on to 'em too long," Jack said, "that'll likely be money down the drain."

"How d'you make that out?" she asked sharply.

"The talk is of more and more grain coming in from America, not less, so you'd better look out or you're going to be left feeling pretty silly."

"Where did you hear this?"

"I heard it in Kevelport this afternoon."

"I'm not too sure I believe you," she said.

But the following morning, the big barn resounded to the noise of flails, and Jack, looking in, found Stretton at work there with his son Harvey.

"I'll say this much for you!" Stretton shouted, without once pausing in his swing: "You've certainly got the measure of that damned woman!"

"He's got the measure of both of 'em, ent he?" Harvey chipped in. "Seeing Miss Nenna's in the family way already?" Then he gave a great howl, for his father, by shoving him sharply in the ribs, had caused him to falter, and the swingle of his flail had come down hard on the top of his skull. "What d'you do that for, Dad?" he demanded, feeling his head very tenderly. "You damn near done for your boy Harvey!"

"She ent Miss Nenna to you no more. She's Mrs Mercybright and don't you forget it. Now get on swinging and not so much fussle. So long as it's only your head that gets dowsed you won't reach much harm, seeing it's mahogany all the way through."

The butter-machine was something of a wonder; even Nenna wanted to see it working; but it was forgotten when the new winnowing-machine arrived, and the new horse-rake, and the new wide drill.

"Laws, ent we modern all of a sudden?" Peter Luppitt said to Paul. "It makes me giddy, watching all this change, honest."

But the greatest excitement was in July, when the new reaper-and-binder arrived, brand new from the Kevelport foundry. It stood in the yard and the men gathered from all over the farm to see it.

"Reaper *and* binder?" said Joe Stretton. "I've heard of such things but I still don't believe it."

"Is there hands on them shafts," asked Peter Luppitt, "with fingers on them?"

"That's right," said his brother, "and they're that clever once they get moving that you've only got to watch a minute or two and out pops a nice big crusty loaf of bread!"

"Does it malt the barley into the bargain?"

"Aye, and passes out a jug of beer!"

"What happens, then, when you put it in to cut the oats?"

"Out pops a Scotchman in a kilt!"

"Does it talk to us and tell us when it's time for oneses?"

"Does it sing?" asked Lacey. "I was always one for a good tune."

"What *I* should like," said William Gauntlet, leaning forward on his shepherd's long stick, his long body steeply inclined, "is an engine that stays up at night while I'm sleeping, delivers my lambs and snips their tails off, then pays me my wages for doing nothing. How about it, Jack? – Could you get me one by next spring?"

"I wouldn't trust it, myself," said Percy Rugg, borrowing Gauntlet's own favourite phrase. "Supposing it never knowed when to stop? That tailsnipping bit would have me worried."

"Who's going to drive this reaper-and-binder?" asked Joe Stretton. "Who's going to have the first go?"

"I am!" said Harvey. "I ent scared of an old machine!"

"Oh no you don't!" Stretton said. "If anyone has first go it's me, not a green sappy half-man like you, boy." Then he turned to Jack. "Unless you want first go, being bailiff," he said.

"No, you go ahead," Jack said. "Try it out on them oats above the Runkle."

Harvest that year went forward like clockwork. It was over and finished in record time. The weather stayed open and ploughing was easy. Jack had been nearly three years at Brown Elms now, and each year had seen an improvement, yet Miss Philippa was far from satisfied.

"How long," she asked him, "before we get rid of the reeds in the Middle Nineteen Acre?"

"Two or three years, most probably. Four, even."

"So long? So long?"

"It takes a lot longer to clean the land than it does to get it soggled up."

"How long before Rummers can be sown with a corn crop?"

"The same, most likely. Two or three years. It's good enough land but sour as a cesspit. It needs nursing and the only answer is time and patience."

"Patience!" she said, and gave an angry sigh.

"There are no short cuts," he said, "not once you've let the land go back so badly."

"It's not my fault this farm's gone back. There was no one I could trust until you came along."

But, having given him her precious trust, she expected miracles in return.

"That sister of yours!" he said to Nenna. "She seems to think I'm some sort of magician. She expects me to work wonders for her."

"You *have* worked wonders," Nenna said. "Nobody else would have worked so hard."

As far as Nenna was concerned, plainly he could do no wrong. She was fiercely protective if she thought he was being put upon, and would take her sister to task about it.

"It was after ten again when Jack got home from work last night. Do you have to run him around as you do?"

"I pay him good wages. Surely he doesn't expect to get them for nothing?"

"That's not what I said."

"Does he talk about me?" Philippa asked. "Does he tell you things, about what I want doing on the farm?"

"Of course he talks to me!" Nenna said. "What do you expect between man and wife?"

She looked at her sister in some surprise, and Philippa turned away to the window.

"And does he complain of the way he's treated?"

"No," Nenna said. "Jack never complains about anything."

"Oh, doesn't he indeed! You're talking rubbish. Your husband, let me tell you, is quite capable of looking after his own interests. *He's* never backward in coming forward or he wouldn't be where he is today."

"And where is that?" Nenna asked scornfully.

"Married to *you!*" her sister said.

It was true that Miss Philippa liked to run him around, and often she kept him after work, calling him into the poky office to talk farm business by the hour. He rarely refused her. He thought she was probably very lonely now that Nenna was no longer with her.

One autumn evening she asked him indoors, into the best front parlour, and gave him a glass of Madeira wine. He was at a loss. He could not understand her. And then John Tuller of Maryhope Farm came in, obviously expected, and he too was given a glass of wine.

"Jack, I think Mr Tuller would be glad of your advice in improving his grassland. Do talk to him about it, will you?"

But the whiskered Mr Tuller, looking down his handsome nose, could scarcely be bothered even to answer Jack's nod.

"I came to see *you*, Miss Philippa, and well you know it."

So Jack drank up quickly and took his leave, noticing that Miss Philippa's colour was heightened, though her manner was dignity itself. He could not decide whether she had invited him in for support or merely to show him that she had an admirer. Either way, he was sympathetic, but Nenna, when he told her, was extremely angry.

"That terrible man? I can't abide him! His wife scarcely cold in her grave, poor soul, and he's already casting about for another!"

"It might not be such a very bad thing. I daresay your sister would prefer to be married and if she likes him—"

"Not John Tuller! He only married his first wife to get his hands on Maryhope Farm and over the years he's bled it dry! He'd do the same for Brown Elms and drive poor Philippa out of her mind. Drinking and hunting – that's all he cares for!"

"Maybe you're right," Jack said, knowing Tuller's reputation, "but I dunno that it's any business of ours exactly."

"Yes, it *is* our business," Nenna said. "What would become of us, do you think, if Tuller were lord and master here?"

Jack laughed. He had never seen her so indignant. But, failing to jolly her out of her temper, he tried to comfort her instead.

"If the worst should come to the worst," he said, "I should just have to look for a job elsewhere."

"After all the work you've put in on this farm, pulling it

together the way you have? Oh, no! I wouldn't hear of such a thing!"

"We'll cross that bridge when we come to it, then. Though I don't see what you can do about it, anyway."

"I can do plenty. I can speak to Philippa for a start."

"Ah, that'll make everything dandy, I daresay."

"Are you laughing at me?" Nenna demanded.

"Good gracious," he said, "as though I would!"

"*I'm* not laughing, let me tell you."

"I can see that."

"Oh, you do make me cross sometimes, you do, really!"

"Hush a minute and listen," he said. "Did you hear that?"

"No. What?"

"My belly rumbling. It's wondering why I'm late with its supper."

"Oh!" she exclaimed, and rushed to open the door of the oven. "There, would you believe it? Just look at my patty!" And she showed him a pie somewhat charred at the edges.

"I like 'em like that, nice and crispy. What's it got inside? Meat and taters? Ah, I knowed it was, the instant I smelt it."

"You!" she said. "A lot you care what it's got inside it, you old bread-and-cheese, you! You're just wanting to change the subject."

"What subject was that?" he asked vaguely.

"You know well enough what subject it was."

Nenna brought a dish of carrots and cabbage to the table, and a jug of gravy. She sat down and began cutting into the pie.

"I'm thinking about the future," she said. "The farm could belong to our children one day. You surely don't blame me for keeping their interests in mind, do you?"

"No, I don't blame you. At least, not exactly. But you don't expect your sister to stay single all her life just so's our children should get the farm?"

"No, of course not," Nenna said, shocked. "But, after all, she is well past thirty. She's not very likely to get a great many chances now."

"She's got John Tuller. Or so it seems."

"He'd bring her nothing but humiliation. And how would you feel if the farm became Tuller's when it might very well have come to your son?"

"This is too much for me," he said. "It's looking too far into the future."

That Nenna should be so calculating was a thing that amazed him. This jealousy on behalf of her young, for the rights and possessions accruing to them, must be something that came with motherhood, just as extra strength came to the heavily burdened body, and milk to the breasts. He looked at her with new eyes, and Nenna looked back without shame. She was now very big and sat with dignity, arranging the folds of her smock in front with a care that made him smile anew.

"How come you're so sure it's a son you're carrying? Did your gypsy friends up in the birchwood tell you?"

"Yes!" she said defiantly. "You may scoff if you like but gypsies often know these things and Mrs Rainbow read my face."

She put a small piece of pie into her mouth and chewed carefully. Everything she did now was done with great care, on account of the baby.

"Besides which, I *want* it to be a son," she said.

"Ah, that just about settles it, then, and no question!"

But the child born to them that autumn was a daughter, and was named Linn, after Nenna's mother. Nenna wept at first with disappointment. She would not have the cot placed anywhere near her. It had to stand against the far wall. But then, seeing Jack's delight in the baby, she recovered and asked for it to be placed in her arms.

"You never said you wanted a daughter."

"I didn't know myself till I got her," he said. "I left that part to the Almighty."

"Do you think she'll forgive me for being disappointed?"

"It depends how you treat her from now on."

"I shall give her lots of brothers and sisters," Nenna said. "She shall never be a lonely little girl as I was."

On a working day late in October she brought the baby, wrapped in a woollen shawl in her arms, up to the farm for the men to see and give their blessing.

"She'll do well," said Peter Luppitt, "born with a waxing moon as she was."

"Peter's right there," said his brother Paul. "I always plants my cabbages when the moon is waxing and you know what mighty things they always grow to."

"Married people should always get their children born with a waxing moon," said Peter. "It's only common sense."

"That ent always easy," said William Gauntlet, with a

slow and solemn shake of his head.

"She ent going to open her eyes at us, is she? I reckon she knows we ent much to look at."

"I don't wonder she's sleeping," Jack said. "She was up half the night screaming her lungs out."

"Got a tooth coming through, I shouldn't wonder."

"More likely wind," said Oliver Lacey.

"You want to go to old Grannie Balsam up at Goodlands. She makes the best gripe-water in the district."

"Have you took her up on Tootle Knap?" asked Gauntlet. "You should always take a new born babby up on top of Tootle Knap. It's the highest point in the parish, you see, and gives the child a good start in life, like being baptised or having a mole on her left elbow."

Jack only smiled, but Nenna wanted to go at once, so he went with her to the top of the mound known as Tootle Knap and there among the elm trees, with the yellow leaves flit-flittering down, he took the baby between his hands and held her up as high as he could.

"There you are, Linn Mercybright! What do you think of the air up here, then? Suit you nicely, eh, does it?" And on the way down again he said to Nenna, "At least she can't say we didn't do all the right things for her!"

"Don't you believe in luck?" Nenna asked.

"I ought to," he said. "The way things are going for me just lately, I never see a magpie without I see two!"

He went back to work drilling wheat in the Sliplands, with Harvey Stretton up behind in charge of the seed-box, and a little while later John Tuller came across on his way to the farmhouse.

"I've been wanting to talk to you, bailiff, about those gypsies you've got camping here. I don't approve of it one iota. You shouldn't allow them to hang about for weeks on end."

"They come every year to help with the harvest. They'll be moving on soon to their winter camp in the quary at Ludden."

"That's not soon enough to suit me! I'm losing chickens every day."

"Then you'd better see Miss Philippa, I reckon."

"I shall, never fear. I'm on my way."

Tuller strode on, smart in breeches and Norfolk jacket, keeping carefully to the headlands. Jack flipped at the horses and they moved off again up the slope, while Harvey Stretton, perched up behind, gave a squawk of laughter.

"Them chickens he's lost! – They most likely fell down a crack in the ground, poor things!"

That afternoon, when Jack led the horses into the yard, Tuller was standing there, deep in conversation with Miss Philippa, and had a basket of eggs in his hand. He was well known for being a cadger.

"I've settled the matter of the gypsies, bailiff. Miss Philippa is sending them packing in the morning."

Jack was surprised. He glanced at Miss Philippa's blank face. Tuller, it seemed, had influence with her.

But a good many mornings came and went and the gypsies continued to camp in the birchwoods, coming and going just as they pleased.

"I thought you was sending them packing," Jack said, and Miss Philippa gave a little shrug. "Why should I?" she said. "They do me no harm and they'll be moving on anyway in November."

So she liked to keep Tuller on a string, plainly, and Jack wondered why. It was quite impossible to guess her thoughts or feelings.

As autumn wore on into winter, Tuller was seen more and more at Brown Elms, striding about over the fields and poking his head into the buildings. Jack took care to keep out of his way, sure that meetings would lead to trouble, but the other men fared badly. They complained that Tuller spied on them and carried his tales to Miss Philippa. He had waylaid the Luppitts after work one evening, demanding that they open the sacks they were carrying, and had then confiscated the two brace of pheasants and the hare and rabbit he found inside. So Joe Stretton, every night after that, carried home a sack full of stones, intending, if challenged, to drop it hard on Tuller's toes.

"But Farmer Tuller keeps clear of *me*! And well he might, too, or I should try straightening his long twisty nose-piece!"

"That's all very well," said Peter Luppitt, "but what if he ups and marries our Missus?"

"If that ever happens I shall emigrate," Stretton said. "I shouldn't stay on under Farmer Tuller."

"Emigrate?" said young Harvey.

"Ah, that's right, over the water!"

"What water's that, Dad? The Atlantic Ocean?"

"Ennen water!" Stretton said. "There's some pretty good farms over the other side from Niddup."

John Tuller was warmly disliked and held in great contempt, too, as the title "Farmer" showed very plainly. For whereas James Trigg of Goodlands and George Ellenton of Spouts Hall, farming their land in the best tradition, were each known as "Mister", the master of Maryhope, frittering his substance away on drink, was everywhere known as "Farmer Tuller".

"Just imagine," said William Gauntlet, "selling *land* to pay for *bubbles*!"

Jack, however, could not always keep clear of Tuller, and one day late in November, when he had five teams out ploughing the Placketts, Tuller came up and asked for the loan of two horses.

"I've seen Miss Philippa about it and she says I can have them."

"Has she indeed? It's the first I've heard."

"I want the loan of a man, too. Perhaps you'd be good enough to oblige me. I want some coal fetched from the station."

"It'll have to wait," Jack said. "I ent wasting good weather like this. Carting coal is a wet-weather job."

Tuller was angry, but made an effort and kept his temper.

"When you've finished, then. I don't much mind so long as it's today."

"It won't be today, no lections of that. When these horses finish this afternoon they'll have done their stint for today, Mr Tuller, and they'll be entitled to shut up shop. But I'll think about it as soon as maybe."

"Damn you to hell!" Tuller said, and this time his temper went for nothing. "Come back at once and ask your Mistress! She'll soon tell you what your orders are!"

"It's no odds to me one way or the other. I'm bailiff here, not Miss Philippa, and I'm the one that says what the horses do or don't do."

"We'll see!" Tuller said. "Oh, yes! We shall see about that, I promise you, man!"

He hurried off across the rough ploughland, and Jack continued up the slope, while, further on along the Placketts, the other men were all agog. A little while later, Tuller returned with Miss Philippa, and they stood together on the lower headland, waiting for Jack to plough down towards them.

"I hear you've refused Mr Tuller the horses."

"I didn't refuse. I only postponed it."

"Is it really necessary for all the horses to be out ploughing at the same time?"

"This weather's a bonus. It won't last much longer. If we go all out for the next few days we shall get the Placketts and the Brant sown with dredge-corn. That's a lot more important to my way of thinking than lugging coal for your neighbours' fires."

Tuller's face was now ugly. He turned to Miss Philippa and thrust out his chin.

"When I first asked you this small favour, your answer was yes, as I recall."

"Only if the horses were not needed here, Mr. Tuller. I said that plainly."

"Are you lending or are you not? I don't much care for haggling about it!"

"When Mr Mercybright says they can go, you can have them by all means, Mr Tuller."

"So! You allow yourself to be ruled by your bailiff?"

"I am ruled by no one," she said stiffly. "Not even by friends such as you, Mr Tuller."

"No?" he said, sneering. "Well, I wouldn't let any labourer of mine speak to me as this lumping clod does to you, madam!"

"You're forgetting, I think, that Mr Mercybright happens to be my brother-in-law as well as my bailiff. He is therefore something more than a mere labourer."

"Not to me, he isn't! And I'm glad I've come to my senses in time!"

Angry at being brought down before his inferiors, Tuller was determined to have his revenge, and made a great show of looking her over from head to foot.

"By God!" he said, in a voice that carried across half the field. "I had plans for making you my wife, madam, but as I've no stomach for welcoming ploughman and pigman at my table, I'm thankful this day has gone as it has done!"

He then walked away along the headland, taking the short way home to Maryhope, and Miss Philippa turned her wrath on Jack.

"I hope you will always remember," she said, "that for your sake I fell out with a neighbour and gave him cause to make me look foolish."

"My sake?" Jack said, but she also was walking away.

The men were well pleased with the outcome of the clash that morning. Oliver Lacey had heard most of what had been said and had passed it on to all the others. For once Miss Philippa found favour among them.

"She told him, didn't she, eh, Jack? She put Farmer Tuller in his place all right *and* sent him off with a flea in his ear-hole. Oh, yes! She took him down a peg right nice and tidy."

"It'd been a lot better," said Joe Stretton, "if she'd never rizzed him up in the first place."

That was Jack's opinion, too. Tuller, he felt, was probably a bad man to quarrel with. There was sure to be trouble. And sure enough, about three weeks later, the dog Roy was found dead in the sunken track dividing Maryhope land from Brown Elms.

"He was after my pheasants," Tuller said, "so my keeper shot him."

There was no evidence either way. Tuller's story was well prepared and his keeper confirmed it. All Jack could do was to be on his guard against further incidents and warn the men to be equally watchful, especially the shepherd, who had three dogs.

"If they kill my Snap or my Pip or my Patsy," William Gauntlet said grimly, "I shall kill them and no bones about it."

And the old man, a fearsome figure when he chose to stand upright and make the most of his six-feet-six-inches, went up to Maryhope straight away to deliver his threat in person.

"You harm my dogs," he said to Tuller and the keeper, "and I'll hang both your gutses with the rest of the vermin on your own gallers!"

There were no more dogs killed on the farm, but Tuller was never at a loss how to make trouble, and scarcely a month went by thereafter without some fresh example of his spite: field-gates broken and the hinges levered out of the gate-posts; ballcocks weighed down in the cattle-troughs so that the water overflowed; an old scrub bull allowed in to run with the Brown Elms heifers.

"There's nothing worse than a bad neighbour," Peter Luppitt said to Jack, "unless, of course, it's two bad neighbours."

One Sunday morning, after church, as Jack and Nenna stood talking to Philippa in the churchyard, Tuller jostled Jack in passing, turned to glare at them all in contempt, then pushed past to speak to Mrs Carrington Wilby of Halls, presenting his back to the Brown Elms party.

The incident was noticed by almost all those gathered in the churchyard. Philippa and Nenna were both upset. But a moment afterwards Mr Tapyard of Ennen Stoke, an important landowner and a magistrate, came up to them and raised his hat.

"How are things at Brown Elms? Fat and flourishing, from all I hear, and improving all the time under Mr Mercybright's supervision. It's a pity there aren't a few more farmers like you, Miss Guff, with cattle and sheep and pigs on their land instead of a handful of half-starved pheasants." And without much pretence of lowering his voice he then added, "If you have any trouble with that fellow Tuller, *don't be afraid to take him to law.*"

Miss Philippa was comforted by Tapyard's show of sympathy and she found the other farmers round about equally friendly. There was not much regard for John Tuller. He was too well known as a spendthrift and a scrounger.

Still, Miss Philippa was a solitary creature, and Jack felt sorry for her, going home to eat her Sunday dinner in the cheerless farmhouse, with only the stone deaf cook for company.

"It's her own fault," Nenna said. "She could easily make friends if she wanted to but she just doesn't try."

"All the same, I feel a bit bad about it, having took you away," he said. "I reckon we ought to do something about her."

"Such as what?"

"Such as having her here to eat dinner with us on a Sunday, so that you and her can enjoy a bit of a chat together."

"Yes," Nenna said. "That's a good idea. And perhaps she will then believe that I really do know how to cook."

The visits were not a success, however, for Miss Philippa was always finding fault with the way Nenna brought up the baby.

"What a terrible mess that child is making, sucking that piece of cheese," she said. "Was it you who gave it to her or was it Jack? Ought she to have it, a child her age?"

"I don't see why not," Nenna said. "It's quite plain she likes it."

"And does she always have what she likes?"

"So long as it's wholesome, certainly."

"She's going to be very spoilt, then, I can see."

"She's going to be happy," Nenna said.

Miss Philippa sniffed, watching the child crawling across the floor towards her. She sat sideways in her chair, her skirts drawn in about her legs, determined to elude the sticky, clutching fingers. Jack leant forward and lifted Linn onto his lap.

"She's got four teeth, had you noticed?" he said. "And another two on the way."

"That's nothing extraordinary in a child of seven months, is it?"

"I wouldn't know. I never had a baby before."

And, catching Nenna's eye, he exchanged a little smile with her. It was difficult to share what they had with Philippa – the more they tried, the more they seemed to shut her out.

Nenna, on the whole, was patient under her sister's criticisms. She had made up her mind to endure them calmly. But acts of interference she would not allow, and one day there were words between them.

It was a warm Sunday morning in summer, and Linn, now nine months, was crawling about the floor barefoot. Nenna went out to the garden for a moment to pick fresh mint and to tell Jack that dinner was very nearly ready. She returned to find Philippa holding the child down hard on her lap, forcing on the second of her tiny shoes, over a twisted, much-wrinkled stocking. Linn was crying bitterly, and Nenna, snatching the child up into her arms, took off both the shoes and the stockings and flung them into a corner of the settle.

"It's none of your business!" she said fiercely. "How dare you make the poor child cry?"

"She shouldn't be going about barefoot like that. On this cold brick floor! On the rough garden path! She'll do herself an injury."

"It's none of your business!" Nenna repeated. "You have absolutely no right to interfere. If you think you know so much about raising children and caring for them, it's time you got married and had your own, before you find you've left it too late!"

Jack came in to an atmosphere that sparked and prickled. He stood glancing from one red angry face to the other. Then he went forward and lifted Linn out of Nenna's arms.

"Them there taters is boiling all over the stove," he said. "They'll put the fire out in another minute. Here, come to your dad, Miss Mercybright, and he'll give you a ride like Jack-a-Dando."

He sat down in the basketwork chair with the child on his knees, facing towards him, and jiggled her about until she laughed.

> "Jack-a-Dando rode to Warwick
> With his newly wedded bride –
> Bumpety-bump up and down,
> Bumpety-bump from side to side –
> Jack-a-Dando's famous ride!"

Linn was now croodling and blowing bubbles, leaning towards him, hands clutching at his waistcoat pocket, where she knew she would find a pod of green peas. Nenna smiled from across the kitchen. She liked to see Jack and the child together. But Miss Philippa took much longer to thaw, and was still rather cool when she left after dinner.

"Well?" Nenna said, defiantly, confronting Jack afterwards. "Whose child is she I'd like to know – hers or mine?"

"Mine," he said, to avoid disagreement. "You can tell

she's mine by the way she's so fond of her bread and cheese."

Often that summer, when Nenna went out to help in the hay-fields, she would take Linn with her and put her to sleep in the shade of the hedgerow, somewhere nearby, where she could keep a watchful eye. And at harvest-time, too, Linn would be out in the fields all day, safe in the charge of the older children, playing in a corner, well away from the reaping machine and the mowers at work with their sharp scythes.

One hot day young Bobby Luppitt caught a large grass-snake and carried it across the harvest field to show it to the other children. Nenna ran up in some consternation, for Linn was awake and would surely be frightened. But when she arrived, Linn had the grass-snake in her arms and was trying to cuddle it against her body, enchanted by its warmth and the way it wriggled in her grasp. She was laughing and gurgling all the time, and cried only when the snake escaped her, vanishing into the shady hedgerow.

"Dolly?" she called, crawling along on hands and knees. "Dolly? Dolly? Cheep, cheep?" Every pet or plaything was "dolly" to her.

She was a forward child from the first, and a happy one, as Nenna had promised. She was pretty, too, and had fair hair with more than a hint of red in it, which Nenna herself kept trimmed short, so that it grew in little fine feathery waves all over her head. Her eyes and lashes were dark, like her mother's, and her skin golden.

"Someone I know is a bobby-dazzler," Jack would say, lifting her up till her hands touched the rafters. "Someone I know is as bright as a button. Now I wonder who it is? You got any idea, have you?"

"Dolly! Dolly!" Linn would say. "Dolly Doucey! Bobby-dazzler!"

She could say many words by the time she was fully a twelvemonth old.

Towards the end of harvest that year there were five days of heavy rain, holding the harvesters back, fretting, and beating down the corn still standing uncut on forty-five acres. And when Jack went up with the other men on the sixth day, determined to cut the oats and barley in the Top Ground, however wet, he found that Gauntlet's sheep had got in from the rough grazing above. The field was a nightmare, the sprouting corn all trodden into the miry ground, and the sheep with their bellies so distended that they lay about, unable to move, having gorged themselves on the undersowing of grass and clover.

"They warnt here last night!" Gauntlet said. "I was up here going the rounds at ten and they was all safe in the leazings then. It's Farmer Tuller that has let 'em in here, or one of the scum that dirties for him!"

When Miss Philippa saw the state of the field, she stood for a time with the tears glistening in her eyes. It really hurt her to see the corn ruined. But then anger got the upper hand.

"I'll have the law on Tuller this time, as Mr Tapyard said I ought."

"There's not enough evidence," Jack said. "Farmer Tuller has seen to that. It's our own sheep that have got in and he's took good care that them holes in the hedge should look as if they was accidental."

"Then what can we do?"

"We can see that it don't happen again."

So every night after that he patrolled the boundary, armed with a double-barrelled shotgun, and one night he challenged a man who was creeping across the sunken trackway. The man turned and ran, and Jack fired one barrel into the branches of a nearby oak tree.

"Tell your master," he called out, "that the next man he sends won't be half so lucky!"

The message, it seemed, went home; there were no more intruders after that; but Jack, working all day to finish the harvest and patrolling five or six hours every night, was in danger of wearing himself to a shadow, and Nenna complained to her sister about it.

"Is it my fault?" Philippa said. "I never asked him to patrol, did I?"

"Then perhaps you'll ask him to stop," Nenna said, "before he kills himself with lack of sleep."

"I shan't stop him. Not until the harvest is safely in. After all, it was all through Jack that I quarrelled with Tuller in the first place, so no doubt he feels himself somewhat to blame."

The harvest was got in at last without further damage. Jack was able to sleep at nights in his own bed, and to put John Tuller out of his mind, at least until the Top Ground fields had been ploughed and re-sown. Then, perhaps, there might be a need for vigilance again.

That autumn, however, there was a change that removed the problem. Maryhope Farm was put up for sale. Jack was driving home from Hotcham and saw a man in the act of nailing up the poster, on the trunk of a tree in Felpy Lane. "Maryhope Farm: two hundred acres of freehold land, with dwelling-house, barns, out-houses, byres, and sundry other buildings pertaining: to be sold by auction on Thursday, October 28th., unless previously sold by private treaty."

Jack went in search of his sister-in-law and found her in the dairy, up to her elbows in the cheese-tub.

"Seems your friend Tuller is selling out. I've just seen a

poster in the lane. Maryhope Farm is on the market."

"Yes, I know, and I'm going to buy it," she said calmly. "I've seen Mr Todds about raising a mortgage and he will be arranging the whole transaction for me."

Jack was struck dumb. He stood watching her bare white arms as she swirled the curds to and fro in the tub. She looked at him with a little smile, enjoying his surprise, making the most of her moment of triumph.

"Are you mad?" he asked.

"No," she said. "I don't think so."

"With farming going downhill all the time? And no sign of any improvement?"

"It means the land is going begging. I couldn't afford it, if it weren't cheap. And things can't stay bad for ever and ever. You've said so often enough yourself. Farming is bound to pick up in the end and when it does this will be one of the finest holdings in the country."

"That land of Tuller's is in worse case than this here land of yours used to be. He's bled it white and you damn well know it. It'd take years to put it back into heart again. Five years at least. Probably longer."

"That's where you come in," she said.

"Ah, I thought it might be. I had this feeling in my bones."

"I hoped you'd be pleased, having a bigger farm to manage."

"I'm happy enough as I am," he said.

"But you will take the Maryhope land in hand, too, won't you? I can't do it without your help."

"Yes, well, I'll do my best about it, surely."

At home that evening, when he passed the news on to Nenna, she was at first inclined to be angry.

"Philippa puts on you," she said. "I will not allow it!"

But the very next time she mentioned the matter, after

discussing it with her sister, she spoke of it as a settled thing.

"The farmhouse at Maryhope will be sold separately and will keep the name," she said. "The land will become part of Brown Elms and a new field-map is drawn up already. It'll really be quite a sizeable holding now."

"You've changed your tune a bit, ent you?" he said.

"It will be for the best in the end," she said, "seeing the farm will pass to our children."

"Oh? Who says so?"

"Philippa says so. She never intends to marry, she said, so our sons will inherit the farm."

"What sons?" he said, to tease her. "Have you been keeping something a secret?"

"No, I haven't!" she exclaimed. "I only wish I could say otherwise!"

"Well, lumme . . . it's early days to be tamping about it. We ent been married two years yet –"

"But Linn came so soon! It was all so easy in every way! I can't understand why other babies haven't followed."

Nenna longed for more children. She felt a hungry impatience for them. And it made her angry that she should be denied.

"Why is it?" she asked. "Why don't I ever get my own way? It isn't a wicked thing to wish for, is it, so why should God deny me more children?"

"Don't worry yourself about it," he said gently. "I daresay they'll come when they're good and ready."

So now he had charge of six hundred acres, a holding which, if he stood at the top of Tootle Barrow, was laid out all round for him to see, spreading its slopes to the south and west.

"Aren't you proud," Nenna said, "to be bailiff of such a farm as this?"

"I shall be a lot prouder when the Maryhope lands is in some sort of fettle," he said.

It all took time. There were no short cuts to salvation on the land. There was only labour. But changes were wrought, little by little, and at the end of two years those changes could be seen plainly: as the wet pastures were drained and sweetened; as the poor starved arable grounds were manured and rested; as the rough grey leazings were cleared and ploughed and sown anew, and slowly, with patience, coaxed into kindliness, the new grass growing close and thick together, bright green and glistening under the spring and summer sun.

"It warms my heart," said William Gauntlet, "to see this land all smiling again."

Jack was somebody nowadays. Farmers sought him out at market and sometimes drove up to Brown Elms to see the improvements he was making there. They asked his advice about grassland and stock and machinery and the use of artificial manures. He was known by name for some miles around and held in some regard, too, and he was pleased because of Nenna. She took such pride in all he did that he could not help but be proud himself. He had never been so cared for before. He had never known such warmth and comfort and satisfaction.

Sometimes, when he worked in the fields nearest the cottage, he would see Nenna's duster fluttering out of an upper window, or would see her going about the garden, scattering corn for the hens and the geese. Sometimes, resting his team at the end of a furrow, he would take off his cap and wave to her, and she would wave back lifting Linn up to do the same.

Sometimes Nenna and the child would come hand in hand across the fields to see him, bringing his midday meal in a basket, with a big stoneware bottle full of cold sweet tea. If the day were a mild one, they would stay in the field and eat with him, sitting on a rug beneath the hedge, and on these occasions, Linn would bring her very own dinner, wrapped in her own red chequered napkin and carried in the tiny chipwood basket that had her initials done in pokerwork on the handle.

"What've you got for bait today, then?" he would ask her. "It's not bread and cheese by any chance?"

And it always *was* bread and cheese, for she had to eat whatever he ate, and would even have had a raw onion, eating it with a knife as he did, but that she knew it would make her cry.

When her dinner was eaten, she would wander off, stepping carefully from clod to clod, to speak to the horses and offer them her last crust. Jack had to watch her, ready to order her away, for she had no fear and would if allowed have passed to and fro under the horses' bellies or gone behind them to pick at the mud drying on their fetlocks. She thought they were all like old

Shiner at home, whose tail she swung on and whose poor, split hooves she polished every day with a little boot-brush.

Shiner always let her do just as she pleased and would stand looking down at her over one shoulder as she rubbed spit on a wart on his leg or pulled the sticky-burrs out of the long coarse hairs on his feet. He would come to her with a little whicker of welcome the moment she squeezed through the bars of the gate into the orchard. She and Shiner were great friends. He knew she always brought him something. All the loaf sugar would have gone to him, had Nenna not kept her cupboards fastened.

Linn wanted to be friends with every living creature on earth and would run after the geese in the garden, her small bare arms outstretched towards them, calling out: "I'll catch you, geeses! – I'll catch you, geeses!" And would then stand forlorn, on the brink of tears, because they would not stay and let her embrace them. The tears seldom came. Something would certainly happen to distract her: a jackdaw perching on the pig's back, or an apple falling, smack, off the tree, and she would be rocking with laughter instead.

When Jack was at home, she hardly ever left his side, but wanted to watch whatever he was doing. Everything he did was such a splendid joke.

Every six months or so, he cleaned the chimney with four long beanpoles tied end to end and a big branch of holly as a brush. Linn would be out in the garden, waiting, and when the "brush" shot out of the chimney, she would go off into fits of trilling laughter.

"Again?" she would call to Jack, indoors. "Dad? Dad? Do it again?"

In wintertime, whenever there was a hard frost, he would lift her up so that she could reach the icicles hanging along the eaves of the thatch. She would break one off and lick its point.

"Ooo! Brrr! It's cold. It's cold."

"Well, of course it's cold! Whoever heard of a hot daglet?"

"I did!" she said, tilting her chin, saucily. "I seen 'em, too."

"Oh? Where was that?"

"Not going to tell you!"

"That's because it ent true."

" '*Tis* true!" she said, and held her icicle against his throat, threatening to drop it inside his shirt. "Shall I?" she said. "Shall I drop it down?"

"You do," he warned, "and I shall put one in your drawers!"

"You wouldn't," she said.

"Oh, yes, I would."

"It'd melt on me. It'd make me wet."

"And jolly well serve you right, too – you with your yarns about hot daglets!"

"How do they come? The icicles?"

"Drip, drip, drip, that's how they come, and get catched in the act when the weather turns frosty."

"Why does the weather turn frosty?"

"Now we're off! We're in for it now – why? why? – sure as Worcester shines against Gloucester. Supposing you ask why little tongues must always waggle?"

"Why must they?"

"Ah. Why? You've got me there. I reckon they must want something to do."

In the springtime one year, when the birds were nesting, he climbed his ladder to put a "cat" on the cottage roof, to scare away the sparrows making holes in the thatch. The "cat" was made of old velveteen, stuffed with straw, and had two green glass beads stuck in for eyes. It had a humpty back and looked ferocious. But its long upright tail was soon pecked to pieces; its glaring eyes disappeared; the birds were just as busy as ever.

"Damn and hammer it!" Jack said to Linn. "I reckon you told 'em that cat warnt real."

"Not me," she said. "I never telled 'em."

"Who was it, then, if it warnt you?"

"A little bird telled 'em!" she exclaimed.

She was always laughing. Everything was a joke to her. Even when she was being scolded, she always managed to turn it aside.

"Whose little dirty black hands've been here?" Jack demanded, pointing to the five tell-tale smudges on the white wall.

"Don't know," Linn said, considering the matter.

"Then let's have a look-see who fits, shall we, and maybe we shall learn something."

He took hold of her hand and put it up against the wall, fitting thumb and then fingers into the smudges. But long before the fourth and last finger was pressed firmly into its place, the child was already wriggling and spluttering with delighted laughter. This was the best joke of all: to see her own hand fitting the imprint on the wall.

"Someone," he said, "is proved to be a dirty rascal."

"You," she said. "Dirty lascal!"

"Someone was told to go to mother and get herself washed in time for bed, warnt they?"

"Did wash. Two times."

"I reckon you're telling me tales," Jack said. "Black paws like them! I reckon you must've been up the chimney."

"Holly bush! Up the chimney!"

"Just look at your pinny, the state it's in. How is your mother to get that clean? And your frock too – I reckon you've been huggling the coal-man."

But the more he frowned at her, keeping his face perfectly straight, the more she spluttered at him, finding him irresistibly funny.

"Old eyebrows!" she said. "Tobacco-face! – Puffing away!"

"Who're you talking to?" he demanded.

"Talking to you," she said, doubling over.

"You're getting too saucy, Miss Mercybright."

"Grrr!" she said. "Saucy your own-self. Old vexatious!"

"Your mother's calling, so you run along before she gets cross and has to fetch you, otherwise there'll likely be ructions, 'cos you've got an appointment with soap and water."

Linn's life was like a bird's: she was always happy to go to bed; always happy to get up in the morning; and in between times she was never at a loss how to fill the hours.

But there were sorrows even for Linn, as when the old horse Shiner died, on a snowy morning in the middle of April, 1900.

It was a Sunday. Jack was lighting the fire in the stove and Nenna was laying the table for breakfast. They had got up in darkness and not yet done more than glance briefly at the outside world. But Linn, upstairs, waking to the sight of the snow falling, tumbled out of bed and went straight to the window, looking out over the garden to the orchard. And there was Shiner, lying stiffly on his side, a dark grey shape on the whitened grass, with the powdery snow falling upon him.

Linn came downstairs sobbing fit to break her heart and threw herself into Jack's arms. He could not understand it. Nor could Nenna. They stared at each other over the child's head.

"What is it? What is it?" he asked, distraught. He had never heard her cry before. "Did you hurt yourself? Did you have a bad dream?"

"It's Shiner!" she said, her voice muffled against his chest. "Shiner's dead! Out there in the snow!"

"Ah, no?" he said, and went to the window with the child in his arms. "He surely ent? Not our old Shiner?" But a glance outside was enough to convince him, for the horse's head was stretched back and his mouth was open. "Poor old boy," he said sadly. "Poor old Shiner, he's gone, right enough. And only last night we was talking about him being so sprightly, warnt we?"

The child would eat nothing all day long, but went about like a small ghost, refusing comfort. When Jack took her out to say a last farewell to the horse, she wanted to stay and sweep the snow from the body; wanted Jack to bring the old horse back to life. And at bed-time that night she cried and cried into her pillow, so that even Nenna got out of patience.

"You'd better go up to her," she said. "I can do nothing with her. She won't go to sleep and she'll make herself ill if she goes on like this."

So Jack went up and sat on the edge of Linn's bed, and her small face accused him wanly.

"Why did Shiner have to die?"

"He was old, that's why. He was tired and frail and he'd got so's he wanted a good long sleep. You don't grudge Shiner his sleep, do you?"

"When'll he wake up again?"

"I dunno about that exactly. Not for a while, I don't

suppose. But when he does wake up in the end, why, he'll be a new horse all over again."

"Mama said he'd gone to heaven."

"Ah, that's right, in heaven," he said. "That's where he'll be when he wakes up. He'll have all his teeth in his head again, and a good clover ley growing all round him, and a bin of oats every morning and evening."

But she was worried because the old horse had died out in the cold, in the snow.

"Why wasn't he in his shelter?"

"I dunno. I suppose he preferred to die out in the open. He never thought much of that shelter I built him. He only used it to scratch hisself on. He always preferred to be out and about under the trees, winter or summer, rain or shine."

He could bring no brightness to the child's face, but as he talked to her, quietly, her eyes closed little by little and sleep claimed her.

In the morning, he brought in a basket containing seven baby chicks, to keep them warm beside the stove, and when Linn came downstairs she was attracted at once by their chirping. In the afternoon, Nenna took her to have tea with Amy Gauntlet, to be out of the way when the knacker came for Shiner's carcass. And the following day, she went with her Auntie Philippa to see some new calves at Spouts Hall Farm.

Time did the rest. The child was only three-and-a-half. There were many things to see and do. Shiner stepped back a pace or two and was soon wrapped round in mist and shadows.

All through the spring of 1900, when the newspapers were full of the war in South Africa, the men would come to Jack and discuss the latest news with him. They plied him with questions. They expected him to know all about it.

"This here Modder River, now," said Peter Luppitt, "whereabouts would that be, precisely?"

"Search me. I dunno much more than you do."

"You was out there, warnt you, back in 1881?"

"It's a big country," Jack said.

"Seems to me you was only wasting your time when you *was* out there," said Joe Stretton, "Seeing we've got it all to do again by the look of things."

"Ah, why didn't you finish the Boers good and proper while you was at it?" asked Oliver Lacey. "Instead of leaving them to breed?"

" 'Cos they finished us, more nearly, warnt it?"

"Well, we didn't lose to them, exactly, did we?"

"We certainly didn't win, did we?"

"Did you kill a few?" asked Percy Rugg.

"No, none," Jack said.

"What, not even one or two extra big ones, them you couldn't hardly miss?"

"No. Nurra one. Not so much as a Boer rabbit."

"I bet I shall bag a few when I get out there," said Harvey Stretton, bright-eyed.

"You?" said his father, with great scorn. "They ent taking half-pint boy-chaps yet, are they?"

"I'm going, though, as soon as I reach my full nineteen."

"It'll all be over by then, you fool. Another month and the Boers'll be beaten."

"D'you think it will, Jack?" Harvey asked.

"I dunno, boy. You'd better write and ask Lord Roberts."

In June that year a recruiting party came to Niddup and drilled for an hour or two on the ham. Harvey gave his age as nineteen and received the Queen's Shilling, along with nine other Niddup lads, and a few weeks later he was walking about in his uniform, showing off to his father and the rest of the men on the farm.

"It's a natty little hat," said Jonathan Kirby, drumming with his fingers on Harvey's pill-box, "but it ent going to keep the sun off your noddle much, is it?"

"What're them stripes down the sides of your trousis for?" asked Peter Luppitt. "So's the Boers can see you better?"

"I shall have a pith helmet to go out there," Harvey said, "and a khaki uniform with puttees."

"I hope they're giving you a rifle," said his father, " 'cos you certainly ent having my old shotgun to go with and you needn't think it!"

"I go into barracks on Sunday night and I start training on Monday morning."

"Leffright, leffright, leffright, leff!" Percy Rugg bellowed suddenly. "Ten! – Shun! All fours!"

"I wouldn't have volunteered, myself," said Will Gauntlet. "Fancy leaving your Dad like that, and your younger brothers."

"Hah!" said Stretton, clapping Harvey on the shoulder. "Somebody got to go, ent they, and I shall be thankful to see the last of him for five minutes. It'll maybe make him buck up his ideas a bit."

Harvey went off with the nine other Niddup volunteers, and his place on the farm was taken by his brother Ernest, aged thirteen.

"I shan't be moving, neither, when Harvey comes back," Ernest said. "He'll have to make do with being second ploughboy under me."

Heifer calves born on the farm that year were given names such as Ladysmith and Bloemfontein. "And as if that ent bad enough," Jack said to Nenna, "the Peter Luppitts is calling their new baby son Kimberley!"

"Another baby son?" Nenna said. "They have three boys already, surely? Why should the Luppitts have so many?"

"Ah, well, that's the way it goes," Jack said. "It's all meant, I daresay."

He was angry with himself for mentioning the matter. He could have bitten out his tongue. For it was a great sadness to Nenna that the sons she longed for never came, and in recent months, especially, she had been growing strangely moody. She was always fancying herself with child and then, when she had to admit that she was mistaken, she would fall into a kind of fretful sullenness, when even Jack could not get a word out of her.

"Don't *you* want a son?" she said once. "Of course you do! It's only natural. All men want sons."

"I'm quite happy to take what I'm given."

"Well, I intend to give you a son, and I shall, too. I'm determined on it."

"Have you been talking to Amy Gauntlet? Listening to her and her old wives' tales?"

"Why not? She's had eleven children, didn't she?"

"That's because old Will is a shepherd. Shepherds always have a lot of children. They're used to dealing with flocks, you see."

"*I'm* not laughing," Nenna said. "It's no good making jokes with me."

"And what did Amy suggest this time? Tinkertations under the moon? Or a glass of parsley wine at bed-time?"

But although he teased Nenna about it, he was often worried, deep down inside, for he too had his superstitions and he felt, somehow, that to ask too much of Providence was to turn it against you.

"We're all right as we are," he said. "I ent worried about having a son so just you forget it and leave well alone."

But Nenna only looked at him with a sly smile, as though she had something up her sleeve. She was young. She was strong. Dr Spray had said she was perfectly healthy. It was wicked that she should have had only one child in four and a half years of marriage. – She was therefore resolved to do something about it. And at harvest-time that year, when the gypsies came as usual to camp in the birchwoods behind the farmhouse, Nenna was up there everyday, talking to Mrs Zillery Boswell.

"How many pegs do they make you buy in exchange for them potions?" Jack asked. "Seems to me we could easy supply the whole of Niddup!"

They were out with Philippa in the Home Field, testing the wheat with a view to cutting, and one of the gypsies had just galloped past on a skewbald pony.

"She ought not to go there," Philippa said. "It encourages them to be familiar. You're her husband – you ought to stop her."

"I shan't stop her," Jack said, laughing. "I'm a man that likes a quiet life."

But there came a time, not all that long after, when he felt obliged to change his mind.

It was a day near the end of the harvest. The men were all up in one of the old Maryhope pieces, cutting the last thirty acres of dredge-corn. They worked late, wanting to get it all up in stooks, because there were showers in the offing. So it was quite dark by the time Jack went home, and as he walked down the fields of stubble he saw a red glow, somewhere up behind the farmhouse.

He turned aside and went on up into the birchwood and there, in the middle of the largest clearing, he found a gypsy waggon burning. The fire from its roof leapt as high as the treetops. The timbers blazed; the paintwork blistered and then crackled; the big red sparks flew up and drifted about overhead. The gypsies stood around, watching the blaze with sombre faces, and Jack saw one of them step forward to throw a set of harness into the very heart of the fire.

"Who's dead?" he asked, going to Mrs Zillery Boswell.

"Old Hananiah," Zillery said.

"What was he sick of, do you know?"

"He was eighty-three. That's a pretty good age for any man. I wouldn't say he was sick exactly."

"How long was he ailing?"

"A few days or so. I couldn't say, not exactly, but it warnt overlong, anyhow. He was an old, old man. He said his Rosanda'd been calling for him. You remember Rosanda? She died a while back, when we was at Dingham."

"Did you have a doctor?" Jack asked.

"No doctor, no. There's no cure for old age."

Mrs Zillery's face was closed against him, and the faces around were so many graven images, redly lit, staring at the burning waggon, now beginning to crumble inwards. Jack turned away, knowing he would learn nothing further from them, but stopped once to call out a warning.

"See that fire don't catch them trees! If there's timber ruined I shall have to run you off the farm!"

And when he got home he spoke very firmly to Nenna about it.

"Keep away from the gypsies. There's sickness among them. Old Han has died and they're burning his waggon."

"What sort of sickness?"

"I dunno. They wouldn't say. But they fetch their water out of the horse-pond and there's no one else would drink such stuff. So be sure to keep away in future – it's always best to be on the safe side."

Nenna nodded. She was frightened of sickness. She went at once to burn all the clothes-pegs the gypsies had sold her.

The following Saturday, Jack finished work at three o'clock, but when he got home, Nenna and Linn were not there, so he went in search of them, guessing that they had set out to meet him and had missed him somewhere, crossing the fields.

He came upon Nenna in the Long Meadow, sitting with her back against a willow, close beside the lower brook. The day was warm and airless, and she was asleep, her hat and scarf thrown down beside her, and a basket of mushrooms nearby. Linn was wading about in the brook, gathering buttercups and cresses, the muddy water washing over her shoes and stockings and wetting her frock whenever she stooped to pick a flower.

Jack pulled her out and scolded her gently, wringing the water out of her frock. He was more severe when he scolded Nenna.

"You should be more careful! The child has got herself drenched all over. And supposing she'd got herself stuck in the mud? It's three feet deep or so, just below. You'd never've heard her calling you, sleeping so fast as you was, neither. I had a job to wake you my own-self."

"I came over tired," Nenna said. "The day is so terribly close and stuffy. But I didn't mean to go to sleep. I only sat down to watch the linnets in that poplar."

She picked up her hat and scarf and basket, and they walked home together, Linn between them, swinging from their hands. Nenna talked of the ketchup she intended making. She had a new recipe from Amy

Gauntlet and was going to try it that afternoon.

"Mushrooms are good for you. Good as meat, Amy says."

When they reached home, she stood for a moment outside the porch, looking up at the roof, where a wagtail was busy running about. She put her fingers up to her forehead.

"I feel rather strange all of a sudden. My head is gone all numb and muzzy."

"It's sleeping out-of-doors has made you feel like that. Come inside and drink a drop of your barley water."

He was intent on changing the child's wet clothes for dry ones, a task that took him a good ten minutes. When he turned again to Nenna, she was standing on the hearth, bent almost double with her arms folded across her stomach, and as he went closer to look at her face, he saw that her skin was grey and yeasty, wet all over with perspiration.

"Here, you're poorly!" he said, frightened. "Sit down in this chair and take things easy."

He made her sit down in the basketwork chair, with a couple of cushions behind her head, then he covered her over with a warm blanket. Her eyes were filmy. Her jaws were clenched hard together. She was shivering all over.

"You sleep for a bit. That's the best thing. I shan't be gone more than a jiffy."

And he turned to Linn, who stood at the window, setting out her flowers along the ledge.

"Don't you move," he told her sternly. "You stay as you are till you see your Auntie Philippa come in at that door there. Understand?"

He went to the farmhouse as fast as he could and sent Miss Philippa down to the cottage. Then he went to Niddup to fetch Dr Spray.

*

"She will need nursing," the doctor said, "And I warn you it may be a long illness."

"Ought she to go to the Infirmary?"

"I think she's better staying here, where she's isolated, at least till we know for sure what's wrong."

"Then I'll come and stay and nurse her for you," Philippa said, her hand on Jack's arm.

"No, no, I'll nurse her myself. You take Linn back home with you, if you please, and keep her there till it's all over."

"How can you nurse her, with so much work to do on the farm?"

"Damn the farm! It can go to hell!"

"What use is a man, anyway, at a time like this?"

"I think it's better," the doctor said, "for Mr Mercybright to nurse his wife, so long as he follows my instructions, of course."

"I'll do whatever you tell me," Jack said. "Anything. Just tell me what." And a little later, seeing the doctor off at the door, he said: "What's wrong with her? What illness is it?"

"I have a suspicion it's typhoid fever. But I can't think how she should have come to contract it."

"I can," Jack said grimly, and told the doctor about the gypsies. "One of 'em died. Didn't you have to sign a certificate?"

"I wasn't summoned. I know nothing about it. It was probably Dr King from Hotcham – He'd sign anything when he's half seas over. I shall have to look into the matter myself. Meantime, well, I'll call on Nenna first thing in the morning."

"Yes. All right."

"She's a strong young woman. She should be all right. She'll pull through – I'm sure of that."

Jack was left staring. It had never occurred to him to doubt it. He went inside and closed the door.

Nenna's illness lasted a full eighteen days. Jack was with her day and night. The doctor came every morning and evening. A nurse came every afternoon.

During the last four or five days, Nenna often lay unconscious. Her poor wrung-out body was thus relieved, though the fever continued to rage in her brain. Jack could not understand most of the things she said in her delirium. It was a perfect stranger talking, and sometimes the words themselves had no meaning.

Only once did she open her eyes and look at him and speak to him, knowing who he was, and that was a few hours before the end. Even then her mind was wandering: she thought she had given birth to a child; and she looked at him with a little smile not of this world.

"It's a boy this time, isn't it? I knew it would be. I told you I'd give you a son, remember, and I've kept my promise as a good wife should. I always knew you wanted it, really, although you would never say so outright. And I shall have more. You'll see."

On his way up towards the birchwood, he passed alongside the Home Field, where the men had already begun ploughing. They saw him passing and Joe Stretton came running up to the corner gateway.

"Hey! Jack! Hang on a minute. We been wanting to ask you – how's your missus?"

Jack made no answer but tramped on up the rise and into the birchwood. The gypsy women were at their fires, with their stewpots steaming, cooking supper ready for their menfolk. The gypsy children gathered round, offering him baskets of damsons for sixpence, but he pushed past them and went to Mrs Zillery Boswell.

"Where are all your menfolk?" he asked.

"At Egham Horse Fair, mostly, I reckon."

"Then send and fetch them back at once. I want all of you off this land by darkfall. Every last pony and every last waggon! Do you hear what I say? Do you understand me? Never mind your suppers, – that's nothing to me – just get the rest of your tribe together and clear off this farm as soon as maybe!"

"But the gentleman surely don't mean it really—"

"If you ent all gone by the time I come back in a couple of hours I shall speed you on your way with a couple of barrels of gunshot!"

Reading his face, the gypsies believed him, and a boy was sent off on a pony to Egham. By dusk that evening, the clearing in the wood was quite deserted, and the procession of waggons was creaking on its way, down the steep track into Felpy Lane, curved roofs and smoking chimneys just visible over the hedgerow.

As Jack stood watching at the top of the track, Miss Philippa came up with Stretton. She glanced at the shotgun under Jack's arm.

"Why are the gypsies moving already? They don't usually go till winter."

"I told them to, that's why," he said. "I sent them packing, bag and baggage."

"What right have you to give such orders without so much as a word to me? This land is mine, not yours, remember, and if there are people here who are not wanted it's up to me to order them off!"

"I've saved you the bother, then, ent I?" he said.

"They're not responsible for Nenna dying. You can't

blame them for what has happened. For God's sake pull yourself together!"

"Get out of my way," Jack said. "Get out of my way, the pair of you, both. I ent in the mood for arguments."

He went into the wood to see that the gypsies' fires were douted.

Sometimes, ploughing the big steep fields up at Far Fetch or around Tootle Barrow, he turned up old skulls and bones and pike-heads and a number of small thick metal coins. The skulls and bones he put into the hedgerow. The rusty pike-heads he ploughed back into the ground. And the coins he took to Sylvanus Knarr at The Bay Tree, where they were cleaned and used in the making of hot rum flip, "to put a bit of iron into our blood" as old Angelina was fond of saying. According to her, the old coins were better than new ones. They had more virtue in them, she said.

Sometimes, that autumn, the clouds came so low over Far Fetch that they swept along the slopes of the fields, bearing down on him as he trudged, until everything was blotted out around him. He would come to a standstill, blind and helpless, wondering if he should go for the swap-plough; but then the cloud would pass on by, rolling across the ribbed brown field, leaving him soaked as though by a shower. In another moment he would be able to pick out his marker on the far hedge. He would click up the horses and trudge on, the ploughshare travelling through the moist earth with a sound like the hissing of an angry goose.

It was very cold all through October. The fall of the

year was swifter than usual. Summer seemed to slip straight into winter.

One day, when he was spreading muck in the Placketts, Miss Philippa came up behind him.

"Linn has been wondering where you've got to. She's asking whether you've gone away. What am I to say to her?"

"Tell her I shall be calling in to see her. Tomorrow, perhaps, or the day after when I ent so busy."

"That's what you said the last time I asked you. And the time before that. Why do you say things if you don't mean them? And what am I to do with her?"

"She's all right with you, ent she? She ent sick nor pining nor nothing?"

"She's in perfect health, if that's what you mean, and I daresay she's as happy as can be expected in the circumstances. But that's not the point."

"Then maybe you want me to come and fetch her and take her back home again to the cottage?"

"No," she said quickly. "I don't want that, the child is better staying with me."

"Well, then!" he said. "Why all the fuffle?"

"I want to know when you mean to see her."

"I'll be along, don't you worry, just as soon as I find the time. You tell her that. Say I'm coming as soon as maybe."

"You ought to come to us for your dinner. I'm sure you're not eating properly by yourself, and what use is that, neglecting yourself and getting run down as you surely will? You need a woman to look after you – to see that you eat good nourishing meals. Come on Sunday at one o'clock. I'll tell Mrs Miggs to count you in."

"Right you are. Just as you say. Sunday dinner at one o'clock."

"You'll come, then?" she said, surprised.

"Might as well. I've got to eat somewhere, like you say, so why not at your place?"

But he said it only to be rid of her. He had no intention of going to the farmhouse. He would just as soon go to The Bay Tree.

"By the way," she said, "Dr Spray was looking for you."

"Oh? Was he? What'd he want? I paid his bill, didn't I?"

"He wasn't best pleased at your driving the gypsies off as you did. He'd been keeping an eye on them up here, he said, in case there were any more outbreaks of fever. He wanted them kept in one place."

"They'll be in the quarry at Ludden all winter. It ent all that far for a man with a pony. He can keep an eye on 'em there if he wants to."

He turned his back on her, forking the manure out over the stubble.

He gave himself work in out-of-the-way parts of the farm. It suited him to be alone. He wanted no one. When the men needed orders, they sought him out. When he had to be with them in the cowshed or barn or working on the threshing-machine, they would speak to him briefly now and then, but the rest of the time they left him to himself.

He wished Miss Philippa would do the same, but she was always appearing to him, seeking him out in remote places, and one day she came to the Twenty Five Acre, one of the old Maryhope fields, where he was laying an overgrown hedge.

"I want to talk to you about the stone."

"Stone? What stone?"

"The headstone, of course, for Nenna's grave. The ground should be settled enough by now and it's time something was done about it. I want you to help me choose the words."

"You're going to get wet, standing there."

"And whose fault is that?" she asked, raging. "If you came to the house as I wanted you to, we could talk things over and get them settled. We could even behave like civilized people! But oh, no, – I have to traipse about the fields in all weathers before I succeed in tracking you down. The other men never know where to find you, or so they pretend at any rate, so perhaps you'll be kind enough to give me your attention just this once and settle the matter here and now!"

"You attend to it," Jack said. "Put whatever words you like."

"It's you that ought to see the mason. Whatever are people going to think?"

"They can think what they like. It's no odds to me."

"That's all very fine. Everything left to me as always! You were Nenna's husband, remember, so why should I have to do it all?"

"You're the one that's wanting a stone."

Jack was working with his back to the wind. He wore a sack folded in half, corner into corner, making a hood of double thickness, and was thus well protected. But Miss Philippa stood on the opposite side of the newly laid hedge, with the sleet driving sharply into her face.

"I don't suppose you would care if Nenna's grave remained bare and nameless?"

"That's right. I shouldn't care tuppence. What good is a stone? It won't bring Nenna back to life, will it?"

"Do you think your behaviour will bring her back? Skulking about at all hours, dragging your tail through muck and mire like a stricken fox in search of a hole? Just look at yourself! Have you no sense of pride whatever?"

"No. None."

"Then you should have!" she said. "For your child's sake – and for mine!"

"Yours? Why yours?"

"I *am* your employer," she said tartly, "even if I'm nothing else."

"If I was you I should stand well back. You might get a wood-chip in your eye, else."

"Coming and going like a thief in the night! Avoiding me at every turn! The only time you set foot near me is when you want me to pay your wages."

"I work for them, don't I? So I might just as well pick them up?"

"Oh, you work, certainly! Even the ox must be given his due. But what do you do when you're not working? Where do you go and what sort of company do you choose? You revert to nature and spend your nights sleeping in the sawdust on the floor of a common village public house!"

Jack ignored her. He bent down a thorn with his gloved hand and sliced at the stem with a chop of his billhook. It was easy enough to pretend the woman was not there. He had only to turn his head a little, till the keen east wind was riffling at both sides of his hood, for the noise of it to cut her out completely. And the east wind it was that eventually drove her away.

One morning he awoke to find himself lying on a heap of hop-waste outside the kilns at Ennen Stoke. He could not remember how he had got there. All he could remember was leaving The Bay Tree with a traveller from Brum and setting him on the road to Egham.

It was still dark when he awoke, but there was a cloudy moon shining. He went straight to the farm and arrived in time for early milking. Joe Stretton had already started. He was on his way out with two full pails.

"By God, you look rough! And you smell like you came down the brewery drain-pipe!"

"It's the hops," Jack said, sniffing his coat-sleeve.

"I know damn well it's the hops, man, and they'll be the ruin of you yet! You look a lot worser than old Nellie Lacey's stinking tom cat and I couldn't say fairer than that by no man!"

Jack sat on his stool and put his pail under Dewberry's udder. He pulled his cap down over his eyes and leant his forehead against the cow's side. And it seemed to him that her body yielded, melting away to nothing beneath him, letting him down and down and down, into a heaving dung-coloured darkness.

"You asleep, Jack?" asked Peter Luppitt, looking in at the end of the stall.

"By God, he is!" said Jonathan Kirby, looking over Peter's shoulder. "He's forty-winking, I do declare, and poor old Dewberry there nearly bursting!"

Jack opened his eyes and the cow's body became quite still. He put out his hands, – his fingers closed over the teats, – the milk went spurting into the pail. Luppitt and Kirby moved away. Joe Stretton appeared instead.

"Jack?" he said.

"Yes, what?"

"Did you have any breakfuss?"

"No. I warnt hungry."

"You look more than just a little bit comical to me. I reckon you've got a fit of the jim-jams. Ent there naught I can do for you?"

"Yes. There is. You can leave me be."

"All right. If that's how you want it. But there must be easier ways of killing yourself, I reckon, even if they ent all so clever as this one."

Stretton still stood, hesitating. He seemed anxious.

"I was going to tell you about the letter."

"What letter?"

"From my boy Harvey. He's coming home. He wrote me a letter from a hospital-place somewhere near Gloucester. Seems he's been wounded in the arm. I couldn't make out every word exactly – he was never much of a hand at writing – but it can't be too bad 'cos he's coming home any minute directly."

"Good," Jack said. "I'm glad to hear it. That's good news for you, your boy Harvey coming home."

A little while later, carrying two full pails across the cowshed, he slipped and fell on his back on the cobbles, the milk from both pails slopping over him, soaking through the sack he wore as an apron and wetting his jacket and trousers underneath. Joe Stretton helped him up and made him sit on a stool in the corner.

"You just sit there and take it easy. Seems to me you're about gumfoozled. Be quiet a minute while I get you a bunnel."

He went to the house and returned with a mug full of hot sweet tea.

"I was in luck. They was just getting breakfuss. I saw Mrs Miggs and she sent you this. Drink it up and you'll feel a lot better."

Jack sipped at the tea, breathing heavily into the mug, and the steam rose up in a cloud to his face, moistening his stubbled jaw and cheekbones and forming a drop on the end of his nose. The tea warmed him. He could trace the course it took inside him, a tingling furrow of heat in his guts. But his head was still an empty vessel; his limbs and body were a burden to him; so he sat for a while and smoked his pipe.

While searching his pockets he came across a trinket bought the night before from the Brummagem traveller:

two tiny Dutch clogs, carved out of pegwood, each the size of his small finger-nail, threaded together on a piece of red ribbon. He got up stiffly and went to the back door of the house. When Miss Philippa answered he gave her the empty earthenware mug and held up the trinket.

"I got this for Linn. Is she up yet?"

"She's up, yes. I'll give it to her."

"Where is she, then? I'd better prefer to give it to her my own-self. Can I come in for just a minute?"

"In that condition? I think not! *I* have some thought for Linn's feelings, though you yourself evidently have none." And she looked him over in disgust. "Have you no idea how the child would feel – have you no idea how it makes *me* feel – to see you so drunken and degraded?"

At that moment, Linn came along the passage behind her and stood, half hidden, peeping out from behind her skirts.

"Here," Jack said. "I've got something for you. Two little clogs like they wear in Holland. I bought them specially last night. How do you like 'em?"

Linn inched forward and looked at the trinket dangling from his fingers. She reached up and took it without a word, stepping back at once into the shadows. Her small face was blank. Her frown was suspicious. "Well, Linn?" Miss Philippa prompted. "What do you say when you're given a present?"

"Thank you very much," the child whispered.

"That's all right – I'm glad you like 'em," Jack said. "I reckon it's time you had a present, seeing it's very nearly Christmas. And how are you going on here lately? You keeping nicely? Everything fine and dandy, is it?"

The child made no answer; only stared at him with Nenna's eyes; and after a moment he turned away. But before the door was closed upon him, he heard her voice as she spoke to her Auntie Philippa.

"Who is that man? He's not my daddy, is he, auntie? That dirty old man is not my daddy . . ."

The day was a wet one and in the afternoon Jack took four horses down to be shod at the smithy in Niddup. Waiting his turn he leant in the doorway, looking out across the dip to where the three main roads came down, meeting in a little open place called the Pightle.

At three o'clock the carrier's cart arrived from Egham, and a young soldier climbed out, shouldering his kit-bag. It was Harvey Stretton and as he turned into Felpy Lane, Jack saw that the boy's right sleeve was empty, folded and pinned to the side of his tunic.

The smith was having some sort of trouble. The Ridlands Hall carriage was in for repairs and was taking longer than expected. He called out to Jack, saying he would have to wait even longer.

"All right," Jack said, "I'll go for a bit of a stroll round."

"Ah, and have one for me while you're at it, will you?"

But although Jack started towards the river, he did not turn right towards The Bay Tree; he turned left instead to the old church, standing at the upper edge of the ham. It was almost dusk, but he found Nenna's grave easily enough, and was able to read the name on the headstone: Henrietta Ruth, beloved wife of John Mercybright: died September 26th., 1900, aged 24. The mound was covered in new grass, little straight-standing blades, very fine and pointed. Soon, he thought, it would want cutting.

Inside the church, someone was moving, carrying a light. Jack stood watching it, glimmering first in one tall coloured window, then in the next, until it reached the eastern end, where it blossomed out in quiet splendour as the bearer lit the candles on the altar. Outside, in the rainy darkness, Jack shivered and turned away.

On Sunday morning he set about cleaning and tidying the cottage. He swept and dusted everywhere, beat the mats on the hedge in the garden, scoured the floors till the red bricks showed their colour again. He even black-leaded the kitchen range and polished all its bits of brass, before lighting a fire in the stove.

He heated the copper in the little wash-house, stripped off his clothes, and scrubbed himself hard all over, using a tablet of strong red carbolic soap. When he came to shave, the ten weeks' growth of beard proved stubborn. It took time; he had to keep on stropping his razor; and when he was finished, his skin felt tender and soft, like a baby's. He found he had a narrow scar, only recently healed, running along the edge of his jaw, and a small cut on his left ear. It was so long since he had last looked into a mirror, the face he saw there was almost a stranger's.

He put on his best Sunday suit and cap and his best soft boots, and, smelling of camphor and boot-polish, set out for the farmhouse. Mrs Miggs let him in and showed him into the front parlour, and there, in another moment or two, Miss Philippa came to him, wearing a full-skirted dress of black silk. She was clearly astonished to see him looking clean and tidy. A little gleam appeared in her eyes. But she stood stiffly, her hands folded in front of her, the fingers entwined.

"Where's Linn?" he asked.

"Why d'you want to know? Have you come with more cheap gew-gaws to give her?"

"No, I've come to fetch her and take her home."

"Don't be ridiculous!" she exclaimed. "How can you

possibly take her home? The state the place is in – it's worse than a pig-sty!"

"Not now, it ent. I've been sprucing it up."

"And who would look after her? Surely not you?"

"I don't see why not."

"You can't even look after yourself properly, let alone a child of four. Oh, you're well enough at this very minute – quite the respectable gentleman, I'm sure – but how long is that going to last, I wonder?"

"I'd like to see Linn, if it's no odds to you. Will you fetch her for me?"

"No!" she exclaimed. "This is all wrong! I will not let you drag the poor child away from me just to suit your whim of the moment. The idea is monstrous. She's better here."

"She's *my* daughter. Not yours."

"Rather late in the day for remembering that, isn't it, seeing you've ignored her all these weeks past?"

"Late or not," he said, "I mean to have her."

For a while she stared at him, hazel eyes very pale and bright, the blood dark on her prominent cheekbones. Then she moved away to one side of the hearth and spread her hands towards the fire.

"How can a man look after a child? It isn't natural."

"It's natural enough, when the man is her father."

"You'll be working all day."

"Linn will go to school with the Gauntlet children. They'll be calling for her on the way down. She's been wanting to go this twelvemonth or more and now I reckon it'll do her good. Then Cissy Gauntlet will stop with her at the cottage after school and look after her till I get home."

"Cissy Gauntlet is only thirteen."

"I know that. But she's good with little 'uns and Linn likes her. I'd trust Cissy Gauntlet anywhere."

"It seems you've got it all arranged."

"That's right, I have. I seen the Gauntlets yesterday evening."

"But why can't Linn stop here in the daytime and then come to you after work?"

"No," he said. "It's better my way."

"And what about when you go to The Bay Tree? What happens to Linn when she wakes up at night and finds herself all alone in the cottage?"

"I shan't be going to The Bay Tree," he said.

"So you say! So you say!"

But it was the last feeble shot in her armoury, thrown off at random. Her expression already showed her resignation. She knew he would never neglect the child – not now he had given his promise.

"Very well," she said. "I'll send her to you."

She went out of the room and a little while later Linn came in, small and pinched-looking, creeping forward as though afraid. She stared at him for fully a minute, her gaze going over him, taking in the familiar clothes, the familiar watchstrap fastened across the front of his waist-coat, then returning at last to dwell uncertainly on his face.

"Well, Linn Mercybright, don't you know me?"

The child nodded but remained quite silent, with-drawn, unsmiling. There was no hint of welcome in her face; nothing of her usual small bright spirit; nothing of the old warmth and fondness. Was she paying him out for his desertion in the past ten weeks? If she was, he deserved it, he told himself, and it was his task to win back her favour.

"I've come to take you home, and about time too, I expect you'll say. I want you to help me make the dinner. We're having a bit of boiled beef – Cissy Gauntlet got it for me – but I ent too sure how to make the pudden. You'll help me, won't you? – You'll give me a hand?"

Still nothing more than a slight nod, but when he made a move towards the door, holding out his hand towards her, she put her own hand into it at once and went with him unquestioningly.

Miss Philippa's face as she saw them off at the back door was difficult to read. She seemed genuinely fond of the child; her fingers rested for a moment on the small fair head; yet her manner was just as severe and abrupt as ever – what warmth she had seemed always to be well battened down.

"Don't be a nuisance to your father, will you? No naughty tricks? No disobedience?"

"Linn'll be good," Jack said. "She's going to help me get the dinner."

With a tiny knife, not too sharp, Linn scraped at the lump of suet, sitting opposite him at the table as he stood peeling the onions, carrots, parsnips and potatoes. The big saucepan hummed on the trivet, and the kitchen was filled with the smell of boiling beef.

"What next?" he said, dropping the vegetables into the saucepan. "A handful of barley? A good whoops of salt?"

"Yes," she said, stopping work to watch him.

"How're you getting on with that there suet? Shall I give you a hand? Take a turn, shredding?" He took a sharp knife and scraped the suet into shreds. "And now I must make this roly pudden. Two handfuls of flour. One handful of suet. Salt and pepper and a good mix round, then make it sticky with this here skim milk. Am I doing it right, do you think? Making a proper molly job of it, eh?"

"Yes," she said, watching as he plumped the piece of dough on the table.

"Jiggle it all about in the flour . . . roll it into a roly-poly . . . and wrap it round in this nice clean cloth. Ah, and how do I do up the ends, I wonder? Do I tie 'em up with bits of blue ribbon?"

"No," she said, and a little breath of a laugh escaped her.

"What, then? Boot-laces?"

"Silly," she said. "You have to tie them up with string."

"String!" he said, snapping his fingers, and went to search the dresser drawer. "What a good thing it is I've got you to tell me how to go on. I'd be making janders of it, else."

While the dinner was cooking and Jack was bringing more logs for the basket, Linn stood on a chair at the gable-end window, watching the birds fluttering and squabbling at the old bacon bone Jack had hung in the cherry tree early that morning. The day was damp and overcast, but with little bursts of sun now and then, slanting down whenever a hole got torn in the clouds.

"Not a bad old day," Jack said. "I thought we'd go down the dip after dinner and take a walk along the Nidd. There was herons there a few days ago. Five or six of 'em. Maybe seven."

"What were they doing?"

"They were standing looking at theirselves in the water."

"Why were they?"

"To see and make sure that they was tidy. They like to look decent the same as most folk. And then, of course, they'd also be thinking of doing a bit of fishing."

"Fishing? How can they?" And the frown she turned on him was puzzled, for she pictured the herons with rods and lines.

"Oh, herons is clever at fishing," Jack said. "They keep

their beaks long and sharp on purpose. Would you like to go down with me and see them? And maybe find some white violets under the trees like we did when we went there once before?"

Linn nodded assent, her eyes wakeful, the glimmerings of pleasure in their depths. She was happy enough in her quiet way. Happy enough to be with him again. As happy, anyway, as he could expect. The old warmth was still missing between them, but that would come back in time, he was sure. It was up to him to see that it did. He must work towards it. He would need that warmth in years to come and so would Linn, for they had nobody but each other.

Every afternoon now, Cissy Gauntlet brought Linn home when school was over, lit the fire and made the place cosy, and kept the child company till Jack got in after work.

Cissy was a fair freckled girl with a long narrow face and something of her father's sorrowful manner. At thirteen she was already a natural mother, delighted to have sole charge of Linn and taking her responsibilities with the greatest seriousness.

Often when Jack arrived home, he would find the two of them going over the twice times table or the words of Our Father or the alphabet, and while he washed himself in the scullery, he would listen to them chanting together.

> "A for an apple on the tree,
> B for the busy bumblebee,
> C for cat and D for dog,
> E for eariwig, F for frog."

Often, too, he would find Harvey Stretton sitting with them, joining in their childish games. Harvey was a special favourite with Linn. He would bring her sprays of spindleberries, or giant fir-cones, or a mumruffin's nest out of the hedge, or a bunch of feathers from a cock pheasant's tail. And, despite his disability, he was always cheerful, always full of life.

"Where's your arm gone?" Linn asked, touching the boy's empty sleeve.

"Seems I must've left it somewhere."

"Why did you?"

"Well, it warnt of a lot of use to me, really. I was silly enough to let it get damaged. So here I am like Admiral Nelson, except that I've still got two good eyes."

"Will it grow again, your arm?" Linn asked.

"Now that's an idea, ent it, eh? I'd like to have two arms again and get two hands on the stilts of a plough. I must hope for the best, mustn't I, and see if this sleeve gets filled up again?"

Harvey was doing odd jobs on the farm, carning only a few shillings, but Cissy Gauntlet had ideas for him. Cissy was an intelligent girl, eager to learn and get on in the world, and her great ambition when she left school was to become a village postmistress. She wanted Harvey to be a postman.

"Well, it's an outdoor job, that's something, ent it?" Harvey said. "Even if it does mean swapping one damned uniform for another. But it's reading the names on the omvelopes – that's the thing that'd flummox me."

"Can't you read, then, for goodness' sake?"

"I can read all right so long as the words is all printed but I ent much shakes when it comes to what's hand-wrote by folks theirselves."

"Then I'll have to teach you," Cissy said.

The boy and the girl were "great" together, as William Gauntlet said to Jack, and although the girl was not yet fourteen, they were fast becoming "acquaintances". It would come to a wedding one fine day and Ciss would be the making of that boy Harvey.

Soon Harvey was calling at Perry Cottage dressed in his postman's uniform and carrying his big canvas satchel. But as it was always at the end of his round, he had no letters to show Linn, and she was bitterly disappointed.

"Why don't *we* get letters?" she asked him.

"I don't rightly know," Harvey said. "Not everyone does. Not by a long chalk. I suppose there ent enough to go round." Then, seeing Linn's face, he said gravely: "I shall have to speak to the postmaster, shan't I?"

So once a week after that, there would always be a letter for Linn, in a small envelope carefully addressed in capitals: To Miss Linn Mercybright; Perry Cottage; Brown Elms Farm; Niddup, near Hotcham. Harvey would pretend to search his satchel; would draw out the letter and squint at the writing; and would place it in Linn's impatient hands. Then, once she had opened it, it was Cissy's job to read it aloud.

"Dear Linn: I hear as you had a cold in your nose the day before yesterday, Sunday, that is, so take good care and don't go out in this cold east wind without you wear your thick woollen scarf . . ."

"Who's it from, who's it from?" Linn would ask, and Cissy, frowning over the signature, would say, "This one's from the Lord Mayor of London" or "Seems it's her Majesty the Right Honourable Queen Victoria writing to you this week from the palace . . ."

Jack, coming home, would hear the three voices upraised in talk, and Linn's light laughter trilling out, and would stand for an instant waiting for the three young faces to turn towards him in the red warm fire-glow. Then his daughter would run to him, as in the old days, for him to lift her up to the rafters.

"You had another letter?" he would ask. "I thought as much when I heard the excitement. And who is it this time? The Shah of Persia?"

"Don't look and I'll show you!" she would say. "It's wrote on blue paper and there's little drawings of Mr Gauntlet with all his sheeps and dogs in the paddock . . ."

His life and hers were linked as before. The warmth was back between them again.

On a dry day in March, when the wind blew, but not too briskly, they set fire to the steep piece of wasteland known as the Moor, up on the slopes above the Placketts. It was a field of sixteen acres, the very worst of the old Maryhope land bought from Tuller, the very last to be cleared and intaken.

It was quite unfit for grazing by cattle and even the sheep got "scarcely enough to starve on comfortably" as William Gauntlet said to Jack. It was grown with great "bull-pates" as Gauntlet called them: tussocks of grass so old and tough that no beast would touch them; and the ground between was so tunnelled by vermin that a man could twist his leg in a pot-hole two or even three feet deep.

The fire was lit at the foot of the slope, and, the wind blowing easy from south and west, it burnt its way slowly and surely uphill, breaking out now and then in a great crackling flare as it caught a thicket of gorse or bramble. lack was there with Joe Stretton and Jonathan Kirby, each armed with a swat on a long pole, ready to run if the flames at the boundaries threatened the hedges. The black smoke rose up across the sun, darkening what should have been a bright day, and as the heat grew on the ground, hares and rabbits and smaller vermin bolted from their holes and ran uphill, where Ernie Stretton lay in wait with his father's shotgun.

"You've started something now, ent you?" Jonathan Kirby said to Jack. "We shan't dare budge from here now till this lot's burnt itself out and douted."

"And what's the use of it?" Stretton demanded. "This stretch of ground will never be nothing worth it neither. It's been naught but wasteland since time unremembered."

"All the land on earth must've been rough like this at one time," Jack said. "Somebody had to start clearing it somewhere."

"Now you've got me beat there," Stretton retorted. "I don't remember that far back!"

During the morning, Miss Philippa came to watch the burning, and asked to see the slaughtered game. Stretton produced four brace of rabbits, three of hares, and a red-legged partridge that must have strayed over from the Came Court estates.

"Is this all?" she asked.

"Well, there's a few stoats and weasels and a mole or two," Stretton said, "but I wouldn't recommend them for eating, exactly."

"No doubt you've put the best bag aside for yourselves," she said. "I know you men here."

"And we know *you*," Stretton muttered, as she walked away. "We ent simple so much as just plain unbewildered."

Going home that evening, when the field-fire had burnt itself out, Jack was covered from head to foot with fine charcoal dust and black ashes. He looked like a collier and Linn, glancing up as he entered the kitchen, opened her mouth in a little "ooo."

"Who's a dirty rascal?" she demanded.

The next morning, when he went up to look at the Moor, the ashes were blowing about on the wind. He hoped for rain and that night it came, a heavy soaker, cooling the ground and settling the ashes.

As soon as the couch-grass and weeds were showing, he and two others went in and ploughed the sixteen acres lengthways. It took six days and was hard going. Then, a month later, when the weeds were showing green again, he mucked the land and ploughed it crossways.

"You'll never get it clean," Joe Stretton said.

"Oh, yes, I shall, given time."

"One year's weeds, seven years' seeds, – that's what the old folk always say – so you'll have your work cut out, that's a promise."

"I depend upon it," Jack said, "to keep me out of mischief."

All that spring and summer, whenever he could spare the time, he went and worked in the sixteen acres, ploughing in crop after crop of green weed seedlings. Or else he went over it with the new cultivator, teasing out the roots of couch-grass and bindweed and thorn and bramble, and burning them in heaps that smoked and smouldered for days on end.

"Where's Jack?" someone would ask. "Up there ploughing his piece again, is he? He'll be getting the hang of it soon directly."

And so, since the sixteen acres could not now be called the Moor, it became known instead as "Jack's Piece" and one of the men wrote the new name in on the field-map hanging up in Miss Philippa's office.

"That's almost as good as having an apple named for you, ent it?" Peter Luppitt said to Paul. "Or a new climbing rose, say, or a new kind of tater."

"He won't get much else in the way of rewards," said Joe Stretton. "*She* won't thank him for working his guts out the way he does."

Jack only shrugged. He worked hard for his own satisfaction; because he hated to see land wasted; because he
would just as soon work as not. And William Gauntlet,
tending his sheep on the high hilly slopes of Tootle
Barrow, where he had the best view, noted the changes
wrought month by month as the old starved Maryhope
lands were given new heart and brought under cultiva-
tion again.

"It does a man a power of good to see these fields all
smiling again."

And Miss Philippa, too, whatever Joe Stretton might
say, seemed well pleased with the way things were going.
She and Jack were in Hotcham one day, attending the
market, and she left him for a while to go to the bank.
When she returned, her face was quite radiant, her eyes
gleaming with something akin to gaiety.

"It's the mortgage I took when I bought Maryhope
Farm," she said. "Every penny is now paid off. Don't you
think that's wonderful news?"

"It's humpty-dinker," Jack said. "Maybe now you'll be
able to afford a few new gates where they're needed."

"More than that. We shall have improvements everywhere. Those new implements you've been wanting . . .
repairs to the sheds and the big barn . . . perhaps a new
cowshed altogether . . ."

She was full of energy and plans for the future; more
outward-looking; more willing to share her hopes and
ambitions than she had ever been before; and as they
walked away from the sale-ring, talking, she slipped her
hand inside his arm. For once they were equal together,
it seemed. A good understanding existed between them;
a sympathy; a fellow-feeling; so that the friendly, comfortable gesture seemed perfectly easy and natural between
them.

"The men's cottages, too," she said. "I know some repairs are badly needed and I mean to make a start before next winter . . ."

Often on fine summer afternoons, Cissy Gauntlet brought Linn up to the fields after school, to where he was working. At hay-making time, the child sometimes rode with him on the reaper, sitting on his lap, within the circle of his arms, and with his big hands covering hers on the ribbons.

"Giddy up! Giddy up!" she would call to the horses, and, when stopping, would lean right back against Jack's body, saying, "Whoa, there! Whoooaaa!" trying to make her voice deep and gruff and manly. Like his, she thought.

At harvest-time, too, she was there with the other children: the Gauntlets; the Luppitts; the little Ruggs; tying up the sheaves until her fingers quickly grew tired and she wandered instead from corn-cock to corn-cock, pulling out vetches and purple knapweed, pink weather-wine flowers and dark red clover, and tying them up in little posies. And when it came to dinner time or tea time, she would sit with Jack in the shade of a hedgerow maple tree, sharing his bread and cheese and cider.

"How many ears of corn are there in this field?"

"I dunno. You'd better count them."

"I can't," she said. "It's too many."

"You'll have to make a guess, then, that's all."

"Hundreds and thousands and millions and billions."

"Ah, that's about it, near enough, I would say."

"Why does barley have whiskers on it?"

"Laws, now you're asking, ent you?" he said. "I'd like to know the answer to that one my own-self. Nasty sharp things, getting inside a man's shirt as they do, prickling him and driving him crazy. I reckon them whiskers is put there on purpose to make us swear."

"You mustn't swear, it's naughty," she said.

"Oh, and who says so?"

"Miss Jenkins says so."

Miss Jenkins was the Niddup schoolmistress: to Linn, a person from another world: not flesh and blood but the Voice of God in sealskin jacket and black snood.

"Don't she ever swear, then, your Miss Jenkins?"

"No," Linn said, in a shocked whisper, then put up a hand to stifle a little spurt of laughter. The idea of it almost overcame her. "Not Miss Jenkins."

"Don't she even say Drat and Bother?"

"No. Never."

"Ah, well, *she* ent never had barley-ails inside her shirt, that's certain."

"Miss Jenkins says . . ."

"Yes? Well? What does she say?"

"Miss Jenkins says . . ."

"We shall hear something now. I can feel it coming."

"Miss Jenkins says *Oh-my-goodness-gracious-me!*"

"Does she, by golly? Now would you believe it?"

"Sometimes she says *Oh-dear-how-teejus!*"

"There you are, then. It's like I said. She enjoys a good swear the same as we all do."

Now and then, on a Sunday, he and Linn had dinner at the farmhouse, where they had to be on their best behaviour. Miss Philippa held that they ought to eat there every day; she was sure a man's cooking could not be good enough for his own needs or those of a child; but he kept the occasions as few as he could, because neither he nor Linn enjoyed them.

"Auntie Philippa," Linn said once, "why ent there any sugar in this here apple pudden?"

"You mustn't say ent, Linn. I've told you before."

"Why *aren't* there any sugar, then?"

"There's plenty of sugar in that pudding. I made it myself."

"I can't taste it."

"Then there must be something wrong with your tongue, that's all I can say about you, little miss."

"Perhaps there's something wrong with the sugar."

"That's hardly polite," Miss Philippa said, frowning severely, and, thinking to teach the child a lesson, she stretched out a hand as though to remove Linn's plate. "Perhaps you'd sooner go without altogether?"

"Yes," Linn said, and pushed the plate across the table. "I don't like it. The apples is siddly. They make me go all funny all over."

Miss Philippa stared. Her lips were tight-pressed. There was trouble brewing.

"I reckon maybe it is a bit sharp," Jack said, to save an outburst. "We've got a sweet tooth, my daughter and me, at least when it comes to apple pudden. D'you think we could have a bit more sugar?"

So a bowl of sugar was brought to the table and the pudding was eaten to the last mouthful. But on the way home that afternoon Linn, remembering, gave a shudder.

"I don't like Auntie Philippa's dinners. They make my mouth feel funny after. They make me feel all *ugh* inside."

Jack felt a good deal of sympathy with her. The mutton stew had been swimming in grease. The cook, Mrs Miggs, was getting old, but Miss Philippa would never admit it. He did his best to make Linn think of other things.

"Where shall we go to get our blackberries? Up Felpy Lane or down Long Meadow? It's your turn to choose. I chose last time."

"Up the Knap and round by the Placketts."

"All that way? You'll be winnelled nearly off your legs."

"You can give me a ride home on your shoulders."

"Oh, I can, can I? And who says so?"

"You always do, when I get tired."

So, on a Sunday, according to the season, they would go berrying along the hedgerows, or looking for mushrooms in the meadows, or collecting fir-cones in the woods at Far Fetch. They always went somewhere, once his stint in the garden was finished, or the clothes washed out, or the house made tidy, and when they returned on cold winter afternoons, he would open the range and stoke up the fire, light the oil-lamp on the table, and see that Linn exchanged her wet boots for dry slippers.

"What would you like for tea today? Welsh rarebit, maybe? Or a nice soft-boiled egg with bread and butter? Or shall we just have a walk round the table?"

"Muffins!" she said. "That's what I should like for tea."

"Who said there was muffins? I never said so, I'm sure of that. I never mentioned muffins once."

"I seen 'em!" she said. "In the pantry. Under the cover."

"Laws, there's no keeping secrets in this house, is there? Not with that sharp little snout of yours poking in here, there, and everywhere."

"It's not a snout."

"What is it, then, a knob of putty?"

"It's a nose," she said. "Only pigs and piglets have snouts."

"It's a snout right enough when it comes to rootling about in the pantry. Them there muffins was meant to be a big surprise. And who's going to toast them, as if I didn't already know?"

She would sit on the milking-stool on the hearth, draw

the kettle-glove over her hand, and take down the polished brass toasting fork with the three curved prongs and the *Cutty Sark* on the end of its handle. As she toasted each muffin and handed it up to him to be buttered, her face would grow very pink and shiny, and she would go into a kind of trance, basking in the heat from the open stove.

Eating the muffins was the grand culmination. She licked each finger afterwards, exactly as he did, with great relish. But it was the toasting of them that mattered most; the encompassing warmth after several hours out of doors; the sharing and the closeness.

Her contentment touched him, so that he was at peace with himself, yet watchful, too. Every evening, when he had seen her into bed, – face and hands washed; hair brushed; prayers said; and a hot stone bottle wrapped in flannel at her feet; – he would stand at the bottom of the stairs, listening, anxious lest fears should come to her with the darkness and aloneness. But all he ever heard was the drone of her voice as she sang to the doll cradled beside her with its head on the pillow: "Little Dolly Daydream, pride of I dunno . . ." After the singing there was only silence. She had very few terrors in her life.

The farm was doing well these days. They had the threshing-machine in November, and all the corn-crops weighed out heavy. Miss Philippa took pride in her neat, clean, orderly fields, and in the produce garnered from them, knowing it could scarcely now be bettered throughout the county.

She was in high spirits and at Christmas that year she went about visiting her neighbours more than she had ever been known to do before. She was more at ease. She talked more freely. She held her head high, proud in the knowledge that she was now a farmer of some repute. And often on these visits she insisted that Jack and Linn should go with her.

"You and the child are all I've got left in the way of family now. It's only right that we should be seen to be united."

The new year came in cold and wet and continued so for weeks on end. February not only filled the dykes but had them overflowing everywhere, and in Niddup village, the river came up to the very foot of The Bay Tree garden. It was just the kind of weather Jack hated and all he wanted was a dry place in a corner of the barn where he could get on with repairing tools and machinery and harness. But Miss Philippa, spending money more freely now, was always sending him off to sales.

One day she sent him to a farm sale somewhere near Egham in the hope of his picking up a corn drill and a horse rake cheaply. But at Nelderton Dip the river was up over the road and a notice announced that the sale had been postponed, so he returned homewards with an empty cart. The early afternoon was dusk-dark, the rain falling in a cold steady downpour, out of a sky full of thick black clouds.

As he drove homewards, through the mud of Hayward's Lane, just before reaching Gifford's Cross, he noticed an elm in the right-hand hedgerow that seemed to lean out of the greyness above, slanting sharply across the roadway.

"That's funny," he thought, "I don't remember that there elm tree leaning so much when I drove this way earlier this morning."

He decided it was probably just his fancy – the tree looking bigger in the rainy darkness – but as he passed beneath it he heard its roots groaning and creaking and heard the plop-plopping of loose clods dropping into the ditch below. And when he looked over his shoulder, he could see the tree falling. He jumped to his feet and flipped the reins, calling out urgently as he did so, and the horse, astonished, pulled as hard as he could along the mud-filled ruts and rudges.

They escaped by inches. An outer branch just clawed the tailboard. But the great noise of the elm tree falling behind them – the screeching of its roots tearing out of the waterlogged clay, the crunching of the branches and the shuddering whoomph as the big trunk bounced to the ground – so frightened the horse that he put up his head and bolted at a gallop. He got the bit between his teeth and Jack could do nothing but hang on, while the cart-axle bumped on the ground between the ruts, and the wet mud flew up in spray from the wheels.

A hundred yards on, when they reached Three Corners, the frightened horse took the nearside turn, which was sharp and narrow and ran downhill. The cart-wheels were pulled clean out of the ruts, and the cart went slewing over rightwards, where it crashed with great force against the corner of Winworth's linhay. Jack was thrown right out of the cart and hurled against the linhay wall. He then fell in a crumpled heap in the roadway while the horse and cart rattled on.

For one slow fractional instant it seemed to him he was given a choice: between light and darkness: living and dying. It was only a question of concentrating. – It was up to him to find the strength. – But the darkness claimed him and he fell forward into the mire.

The horse returned home to Brown Elms, trailing the splintered remains of the cart. Joe Stretton and the rest of the men set out immediately to search the back lanes between Niddup and Egham, but it was young Harvey, out delivering letters at Gromwell, who found him and ran to Winworth's for help. By then, Jack had lain unconscious for five hours, with the rain falling on him without pause.

He was taken home to his own cottage. He was still unconscious. Cissy Gauntlet helped to strip off his sodden clothes and to get him to bed wrapped in hot blankets. Linn was frightened by the sight of her father being carried so blue-looking into the house, and Cissy stayed to comfort her while Alfie Winworth went for the doctor and Harvey went for Miss Philippa.

Dr Spray was sure that Jack would die. Pulse rate was critically low. Breathing was almost inaudible. He would send a reliable nurse, he said, to do what little there was to be done. It was probably only a matter or hours. Then the nurse must go to Ridlands Hall.

But Miss Philippa would have nothing of it. She called Dr Spray a stupid fool. She would look for more sense from the drunken Dr King, she said, or old Grannie Balsam with her herbs and simples.

"This man is most certainly not going to die, Doctor, – not if I have anything to do with it! And as for your reliable nurses, you needn't put them to any trouble, – I will nurse him myself, better than they would!"

Sometimes he thought it was Nenna's presence he felt
in the bedroom; Nenna's hands sponging his burning
face and body; Nenna's eyes watching over him at all
hours. At other times he remembered clearly that Nenna
had been dead for seventeen months and was buried
under the chestnut tree in the church-yard at Niddup.
The woman in the room must therefore be a stranger.

Once he thought he was drowning in the muddy,
chopped-up waters of Ennen. The bridge was crumbling
underneath him, the stones tumbling as though they
were nothing but a child's building-blocks, kicked from
underfoot. The flooded river would have him this time,
and he didn't really mind, for it took too much strength
to swim against such an angry current. He would have to
give in. He would let his lungs fill with cold water.

"No! No! You are *not* to give in! I am not going to let
you! Jack? Do you hear me? You must think of your
daughter. – What would become of her, do you think, if
you gave up now?"

So the woman was not such a stranger after all. She
knew all about him. She called him by name. Yet the
calm, perfect face was quite unknown to him, leaning
towards him in the soft lamplight. And her quiet voice,
speaking with such strength and assurance – surely he
had never heard it before?

"Philippa?" he said once, and the quiet voice answered him: "Yes? I'm still here. Drink a little of this barley water."

Sometimes the pain in his chest was such that he wished he knew how to stop himself breathing. The pain was everywhere more than he could bear. He wished the quiet voice would release him, give him leave to slip down into the darkness, where the cold river waters would ebb and flow throughout his frenzied blood. But then a picture came into his mind, of a small child in a blue frock, wandering all alone in a meadow, lost among the buttercups and ragged-robin.

"Linn?" he said, leaning forward, off the pillow. "Where's Linn?"

"Linn is all right. She's with Cissy Gauntlet down in the kitchen. I shall bring her to see you as soon as you're well. Tomorrow, perhaps, or the day after."

"Tell her," he said.

"Yes? Tell her what?"

"Just tell her," he said. "Tell her I'm here. Tell her I'm going to get a lot better. Tell her I shall see her soon."

Sometimes, when Philippa held a cup to his lips for him to drink, or when she leant over him, arranging the pillows at his back, a sense of freshness and strength seemed to pass from her to him. It was in the cool touch of her fingers on his; in the way her arms supported him, holding him up, strong behind his shoulders, as she made the bed smooth and comfortable and wholesome again. And once, when his head lay for a moment against her breast, the scent of lavender that hung about her was like the breath of pure sweet air blowing from a summer garden.

"I can't rightly see you."

"Then I'll turn up the lamp."

"What time is it?"

"It's half past seven."

"Evening or morning?" he asked, puzzled.

"Evening," she said. "I've just been seeing Linn to bed."

"Is it still raining?"

"No. Not now. It hasn't rained for a week or more. There's a brisk wind blowing now and the land is drying out very nicely."

"A peck of dust in March . . . " he said, with an effort, and fell into a deep, quiet, sweet-tasting sleep.

When he awoke, Dr Spray stood before him.

"You're a lucky man, Mercybright. I have to confess that I myself had given you up as lost. And so you would have been, no doubt of that, if it hadn't been for Miss Guff here. You couldn't have had a better nurse if you'd searched all through England."

"Am I past the worst, then?"

"Just stay as you are and obey Miss Guff in everything, and you'll soon be up again, breathing God's air without any undue strain."

That afternoon, sitting up in bed, washed and made tidy and wearing a clean white nightshirt, he was ready to receive Linn, who came on tiptoe to the side of the bed.

"Why, bless my soul, you've brought me some prim-roses, ent you?" he said. "I bet I can tell you where you got 'em."

"I didn't get them in Long Meadow."

"Then you got 'em in the woods at Far Fetch. Am I right? Eh? And I bet they took some finding, too, so early in the year as this."

He took the primroses and put them to his nose. Their cool creamy scent was to him at that moment the purest thing in the whole world. He gave them back to Linn and watched her put them in the pot on the table.

"That'll cheer me up, seeing them primroses there beside me, knowing the spring is under way."

"Why is your voice gone funny, father?"

"Got a frog in my throat, I suppose," he said.

"Are you better now?"

"I should think I am! I'm very nearly fighting fit. Just another day or two and I shall be up like Punch and Judy."

"Auntie Philippa's come to live with us now. Did you know?"

"It's only for the time being, while she's looking after your dad."

"She brought a pallet and sleeps next to me in my room."

"Ah. Well. And is she comfortable, do you suppose?"

"I dunno," the child said, shrugging.

"Then you ought to ask her. She's gone to a hang of a lot of swither, you know, looking after me like she has done, and it's up to us to show we're grateful."

"Why are you growing a beard, father?"

"To keep my face warm in winter," he said.

"But it's not winter now – it's spring," she said. "Mr Gauntlet's got twelve lambs already."

"Has he indeed? Who would've thought it? But hang on a minute – what's all this 'father' business all of a sudden? You always used to call me 'dad'."

"Auntie Philippa said I must call you father."

"Did she by golly? Well, maybe she thinks it goes a lot better with my beard. But I'd just as soon you called me dad the same like you have done herebefore."

The bedroom door opened. Miss Philippa came in.

"You must go now, Linn, before your father gets too tired. You'll be able to see him again tomorrow."

Linn stared at Jack for a long moment, then left the room and went downstairs.

"She ent feeling lonely, is she, d'you think?"

"Oh, no, why should she?" Philippa said. "Cissy Gauntlet is down there with her. Cissy is teaching her how to knit."

Sometimes, waking up, he would find Philippa sitting a little way away, in the wickerwork chair from downstairs, with the lamp on the table at her elbow, and a piece of needlework in her fingers. She always knew when he was awake, however still he lay there, watching. She seemed to sense his eyelids opening.

The lamplight was kind to her, softening her rather strong features, giving her eyes great depth and darkness, and shining on her smooth dark hair, the colour of red-brown sorrel flowers seen in sunlight. There was something very quiet about her. He found it restful; reassuring; he had never known her so serene.

"There's a little arrowroot in this basin. I brought it up ten minutes ago. If you take it now, it'll still be warm."

"I shall be getting to look like arrowroot directly."

"Perhaps so, but you're not yet ready for bread and cheese."

Even her smile had something about it that surprised him. He sat up in bed, looking at her, and accepted the basin of arrowroot. He took the spoon.

"How are things doing on the farm?"

"Kirby and Rugg were out harrowing the Breaches this morning. I shall sow it with beans as you suggested. The others were ploughing in the Upper Runkle. The weather continues dry, thank God, and Stretton thinks we shall soon be quite upsides with the sowing."

"Has that kale-seed arrived?"

"Yes. And the clover-seed for undersowing in the Sixteen Acres."

"That'll need a good going over with the roller and harrow first. But I hope I'll be out and about in a day or two."

"You ought to be. The doctor has given his sanction to it. But you won't worry too much about the work, will you? The farm is all right. You're not to worry."

"I'm not worrying. Only asking, that's all."

And it was true. He was not worried. He knew how things went on a well-ordered farm. A man fell out, – his place was taken by someone else, for a time or forever, as the case might be – and the work went forward as before. Yet, although not worried, he kept having the same strange, disquieting dream.

He dreamed he set out to plough twenty acres of barley stubble. He knew the place he was making for. It was close behind Will Gauntlet's cottage and was known as the Scarrow. But when he arrived there, instead of a field of barley stubble, he found a field full of yellow wheat, the grains plump and round in the braided ears, crying out with fullness and ripeness. So he turned and went back to the farm for the reaper. But now, on reaching the field again, he found it full of seeding thistles, standing tall and thick, crowded together throughout the whole of the twenty acres, and the tufts of grey down were blowing away on the boisterous wind, which sowed the seed broadcast over all the innocent land around.

He woke up with a shout, and in a moment Philippa was beside him, dressed in her night-clothes, her dark hair twisted into a single plait that hung forward over her shoulder. In one hand she held a candle in its holder. With her other hand she touched his forehead.

"Jack, what is it? Are you bad again? Is there anything I can bring you?"

"It's all right," he said, feeling ashamed. "I had a funny

dream, that's all, about ploughing the Scarrow."

"I told you," she said, "you are not to worry about the farm."

"Did I wake the child?"

"No, no, she's still fast asleep."

"I woke you, though. I'm sorry for that."

"It doesn't matter. Don't fret yourself."

Her hand was cool and soothing on his brow. Her fingers pushed back the moist, lank hair from his forehead. He closed his eyes and was gone again, to sleep till morning.

On his first day out of doors, walking over the fields to speak to the men, he felt as though the keen March wind was blowing straight through him.

"My God," said Joe Stretton, "you look like a walking ghost, man!"

"I feel like one, too. I feel as though I was made of muslin."

"Then get back home in the warm for God's sake and don't come haunting us again till you've put a bit of flesh on them there boneses."

"I wouldn't have come out, myself," said Will Gauntlet, sparing a moment from his lambs, "not on a sharp old day like this one."

"I've got to come out sooner or later," Jack said.

Within a week he was doing a full day's work again, and within a fortnight he was very nearly his old self. His illness had at least meant a rest for his knee, and for once his left leg was as good as his right one. He decided not to shave off the beard and moustache that had started growing during this time, but trimmed them neatly and let them remain, brindled and streaked with grey though they were, giving him the look, Joe Stretton said, "of some damned prophet out of the Scriptures."

"It's to keep his face warm," Linn explained to all and sundry.

Miss Philippa was still at the cottage. She would stay, she said, until satisfied that he was quite fully recovered. And he had to admit there was much comfort in having a woman in the house again; in finding his supper already cooked when he got home; in having someone to talk to in the evening.

She would sit in the old Windsor chair, with her tapestry-work or a shirt of his that wanted mending, and he would sit in a corner of the settle, opposite, remarking on the news in the daily paper, or discussing future plans for the farm.

"Why don't you smoke a pipe?" she said once. "Your lungs are not troubling you now, are they?"

"My lungs is fine. But I had an idea somehow that you was against tobacco smoking."

"Why should I be? My father always smoked a pipe and I liked to see him looking contented. Besides, a man is entitled to do as he pleases in his own home, surely?"

"Right, then, I will. So long as Linn ent took all my pipes for blowing soapy bubbles with. It's a trick she's fond of."

"No, they're up on the shelf. I put them there out of Linn's reach."

"They say there'll be peace in South Africa soon. Did you see it in the paper?"

"They've been saying that since the new year."

"That's true," he said, sitting down again, puffing at his pipe. "But it's got to come in the end, I suppose, when they've all done arguing the toss about it."

"Jack, I've been wanting to speak to you," Philippa said suddenly.

"Oh, ah? Well, speak away."

"It's about Linn . . . I'm sorry to say it but the child has been stealing."

"Stealing? Good heavens! What *do* you mean?"

"She keeps taking the eggs from out of the larder. It's happened two or three times just lately. I found them under the orchard hedge and when I asked her how they got there, she said she was giving them back to the hens."

"There, now," Jack said, straight of face. "Would you believe it?"

"She takes no notice of me, you know. I'm afraid you've spoilt her. She's very rude and impertinent sometimes."

"Right, then. I shall have to speak to her about it."

The next night at bed-time, when he mentioned the matter to Linn, her face became very set and stubborn.

"How long is Auntie Philippa stopping in our house?"

"Why? Don't you like her?"

"She put sour cream on my porridge this morning and made me eat it."

"Any more reasons besides that one?"

"This isn't *her* house. Why should she always give me orders? It's your house, ent it, not hers? Why don't she go home and leave us by our own-selves like we was before?"

"You know why she's here. She's been looking after you and me. We'd have been in a rare old pickle, you know, if it hadn't been for your Auntie Philippa coming here. Still, it won't be much longer now, I reckon, before she ups sticks and goes back off home."

But Miss Philippa continued to stay at the cottage, and the men on the farm were beginning to make remarks to Jack.

"You cosy down there, you and the Missus, tucked in

together all this time?" asked Peter Luppitt, winking at
his brother Paul. "Looking after you nicely, is she?"

"All the home comforts?" asked Jonathan Kirby.
"Without the strings?"

"Supposing you just attend to your business!"

"Who would've thought it of our Miss P?"

"Them prudish ones is always the worstest."

"Sooner you than me, Jack, but everyone to their own
taste as the old lady said when she kissed the cow."

"D'you want to know what I think?" asked Joe Stretton.

"No," Jack said. "You can damn well keep your mouth
buttoned!"

At home that evening, sitting opposite Philippa as
usual, he broached the matter without beating about the
bush.

"It seems you've been here long enough. It's beginning to cause a bit of gossip."

"Oh?" she said, and dabs of bright colour appeared at
once on her high cheekbones. "Among the labourers, do
you mean? How dare they gossip behind my back!
They've no right whatever to discuss my affairs."

"You can't stop folk talking. It's meat and drink to
most of them. You know that as well as I do."

For a time she was silent, sitting straight-backed in the
Windsor chair, her hands together, resting on the
tapestry in her lap. She looked at him with a still gaze.

"In that case," she said, "I'll go tomorrow."

"Yes," he said. "I reckon it would be for the best, all
told, really. You've done well by me. I'm grateful for it.
But I'm perfectly healthy again now, and quite well able
to take good care of myself and Linn."

She watched him intently. There occurred another
long silence. He even heard the deep, slow breath she
took before she finally spoke again.

"I have a suggestion to make," she said. "You may have some inkling of what it is. I suggest that you and I should marry."

Looking at her, – meeting the stillness of her gaze; trying to see past her composure – there was a moment in which he almost felt something for her. There were lines of tiredness in her face, especially about the eyes: they were there because of him; because she had spent so many vigilant nights at his bedside; he saw the little signs of strain and was touched by them. Then the moment was gone. He knew the feeling for what it was. Gratitude. Nothing more.

"No," he said, and his glance fell away, seeking refuge elsewhere. "No. It wouldn't do. Such a thing is not to be thought of."

"Nenna and I were not really sisters. We had no tie of blood whatever, so there's no impediment, if that's what you mean."

"As far as I'm concerned you *are* Nenna's sister."

"That's just stupid. I've no patience with that. A man needs a woman to take care of him and run his household. He's all at sea otherwise."

"I can manage all right. I have done so far."

"Can you? Can you?" she demanded. "Were you able to manage these few weeks past, lying helpless as you were, with only me to care for you?"

"I was pretty far gone. I'm aware of that. I've got a lot to thank you for, and I do thank you with all my heart."

"You were very near death. You should ask the doctor. It was only my nursing that pulled you through."

"I'm aware of that too. I heard what the doctor said right enough."

"Then what's the point of boasting that you can look

after yourself and your child? How can you think it? You have no one else in the world but me."

"Philippa," he said, but could think of nothing more to say.

"Well? What? I'm waiting and listening, as you see, so what is it you're trying to say?"

"Nothing," he said. "Nothing more than I've said already."

"Supposing you were to fall ill again?"

"I shan't, I promise. I shall see to it."

"How can you be so arrogant? Do you think you have control of the future?"

"No," he said. "I don't think that."

"Then just supposing?"

"I shall cross that bridge when I come to it."

"No doubt you think I should always be at hand! Always ready to pick up the pieces? Always at your beck and call when needed? Is that what you think? Is it? Is it?"

"No. It ent. I've never thought about it at all."

"No," she said, in a quieter tone. "You haven't thought of it, that's just the trouble." She threaded her needle into her work, folded it neatly, and put it away into its bag. "Perhaps we both need time to think . . . to consider the future . . . and perhaps a night's sleep will help us both to think more clearly."

She rose to her feet and went to the dresser, to put her work-bag away in a drawer. She returned with her candle in its holder and lit it at the fire in the stove. On her way past again she paused close beside him, and allowed her hand to rest on his shoulder.

"We're both of us quite alone in the world, you and I . . . It's worth considering my suggestion . . ."

"I'm not alone – I've got Linn," he said, and then, per-ceiving the cruelty of his answer, he put up a hand to cover hers where it lay on his shoulder. "Ah, no!" he said. "I didn't mean to say it like that—"

"But exactly so!" Philippa said. "You've got Linn and I've got the farm! And what I'm suggesting is that we both plan our future lives together around the things that really matter! It's only common sense. I'm sure you must see it."

A burnt-out log collapsed in the stove and a shower of sparks sprayed out in the hearth-place. Jack leant forward and swept them under with the hearth-brush, and Philippa's hand fell to her side. She thought the withdrawal was deliberate – perhaps it was; he could not have said – and when he looked up again, her hands were folded, holding the candle, and her gaze was entirely without warmth.

"This is a practical proposition, Jack, based on matters of mutual convenience."

"Aye? I daresay."

"Good God!" she said harshly. "Did you think otherwise by any chance? Did you think I was troubled by girlish considerations of love?"

"No," he said, "I didn't think that."

"I don't *love* you. – You needn't worry yourself about that! I'm a woman of thirty-six. – I'm not a foolish, romantic girl of twenty. You mean nothing more to me in that way than if you were just a block of wood! Do I make myself clear to you, I wonder?"

"I get the drift," he said, nodding.

"Then I'll say goodnight and leave you alone to consider the matter."

"I ent got nothing to consider."

"Oh, yes, you have," she said, quietly, "if you really put your mind to it."

*

The following morning she packed her things and returned to the farmhouse. They had the cottage to themselves again, he and Linn, and the child's satisfaction was plain indeed.

"This is *our* house," she said to him. "You're the master here, ent you, and I'm the mistress?"

"That's right," he said. "We pull together like a good team of horses. Like Spindleberry and Dinkymay. Like Minta and Maisie. Like Diamond and Darky and Jubilee. And that's the way it'll be always, you and me in harness together."

It was now the second week in April. There was a softness in the air. The green, growing season was under way. Jack was out in the sixteen acres reclaimed from wasteland the year before, going over it with roller and harrow, reducing it to a powdery tilth, ready to receive its first sowing in more than twenty-five years. He had Ernie Stretton and Jonathan Kirby harrowing with him.

On Saturday morning, in an interval between showers, Miss Philippa came to the gate of the field and leant there watching. Jack took no notice but continued on up the slope, turned at the headland, and descended again, keeping the horses to a slow walk. Miss Philippa pushed the gate open, and, lifting her skirts above the ankles of her buttoned boots, made her way across the field to meet him.

"Have you been avoiding me on purpose?"

"I've been busy, that's all, making up for lost time."

"It's three days since I left the cottage. I want to know what conclusion you've come to."

"The same conclusion as before."

"I don't understand you. I simply cannot make you out."

"Perhaps you don't try," he said, shrugging. "Though, come to that, I don't understand you, neither."

"It's perfectly simple. An unmarried woman is always at a great disadvantage in this world. I therefore want a husband."

"If that's all it is, you'll soon find one easy enough, I daresay."

"But I happen to trust *you*!" she said, with sudden passion. "You're the only man in the world that I *do* trust! Do you realize that? Have you any idea what a precious gift trust can be between people?"

"Precious, yes, but it still don't buy a man body and soul as you seem to think it does," he said, "and the trust has to be on both sides."

"Brown Elms would be yours. Do you realize that? A farm of over six hundred acres! You would be its master. Surely that must mean something to you?"

"I'm master now, as far as the work is concerned," he said. "I *made* this farm what it is today. That means something, I don't deny, but it's no odds to me whose name's on the deeds."

"And where would you be if it weren't for me? What were you, in fact, when I first found you, skulking in the old ruined cottage? What were you then – you answer me that!"

"The same as now, just a man," he said.

"You were nothing!" she said. "And nothing you'll remain if you go against me, for I can make you or break you just as I choose, as simply as though I were snapping my fingers. Everything comes from me, remember. – The house you live in. – The wages you draw. – Everything you have you get from me!"

"I work for my wages. I don't pick 'em like apples off the tree."

"Work!" she said. "What is work to me when I can get labourers two a penny?"

"And d'you think marriage would make us equal? In your own eyes, I mean, not in mine. Do you truly believe it?"

"You would be my husband. What more could you want?"

She turned from him and left the field, and he stood for a moment looking at her footprints, clearly marked in the soft, fine, crumbly brown soil. Then he clicked at the horses and went on down, and the harrow jiggled the footprints out.

When he finished that day, the field was ready for sowing on Monday, and he said so to Stretton in the stables.

"Ah, well," Stretton said, "I reckon you'll want to sow them oats yourself, seeing it's your own piece of ground so especially, that you cleared and reclaimed from the very start."

Jack gave a shrug.

"It don't much matter who sows it," he said, "just so long as it gets done."

At bed-time that evening he said to Linn, "How would you like to go on a journey?"

"Where to? Where to?" she asked, wide-eyed.

"Well, as to that, I reckon we'll have to see when we get there."

"Both of us together?"

"Why, of course!" he said. "You wouldn't go off and leave your poor old dad on his ownsome, would you? Where's the fun in that? We're a team, you and me, like I said to you the other day, and we pull together like a pair of good horses. We shall always stick together, you and me, come rain or shine, thunder or hailstones. So what do you say to my new idea?"

"Yes!" she said. "Let's go on a journey!" And she gave the bedclothes a little shake, sending them rippling over the bed. "Shall we go on a train?"

"Not on a train, no. Shank's pony. We'd miss the best places if we went on a train."

"When are we going?"

"First thing in the morning, if that's all right with you," he said.

"First thing?" she said, doubtfully, and her eyes opened wider still.

"That's the ticket. Bright and early. Up with the lark while the dew's still falling! And if we look smartish, we shall see the morning daisies growing, yawning and stretching and waking up out of the grass."

"Shall we?" she said. "Shall we, honest?"

"Of course we shall! And see all the cockerels perched on their mixens, crowing away to wake the world up. You'll like that, I know, 'cos you was always one for getting out and abroad bright and early."

"What time will you wake me?"

"First thing, like I said. And we must hope for a fine day, without too many April showers."

"I'll ask for sunshine in my prayers."

"Ah, you do that," he said, "and then go off to sleep nicely so that you're full of beans tomorrow."

He woke her in the morning at first light; ate breakfast with her in front of the fire; then packed a few of her clothes and his into his old canvas satchel.

"Can I take my doll?"

"Why, surely, yes! We can't go and leave Dolly Doucey, can we? You pop her in on top of my shirt there, so's she rides nice and comfortable."

"Are we taking bread and cheese?"

"Lashings of it. Every bit we've got in the house. I

never went on a journey yet without I took plenty of bread and cheese."

He tipped his savings out of the old earthenware jug and put the money in his pocket. He poked the fire down low in the stove and closed the damper. Linn was still sleepy, but became bright and fresh and she stepped out into the morning air.

"Shall we be coming back?" she asked.

"No, my chilver, we shan't be coming back," he said. "Neither late nor soon. Not ever nor never."

He locked the door and pushed the key up into the thatch. The child watched him with uncertain face. Her lip trembled.

"Aren't we going to say goodbye to Auntie Philippa up at the farm?"

"What, at this time of day? She'll still be in bed, tucked up tight and fast asleep."

"Nor Cissy, nor Harvey, nor Mr Gauntlet?"

"Better not," he said, "or we should take all day about it and never get going at all, should we?"

"Do we have to go?"

"I reckon we do. We promised ourselves a journey, remember, and think of the things we shall see on the way."

"Daisies!" she said. "Waking up!"

"Right the first time. But we'll have to keep our eyes skinned, won't we, all the time as we're going along?"

He lifted her up and she sat on his shoulders. The gate closed behind them and they set off down the winding lane, between fields still milky-white with mist.

"You comfy up there, Linn Mercybright?"

"Yes," she said.

"Seems we're lucky with our morning. I reckon it's going to be a fine day."

"Will it be nice, where we're going? Shall I go to school there and make new friends? Will there be a river and woods and hills?"

"It's up to us to choose," he said. "When we come to a place we like the look of, that's where we'll stop, and see what we make of it, you and me."

"Will there be horses at this place?"

"I never yet saw a place without 'em!"

"And will the people be nice there?"

"They'd better be middling. We shan't stop, else."

He took the back lanes out past Niddup until he came to Darry Cross. There, a signpost stood in the grass in the middle, and they had a choice of three roads.

"Well?" Jack said. "Which way would you like to go?"

"That way," she said, and pointed along the straightest road, where sparrows were bathering in the dust, and where stitchwort flowers were white in the hedgerow at either side.

"Very well," he said. "Whatever you say. It's up to you." He looked at the signpost, which, pointing that way, read: Yarnwell; Cranfield; Capleton Wick. "It sounds all right. We'll give it a try."

So he took the road Linn had chosen, and the newly risen sun was warm on his back.

THE SORROWING
WIND

Within the woodlands, flow'ry gladed,
By the oak tree's mossy root,
The sheenèn grass-blades, timber-shaded,
Now do quiver underfoot;
An' birds do whissle auver head,
An' water's bubblèn in its bed,
An' there for me the apple tree
Do lean down low in Linden Lea.

William Barnes

Betony and the young Army officer, Michael Andrews, had sat opposite each other all the way from Paddington, but they might never have struck up a friendship had it not been for the scene that occurred between two other people in the compartment: a stout district nurse and a young man who looked like a clerk.

At Paddington the train had been crowded. After Oxford it ran half empty. The nurse got in at Long Stone, the clerk at Milston, and right from the first she fixed him with a stare calculated to discomfit him.

"I wonder you aren't ashamed!" she said, when he was foolish enough to meet her gaze. "A sturdy young man in the prime of life, fighting-fit and full of beans, yet still wearing civvies! *I'd* be ashamed. I would, honest!"

"It so happens I suffer with asthma," the young man said, red with embarrassment, and hid himself behind his paper.

"That's what they all say nowadays, but you look healthy enough to me, young fellow, and if you were a proper man you'd be up and doing like the captain there, and all our other gallant soldiers."

The woman glanced across at Michael. Plainly she expected his approval. Then she leant towards the clerk and rattled the newspaper in his hands.

"It's funny what a lot of asthma there is about lately,

not to mention gastric troubles and the odd cases of housemaid's knee, but I could give it another name if anyone was to ask *me*!"

Michael, in his corner, could bear no more.

"Madam, be quiet!" he said sharply. "Leave the man alone and hold your tongue!"

The woman was shocked. Her mouth fell open a little way, showing teeth stained mauve with the sweets she was eating.

"You've got no right to speak to me like that! If my husband was with me you wouldn't dare!"

"If your husband was with you I hope he'd keep you in better order."

"Well, really!" she exclaimed. "Well, really! I'd never have believed it!"

But she leant back again in her seat and remained silent for the rest of her journey, glaring at the newspaper shielding the clerk. Michael turned again to the window, and Betony looked at him with new interest. Straight sandy hair, rather untidy; beaky face and brown skin; tired grey eyes and tired mouth with lines at the corners: the sort of face, young yet old, which she had grown accustomed to seeing in the fourteen months since the start of the war.

The train was now stopping at every station. When the clerk and the nurse got out at Salton, Michael turned to Betony.

"I'm sorry about that," he said, "but the damned woman got my goat."

"It's the new blood sport, baiting civilians," Betony said.

"If she only knew what it's like over there – if she could see for just five minutes – it would soon wipe the smile from her smug pink face."

"But somebody has to go and fight."

"Yes, yes," he said, with some impatience. "But everyone here is so complacent! So glib and self-righteous and so damnably bloodthirsty!"

"How would you like us to be?" Betony asked, and he gave her a smile.

"Quiet . . . comfortable . . . calm . . ." he said, "talking of cricket and fishing and the crops, and whether the hens are laying at the moment . . ."

Betony nodded. Looking at him, she could feel his tiredness. Her own flesh ached, as his must ache.

"You've been wounded, haven't you?" She could see how stiffly he held his shoulder.

"I've been wounded three times yet up I pop again good as new. A charmed life, apparently. I was gassed, too, on this last tour. That's why my voice is rough at the edges. Not badly, of course, or I shouldn't be here to tell the tale."

"How long is your leave?"

"Until I'm fit. A month, perhaps."

"And then what?"

"Back again to face the music."

"How can you do it?" Betony asked, marvelling.

"No choice," he said, and turned the talk towards her instead. "Do you travel a lot?" He glanced at her briefcase on the rack above.

"Quite a lot, yes, though not usually as far as London. I've been to a sort of conference there. But mostly I travel around the Midlands, seeing to the welfare of women workers in munitions factories."

"Do you enjoy it?"

"Yes. In a way. At least it's something that needs doing. But I'm always glad to leave the towns and get home to Cobbs where it's quiet and peaceful."

"Cobbs? Where's that?"

"In a village called Huntlip, near Chepsworth."

"I live in Chepsworth, myself," he said. "It's a nice walk from there out to Huntlip. Can I come and see you sometimes?"

"Yes, come and meet my family," she said. "I can't guarantee they'll talk about cricket, but someone is sure to mention hens."

"There's one good thing about the war. We can take short cuts in making friends, even with members of the opposite sex."

But he felt she would not have rebuffed him, anyway, war or no war. She was at ease with him; sure of herself; quiet and calm and straightforward. She was also very pleasant to look at: he liked her bright fairness and the clarity of her blue eyes. She had the serenity he longed for.

"Tell me about your family," he said.

At Chepsworth station, Jesse Izzard was waiting for his daughter, eager to take her bag and brief-case, carrying them for her with a sense of importance. His fair face shone, as it always did when he welcomed her home, and his pride increased when she introduced Michael Andrews.

"Captain Andrews will be coming out to visit us, dad. He wants to see the carpenter's shop."

"Why, yes," Jesse said, as he shook Michael's hand. "Very welcome, I'm sure. Are you Captain Andrews of King's Hill House?"

"That's right," Michael said. "Just up there, behind the station."

"I put a new fence round your paddock once. Years ago, now, when your father was alive."

"You'll be glad to know it's still standing."

"Ah, well, it would be," Jesse said. "It was good oak fencing."

His sense of importance knew no bounds. He walked with a very slight swagger. The Andrewses were well-known people. They had lived in Chepsworth umpteen years. But there was a blot on Jesse's day, for, outside the station, instead of the smart little pony and trap, stood the old workshop waggon with sacks of sawdust and shavings aboard and the scruffy horse, Collier, between the shafts.

"It's your great-grumpa's fault," he said, muttering to Betony. "He took the trap to go to Upham." And, clearing his throat, he said to Michael: "Can we give you a lift, captain?"

"No, thanks," Michael said. "I shall enjoy the walk up the hill."

He stood on the pavement and waved them off. Jesse saluted, rather stiffly.

"D'you think he refused on account of the waggon?"

"No, of course not," Betony said. "He's not such a snob as you are, dad."

And, sitting beside him, she squeezed his arm to reassure him. He did not always know when he was being teased.

The old house at Cobbs was quiet under its oaks and elms. There was no noise from the carpenter's shop, for work stopped at twelve on a Saturday now. Only Great-grumpa Tewke found things to do.

"You've had the sign painted," Betony said. They were passing the gate of the workshop yard, and the two names, Tewke and Izzard, stood out black and shiny on the white ground. "The things that happen when I turn my back for a few days!"

"Young Tom done that. He's good with a paint-brush. He gets it from his poor dead father."

In the big kitchen, as Betony entered, her mother was laying the table for supper. She paused, looking up with a welcoming smile, and her flickering glance delivered a warning – that somebody lurked behind the door. Betony pushed it open wide and squeezed her youngest brother, Dicky, who emerged crestfallen, holding his nose.

"Aw, they told you!" he said, disgusted. "And I was going to make you jump!"

"You're too fond of making folk jump," Jesse said. "Here, take this bag up to your sister's room."

"No, don't take it up," Betony said. "I've got things to show you when everyone's in."

"She's brought us presents," Dicky said.

He was young enough, at fifteen, to have waited indoors for his sister's return, but William and Roger, with manly interests to pursue, sauntered in casually a little later.

"Had a good journey?" William asked.

"A slow one, I bet," Roger said, "stopping at every way-side halt."

"What happened in London, when you saw them high-ups?"

"Your sister's been put in charge," Jesse said. "She's to superintend the whole region."

"That'll suit our Betony," Dicky said, "telling folk what to do."

By supper-time, Granna Tewke had come out of the parlour, spectacles pushed up high on her forehead, and Great-grumpa Tewke had returned from Upham, having looked at a stand of timber there and rejected it because of the price.

"Taking advantage!" he said, swearing. "They're taking advantage everywhere you go nowadays but nobody's going to profiteer me!"

"Where's Tom?" Betony asked.

"Late as usual. We'll start without him."

"I reckon he's courting," Dicky said.

"More likely drinking in The Rose and Crown."

"He'll go to the bad, like his father, that boy," said Granna Tewke, looking everywhere for her glasses. "Ferrets indeed! What's a decent boy want with ferrets?"

"Our Betony's made a new friend," Jesse said. "Captain Andrews of King's Hill House. They was talking together on the train and he's likely coming out here on a visit."

"What, one of that lot with all the money?"

"All made out of mustard," said great-grumpa, "and now they live like landed gentry."

"The captain's all right," Jesse said. "A nice young gentleman, straight off."

"He'll think hisself somebody," William said, his mouth already full of food, "being in uniform and all."

"And isn't he somebody?" Betony asked.

"No more'n the rest of us," William said.

"Oh, no, of course not!" Betony exclaimed. "*You* risk your life every day in the workshop, whenever you take up a hammer and chisel!"

"So that's it?" said William. "Now we're hearing a few home truths!" His clear-skinned face became crimson, and his blue eyes glittered. "You want me in uniform, out at the Front, living in trenches like a rat!"

"No, I don't," Betony said. "I just don't like to hear you sneering at those who are."

"No more don't I," Dicky said. "I'd go tomorrow if only they'd have me."

"Me, too," Roger said. "I'm as big as many chaps of eighteen."

"Go and good luck to you!" William said. "You're both too wet behind the ears to know any better!"

He sprang from his chair and would have hurried from the room, but that his mother spoke out sharply.

"Sit down, William, and stop jogging the tea on the table. We'll have no arguments on this subject, nor on no others for the time being. Roger, cut your father a slice of bread."

William sat down, though still in a temper, and the others talked to cover his silence. Often a word was enough from their mother. She had great-grumpa's forcefulness, coupled with a coolness of her own. It was she who ruled within the household, just as great-grumpa ruled in the workshop.

At King's Hill House, Michael had soaked for an hour in the bath, and now, in his bedroom, dressed in grey flannels and a white shirt, he was combing his hair in front of the mirror. Behind him, on the floor, his uniform lay in a crumpled heap, where he had stepped out of it, trampling it underfoot in the process.

His mother knocked and came in. She watched him putting on a tweed jacket.

"Oh, dear! They don't fit you, do they, your old clothes? You've grown so much thinner." She turned to the crumpled heap on the floor and picked up his tunic. "Really, Michael, that's surely no way to treat the King's uniform!"

"The King is welcome to it," he said, "and its livestock, if any."

"Livestock?" she said, and dropped the tunic with a shudder. "You're surely not serious? I don't believe it!"

"Perfectly serious, mother," he said. "Now perhaps you understand why a man likes to get into ordinary clothes."

"Doesn't your servant look after you properly?"

"It's not his fault. It can't be helped. We're all the same over there – lousy as hedgehogs."

"But you've been in hospital. Surely – '

"Oh, I've been deloused, certainly, but the eggs survive the fumigator and live to hatch another day."

"Good heavens!" she said. "I couldn't bear it if it started here."

"Neither could I. It's bad enough over there."

"My poor boy! How thoughtless of me. What must I do with all your things?"

"Leave it to me. I'll take them down to Cook and get her to bake 'em in one of the old wall ovens. A few days of that should do the trick."

Returning a little while later to the bedroom, he found her at work with a spray of disinfectant. She stopped spraying and looked him over.

"Are you going out, dear? You won't forget dinner's at seven?"

"I won't forget. I'm only going down to the town for a drink."

"At a public house?" she said, astonished. "But there are plenty of drinks in the sitting-room."

"I feel like a long cool draught of beer."

"I'm worried about you, going out dressed like that. People are often unkind to civilians, you know."

"I know about that. I witnessed a sample on the train today."

And, having related the incident, he went on to talk about Betony.

"She travels round the midlands, arranging facilities for women working in the factories. It's amazing what girls are doing now. They're really breaking out and showing their mettle."

"A carpenter's daughter, did you say? How extraordinary!"

"She didn't have tin-tacks between her lips, mother, or a pencil stuck behind her ear."

"No need to be so touchy, dear. I didn't think she sounded like your sort of girl, that's all, but if I'm mistaken, perhaps you'd like to invite her to tea?"

"Now you're going a bit too fast."

"Yes, well, perhaps it's not such a good idea. Food is so scarce here now, you know, that meals are becoming quite a problem."

Michael smiled, having seen the dinner Cook was preparing in the kitchen. His mother, interpreting the smile correctly, gently reproved him.

"Today is rather a special occasion. We don't always eat so well."

"I'm sorry, mother. Don't take too much notice of me. I'll be less sour in a day or two."

Walking down into the town he experienced a feeling of well-being so all-suffusing that the pain of his wound almost gave him pleasure. He felt pure and clean and not-of-this-world. Yet his mood was supremely physical, too: the scent of chrysanthemums in people's gardens; the sight of the chestnut trees turning a fiery red-and-yellow; the sound of the great cathedral clock striking as he crossed the close and turned down beside the river: he apprehended all these things in every particle of his body.

And when, drinking a pint of Chepsworth ale in the bar of The Swan, where four farm labourers sat with the landlord and the talk was of turnips and winter wheat, he smiled to himself and listened greedily to every word, till one old man drew him into an argument about the virtues of home-baked bread.

At King's Hill House, his mother, worrying, hoped the war would soon be over. It seemed to be giving Michael a taste for low company.

*

The orchard at Cobbs was at its best, the apples so thick that many branches were borne down low, and Betony, walking among the trees, often had to bend her head. She had never known such a year for apples. She kept touching them with the tips of her fingers: the big green quilters, the rusty red pippins, and the crimson winesaps much loved by wasps. She was choosing a pippin for herself when she saw Michael coming towards her from the house.

"I met your brother William," he said. "He told me where to find you."

"Was he polite to you?" Betony asked.

"Perfectly. Why do you ask?"

"He's in a sullen mood lately. Anti-military. Anti-war."

"Then his feelings run with mine exactly."

"I think he feels guilty at not enlisting."

"It'll all be decided for him soon, when conscription comes in."

"Poor William," she said. "He so loves his home and his family, and the work he does in the carpenter's shop. He so loves everything to be neat and tidy. He'll hate all the mess and confusion and waste . . ." She looked at Michael. "Where will it all end?" she asked. "And when, oh, when?"

Michael shrugged. He knew he ought to say comforting things: that the Germans were beaten and it was only a question of finishing them off. Such was the spirit promulgated by the commanders. But his own feeling was that the war might last for ever and ever. He could see no solution; no victory on either side; no other outcome except complete annihilation. Perhaps it was just that he was so tired. Once he was perfectly fit again, his old optimism was bound to return.

"It's got to end somewhere, sometime," he said. "But don't ask me when. I'm no strategist, God knows. I just obey orders – with my eyes shut mostly – and do my best to stay alive."

They were walking slowly through the orchard and he noticed how, whenever she stooped beneath a low branch, her skirts went out in a billowing flare, sweeping the grass. The dress she wore was a very dark red with black threads running through it in waves, and, watching the way the skirts flared out at every curtsey, he knew he would see the pattern they made whenever he thought of her in future.

"You said you'd show me round the workshop."

"It's shut up on Sundays. Great-grumpa Tewke is strict on that score."

But she took him and showed him the workshop buildings – stables, once, when Cobbs had been a farmhouse, long years before – and the yard where oak and elm planking lay criss-crossed in piles, with laths between to let the air blow through and dry them. She showed him the sawpit and the timber-crabs and the store-yard full of ladders, field-gates, cribs and troughs. And she told him all she knew of the business, founded by Great-grumpa William Tewke in the year 1850, when he was a boy of nineteen and had scarcely enough money about him to buy his first tools. Now the workshop employed twelve men. Or would do, she said, if two had not gone into the Army.

They walked and talked until dusk was falling, when her father came in search of them, saying supper was on the table and would the captain care to stay?

In the big kitchen, under the low black beams and rafters, they sat down to eat at a long table covered over with a stiff white cloth. There were nine in the household.

A clan indeed. Ten, he was told, if they counted Janie, but she was married to Martin Holt and lived at the neighbouring farm of Anster. Michael himself, an only child, was glad to be sitting with this family. He wished he belonged there, sharing the strength their unity gave them. He had often been lonely in his own home.

At the head of the table sat William Tewke, quick of eye and ear although he was turned eighty-four, and next on his left sat Kate Tewke, his dead son's widow, vague and shortsighted, known to the younger ones as granna. At the foot of the table, Beth, Kate's daughter, fresh-faced and comely, her corn-coloured hair in a braid round her head, looked on them all with a calm blue gaze and saw to it they had what they wanted. Next to her, her husband, Jesse, was just as yellow-haired as she, so that it was no wonder the two of them together had produced children of such harvest fairness.

But there was an odd-man-out among them: the boy named Tom Maddox: black-haired and brown-eyed, with the hollow cheeks and smooth dark skin of a gipsy, and the same slender build. He was very quiet, with an almost unnatural stillness about him, and although he was one of the family, he was yet apart from all the rest, watchful, intent, aware of everything that passed yet speaking, it seemed, only when someone spoke to him. He was an oddity indeed; an orphan brought into the family and raised with them from the age of nine; standing out from all the rest like a blackbird in a sheaf of corn.

"You can see he ent one of us, can't you?" said young Dicky, showing off to Michael. "Mother's never been able to scrub him clean."

"Tom is courting," Roger said. "Did you know that, dad? It's Tilly Preston at The Rose and Crown."

"Is that really so, Tom?" Jesse asked, assuming a father's

gravity. "And if it is, shouldn't you be asking my advice?"

"No," Tom said, "it ent true."

"Well, Till Preston is sweet on *him*. She drew him a pint of ale for nothing when we was there on Friday night."

"That's another bloody lie!"

"Now, then, Tom, mind your language in front of strangers."

"Hah!" said great-grumpa. "I daresay the captain's heard worse'n that."

"Yes, indeed," Michael said. "It's a true saying, 'to swear like a trooper'. "

"But you're not a trooper," Dicky said. "What are you, exactly, since you ent in uniform for us to see?"

"Infantry," Michael said. "Second Battalion, the Three Counties Regiment."

"Then you've seen some action, probably?"

"Oh, there's plenty of action out in France at present, yes."

"Them French!" said granna, suddenly, adjusting her glasses to glare at Michael. "You give them what-for and teach them a lesson!"

"What're you on about?" asked great-grumpa. "The French are our allies, same as the Belgians."

"Allies?" said granna. "I thought they was meant to be on our side!"

"Let's not talk about the war – Michael gets enough of that," said Betony.

"Don't he like talking about it? – He's different from most, then," William said.

"Let's talk about the chickens and whether they're laying well lately."

"Chickens?" said Dicky. "Why talk about chickens for heaven's sake?"

"It's as good a subject as any other."

And, across the table, Betony exchanged a smile with Michael.

He was often at Cobbs after that. It became for him a place apart. And the family accepted him, even William.

Having done his duty by his mother, going with her to luncheon parties, allowing her to show him off in his new uniform, he would then change into comfortable clothes and escape on long walks into the country, where he ate bread and cheese in quiet pubs, and drank beer. He could not have enough of days like these and often at the end he would come to Huntlip; to the old house at Cobbs; to Betony, whose day's work ended at six o'clock.

One evening they walked in Millery wood, half a mile away, on the north bank of the Derrent brook. It was just about dusk and as they climbed the steep path they passed a figure standing perfectly still in the shadows.

The man's stillness was uncanny, and immediately Michael was back in France, creeping at night along derelict trenches, where at every turn an enemy guard might loom up darkly. His flesh crept. He almost sprang at the man and struck him. But Betony's voice said, "Tom? Is that you?" and her foster-brother stepped out to the pathway. Michael's breathing became normal. The sweat cooled on his lip and forehead.

"Yes, it's me," Tom muttered, and slouched past them, hands in pockets, down the path towards the Derrent.

"Extraordinary fellow!" Michael said. "What does he mean by it, skulking about in the dark like that?"

"It's nothing unusual for Tom. He's always been a night-creature."

"Was he spying on us by any chance?"

"Goodness, no!" she said, laughing. "Badgers, perhaps. Foxes, even. Or he may have been lying in wait for a pheasant. But he'd never bother to spy on people. They don't interest him enough for that."

"Perhaps he had an assignation. That girl your brother Roger mentioned."

"I hope not," Betony said. "Tilly Preston is a slut."

She was rather protective where Tom was concerned. Michael had noticed it often before. And he wondered that she should concern herself with a youth whose manner towards her was always surly and indifferent. He had learnt a little of the boy's history: Tom was illegitimate; granna had spoken of bad blood.

"Bad blood! What rubbish!" Betony said. "I don't believe in all that. Tom's father had a terrible temper. He killed Tom's mother in a drunken quarrel and afterwards he hanged himself. Tom was a baby of twelve months or so, neglected until he was skin and bone. Then he was raised by my Grannie Izzard, well-looked-after but allowed to run wild. Those are the things that have made him strange. It's nothing to do with bad blood."

"You're certainly a loyal champion."

"I was cruel to him at first," she said. "When Grannie Izzard died and Tom came to us, I made his life a misery."

"How did you?"

"Oh, tormenting him about his parents . . . making him feel he wasn't wanted . . ."

"Did your brothers do it too?"

"No. Only me. I was horribly spiteful."

"That explains why you leap to defend him. You're trying to pay off a debt of guilt."

"I suppose I am, though there's nothing Tom ever wants from me, and the silly thing is, he bears me no grudge."

"Are you sure of that? He's very churlish."

"He still doesn't trust me," Betony said, "and I can't really blame him."

Coming out of the wood, onto high ground, they were met by a big full golden moon shining on the skyline, and Betony's face, when he turned towards her, had the moonlight bright upon it.

She looked serene. Her glance, meeting his, had a smile in it. But when he put out a hand to touch her, intending to hold her back a while, just as she was, with the moonlight on her, she walked quickly past and swung along the ridgeway path.

"I can hear the trains at Stickingbridge . . . that generally means we'll get a shower . . ."

The orchard at Cobbs presented a different picture now. The apples had been picked and the boughs, relieved of their heavy burden, had sprung back to their proper place. The forked supports had been removed; Martin Holt's sheep had been put in to graze; and now the leaves were falling fast, a luminous yellow in the long lush grass.

Michael was aware that the days were slipping through his fingers. His month's leave was almost over. He wished he could choose a specific moment and call for time to stand still. This moment, for instance, with Betony laughing in the sun, standing on tiptoe under a plum tree, trying to reach a globule of gum that hung on the branch like a bead of amber.

Yet what was the use of asking time to stand and deliver? All living creatures must take what they could. There was no fulfilment otherwise. Betony, with her arms upraised, the shape of her breasts inviting his touch – surely she was aware of herself, aware of the sun going round the sky, faster and faster every day?

Feeling him near her, she turned quickly, letting her arms fall to her sides. She was laughing and breathless and flushed with exertion, but as she looked at him and read the sick appeal in his eyes, her laughter faded away to nothing. His hands touched her face, her throat, her hair, and she stepped back a little, pushing him away. Her eyes remained steady. She tried to think of something to say. But it was Michael who spoke first.

"I want you to marry me. Soon. Straight away. I thought I'd get a special licence."

"No, Michael. It's too soon. I don't really know if it's what I want."

"I know my own feelings. I've no doubts whatever."

"How can that be? It's impossible. We've known each other eighteen days! Afterwards, perhaps, when the war is over – "

"There may not be any afterwards for me."

"You mustn't say that! It isn't fair to say such things."

"It's true all the same. Do you know what the chances of survival are over there? I'm already living on borrowed time."

"So you'd marry me quickly just to go off and leave me a widow?"

"No! That's just it! I know it's silly, but somehow I feel if I had your love, it would keep me safe from everything. I'd damn well make sure I got through safely!"

He knew he was playing on her feelings, but when he saw the pity in her face, he became ashamed.

"This is what it does to us! – Turns us into abject beings, preying on people, demanding their love. I'm sorry, Betony. Don't judge me too harshly. Let's forget about it and try to be as we were before."

He took her hand and drew it into the crook of his arm, and they walked together towards the house, talking quietly of ordinary things. But all the time he wondered about her; tried to guess how she felt towards him; for he had pinned his faith on her and looked to her as his protection.

In the cobbled fold at the back of the house, Jesse Izzard was pumping water, filling two old wooden buckets. He saw Betony walking with Michael through the garden but pretended he had something in his eye. When they had passed, he picked up his buckets and went into the dairy, where his wife was busy bottling honey.

"The captain seems smutten on our Betony. Think it'll come to anything, do you?"

"Maybe. Maybe not." Beth for once had no sure opinion. "But Betony's a girl who will find it hard to give herself heart and soul to someone."

Often when Tom was in The Rose and Crown, someone would bring him a chunk of wood and ask him to carve a bird or a fish or an animal, and today Tilly Preston, the landlord's daughter, had brought out an old maplewood beer-mug, for him to carve her likeness on it.

It took him perhaps half an hour, using only a pocket-knife, but the face on the mug was Tilly's exactly: the wide-set eyes under fine brows; the small straight nose with flared nostrils; the pretty lips parted a little, showing teeth with spaces between them; and the wisps of hair curling down over her forehead.

Tom, as he worked, was shut away from the noise around him, and Roger, watching his clever fingers, wished he had half Tom's skill in carving.

"Why, you've made me look flat!" Tilly complained, when she held the finished mug in her hands. "Still, I reckon you've earnt your pint of Chepsworth."

She filled the mug brimfull, and Tom drank it down in one long draught.

"That's the idea, Tom," said Oliver Rye. "Up with her until she's empty!"

"Is that all he gets?" asked Billy Ratchet. "Don't he get a kiss and a bit of a huggle?"

"Go on, young Tom. Tilly's agreeable, I'll be bound."

"Perhaps he's frightened," said Henry Tupper.

"Perhaps he don't rightly know the motions?"

"D'you want a few pointers, Tom, lad, from one of us old hands that've had some experience?"

Tom said nothing. He wiped his mouth with the back of his hand. His dark face was flushed, and he couldn't look at Tilly Preston. But Tilly herself was leaning towards him, and when Billy Ratchet pushed Tom forward, she put her arms up round his neck. Her small round breasts rested against him, and her face came slowly closer to his, her lips parting as they touched very softly against his own.

The little gathering sent up a cheer. Glasses were thumped upon the tables. Then, abruptly, there was silence. The girl sprang away from the boy's arms and turned to her father who stood scowling in the open doorway.

Emery Preston was a well-built man. His chest was like one of his own barrels. And, going up to the slim-built Tom Maddox, he looked like a bulldog approaching a whippet.

"If I catch you touching my daughter again, I'll make you sorry you was ever born!"

"Father!" said Tilly, pulling at his arm. "You mustn't speak to my friends like that."

"No lip from you or you'll get my belt across your bottom! You're supposed to be courting Harry Yelland. 1 won't have you meddling with this chap Maddox."

"Why, what's wrong with Tom?" Roger demanded, hot in defence of his foster-brother.

"I knew his father!" Emery said. "He was the nastiest-tempered brute in Huntlip and he once hit my mother across the mouth because she refused him drink on the slate."

"When was that? In the year dot? It warnt our Tom that done it anyway!"

"Like father, like son, so I'm taking no chances," Emery said. "Just mind and keep him away from my daughter!"

"Don't worry!" Roger said. "We'll keep away from you *and* your daughter and be damned to both of you good and all!" And, taking Tom's arm, he led him to the door. "Come on, Tom, we'll drink elsewhere. There's plenty of places better'n this one."

Outside the door Tom pulled away from Roger's grasp and thrust his fists into his pockets. He turned along the Straight and Roger followed.

"Take no notice of Emery Preston. Who cares about him? Or Tilly neither?"

"Not me," said Tom. "I ent grieving over them."

"San-fairy-duckwater, that's the style."

"He was telling the truth, though, all the same. My dad was a bad 'un. There's no doubt of that. He murdered my mother down in that cottage at Collow Ford and then went and hanged hisself in a tree."

"So what? It's all ancient history, over and done with. You don't want to worry yourself over that."

"I don't," Tom said. "It's other folk that worry about it, not me."

Sometimes he tried to picture his father: the drunkard hitting out in a rage; the fugitive run to ground by guilt; the despairer saving the public hangman a task. But no picture ever came to mind. It was just a story, and the man in the story was shadowy, faceless.

Could he picture his mother? Yes, perhaps. For sometimes he had a memory of white arms reaching towards him; of warm hands receiving his body into their strong, safe, thankful grasp. But the memory, if memory it was, always slid away when he tried to catch it, and then there was only a pitchblack darkness.

"Let's go to Chepsworth," Roger said. "We'll have a drink at The Revellers. They've got a skittle table there."

At The Revellers, in Lock Street, a coloured poster hung on the wall, showing the ruins of Louvain cathedral after its capture by the enemy. It was an artist's impression, it said, and it showed the German cavalry stabling their horses in nave and transept. One German trooper was smashing a painted plaster madonna by hurling it against the wall. Another was tearing the sacred vestments. Several others were burning carved wooden statues, including one of Christ blessing the loaves and fishes, to boil a pot of stew on a tripod, while, in the broken doorway, a few Belgian people, mostly old men and women, stood with their faces in their hands.

"I was just thinking," Tom said, "supposing that was Chepsworth cathedral, in ruins like that, with soldiers breaking everything up?"

"You ent religious, are you, Tom?"

"No, not me, but I think it's wicked all the same."

"What about all the people killed? That's a lot more wicked than bosting statues."

"Ah, well, that's right, of course," Tom said. "People is more important than statues."

But he hated the thought of all those carved figures fed to the flames in Louvain cathedral, just to boil a stewpot for German soldiers.

"You've gone and done *what*?" Jesse asked, openmouthed. "You surely didn't say enlisted?"

"Ah," said Tom. "Enlisted, that's right. Three o'clock this afternoon."

"And you?" Jesse said, staring at Roger. "You surely never went in too?"

"They wouldn't have me. They wouldn't believe I was eighteen."

"God in heaven!" said great-grumpa. "Anyone with half an eye could see you was only just weaned."

"They took my name, though," Roger said. "They'll be sending for me in due course."

"Due course," said Jesse, relieved. "Why, it's more'n a year before you're eighteen, and the war will surely be over by then?"

"It'd better be!" great-grumpa said. "It's damn near ruining the business."

"So Tom is to go? Would you believe it! I can't hardly credit it even now." Jesse looked doubtfully at his wife. "Ought we to let him, do you think, or are you going to put your foot down?"

"We can't stop him," Beth said. "He's well past eighteen and a grown man. If all I had to do was put my foot down, this war'd have been over before it started." She looked at Tom, standing before her. "When d'you have to go to the barracks?"

"They'll be sending my papers, the sergeant said."

"You done right to enlist," granna said. "I'm only glad it ent our William."

Tom went off to bed-down the pony in its stall, and there Betony found him later, having heard the news from her father and mother.

"Why did you go and enlist like that, without a word to anybody?"

"I just thought I would, that's all."

"Do you think it's easy being a soldier?"

"I dunno. I ent considered."

"I suppose you were tipsy as usual."

"I suppose I was," he said, shrugging.

She could never get near him, try as she might. He

spoke to her only to answer her questions. It had always been so from the very beginning; from the moment he had come to Cobbs, when she had made him feel an outcast and had driven him into himself like a crab. Nothing would change him now, it seemed. He would never believe that she minded about him.

"I can't imagine Tom as a soldier."

"You seem to be worried," Michael said, "yet it's no different for him that for any other volunteer."

"Tom's known so little happiness. It would be wicked if he were killed."

"He's been happy enough with your family, hasn't he?"

"But he's known no *joy*," Betony said.

"How many people ever know joy?"

"Not many, I suppose, and then only in fleeting moments."

They were walking in the garden at King's Hill House. Betony had sat through afternoon tea and had weathered his mother's interrogation. But her thoughts, obviously, had been elsewhere.

"There ought to be *special* joys in the world for people like Tom," she said, "though I've no idea what they might be."

"You don't seem to mind that he treats you so boorishly all the time."

"I know I deserve it, that's why."

"Oh, come, now!" Michael said. "You can't have treated him that badly."

"You don't know. You weren't there. Children can be very cruel."

"It was all a very long time ago."

"I still feel guilty all the same."

"I'm glad it's nothing more than that. I was beginning to be afraid you loved him."

"But I *do* love him!" Betony said. "I love him dearly and I wish to God I could make him trust me. He's a creature all alone in the world yet I can't get near him – I can't do anything to help him. Oh, yes, I love him. I love him very dearly indeed."

Then, suddenly, she saw the expression in Michael's eyes.

"Ah, no!" she said. "It isn't like that! Not *that* sort of love. How can I make you understand?"

And because she could not bear to see him unhappy, she reached up and kissed him, holding his face between her hands.

"You mustn't look like that," she said. "You've got no reason to look like that."

"Betony – "

"Yes, yes, I know."

"You do feel something for me, then?"

"Of course I do. How can you ask?"

"Are your feelings the same as mine?"

"I think they will be, given time."

"Time," he repeated. "Ah, time!"

But he had her promise, and it was worth more to him than her surrender. He told her so by taking her hand and raising it formally to his lips. His eyes were not so desperate now.

Mrs Andrews, watching them from the French window, gave a little sigh of resignation. The girl meant to have him. That much was obvious.

Towards the end of his leave, he went before a medical board. The wound in his shoulder had healed well. The effects of gas poisoning were passing away. He was fit for duty.

"You're very lucky," the elderly doctor said to him. "You've got an excellent constitution. Still, I'm taking no chances with those lungs of yours, so it's home service only for at least six months. Then we'll have you along again."

Michael's heart leapt. Six months in England! He could hardly believe it.

"Disappointed?" the doctor asked dryly.

"I think I can bear it," Michael said.

"You've earnt your respite. I wish I could give it to all the men who pass through my hands, but I have to send most of 'em back out there, like so many pitchers going to the well."

Michael went home to enjoy the last few days of his leave and await his posting.

"I'm so relieved," his mother said. "Perhaps it will all be over soon, before you're ready for foreign service."

"Perhaps it will. Who knows?"

That was November, 1915. The war must end sooner or later. Why not look on the bright side?

The new year came in, bringing a new determination. 1916! There was a certain sound about it. Great things were expected from the start, and people in Britain were pulling themselves together again, preparing for a new effort.

Michael was now at Yelmingham, attached to the new Tenth Battalion. He was lecturing recruits on trench warfare.

Tom, in training at Capleton Wick, had a weekend pass every third or fourth week, and the family at Cobbs grew used to seeing him in khaki. Dicky still jeered at his skinny legs, bound tight in puttees, but Great-grumpa Tewke thought him much improved.

"They've smartened you up, boy. They've made you walk straight instead of lolling about like a ploughboy.

There's something to be said for discipline."

Early in April, Tom was at home for the last time, on twenty-four hours' draft leave. There were three other Huntlip boys due to go, and the four were given a noisy send-off at The Rose and Crown. Tilly Preston hung on Tom's arm almost all the evening and her father for once said nothing about it. The family, too, gave him a send-off, drinking his health in a bottle of Beth's strong colts-foot wine, and presenting him with a pocket-bible.

"Are you sure you don't know where you're going?"

"No, they ent told us, but the chaps think it's France."

"Well, wherever it is," granna said, "always take care that you air your clothes."

Later that evening, Tom was missing from the family party. Betony went out to the fold, where the cobbles were frosty underfoot, and saw a light in the old wood-shed. Tom kept his ferrets in a hutch there, and when she went in, he had the two of them in his arms. His stub of candle stood in the draught, so that his face was lit and unlit ceaselessly, cheekbones and jawbones sharply outlined, deep dark eyes now seen, now unseen, as the flame leapt and flickered, trying to pull itself free of the wick.

"Will you look after my ferrets for me?"

"Why me, for mercy's sake?"

"The boys'd forget. They're not keen on ferrets."

"I'm not keen myself. Nasty smelly things. But yes, I'll look after them, that's a promise."

It surprised her that he should entrust this duty to her. He had never asked a favour in his life before. It pleased her, too, and she stroked the ferrets in his arms.

"I suppose you think you're going on an outing?"

"Ah, that's right, a regular dido."

"Or out poaching with old Charley Bailey."

"I know what it's like. I read the papers."

"You'll write to us, won't you, and tell us how you're getting on?"

"I ent much of a hand at letters."

"Well, I'll write to you," Betony said, "and that's the second promise I've made."

Tom merely shrugged. He was feeling a wart behind Nipper's ear. It might be serious and need a spot of something on it. He showed it to Betony and made her feel it, telling her what she must do about it if it got worse while he was away.

Out there in France, in the trenches, however, letters were precious and were read over and over again. They were kept until they wore through at the folds and even then they were sometimes mended. All except the most intimate letters were passed round and shared, and Betony's letters were great favourites, being full of things that made the men laugh. And because she addressed them to "Private Thos. Maddox" Tom was newly christened "Toss".

"We can't call you Tom," said Pecker Danson. "We're all Tommies out here!"

"What's she like, this Bet of yours? – Is she well-built?" asked Big Glover. "I like 'em well-built, with some shape about them. Fair, did you say, and nice-looking? Soft and sweet and gentle, is she?"

"No," Tom said, and the thought brought a faint smile to his lips.

"Whatya mean, no?"

"I wouldn't call her sweet and gentle."

"Are you saying she's a Tartar?"

"Well, a bit on the bossy side, you know."

"We might've known there was snags in it somewhere.

God preserve us from bossy women!"

But their disappointment did not last long. They would have nothing said against Betony. They had made her their mascot.

"It's a good thing sometimes, being bossy," said Bob Newers. "I wish we had her out here with us. She might get the rations up on time."

"Ask Bet if she'll marry me when I get back to Blighty, will you?" said Big Glover. "Say I'm six-foot-four and handsome with it. Don't mention the mole on my left elbow. I'd sooner keep it as a surprise."

"She's got a chap already," said Danson. "An officer in the Second Battalion. That's right, ent it, Toss? Name of Andrews?"

"Ah, that's right," Tom said.

"Sod hell and damn!" said Big Glover. "The officers get all the luck."

"Stands to reason," said Rufus Smith. "Bet ent like Toss. She's educated. You can tell by the way she writes her letters."

"It makes me laugh whenever I think of it," Pecker Danson said, choking. "What she said last time, about the girls at Coventry writing messages on the shells. It makes me wish I was an artillery man. I might've learnt a thing or two."

Rain was falling steadily. The trenches fell in as fast as the men worked to repair them. They stood to the knees in icy water, filling sandbags with the chalky mud.

"Why don't you never gamble, Toss? Why don't you never cuss and swear?"

"He don't need to, Pecker old son, 'cos you do enough for him and you both."

"He ent hardly human, the way he never grumbles nor

nothing. Don't you feel the cold and wet, Toss, the same as all us other chaps?"

"I try not to think about it," Tom said.

Somehow he was able to shut out the cold teeming rain and the tiredness. He was able to shut himself up inside, with his own thoughts, while his body moved automatically and his arms went on working. Yet when they asked what these thoughts were, he could never tell them.

"The same as yours, I suppose," he said.

"You're a dirty little tyke, then, if you think the same thoughts as the rest of us."

After their spell at Hébuterne, which Danson said was to get them used to shellfire, they marched to billets at Beauquesne. The weather improved. They had ten days of intensive training, mostly in sunshine.

"Why bayonet practice?" Glover said, during a respite. "Are we running out of bullets?"

"I saw a general this morning," said Ritchie, "the first I've seen since coming over."

"You didn't see the C.-in-C.?"

"I wouldn't know him from Adam, would I, except that he'd be wearing khaki?"

"Who *is* C.-in-C.?" asked Pecker Danson.

"Blowed if I know. Does anyone else?"

"Charlie Chaplin," Glover said.

"Mrs Pankhurst," said Rufus Smith.

"Angus Jock Maconochie."

"Alexander's Ragtime Band."

"Here, sarge!" said Bob Newers, stopping Sergeant Grimes as he came by. "Who commands the B.E.F.?"

"I do!" said Grimes. "And next after me, General Sir Douglas Haig."

"Haig," said Newers. "Any whisky coming our way?"

The sergeant fixed him with a pitying eye.

"D'you mean to tell me you didn't know the name of the C.-in-C.? You're ignorant, Newers, that's what you are."

"I am," agreed Newers, nodding sadly. "I'm that bloody ignorant they'll give me three stripes if I ent careful."

"Enough of that!" Grimes said, without rancour. "Too much sauce and I'll make you caper."

Not all the instructors were like Grimes. Sergeant Townchurch, for instance, was out of a different mould entirely. He liked to pick on weaker men and humble them before the others, and one such was a Welshman named Evans, a small thin man with sunken chest who had trouble with his breathing: a man, Newers said, who should never have been in the Army at all.

"Evans?" said Townchurch, during a mock attack one morning. "A Welshman and a miner, eh? In other words, a bloody slacker! We've heard about your lot, going on strike for better pay while we sweat our guts out fighting the Huns!"

Evans said nothing. His eyes were glazed and his skin looked like putty. He was almost choking, for Townchurch had run him about at the double, weighed down by pack, rifle, entrenching tool, and two canvas buckets full of grenades.

"How come you're in the Three Counties? Won't they take slackers in the Royal Welsh? Or even in the South Wales Borderers?"

"Leave him alone," Tom said. He was standing next to Evans and could hear how the man struggled for breath. "If he was a slacker he wouldn't be here."

Townchurch came and stood before Tom. He looked him over from head to foot.

"Are you another bloody Welshman? No? Perhaps not.

A gipsy, then? It's what you look like. And what, might I ask, is your sodding name? Maddox. Right. Be sure I'll remember."

So Tom and Evans became his victims. Luckily their stay at Beauquesne was brief. The party in training broke up, and the Sixth Battalion went into the line, taking over trenches at Mary Redan. Evans was now in C Company, in the same platoon as Tom and Newers, and by a strange unlucky chance, when their sergeant was injured by shrapnel, his place was taken by Sergeant Townchurch.

Tom's letters home were few and far-between, and, although written with immense labour, were never more than half a page long. "I am well. I got your parcel. How are Nipper and Slip and the workshop?" There was not much to say. The censor would only cut it out. So he wrote about the yellowhammer, heard so often in the hedgerows, saying A *little bit of bread and no chee-eeese,* just the same as it did in England. And he pressed speedwell flowers and herb robert between the folded sheet of paper. It astonished him daily that the same flowers grew in Picardy as grew in the fields and lanes at home.

"Things can't be too bad over there," Jesse said to Betony, "if young Tom's got time to gather flowers."

In England, now, the May was out and the wild June roses would soon be coming. The weather was good. Hay harvest had started at Anster and in the evenings Jesse and his sons were out in the fields, helping Janie and her husband Martin with the haymaking. William had now had his eighteenth birthday. Jesse was rather worried about him.

"Won't you get into trouble, boy, stopping at home now conscription's come in?"

"It's no odds to me. I still ent going."

"If William was to work on the farm full-time he might be exempt," Janie said.

"I don't care to be exempt – I just ent going," William said. "I didn't start this damned war so why should I down tools and go fighting in it?"

"Yes, but suppose they put you in gaol, boy?"

"They'll tarnal well have to catch me first!"

One day soon after, William and Roger were delivering ladders at a shop in Chepsworth. Roger disappeared for a little while and returned triumphant.

"I've been along to the recruiting centre. They took me this time. No questions asked."

"Are you gone in the head, you stupid fool? You've got no right! You're still under age."

"If I look eighteen then I'm good enough to be eighteen. I'm a lot stronger than some of the chaps I seen there today."

"I'm going down there to get your name took off their list!"

"If you do that," Roger said, "I'll run away south and join up there."

William saw that Roger meant it. He stood for a moment in a quivering rage. Then, suddenly, he was calm.

"All right," he said, "if one of us goes, we're both going."

"But you don't want to!" Roger said.

"I ent letting you go by yourself. A kid like you needs looking after. Besides, what'd I look like, do you think, with my younger brother gone and not me?"

So William and Roger joined together, and together confronted their parents at home.

"Don't worry, mother," William said. "I'll take care of Roger for you and I'll make certain-sure we don't get parted."

Within a month, they were in camp at Porthcowan, training with the Royal Artillery.

"It's not a bad life, considering," William wrote in a letter home. "In fact I reckon it suits me fine." And at the end, in a casual postscript, "I came out top in the ranging tests yesterday morning. The instructor says I'm a born gunner. I might put in for a stripe directly if everything goes according to plan."

Being William, now that he had become a soldier, he was determined to be a good one.

One Sunday in May Betony went up to London and spent the afternoon with Michael. He was looking better: stronger; more relaxed; yet when she told him so, his eyes darkened and a shiver went through him.

"I'm practically one hundred per cent, which means I'll soon be posted abroad."

"Are you sure?" she said. "Sure you're fit again, I mean."

"You just said so, yourself."

"I said you looked it, but I'm no doctor."

"No, well, we've got plenty of those, and they look me over now and then." Then he said abruptly: "How are things in munitions nowadays?"

"Frightening," she said. "I was in Birmingham yesterday, where they're making shells. The output is tremendous, and it's just the same wherever I go."

"That's the stuff! We might get somewhere if we've got things to throw."

"Is something coming?" Betony asked. "A big offensive?"

"Shush," he said, smiling. "How do I know you're not a spy?"

They were having tea at The Trocadero. He passed his cup across the table and watched her, secretly, as she filled it. There was something about the shape of her face, and her calm expression, that took him by surprise each time he saw her. She seemed so unconscious of herself; of the way she looked, the way she smiled. He had not been mistaken. He wanted her badly.

"Betony," he said, "do you have to go back to Chepsworth tonight?"

"Yes. I've got to be in Gridport at eight in the morning."

"Oh, that work of yours!" he said. "Couldn't you be late just once in a while?"

"No, Michael, I'm afraid not."

"Would you have stayed with me, had you been free to?"

"I'm never free for more than one day."

"You're just trying to spare my feelings. The answer is no, obviously." His gaze fell away and he stared at the sugar-bowl on the table. "I'd like you to know," he said slowly, doing his best to make light of the matter, "that I don't try it on with every young woman I meet."

"Do you meet so many, at Yelmingham?"

"You'd be surprised at the number of homes we officers are made welcome in. It's all meant to sustain our morale and there's a certain titled lady at Gaines who takes her task very seriously indeed."

"Are you trying to make me jealous?"

"Drink up," he said. "We ought to be moving if we're to catch that train."

He drove with her in a taxi to the station, and kept up the same light-hearted conversation till her train pulled out.

"Give my regards to your family," he said. "And don't forget to call on my mother. She's very anxious to get to know you."

Towards the end of May he was pronounced fit for

general service and ordered to rejoin his old battalion. He had forty-eight hours' leave and arrived at Chepsworth at eleven o'clock on Saturday morning. After lunching with his mother he walked out to Huntlip, but Betony was not at home. She had gone to Stafford on a special course and was not expected back until Sunday.

"What time on Sunday?" Michael asked.

"We don't rightly know," Jesse said. "She didn't go by train, you see. She went in a special motor bus, along with some very important people."

"Can I get her on the telephone?"

"Laws!" Jesse said, and his blue eyes opened very wide. "I shouldn't think so!"

So Michael left a note and returned home. His leave slipped away, pointless and empty, with his mother pretending not to notice his silence. She feared for him dreadfully, three times wounded yet returning once more to the battle zone, and she thought it wrong that the same young men should be called upon again and again for duty.

And yet at the same time she took pleasure in the sight of him in his uniform, with the three stars on each epaulette, and the three yellow wound-stripes on the sleeve. She took pride in him because he was her son, and because he had been among the first to answer his country's call for men. She forebore to reproach him for his silence. Her only complaint came at the end, when he refused to let her see him off at the station.

"Is it because of that girl?" she said. "The carpenter's daughter? Will she be there?"

"I don't even know if she got my message."

"If she hasn't, you'll be leaving all alone."

"I'll chance that," he said. "I'd much rather say good-bye here."

"Very well. It's as you wish. I will be praying for you, my son, and thinking of you constantly."

"Good," he said, and stooped to kiss her. "I may be too busy to pray for myself."

His train left at nine that evening. It was drawing out as Betony ran down onto the platform. She saw him at once and hurried forward, trying to take his outstretched hands as he leant towards her, out of the window. Their fingers were joined momentarily, – a brief exchange of warmth and softness – then the train gathered speed and tore them apart. Betony hurried along beside it, and Michael looked down at her with anguished eyes, his lips apart but no words escaping between them. He wanted to open the door and jump out. She was growing smaller all the time. She had come to a standstill.

"Michael, take care, take care!" she called, and he heard her even above the noise of the engine. "Come back safely! I'll be waiting for you!"

Staying in London overnight, he heard much talk of the coming offensive, even among the hotel staff. He mentioned the matter to Morris Tremearne, a fellow captain in the Second Battalion, also staying at The Kenilworth.

"Even the bootboy knows there's going to be a push. And now there are hints in the newspapers. We may as well send the Kaiser a telegram, stating the exact time and place!"

"Ah, that's the beauty of it!" said Tremearne. "The fuss we're making, the Germans'll never believe it's going to happen, don't you know!"

Michael turned away, catching the eye of his new batman. Lovell was discretion personified, but his glance was expressive.

Three days later they were with their battalion in Bethune. Michael was glad to see men he knew. Six months was a long time. He tried not to think of those who had vanished in the interim. He tried not to keep counting them.

"My God, you look smart!" Lightwood said. "I hardly knew you."

"Plenty of new chaps coming up, not all of them hopeless," Ashcott said. "This specimen here is a good man. – He's brought the latest gramophone records." And he waved a hand at the new young subaltern standing beside him. "His name's Spurrey. We call him Weed."

"What's the new C.O. like? Big man or small?"

"Big and fatherly and serious-minded. Has a proper respect for flesh and blood. Treats us almost as human beings."

"What's happening here at the moment?"

"We're up and down the canal mostly. We know it like the backs of our hands. Still, the big push is coming, so they say, and soon we'll be sleeping in the Kaiser's palace."

"Has he *got* a palace?" Spurrey asked.

"I'm damn sure he doesn't live in a dugout!"

"Four miles," Michael said, listening to the guns firing at Givenchy. "It sounds nearer."

"That's because you've been away. You've got used to the hush at home in England. What did you do with yourself, all that time? Pickle the onions?"

"It's mustard, not pickles," Michael said. He was used to jokes about the family business. "But I never go near the factory if I can help it."

"Mustard! Of course! That explains your famous coolness under fire. You've had it hot and strong all your life, what?"

"Besides, I haven't been in Chepsworth all the time."

"No, you've been manning a desk at Yelmingham, you lucky devil. Still, I expect you're glad to be back in the swim. It must be pretty dangerous in England now, with all those women driving the trams."

The next day, they were in the front line, in the Cuinchy sector. Michael had command of B Company, and his sergeant was a man named Bill Minching, a veteran of Mons and Festubert: quiet-spoken; steady-eyed; unupsettable, as Lightwood said. Almost half the men in the Company were new drafts but they looked on Michael as the newcomer.

A working party, under Minching, was out one night digging a new communication trench. Some rain fell and in the morning, when Michael inspected the finished work, there was water at the bottom of the trench. The men slopped about in it, thinking it nothing, but Michael gave orders that duckboards were to be laid down immediately.

"One of those, is he?" a private named Biddle was heard to say. "Believes in giving us plenty to do!"

Minching tapped him on the shoulder.

"You may have webbed feet, Biddle, but the rest of us are not so lucky."

Two men were killed by shellfire that day, and two were wounded. One of the wounded was Private Biddle. He was carried away with a deep jagged gash spouting blood from breast-bone to navel, and, passing Minching, he spoke weakly.

"Seems I'm a goner, don't it, sarge?"

"Oh no you're not!" Minching said. "You'll just be laid up for a bit, that's all. You've got a Blighty one. – Ent that the answer to your prayers?"

Biddle believed him. New hope came into his eyes. He lay back smiling.

"Carry on, my good men," he said to the bearers, "the surgeons are waiting."

"Will he live?" Michael asked Minching later.

"I don't know, sir, but faith can work wonders, so they say."

One afternoon, during an off-duty period in Annequin, a young subaltern, exploring the ruins of a bakery, set off an old enemy shell that had lain there, rusting, for over a year. He was blown to pieces.

"It's a bad place, this," Spurrey said to Lightwood at

mess that evening. "I don't like it. It gives me the creeps."

He was nineteen and had come out in April with his friends Hapton, Challoner, and Wyatt. All three friends were now dead. Wyatt was the man killed by the old "sleeping" shell.

"Don't like La Bassée?" said Hunter-Haynes, as though offended. "You surely don't mean it!"

"How about a stroll down to the brickstacks?" Ashcott said, patting Spurrey's shoulder. "Plenty of souvenirs to be had there . . . such as a bullet in the head."

"You should look on the dark side, young Weed," said Spencer, "then every day is a kind of bonus."

"Blessed are the meek, for they shall inherit the earth," said Lightwood, "though I must say the will is a hell of a long time in probate."

"You're quiet, Andrews," Ashcott remarked.

"He's got inside knowledge, I bet," Lightwood said. "How do you do it, Andrews, old man? Have you got the colonel's ear?"

"I've got Minching's ear. He's good at sorting out the rumours."

"And what does the omniscient Minching predict?"

"A move southwards in the near future."

"Nothing more specific than that?"

"I'm afraid not."

"Ah, well," Lightwood said. "I doubt if Staff themselves know very much more. I don't suppose they've stuck a pin in the map yet."

After their tour of duty in the trenches, they returned to Bethune and had a fortnight's training there, mostly mock battles. They now knew, officially, that the great offensive had begun, thirty miles southwards, on the Somme.

"Shall we be in it?" Spurrey asked.

"Up to our necks," Ashcott said, "but not yet, I hope."

"Why not yet?"

"There's a marvellous girl living near the soapworks, and I mean to have her, that's why."

"You and whose army?" Lightwood murmured.

On July the eighth, after dark, the battalion entrained at Lillers station and travelled southwards through the night. Early next morning they arrived at Saleux, and from there they marched nine miles to St Sauveur.

After the coal-pits and slag-heaps of Artois, Picardy was lovely indeed: a district as yet hardly touched by war: a country of orchards and big sweeping fields full of green standing corn, where poppies flared along the roadsides, and the air smelt sweet and fresh and clean.

At every farmhouse, every hamlet, people turned out and watched from their doors. A very old man bowed gravely, straightened and gave a military salute. An old woman wept into her apron. Children ran beside the soldiers.

"Tommee! Tommee! Soldats anglais!"

"Napoo lay boutons!" the soldiers said, as many small hands plucked at their tunics.

"Napoo lay badges!"

"Napoo nothing! Allay bizonc!"

"Après la guerre finee. Maybee. Ah, and viva to you, too, you cheeky monkey!"

But the men were tired. They grew more silent with each mile that passed. The day was a hot one and they marched in a cloud of thick white dust that dried out their mouths and gave them a terrible raging thirst. So at St Sauveur they stopped for rest, drink, and food, before pressing on another eight miles towards the banks of the River Ancre.

They came at last to Vecquemont, a glimmer of lights

in the dusk now falling, and here they stayed, the men flopping down beside the road while the officers went to arrange billets. The people of Vecquemont were not best pleased. They stood about, blank-faced, unmoving. Yet when a battalion of the Glasgow Highlanders marched through half an hour later, with the pipes playing, they were given a rousing cheer.

"That's what we're here for," one of their officers said to Michael. "The Scots turn-out is good for morale. It gives the civilians a bit of a boost. And you English fellows, too, of course."

"Cocky bastards," Lightwood said, as the Highlander turned and swaggered away. "Strutting about in their fancy dress!"

All next day they remained at Vecquemont, giving the men a chance to recover from their seventeen-mile march and make themselves ready. They left early the following morning, and, determined not to be outdone by the Glasgows, marched smartly out of the village.

"We may not have a howling cat to lead us," Sergeant Minching said to his men, "but there's nothing wrong with the way we march."

"Good old Three Counties!" a voice shouted from the ranks. "Especially Leominster!"

At Morlancourt, eight miles westwards, they rested again for twenty-four hours, and the men handed in unwanted equipment, including greatcoats. They were now within close sound of the guns. No civilians were to be seen. The villages here had all been evacuated some time before. After dark on the twelfth, they marched three miles to Becordel, close to the old front line of 1914. There they met up with other battalions, and the whole brigade went into camp.

In the morning, Michael rode up with the other company commanders to a ridge called Calou, from whence they could see the new battle zone, a mile or so distant, under bombardment by British artillery. The noise was deafening. The enemy line danced and quivered under the smoke. The air was never still for a moment.

"I feel almost sorry for poor old Fritz," a man named Logan said to Michael. "We've been pounding him for three weeks. I shouldn't think he could stand much more. It should be a walkover, when we attack."

As they rode back again, down onto the fields where the whole brigade lay in bivouac, Michael felt an upsurge of hope. There were two thousand men mustered below, and everywhere else along the line the concentration of troops was enormous. Surely the offensive must carry the war? Official communiqués were encouraging. They told of successes further south. And yet, somehow, sneaking in under the official news, there were rumours that spoke of bad setbacks everywhere; of terrible losses; of whole divisions cut to pieces on the enemy wire. How did the rumours get about? he wondered. Were they, as the colonel stated, merely the work of German spies?

That night was cold, and because the encampment was hidden from the enemy by two or three ridges of high ground, the men were allowed to light fires. They flickered up everywhere, small ghosts of fires in the damp darkness, each with its close-packed ring of men. Some groups told stories. Some sang songs. From a few came the sound of a mouth-organ playing. And, going about from group to group, Colonel Nannet in his British warm, with his collar up and his cap pulled well down, stopped to exchange a word or two with the men of his battalion.

Michael, with the other officers of his company, stood

at the opening of their tent. Lightwood was smoking a large cigar. The scent of it wafted on the damp air.

"There goes the old man, dishing out his eve-of-action comfort."

" 'A little touch of Harry in the night,' " said Ashcott. " 'Oh, God of Battles, steel my soldiers' hearts!' "

"Something the poor devils could well do without," said Lightwood. "Still, he's not a bad old cock, really."

The colonel retired to his quarters at last. B Company officers retired to theirs. Michael sat looking towards the west, where gun flashes lit the cloudy sky, beyond the contours of Calou Ridge. Underneath, in the darkness, the camp fires still flickered, kept alive assiduously with twigs and leaves and bits of grass. Some of the men were still singing.

> "When this lousy war is over,
> Oh, how happy I shall be!
> I will tell the sergeant-major
> Just how much he means to me . . ."

From first light onwards, the Allied bombardment was intensified, all along the enemy lines. It was Bastille Day and the French guns were particularly active. At ten-thirty, the sun was already very warm, shining down on the columns of men marching along the Fricourt road.

They were among the trenches again; on ground that covered, all too shallowly in places, the dead of two years' warfare. All along the old front line, the bodies of those killed in more recent fighting still lay about, and the stench of corruption was everywhere. Sometimes these bodies appeared to heave, because of the flies seething upon them, and because of the movement of scavenging rats.

At the village of Fricourt, now in ruins, the battalion rested for several hours, awaiting orders. They got food and drink from a field kitchen, but every mouthful tasted of lyddite from the batteries of guns firing nearby. Such news as came was so far good. The enemy line was reported broken and the Germans were said to be giving way. Our Indian cavalry had been in action and were at this moment riding the enemy into the ground. Certainly a great many prisoners had been taken. Whole columns of them kept coming down, eyes staring out of blackened faces; exhausted, shrunken, scarcely able to lift their feet.

From Fricourt the battalion marched to the village of Mametz, now no more than a heap of rubble. Among the ruins stood a column of motor ambulance cars, and there were crowds of British wounded awaiting attention at the medical aid post. They seemed cheerful and said the day was going well.

"We've cleared the way for you up there. You've got nothing to do but go round with the mop."

"Jerry is running for all he's worth."

"Bazentin is in our hands . . ."

"Mametz Wood is in our hands . . ."

But one man, with bandaged head, sitting smoking a cigarette, gave a cynical laugh.

"Dead hands, mostly, you'll find," he said.

Leaving Mametz, the battalion moved down a sunken road, then forked off into a valley. On their right rose a long escarpment. On their left the ground sloped, open, all the way up to Mametz Wood. The noise of the bombardment was almost more than they could bear, for, all across the open area, batteries of British field-guns kept up an incessant fire, and beyond the escarpment were the French seventy-fives. The shriek of shells overhead never stopped, for the British heavies were also at work, some way behind.

The rough road was strewn with dead. Michael tried not to look too closely, for it seemed to him there were many more khaki-clad bodies than field-grey, and now the number of walking-wounded had grown to a never-ending stream. Silent men, trudging past as though indifferent; mere shadows of men, hollow-eyed, the same as the Germans; men whose last remaining strength was needed to carry them along the road.

"What lot are you?" Minching asked, as one group passed.

"Manchesters," came the brief answer.

"What lot are you?" he asked another.

"South Staffords – what there is left of us!" a man said, snarling.

Everywhere along the valley lay the carcasses of dead horses, their heads thrown back, their legs in the air. Some were transport horses, and their smashed limbers lay nearby; but some were cavalry horses with braided saddles and gleaming stirrups, and their riders lay only God knew where.

Down the road now came wounded troopers of an Indian regiment, some leading their terrified mounts, others slumped as though dead in their saddles. One elderly Sikh, having watched his wounded horse collapse, was on his knees beside it, and the tears were running down his bearded face. His lips moved as though in prayer. His hands made a little secret sign. He took his revolver from the saddle and shot the dying horse in the head. He knelt, watching, until it was still. Then he turned the revolver on himself and fell across the horse's body.

"Christ!" said a soldier to his mate. "Did you see that?"

"No one saw nothing!" shouted a sergeant, determined to keep the column moving. "Close up, there, Number One Platoon! Keep your dressing by the left!"

The men marched on along the valley, passing between the two flanking storms of the great bombardment, under a sky that shrieked and sizzled with the flying shells.

Logan came up and rode with Michael a little way. He had been talking to a wounded officer of the South Staffords.

"He says he's been here since the big push started. A whole fortnight in the front line. No wonder they all look such wrecks, is it?"

"What's the name of this place, did he say?"

"Seems they call it Happy Valley."

They came out into the open, among fields of tobacco and turnips and corn, the crops all trodden into the ground. It was now seven o'clock in the evening, and the battalion dug itself in for the night, close beside a wood known, from its shape, as Flatiron Copse. Enemy shells were falling all the time. Eight men were killed before the shelter-trenches were dug. Another six were badly wounded.

Nobody slept. The shelling was too close for that. It was also very cold, and the men, having left their greatcoats at Morlancourt, lay huddled close together for warmth, trying to make the most of their groundsheets. Dawn, when it came, brought some relief, and there was breakfast of a sort, with hot sweet tea and a tot of rum.

The battalion fell in, and the whole brigade moved off eastwards in a thick white mist, forward into the battle area. The ground was broken and badly cratered, littered with debris and dead bodies. There were wounded men,

too, who had lain out all night and who now reached up
with pleading arms as the marching columns tramped
by. One or two soldiers, not yet hardened, stepped out of
line, reaching for their water-bottles, but were herded
back by a watchful N.C.O.

"Leave that to the stretcher-parties! You'll need them
water-bottles yourselves directly!"

The brigade formed up in a valley south of High
Wood. The Second Three Counties were in reserve. They
held a position at Trivet Spur, beside a rough track
known as Windy Lane. The Second Worcestershire were
nearby.

A mile to the north, the Glasgows and the Queen's
formed the front line, and some of the Glasgows had
already been in action during the night, in High Wood
itself. Now they were attacking the main Switch Line,
where the Germans, contrary to earlier reports, were as
strong as ever. High Wood was thought to be safe, but as
the Glasgows advanced across the open, they were cut
down by enemy machine-guns firing from among the
trees.

Michael, watching through his field-glasses, could see
it all: the double lines of kilted figures advancing up the
open slope; the glint of a bayonet here and there; and
then the terrible thinning-out as the Maxims raked them
from front and rear. He could see the depleted line
pressing onwards, with men of the King's and the First
Queen's going up to fill the gaps; could see the line fal-
tering again, the bodies thick in the green corn; and now
the live men were falling, too, crawling to the cover of
shell-scrapes and craters. He saw the Worcesters go up
to help: two companies into the wood; two attacking
across the open; and he saw the pitiful remnants returning, dragging themselves back to their line.

"What do you think, sir?" Logan was saying to the colonel. "Shall we be sent up to help, d'you suppose?"

Michael put down his glasses and turned a little, waiting for the answer, which was slow in coming. The colonel's face was deep-lined, and his eyes were full of angry tears.

"Is that what you want? – To go the same way as those poor devils out there?" But he quickly relented. "I'm sorry, Logan. I didn't mean to snap your head off. I've no idea what our orders will be. All I know is that it's madness attacking across that space while Fritz still holds that bloody wood. I'm sending along to Brigade H.Q. to tell them so."

At twelve noon, for half an hour, there was another bombardment by British guns, but it short-ranged and the shells fell on what was left of the Glasgows' own forward line. German shells were exploding in the southern half of the wood, driving out the Worcesters and the South Staffords, many of whom were mown down by their own machine-guns before they were able to make themselves known.

At four o'clock in the afternoon, two companies of the Second Three Counties were sent up into the wood: C Company under Logan and D Company under Tremearne: roughly two hundred men in all. The other two companies remained in their trenches, with enemy shells falling close, and at half-past-four orders came for them to advance up the open hillside.

Colonel Nannet delayed. He wanted to be sure the wood was safe. He sent up a runner, who failed to return, and was about to send another when a message arrived from Brigade H.Q.: "High Wood is ours. Proceed as ordered." So, at six o'clock exactly, A Company under Ashcott and B Company under Michael climbed out into the open and began advancing up the slope towards the enemy Switch Line.

The hillside was strewn with the dead and dying, the ground was broken everywhere, and black smoke drifted from left to right as enemy shelling intensified. Visibility was bad, and the slope grew steeper all the time, so that progress was slow, but once up and over the brow, the smoke lessened and it was like coming out into a brighter light again.

Michael turned/ his head, first right, then left, to see how many of his men had gone, falling, unseen, behind the smoke. It seemed to him the line was still strong, the forward movement still determined, and he caught a glimpse of his sergeant's face, calm, intent, open-eyed, under the brim of his steel helmet.

Towards the top of the first slope, crossing a road, Michael turned aside to avoid a deep crater, and as he did so, three men with rifles rose from its shelter and fell in behind him: kilted men of the Highland regiment: survivors of the earlier attack.

"We're wi' ye, laddie! And whoever you are you're doing fine!"

They were out past the corner of the wood now, moving across the wider space, inside the range of the worst shelling, though shrapnel was bursting overhead. A Company was on the right, B Company on the left, the two lines straggling but still moving forward in good order. The ground had flattened out again. The enemy line was only two hundred yards away.

But now, suddenly, from the northernmost boundary of the wood, came a burst of machine-gun and rifle fire, and Michael, glancing back, saw his three Highlanders fall to the ground. Over on his right, A Company had received the first and the worst of the fire, and nearly half its men had fallen. The remainder struggled on, only to meet the same destructive fire from in front, as they tried to reach the enemy line. The task was beyond them and the few men remaining faltered badly, seeking shelter instinctively behind B Company, still advancing. Only Ashcott kept to the front, and, running close beside Michael, sobbed out, swearing:

"The liars said the wood was ours! Why do they tell such lies, the bastards?"

Then, abruptly, he was no longer there. His body was being trampled underfoot. His place beside Michael was taken by Gates. The noise of the Maxims was very loud. Their fire was withering, murderous, keen. Michael felt himself blinking, averting his face as though in a hailstorm, and all the time as he ran forward he felt he was pushing through a great bead curtain of spent bullets. He had the strange fancy that this bead curtain was his protection: that a deadly bullet would not get through: that all he had to do was to keep pushing forward.

Gates was hit and fell with a terrible high-pitched scream. The man who took his place was sobbing and swearing, snorting for breath through wide-open mouth and wide-stretched nostrils. He was hit in the chest and fell headlong, and his rifle was thrown between Michael's feet, causing him to stumble.

Now, whenever he glanced to left or right, there were great gaps all along the line; gaps that were no longer filling up; gaps that grew bigger as he looked. He pressed on, leaping over a huddle of corpses, and as he did so he was hit in the thigh. He fell among the dead bodies.

Twenty yards away lay a crater. He began crawling on his stomach towards it. A man looked over the edge and saw him. It was Alan Spurrey, his new young subaltern, bare-headed, having lost his helmet. Spurrey was wounded in both feet, but he crawled from the crater and wriggled forward, arms outstretched to help Michael.

"Get your head down!" Michael shouted. "Get down and get back, you bloody fool!"

A machine-gun rattled, and Michael pressed his face to the ground. Bullets struck the turf beside him and ripped on in a curving line. When he looked up again, Spurrey was dead, his head shattered. Michael crawled on into the crater.

It was not a bad wound: the bullet had entered the fleshiest part of the right thigh and had passed out behind; but the bleeding was heavy and soon soaked the dressing, so he used his tie as a tourniquet.

When he looked out over the edge, there was no advancing line to be seen, for those few men who were left alive had sought shelter in the broken ground. He could see some of them nearby, crawling on their stomachs, and after a while two men joined him in the crater, one of them wounded in the chest.

The wounded man, Aston, was in a bad way. Michael helped the other, a corporal named Darby, to dress the wound. He gave him a drink from his water-bottle.

"What a mess it all is!" Darby exclaimed. "What a stinking awful bloody mess!" He looked at Michael with bitter defiance. "We never stood a chance of reaching the Germans. Neither us nor the other poor sods this morning. Surely the brasshats should've known?"

"They know now," Michael said.

"If I get back safe I swear I'll get some bloody rednosed brigadier and stick him through with my bloody bayonet!"

"Is Aston your particular friend?"

"He's my brother-in-law. He married my sister before coming out. And what'll *she* say when she hears he's hurted?"

"He may be all right. We must get him back as soon as we can."

"What a hope!" Darby said. "What a bloody flaming hope!"

A burst of machine-gun fire shut him up. He crouched low in the loose earth. Michael was wondering what had drawn the fire when a man rolled over the edge of the crater and lay down beside him. It was Sergeant Minching.

"You all right, sir? I see you're hit."

"Not too badly, though I've bled like a pig. It's Aston here who's in trouble."

Aston was only barely conscious. Minching bent over him, listening to his heartbeats and his breathing. Darby watched him.

"Any hope, sarge?"

"There's always hope," Minching said. "The bullet's missed his lungs, I would say, but we'll have to be careful how we move him. Might be better to leave him here – let Jerry find him and patch him up."

"Hell, no!" Darby said.

"He'd get attention that much sooner."

"What sort of attention, though, by God?"

"The Jerries aren't monsters. They'd take care of him all right."

"I'm getting him back," Darby said, "even if I have to do it by myself."

"All right, we'll do it between us, don't worry, as soon as it's dark enough to move." Minching turned towards Michael. "What about you, sir? Can you walk?"

"If not, I can always crawl."

A shrapnel shell burst in the air nearby, and they pressed their faces into the earth, while the balls blasted the crater's edge. When Michael looked up, the smoke was drifting overhead. He called to Minching, who was looking out.

"What's going on out there? Can you see?"

"I can see a bunch of our men, sir, falling back down the side of the wood. They're making a dash for it, back to the line."

"No sign of their rallying?"

"There's nothing much left to rally, sir. A couple of dozen at the most."

"What happened to our Lewis-gun sections?"

"Copped it, sir, quite early on. A shell got one of 'em – Mr Rail's – and the gun was useless. I know it was 'cos I went to see. The other lot stopped at the corner of the wood, trying to get that bloody Maxim. They were cut down in seconds. They never even got their gun into action."

A rifle cracked from the German line, and a bullet struck the edge of the crater. Minching wriggled back at once.

"The colonel was killed, sir, did you know? So were Mr Lightwood and Mr Haynes."

"And Mr Spencer?"

"Badly wounded in the head. A Company's worse off than us. I reckon they're pretty well wiped clean out."

Michael turned away and closed his eyes.

Just before darkfall, Minching opened their iron rations. They ate corned beef and hard biscuit. Aston, though conscious, could eat nothing. He asked for water all the time. Darby kept giving him his own bottle.

"Hang on, Fred, it won't be long now. We'll get you

back, don't worry. But for God's sake remember to keep
mum or we'll have Jerry down on us as sure as fate."

As evening came on, artillery fire was renewed on both
sides, and the air above was filled again with the shrieking
of shells; but after a while, as night fell, it eased off and
became intermittent; and between the two flashing sky-
lines, darkness settled along the ground.

"Now," Minching said. "It's time we started."

He and Darby hoisted Aston till he hung with an arm
round each man's neck. Aston gave a cry but choked it
back quickly, sucking his breath between clenched teeth.

"Easy does it," Minching muttered. "Hold on, my lad,
and bite on the bullet. It's a long way to Tipperary."

He turned his face towards Michael, who lay trying to
bend his knee.

"You coming, sir?"

"No, not yet. Better for you to go ahead."

"Supposing you was to need help?"

"Don't fuss, man! Just get a move on and do as I say."

"Very well, sir, but don't dilly-dally too long – the Jerry
patrols'll be out soon."

"I know that. I'm not a fool."

"All right, sir, and good luck."

"Good luck, Minching," Michael said, and watched as
the three men stumbled over the edge, vanishing into
the misty darkness.

He crawled to the rim and lay listening. All around in
the darkness, wounded men groaned and whimpered,
and sometimes he heard slithering noises as somebody
crawled along the ground, inching his way down the
slope. Sometimes he heard tortured breathing. Once he
heard a man praying.

Half a mile below, shells were bursting in High Wood,
great yellow flashes splintering the darkness between the

trees, while, on the horizons, north and south, as the big guns answered each other, the sky flickered, pulsing whitely. Now and then a starshell rose, green-spiked, beautiful, a manmade meteor rising and sinking like a sigh. And every few minutes the bright Very flares blossomed overhead like Japanese flowers, spreading their light over all the earth.

Michael lay back again, looking up at the throbbing sky. He had lost much blood; he was weak and light-headed; a deathlike weariness numbed his limbs. Somewhere nearby he heard voices speaking in German, and heard the tread of booted feet. The first patrols were going out, picking their way among the dead and wounded.

"Ach, Du liebe Güte, was fur ein wüstes Durcheinander!" a voice said, quietly but clearly. Then the voices and the footsteps went further away.

Michael knew he ought to move. His wound was not crippling; he could easily find the strength to crawl; and the doctors at Douvecourt would soon patch him up as good as new, so that he could fight again another day. But his will was paralysed, his soul inert, and his body obeyed its own dictates. So he stayed where he was in the shell-crater and waited for the Germans to come and take him prisoner.

Betony, receiving a letter from Mrs Andrews, went at once to King's Hill House. She was shown into the morning-room, which was full of sunshine and the scent of roses. Mrs Andrews sat straight-backed, her face impassive, but when she began talking of Michael, she broke down and wept and it was some time before she could continue. She felt ashamed, weeping in front of this carpenter's daughter, this girl of twenty whose own eyes were dry, whose manner was strangely matter-of-fact.

"I'm sorry, Miss Izzard, but I haven't yet got over the shock. I didn't expect you to come so soon."

"Have you heard from Michael himself?"

"Yes, but only one of those printed postcards. A letter is following, it said."

"Is he wounded badly?"

"The Red Cross people say not. But he's in a German hospital and I cannot believe they will treat him properly."

"I'm sure they will. The Red Cross are there to see that they do."

"I wish I could share your confidence, but we hear such terrible tales sometimes . . ."

"At least he's safe. That's the main thing."

"My son is a prisoner-of-war with the Germans. I find little in that to comfort me."

"But he *is* alive!" Betony said. "He *will* be coming back again, eventually, when it's all over. Surely that must comfort you?"

And she thought of the thousands of men who had died since the great offensive had begun, for, travelling about England as she did, visiting factories, she met grieving women everywhere and had lost count of all those whose menfolk lay dead on the Somme.

Mrs Andrews got up.

"I'm glad you're taking the news so calmly. I was afraid you might be distressed. I expect you young women are getting quite hardened, which is probably a blessing in its way."

"Is there an address where I can write to Michael?"

"Yes. Of course. I'll give it to you." Mrs Andrews went to her desk. "He'll be very glad to hear from you, I'm sure."

All through summer and on into autumn, fighting continued on the Somme. Pozières. Longueval. Delville

Wood. Morval. Le Transloy. Then, in November, it ground to a halt. A few miles of territory had been gained. 500,000 lives had been lost. The big push had failed. But the Germans, it was said, were demoralized by their own losses. It was bound to tell on them in the end. Meanwhile there was deadlock again; the two opposing armies dug themselves in; and winter advanced upon them both: the worst winter for twenty years.

"D'you think it's as cold as this at home, Woody?"

"Definitely. My missus wrote she was getting chilblains."

"We're practically strangers, my feet and me, not to mention other members."

"Anyone here called Winterbottom?"

"Hey, Toss, remember how hot it was at Monkey Britannia? I could almost wish myself back there now. Or Devil's Wood, say, when the trees was burning. I'd sooner've been burnt like poor old Glover and Verning and Kyte than froze to death by bloody inches."

"How can you talk like that?" asked Costrell, one of a new draft out from England. "As though it was all a huge joke?"

"It *is* a huge joke," said Danson. "A killing joke for some, it's true, and has a lot of the rest in stitches. But you new chaps don't understand."

Costrell was silent. He thought them callous, ghoulish, disgusting. He could never share their attitude. He was always aware of the frozen corpses lying out in no-man's-land, many of them visible from the front trenches, some quite close to the picket wire, only a few short yards away. And when Danson said, as he often did, "D'you reckon old Bill could do with a blanket?" or, "I could swear John Willie has turned hisself over since this morning," Costrell could not help shuddering.

"It's all right, son," Bob Newers said to him. "*They're* all right, the ones out there. *They* don't feel the bleeding cold, or hear the ruddy shells come over, or get told off for san fatigues. They're better off and they bloody well know it."

"Did you notice that subaltern smelling of scent?" said Pecker Danson.

"Poor sod," said Dave Rush. "He's probably plastered with anti-louse cream."

"Get away!" said Privitt, looking up from the letter he was writing. "Do officers have chats, then, the same as us?"

"Not the same, no. The chats they got is bigger and better, with pips on their shoulders and Sam Browne belts."

"What about Fritz? Has he got 'em too?"

"It's him that flaming well sends 'em over. He fires them in canisters, same as gas. It's the Kaiser's most successful weapon."

Privitt, going back to his letter, wrote for a moment or two in silence. He was having a bit of fun with the censor. He looked up again to read what he had written so far.

" 'Dear Brother Humphrey, Last Saturday night I slept with three French girls and their mother. The mother was best though not as good as the Friday before when I spent the night in a high-class establishment kept by a Chinese lady who used to run a laundry in Solihull.' There! That'll make 'em open their peepers! When the major reads that he'll be after me to know the address."

"It isn't true, is it, Privy?"

"Hah! Get away! All I've ever slept with is a woolly rabbit."

A shell came over and exploded, crump, behind the parados. The men ducked low, and a shower of hard-frozen clods fell upon them, bouncing off their steel helmets. Privitt sat up again, wiping the debris from his notepad.

"The way things are here, I shan't get much chance to graduate, neither!"

"The Lord be thanked for tin bowlers," said Pecker Danson, adjusting his helmet. "Or do I mean Lloyd George?"

"Get a move on there!" shouted Corporal Flinders, coming quickly round the traverse. "Clear that mess away, quick sharp, and no sweeping it under the carpet!"

The men got to work with entrenching tools, shovelling up the fallen earth and tossing it onto the broken parados. They filled new sandbags and repaired the gap.

"Entrenching tool," Costrell muttered. "Why can't they call a spade a spade?"

"I'm thinking of changing my name," said Privitt. "It's no joke, you know, being called Private Privitt, nor Privy neither, seeing the privies here ent all that private."

"Say that faster and you'll find yourself in the next camp concert."

"How many shells has he sent over this morning, Toss?"

"I dunno. I ent been counting."

"Seems quiet to me. Perhaps he's busy doing the crossword." Newers, on the firestep, sniffed the air. "He's got bacon for breakfast again this morning. Smoked, I reckon, the lucky sod."

The two lines at Brisle were certainly very close together, and there was a live-and-let-live policy there, so that rifle and machine-gun fire was only rarely exchanged, and that, as Corporal Flinders said, just as a sort of formality. No-man's-land was scarcely fifty yards across, and when some Tommy sneaked out and raised a notice there, saying *Trespassers Will Be Prosecuted,* the Germans, instead of blasting it to smithereens, merely pelted it with snowballs. Even the officers turned a blind eye to these unwarlike pastimes.

One freezing night, when the men were huddled in a dugout, warming themselves at a small brazier, Dave Rush got out his wheezy old mouth-organ and began playing popular tunes. The men sang, swaying together from side to side, for the singing and the movement kept them warm. And then, half way through *There's a long, long trail a-winding*, Burston, on sentry, suddenly pulled aside the curtain.

"Shut up and listen," he said to them, and when they obeyed him they heard the Germans finishing the song.

"Would you believe it!" Rush exclaimed. "They've got a nerve, pinching our songs. But I'll soon fix *them*. Just listen here."

He raised his mouth-organ to his lips and played the first verse of *God Save The King*. At the end he stopped and listened again, and across the way, in the German trenches, there was utter silence.

"That's foxed 'em!" he said. "They're not singing *that*, the saucy buggers!"

"No more ent we," said Pecker Danson, and, taking the brazier outside, swung it about till the charcoal glowed redly again. "The new moon is up," he said, returning. "Anyone got a franc to turn?"

The Germans now, recovering, were singing *Deutschland Uber Alles*. The Sixth Three Counties retaliated and noisily drowned the rival song.

> "Oh, the Kaiser fell in a box of eggs,
> Parleyvoo!
> The Kaiser fell in a box of eggs,
> Parleyvoo!

The Kaiser fell in a box of eggs
And all the yellow ran down his legs,
Inky-dinky-parleyvoo!"

There came a day when Sergeant Townchurch was with them again, after a month in hospital. No one knew what his illness had been, though rumour gave it as "a bout of German measles and a bad cough". He himself gave no explanation. He preferred to forget he had ever been ill. And he reasserted his authority by reporting Corporal Flinders, acting platoon sergeant during his absence, for letting the discipline run down.

One morning, after a heavy fall of snow, two excited German soldiers, fair-haired boys of about seventeen, climbed onto their parapet and began making a snowman there. Tom and Newers, looking through a loophole, watched with amusement as the snowman grew to lifelike proportions and was given a field-grey comforter and cap and a few bandoliers slung over his shoulder.

Sergeant Townchurch came along. He pushed between Newers, Tom, and Evans, and peered out at the two Germans dressing the snowman on their parapet. He unslung his rifle, put it to his shoulder, and took careful aim through the narrow loophole. Newers moved along the bay and apparently tripped on a loose bit of duckboard. He lurched against Townchurch and the shot went wide. The two German soldiers dived for cover.

"Clumsy swine! You done that on purpose! You got friends over there, have you?"

"Sorry, sarge. It's these loose slats. I'll go and get a hammer and nails before someone breaks his silly neck."

A few minutes later, an arm appeared above the German parapet, and a well-aimed grenade exploded inside the British trench. Then a second and a third.

Costrell and Rush retaliated. Six grenades were returned for three. The sector quietened down again. But Burston and Trigg had each lost a hand and Corporal Flinders had been blinded; and Dick Costrell, hearing this news, would have gone for Townchurch with a pick-axe if Tom and Newers had not restrained him.

Quite soon afterwards, the silence in the enemy lines became uncanny. Patrols going out after dark found the trenches deserted. The Germans had withdrawn, noiselessly, to the strongly fortified Hindenburg Line, ten miles or so behind their old trenches.

"Why not to Berlin while they was at it?" said Dave Rush.

"The Hindenburg Line," said Bob Newers. "Is that part of the Great Western?"

"That's right," said Danson. "Paddington, Oxford, Cardiff Docks, and all stations to Haverfordwest."

"If Jerry's gone we can maybe go home – I don't think!" said Dick Costrell.

Two days later they were relieved by the North Warwicks and went into billets at Doudelanville. When they returned to the line again, it was to take over newly dug trenches in the Vermand area.

The weather continued bitterly cold. Men who stood still for a few seconds found themselves frozen to the boards. They could scarcely bear the touch of their rifles, so cold was the metal in their hands, and they fired off round after round at nothing, to warm the barrels and prevent the bolts from freezing up.

But worse even than the cold was when the thaw came, and they lived always in a world of slush, wet through, waking or sleeping. A man named Thompson complained of trouble with his feet. They were badly swollen and had gone numb. He could not get his boots off to rub in the oil that might have brought him some relief.

"Move about a bit more!" Townchurch said. "Of course you'll get trench feet if you never shift yourself, idle bastard!"

Three days later, when their spell in the forward area ended, Thompson was quite unable to stand. He had to be carried out of the line, into the rest camp three miles behind, and there he went for a medical.

His boots were cut away and the feet were revealed, swollen and shapeless, the colour of raw meat putrefying, with the woollen socks darkly embedded, making a pattern in the rotten flesh. Thompson, watching, said not a word. He merely swallowed, making a noise. Then he looked away, into the distance, whistling tunelessly between his teeth.

The doctor took Newers on one side. He said Thompson would probably lose both feet.

"Why wasn't he sent before?"

"Sergeant Townchurch thought he was swinging the lead."

"I must have a word with your Sergeant Townchurch."

But the doctors at Vraignes were busy men. They worked a twenty-hour day. And when the battalion returned to the line, at Gricourt this time, Townchurch went on as he always had done.

"Evans! Maddox! Newers! Rush! I want you in a raiding party. The colonel has asked for a couple of Boche prisoners. It's up to us to try and oblige him."

"Why always Evans?" Newers asked.

"Why always *me*?" Townchurch retorted.

Townchurch himself was without fear. Rush said he meant to get a decoration. He had more than once been mentioned in dispatches, and was held in some regard by

the C.O. Townchurch knew it. It was only his due. He
worked hard and he had courage. He could do great
things if only he were given the chance, and he told his
fellow N.C.O.'s that he meant to make the Army his
career. He wouldn't go back to being coachman at
Capleton Castle. The gentry would never wipe their boots
on him again. He was somebody now and his great ambition was to gain a commission in the field.

There was hard fighting again that spring. The British
were following up the German withdrawal. They were
pushing on towards St Quentin. The bombardment was
heavy on both sides.

In the Gricourt sector, shells were falling with great
accuracy, aligned exactly with the front line trenches for
a length of fifty yards or so, reducing the earthworks to a
mass of debris. The noise of the British guns answering
was overwhelming. It was like living between volcanoes.
And under the storm, human nerves were stretched and
broken, human minds were dislocated.

Tom, in a hole scooped out of the trench-side, felt the
earth would never stop shaking. He felt it would open
and swallow him up. Opposite him was a man named
Lambert, who crouched on the firestep with terrible
tremors running through him, and who plucked with his
fingers at his lower lip till blood splashed down onto his
tunic.

Suddenly Lambert sprang to his feet and hauled himself over the parapet. Tom tried to catch him but was too
late. Lambert was already through the wire, running
towards the enemy, lobbing imaginary grenades as he
went.

"Bloody guns!" he shrieked. "I'll soon shut you up! I'll
shut you up once and for all!"

Tom was following, running like the wind, when

Lambert fell dead, a sniper's bullet through his forehead. Tom veered and doubled back. He leapt head first towards the trench and rolled over into safety. His left foot felt as though he had hit it with a heavy hammer. A bullet had taken the heel off his boot.

Sometimes, during a period out of the line, housed in a barn or ruined cowshed, a man might throw himself down in the straw and sleep for ten or twelve hours at a stretch. He slept through anything. The world could end for all he cared. The last trump could sound and he'd never hear it.

But in a day or two he would revive. Hot food eaten in safety; hot tea made with clean water; time to sit and smoke a cigarette; and perhaps after all the end of the world had better not come yet. A wash and a shave could make a new man of one who had thought himself played out. There were things to do. Pleasant things. And if he were lucky he could stroll in places where grass still grew and leaves were opening on the trees; where the air still smelt wholesome; and where, from fields of green corn, larks flew up and hung singing in the blue sky.

"It's funny," Tom said, "how many things is just the same as they are at home."

On the farm where they were billeted, there was an orchard of apple trees, and the blossoms were just beginning to open. Tom sat on the ground and watched the swallows building in the eaves of the ruined farmhouse. Some chickens were pecking about in the grass, and a little way off, sitting on a hencoop, a solemn-faced girl of seven or eight was keeping guard over them.

The house was no more than a broken husk, but the elderly farmer lived there still, with his family of women-folk and small children. The younger men were away fighting. The old man was up on the roof, nailing canvas over the beams, a short clay pipe between his teeth, a straw hat on the back of his head. The women were working in the fields. One was ploughing with a team of cows.

Tom got up and walked towards the child on the hen-coop. She looked at him with frowning eyes.

"You needn't worry. I shan't steal your hens."

"Comment?"

"Chickens," he said, and pointed to them. "I shan't steal them. Nor the eggs neither."

"Comment?"

"I was watching the swallows, that's all, and looking at the blossoms on the trees. I reckon you'll have a nice crop of apples, so long as there ent no nasty late frosts."

The child said nothing. She did not understand him. She sat with her hands tucked into her apron and frowned at him harder than ever.

"Look at this here," he said to her, and took a snapshot from his pocket. It had come with a letter from Betony and it showed her mother in the orchard at Cobbs, a straw beeskep between her hands, about to take a cast of bees that were swarming on the trunk of an apple tree. "You know what those are, I'll be bound. I see you got stalls of your own up yonder. This is in England. Blighty. *You* know. See the blossom on the trees there? Just the same as you got here."

The child took the picture and looked at it for a long time. She handed it back and her hands disappeared in her apron again.

"C'est la ruche," she murmured, "pour les abeilles."

"Ah. Well. Like I say, that picture was took in England."

Tom walked on. Newers and Danson were coming towards him. So was Evans. They were stopping to smell the apple blossom.

"Hello, Toss, been fraternizing?"

"I was trying to tell her I wasn't after her eggs and chickens."

"*We'd* be after 'em fast enough if it warnt for her grandpa. The old devil keeps a shotgun."

"I wish I could talk to the people here. It don't seem right, not to be able to talk to them."

"What's that to you, Toss? You don't hardly talk much even to us. You was always a silent sort of bastard."

"I talk when I think of something to say."

"Ah, Tuesdays and Fridays usually, ent it?"

"Take no notice of Pecker," said Newers. "He just lost his pay in a game of poker."

Tom had picked up a rounded chump of sweet-chestnut wood, roughly the size of his own fist, and had carved the little girl's likeness from it. Whenever he had a moment to spare he worked away at it, shaping the neatly rounded head, set so gracefully on the fine neck, and perfecting the features from memory.

The battalion was under notice to move. The men were mustering outside the village. Tom walked out to the old farmhouse and met the child driving cows up the lane. He took the carved wooden head from his pocket and gave it to her.

"For you," he said. "A souvenir. I done it myself, see, with this here knife. I hope you like it."

The child looked at the carved head, then at Tom. Her face remained blank. She said nothing.

"Well!" he said. "I've got to go or I'll land in trouble. We're moving in a little while."

He turned and hurried back towards the village, his boots thudding in the dust of the roadway. When he got to the bend and glanced back, she was still standing, a tiny figure, the carved head clutched against her chest.

At ten o'clock that morning, the whole of the battalion was assembled outside the village, fully accoutred and ready to move. The day was a warm one and the air smelt sweetly of trampled grass. The men sat about on the roadside verges, smoking and talking, awaiting orders. Newers and Danson were throwing dice. Tom was adjusting Evans's pack.

"Hey, Toss!" said Newers, nudging him. "Ent these the people from the farm?"

An old man and a small girl were coming slowly along the road, scanning the crowds of waiting soldiers. The old man had very white hair and black eyebrows. He wore a blue cap and smoked a pipe. The child wore a pinafore striped white and brown. They came along the road hand in hand, and one or two soldiers called out to them, making jokes in broken French. Suddenly they came to a halt. The child was pointing a finger at Tom.

The old man nodded, puffing at his pipe. He took something from his pocket and gave it to the child. She in turn gave it to Tom. It was a wooden crucifix, six inches long and four wide, with Christ carved very plainly and simply: the sort of crucifix he had seen so often lately, hanging on the walls of ruined houses throughout the district.

"It is for you," the old man said, in careful English, "to keep you safe from harm in battle."

"Laws," Tom said. "You shouldn't have walked out all this way – "

"The little one wanted so much to find you. It was important. *Very.* Yes. You are her friend and make her a present. She will keep it always, and remember you. Me too. We will remember."

"Ah," Tom said, and rose awkwardly from his knees,

aware of the men listening all round him. "Thank you. Merci." His hand rested briefly on the child's head.

"Bonne chance," the old man said. "God be with you, and with your comrades."

He and the child went back hand in hand. They were soon lost to sight, for the soldiers were moving now, thronging the road. Tom stood looking at the crucifix, turning it over in his hands, feeling the smooth-worn corners and edges, and the smooth grain. It was carved from boxwood and felt very old.

Sergeant Townchurch came along, shouting orders. He saw the crucifix in Tom's hands.

"What the hell's this? You aren't a bloody Catholic, are you, Maddox?"

"No, somebody gave it to me," Tom said.

"Some tart, I suppose," Townchurch said, and passed on, shouting his orders. "On your feet, all you men! What d'you think this is, a jamboree?"

So the Sixth Battalion marched away, leaving the village of Nobris behind them. Larks sang overhead and sparrows whirred from the roadside hedges. The sun was in the soldiers' eyes. They were marching again to the battle area.

"I *was* married," Evans said, "but my wife died ten years ago, and our baby with her."

"How long was you married?" Danson asked.

"Two years, that's all."

"Ent you got no family at all?"

"None that I know of," Evans said. "There's no one to miss me when I'm gone. That's one good thing."

"Gone?" said Braid. "Why, where're you off to, Taff? Monte Carlo?"

Evans gave a little smile.

"I shan't come through this war alive."

"Oh yes you will," Newers said. "I bet you a pound."

"You got a foreboding, Taff?" asked Dave Rush. "You're all the same, you bloody Welshmen. – All as superstitious as hell."

"You was exempt, being a miner," said Dick Costrell. "Why didn't you stop down the pit?"

Evans looked up at the blue sky.

"I wanted to come up out of the darkness."

"You warnt very clever, choosing your moment."

"It's being afraid all the time, you see. I thought I'd left all that down the pit. I thought, out here, I should either be killed or not killed. I hadn't bargained for *living* with death as though it was a presence in itself. A presence lying in wait everywhere, preying on the minds of men."

"It's time you put in for a spot of home leave."

"I have," Evans said. "But somehow I don't think I'll ever get it. I've got this feeling all the time, that something is about to give."

"We all get that feeling," Danson said. "It means another bloody button going!"

Evans laughed along with the rest. He leant across and punched Danson's shoulder. But the long period out of the line had not built him up as it had the others. He was white-faced and worn, and his hands, when he lit a cigarette, shook like those of a very old man.

There was heavy shelling in the Seiglon sector. The village was soon a heap of rubble. Both the front line trenches and the reserve were blasted in repeatedly, for the enemy had them registered "right to the fraction" a Corporal Stevens said to Braid. One morning, early, a shell fell directly on a forward observation post, and afterwards there was silence there. The post had been manned by Lieutenant Bullock and two men, Bremner and Evans.

Tom and Newers crawled across, under fire from a machine-gun. They reached the post and began to dig. The officer and Bremner were both dead, but Evans, buried under four feet of earth, was still alive when they dug him out. His mouth and throat were full of earth; they had to scoop it out with their fingers; it was almost an hour before his lungs really filled with air.

They thought he would die if he didn't have prompt medical attention and so they decided to run for it, although it was now broad daylight. They lifted him up and started off across no-man's-land. They had about two hundred yards to travel. The German machine-gun opened fire and the bullets perforated the ground behind them. A rifle whipcracked three times. Then, abruptly, the firing stopped. The Germans were letting them cross in safety.

Evans went to the medical post at Rilloy-sus-Coll. Tho doctor pronounced him a lucky man and sent him back to duty again. A fallen rider should always remount at once, he said, and a shell-shock case should face the barrage. Sergeant Townchurch was of the same mind. He carried the principle one stage further. And only forty-two hours later he named Evans for a wiring-party.

"You can't take Evans," said Corporal Stevens. "He's a sick man. He shouldn't be in the line at all."

"All that twitching and jerking, you mean? He's putting that on. He's swinging the lead like he always has done."

"That man was buried alive in the O.P. on Monday. Newers and Maddox had to dig him out."

"So what? It's only when he's buried *dead* that he'll be excused his whack of duty. Till then he takes his turn."

So Evans went with the wiring-party, fifty yards out into

no-man's-land, carrying a coil of new barbed wire. There were ten men including Townchurch and during the night they were fired on by an enemy patrol. The party returned with two men wounded. Townchurch reported another missing. The missing man was Private Evans.

"Was he hit?" asked Captain Edman.

"Not him!" said Townchurch. "He's bloody well skipped it, that's what he's done. I always said he was a slacker."

Some days later, Evans was discovered sitting in the church at Basseroche, and was brought back under arrest. He went before a court martial, charged with desertion. Sergeant Townchurch gave evidence against him. So did the fox-hunting doctor from Rilloy, who stated that Evans was in good health, physically and mentally. Certainly Evans seemed calm enough now. No longer twitching. Only tired. He was found guilty and sentenced to death.

The battalion moved into camp at Berigny. The weather was broken. There were thunderstorms. The men of Number Three Platoon were digging drains to carry away the surface water. Sergeant Townchurch sought them out. He wanted Tom.

"Maddox!" he shouted. "Follow me!" And, as soon as they were out of earshot: "I got a job lined up for you. One of twelve for a firing party. Little matter of an execution, first thing tomorrow morning."

"I won't do it," Tom said.

"Not all the guns're loaded live. You might get a blank."

"It makes no difference. I still won't do it."

"You don't seem to realize – this is an order. D'you know what'll happen if you refuse?"

"I don't care a sod. You've got no right to pick men out from the same platoon. You won't get none of the others to do it neither."

"Somebody's got to do these things. I reckon it's better, keeping it in the family as you might say."

"Let them who sentenced him do the shooting. I came out to kill Germans, not to kill my own mates. Ah, and I sometimes wonder why the hell I should kill *them*, seeing they're people the same as us."

"Maybe you'd like to join up with them? There's sure to be lots like you in their lines. You'd find yourself at home with Fritz. *Don't turn away when I'm talking to you!* Where the hell do you think you're going?"

"I'm going back to my platoon."

"Oh no you're not! I'm putting you under arrest, Maddox, and tomorrow you'll find yourself up on a charge. It's easy enough to disobey orders. We'll see if you like the consequences."

Tom was taken to the edge of the village and locked in a cowshed for the night, next to stables occupied by Evans. There was only a wooden wall between, and Evans heard Tom arrive.

"Who's in by there? Someone I know?"

"It's me," Tom said. "Toss Maddox."

"What you been crimed for, Toss, man?"

"I was late on parade," Tom said. "Third time this week, according to the corporal."

"They're going to shoot me in the morning. Did you know that, Toss? Did you hear what happened?"

"Yes. We heard. The chaps was wanting to come and see you but somebody said you'd asked them not to."

"I'd just as soon be left alone. They weren't offended, were they, Toss? It's just that I need to have time to think."

"They warnt offended," Tom said.

"It's nice and quiet here, considering. I can hear a blackbird singing somewhere."

"You got a window in there, Taff?"

"There's a small round window above the door. I can see the sky, anyway. Looks like we're in for another storm. It'll get dark early tonight, I'd say, but I've got a candle and matches here."

"You got plenty of cigarettes?"

"Diawl, yes! A tin of fifty. But I was never much of a smoker. Just the odd one now and then."

"Me, too," Tom said.

When darkness came, Evans struck a match and lit his candle. Tom sat on his bunk in the shed next door and looked at the cracks of light in the wall. A little while later he lit his own candle. Outside the shed, footsteps sounded occasionally, and men's voices. Further away, north of the village, wheels rumbled on the stone-paved roads as the ration-limbers went up to the line, and further off still was the noise of the guns. In a lean-to shed next to the stable, a few chickens rustled on their perches during the night, querking sleepily now and then and changing places with a flutter of wings.

"Toss?" Evans said. "Are you awake?"

"Yes, Taff, I'm awake."

"Are you sitting up with me till the end?"

"Might as well. Company, like. But you don't have to talk if it don't suit you."

"Have you ever been to Wales, Toss?"

"No, never," Tom said.

"There's a little village outside Merthyr with a stream running through it and an old crooked bridge over the stream and silver birch trees growing beside it. The water in the stream is so clear that if it weren't moving over the stones you would never know it was there at all."

"I should like to see that place," Tom said.

"When I go out tomorrow morning, I shall think I'm going to walk by that stream. It's nonsense, I know, – I've never believed in the life everlasting – but that's what I shall be thinking about, and that's what I'll see in my mind's eye. I'll follow the stream till the ground rises. I've done it often and I know exactly where I'll come to. A green hillside and someone waiting."

Just before first light, the stable door was unlocked, and the padre entered. He sat on a stool at the makeshift table and looked at Evans opposite. The condemned man, he thought, looked quite composed.

"Well, Evans?"

"I told them I didn't want a parson."

"I thought you might have changed your mind."

"I have not changed my mind."

"Are you a chapel man, perhaps? I can find the Methodist padre if you want him, you know."

"No, no. I was brought up Church," Evans said. "But I'm nothing now. I'm an unbeliever."

The padre was silent, looking at Evans in the light of the candle. His hand, with the crumpled prayerbook in it, was long and slender, like a woman's. His face was childlike. He was trying hard to understand the condemned man's mind.

"Obviously, then, it is lack of faith that has brought you to this sorry state."

"Go away," Evans said.

But the padre remained, hesitating. He felt it was his duty to try again.

"You call yourself an unbeliever, yet when you were arrested you were found sitting in a village church."

"It was quiet there."

"If you cannot believe in God, can't you at least have faith in your fellow men?"

"I come from South Wales," Evans said. "I have seen where certain men have laid their hands, and the place is left black and smoking ever after. I have seen where other men have laid their hands, and the place is greener than it was before."

"So? What then? It follows that you believe in good and evil."

"They exist together, and will do always."

"You don't believe that good must ultimately win a victory over evil?"

"It is a victory that good exists at all."

"*I could* give you comfort, you know, if only you'd let me."

"I don't need it," Evans said.

The padre went. The two halves of the stable door were closed and bolted. Light came gradually in at the round hole above and Evans douted the flame of his candle. He put the stump into his pocket.

Tom, in the cowshed, sat on his bunk with his knees up and his arms clasped round them. He watched the daylight growing brighter through the slatted window. Outside, in the yard, the hens had been released and a cock was crowing. Someone was working a chaff-cutter. Next door, Evans was making himself tidy.

When the escort came to take him away, Evans stood up and knocked on the wall.

"So long, Toss. Look after yourself. Thanks for sitting up with me."

"So long, Taff."

Tom got up and looked out through the slats of his window. He saw them marching Evans away. In the straw-littered yard an old woman with a black knitted shawl over her head was scattering a panful of grain for the hens. She came to a standstill, crossing herself, as Evans passed by between his guards. Tom craned his neck and looked at the sky, overcast with purple stormclouds, under which the morning light shone out levelly over the earth. He saw three seagulls flying over, silver-white against the dark clouds. From somewhere not very far away came a quick volley of rifle fire. The old woman got down on her knees.

Tom, appearing before the court martial, was charged with refusing to obey an order. He admitted the charge and was found guilty. Townchurch, of course, had been in the wrong. Tom knew it; the officers knew it; but discipline had to be maintained, so no one asked what the order had been.

He was sentenced to five days' Field Punishment Number One. This meant extra fatigues, parading on the hour in full marching order, and confinement in the guardroom. It also meant that every evening of the five-day period he spent two hours tied to the wheel of a gun limber, stretched crossways with his feet off the ground, his wrists and ankles strapped to the spokes. Sergeant Townchurch was there to see that the straps were pulled tight; he was there again later to see Tom released; and every evening, as the straps were removed, he would ask the same question.

"Well, Maddox? Don't you wish you'd obeyed that order?"

Tom never answered the sergeant's question. He tried to pretend the man was not there.

At the end of July, the Sixth Battalion left the Somme and moved north into Flanders, up into the martyred city of Ypres, under bombardment day and night. A group of signallers stood watching as they marched in.

"Welcome to the capital of the salient! – Kindly leave it as you find it!"

"Come to Wipers and be wiped out!"

"Hope you're nifty, catching whizzbangs."

"The barracks is over there on your left, or it was this morning."

"The password is knife. You never get time to say nothing more."

That evening, Tom and Newers explored the city, once a place of proud spires. They gazed at the ruins of the old cathedral, the skeleton of the Cloth Hall.

"Someone's going to have to do some building here when it's all over. I wonder how they'll ever have the heart to begin."

"Will you come back?" Tom asked. "Afterwards, I mean, to see how it looks?"

"It's an idea," Newers said. "How about us two coming together? Ten years after the end of the war, say, on a special trip?"

"Right, it's a deal," Tom said, "so long as we're alive to do it."

"If we're dead we'll come in the spirit. There'll be plenty of ghosts wandering through France and Belgium in the years to come."

Throughout the salient, troops were massing for the new offensive. Every acre of open space was packed with men, horses, guns, equipment. And the enemy, occupying the higher ground north-east of the city, could look down over the bustle below as though looking on a human ant-heap. His observation posts were supreme. His gunners could place their shells as they chose. The bombardment intensified every day.

"Talk about sitting ducks!" Dick Costrell said to Newers. "What the hell are top brass waiting for, for God's sake?"

"They're finishing their game of bowls."

"Another day or two of this and there'll be nothing left of us to attack with."

Costrell spoke bitterly. The waiting was getting on his nerves. Rain had begun falling now. The ground was receiving a thorough soaking.

On the last day of July, as first light came, the British guns redoubled their fire, and all along the salient front the British infantry climbed out of their assembly trenches and, following the creeping barrage, advanced towards the enemy lines. The great new offensive had begun.

The Sixth Battalion was in support. They had orders to push through the line established by the Worcestershires and press on to the next objective. Tanks were coming up to assist. But the ground had been thoroughly soaked with rain and the tanks were either bogged down in the ditches or moved so slowly that they were destroyed by enemy shells.

The Sixth Battalion went into the attack but were beaten back by murderous gunfire. They had to dig in short of their objective. And in the evening came more rain.

They lay out all night in shallow trenches full of water. The rain continued all next day, and the day after.

On the fifth night they were relieved by a sister battalion. They marched along the Menin road and went into camp outside Ypres. They were given dry clothes and hot sweet tea with rum in it. Food when it came was bully beef stew ladled piping hot into mess-tins, but, because of the undiminished shelling, it contained a few unwelcome ingredients.

"What's this?" Newers asked, fishing out a piece of shrapnel and showing it to the sergeant cook. "Iron rations?"

"That's something you leave on the side of your plate."

While they ate, they tried to glean news of how the big attack was going, but nobody seemed to know for sure. They heard only rumours and some of these were bad indeed, like the post corporal's story of how the British guns had pounded a position already captured by British troops. They heard, too, of a whole company of the Third Three Counties lost for eight hours in the darkness up near Pilckem Ridge. And they heard – was it true? – that the Fifth Battalion West Mercia had lost three quarters of its strength in the action outside Rannegsmarck.

"The bloody Somme all over again," Pecker Danson said to Tom, "only bloody worse if anything."

August was always a wet month in Flanders, but August 1917 was the worst known for forty years.

"It's the guns that bring down all this rain," Danson kept saying. "I've noticed it time and time again – get a big bombardment and down it comes!"

They were in trenches near Hooge, soaked to the skin for days on end. There was no sleep because of the shelling. Tempers were short and nerves ragged. Only Newers remained cheerful.

"You should've brought your brolly, Pecker."

"I should've brought my bleedin' canoe. I can see why Fritz is so keen on his submarines. He'll be using them in the trenches soon."

"Listen!" said Newers, a finger to his lips.

"What the hell is it?" Danson asked.

"Darkness falling. Stand-to!"

"I'll bloody well brain you in a minute."

The enemy bombardment, heaviest at dusk, gradually lessened as darkness came. Shells were fewer. More widely spaced. "Fritz is getting ready for bed," Newers would say, as the shelling eased. "He's putting the cat out and leaving a message for the milkman." *Womp. Womp.* Away on the left.

"Two pints," Newers said.

Womp. Womp. Away on the right.

"He's fallen over the milk-bottles."

Womp. – Womp. – Womp. – Womp.

"Now he's going upstairs to his missus. She's lying there listening to his steps on the stairs. She's been warming the bed like a good wife should."

There followed a silence. Newers sucked at his empty pipe.

"I don't like to think what they're doing now."

Womp. Womp. Very close.

"Seems he's fallen out of bed."

"Don't you ever shut up?" Costrell shouted suddenly.

"Sometimes I do," Newers said.

"I'm sick to death of your endless clacking! For God's sake let's have some peace and quiet!"

"All right, keep your hair on," Newers said. "I can take a hint as well as the next man."

Costrell was in a state of nerves. He twitched and trembled all the time. Tom was reminded of Lambert and Evans. He leant across the tiny dugout and offered Costrell a cigarette. Costrell knocked it out of his hand.

"Steady on," Danson murmured.

The next night, wet as ever, Tom and Danson were on sentry. So was Costrell. Tom heard a commotion in the next bay and went along to see what was wrong. Costrell lay stretched out on the duckboards, a rum-jar beside him, and the other sentries were trying in vain to wake him up. "He's dead to the world! Where'n hell did he get that jar?"

"What shall we do?" Rush whispered, and there was panic in his voice. "If Townchurch sees him like this he'll end up the same as poor Taffy Evans."

They raised Costrell and slapped his face, but he remained lifeless in their grasp. Tom ran back to his own bay and called Newers out of the dugout. Newers came, turning his pipe-bowl upside down, and lifted one of Costrell's hands. He put his thumb-nail under Costrell's and pressed down hard into the quick. There was a sudden loud cry. Rush put his hand over Costrell's mouth and Danson rubbed the boy's wrists. They stood him on his feet and ran him quickly to and fro. He was soon sick and began to recover.

"Where'n hell did you get that jar?"

"I dunno. I won it somewhere."

"Can you stand now? Can you walk about?"

"Think so," Costrell muttered.

"You better had!" Danson said. "You know the penalty for being drunk on sentry, don't you?"

"Christ!" Costrell said, and began crying. "I feel so ill!"

"Pull yourself together, lad. Townchurch'll be along in a minute."

"Oh, Christ!" Costrell said, but he stood up straight and took his rifle from Dave Rush.

"If it wasn't for Newers you'd still be out cold," Danson said. "We couldn't do nothing to bring you round."

Costrell's glance slid to Newers.

"Thanks, chum. I'll buy you a drink in 'Pop' on Friday."

"Chew some of this," Newers said, and handed him a plug of tobacco. "It'll maybe soak up the smell of rum."

Newers went back to his own dugout, taking the half-empty rum-jar with him. A few minutes later, Townchurch came by with the platoon officer, Mr Coleby. All the sentries were up on the firestep. Everything was as it should be.

The low-lying land north of Ypres had long ago been reclaimed from the sea; it was kept drained by a series of dykes; but these dykes had been broken down by the British bombardment and the waters, overflowing, were turning the area back to swamp. Over this swamp the Allied forces were attempting to advance, against the Germans firmly entrenched on the ground above.

"Talk about Weston-super-bloody-Mare!" said Dave Rush, dragging one leg from the mire as he spoke. "It's only sheer will-power that's keeping my boots on my bloody feet."

"The continong is not all it's cracked up to be," said Pecker Danson. "I'll stick to Skegness in future."

"I'll stick to everything after this!"

Newers had been caught in a shell-blast that had bowled him over into the mud, yet he still had his empty pipe in his mouth and was blowing through it to clear out the muck.

"A mud-pack is said to be good for the complexion. We'll come out looking like the Oxo Boy. There's ladies in London who spend a mint of money to get what we're getting here for nothing."

"I bet their mud-packs don't smell like this."

"You mustn't mind that – it's only the smell of rotting bodies."

"Yes, my pal Jim Baker's buried here, somewhere. He was out in 1915."

"Well, we won't stop and look for him now, Pecker. We got an appointment with Fritz in the morning."

It was towards the end of August, a night of rain and intense darkness, and they were moving up to the line, feeling their way yard by yard into the forward assembly trenches, ready for the engagement next day.

"What we need," said Dave Rush, "is an electric torch with a black light."

"No smoking!" came the order, passed along from man to man.

"I ent ready for this engagement," Pecker Danson said to Tom. "I haven't bought the bleeding ring."

"No talking from now on!" shouted the corporal, just behind them.

The columns of men filed forward very slowly, slock-slock, through the mud. It was still raining. The assembly trenches were all flooded. The water reached above their knees.

Dawn, when it came, showed itself first in the flood-water lying out in front. No-man's-land was a waste of puddles and the light in the water seemed paler, brighter, than the light in the heavily clouded sky. Rain was falling steadily, a grey curtain reluctantly letting the daylight through, to reveal the desolation on the ground. Ruined field-guns lay lopsided in the mud and smashed tanks were bogged to the turrets. One great tank had lost its tracks. Dead men and horses lay everywhere, sunk in black slime, unrecognizable except that in places, here and there, a hand or a hoof stuck out and pointed to the sky.

"If I get out of this war safely," Dave Rush said to Tom, "I never want to see another dawn as long as I live."

Communications were difficult. They lay out all morning in the rain waiting for orders. At two o'clock the British guns opened up an intense fire. The attacking platoons crawled from their trenches and began pushing forward through the mud, following the barrage as it moved slowly up the slope.

Weighed down as they were with battle equipment, moving through mud which in places reached to the very thighs, their progress was dreadfully, painfully slow.

"It's all right for Jerry," Danson said. "He's got the best place up there on that ridge."

"Then you know what to do – take it from him!" said the young lieutenant commanding the platoon, and pushed forward, his rifle held high.

"Easy, ent it?" Danson said, as Newers drew alongside. "Nothing to it, if Jerry'll just wait while I get my bleeding feet up, out of this bleeding rotten muck."

Townchurch, ahead, had stepped up onto a slab of concrete and was urging the men to make more effort.

"Come on, you grubs! Shift yourselves and get a move on! I want some progress bloody forward! I want my platoon up there in front!"

"We know what *you* want!" Costrell shouted, hardly aware of what he was saying.

"Yes, Costrell, what do I want?"

Costrell was struggling in the mud. Townchurch splashed across to him and helped him on with a shove from behind. Costrell fell forward onto his face.

"I said get a move on!" Townchurch bellowed. "I said to shift yourselves and show some spunk! You'll get on forward up that slope if I have to push you all the way!"

Costrell floundered onto his knees, choking and crying, trying to wipe the mud from his rifle.

"Just look! Just look! How the hell can I use that? I can't go on without a rifle! What the hell am I going to do?"

"You've got your bayonet!" Townchurch said. "If you ever get close enough to use it! Now get on or I'll bloody well put you on a charge!"

Tom and Newers helped Costrell up.

"Keep with us," Newers said, "and if one of us falls, grab his rifle."

Townchurch was now splashing forward to another group stuck in the mire.

"Shift yourselves, can't you? I want you up there behind that smoke! If I can move, so can you!"

The barrage, creeping forward, was gradually leaving them behind. They could not keep pace with it, slow as it was, and now, as the smoke around them drifted away, there was nothing to hide them from the enemy. They were out in the open, in a sea of mud, though the enemy lines were still some way off, under the smoke and the driving rain.

"Which way? Which way?" a man was screaming, off his head. "I don't even know where the Germans are!"

"Nor me neither," Newers said. "I'm following them two up there." He pointed to Townchurch and the subaltern, moving twenty yards ahead. "Let's hope *they* know where we're going!"

Tom, sharp-eared, heard an order shouted in German, somewhere on the right, not far away. A Maxim opened fire from there, followed by another on the left, and the men in front went down like ninepins. A few that were left crept into shell-holes. Others, stuck, unable to move, burrowed into the mud where they were. Tom found himself treading on a man's shoulders.

The Germans had set up machine-gun posts in shelters of sandbags out in the open, and now the barrage had moved over, they came into action everywhere. The attacking platoons were in an ambush, receiving fire on both flanks, and the second wave went down like the first. D Company had suffered badly: all its officers had fallen and the remnants, pushing on, followed a subaltern of B Company, who had lost touch with his own men. He was calling to them and waving them on when a Maxim opened fire from the main German line, now visible a hundred yards off. He fell, wounded, and lay on his elbows watching men falling all round him.

"It's no good!" he shouted, as the stragglers reached him. "Save yourselves! We can't get through!"

But Sergeant Townchurch was urging them on.

"Don't listen to him, he's raving!" he said. "Of course we'll get through! Follow me!"

Then his arms flew up and he toppled over into the mud, and everywhere behind him men took cover in the broken ground.

Fighting continued all day: fierce little battles conducted from shell-holes; and all the enemy machine-gun posts were at length destroyed. But the main attack was not renewed. Those men who were left were too few and too tired; there was no hope of reinforcements; and early darkness put an end to the day. Orders came to dig in. Rain fell harder than ever.

All next day, stretcher-parties were out from both sides, retrieving their wounded. The big guns exchanged some token fire, but all along the forward area an unofficial truce was observed, and the bearers moved across the open, searching the shell-holes. Enemy losses had not been great, and sometimes the German stretcher-bearers, having rescued British wounded, would set them down near the British lines.

Tom and Newers, with Braid and Costrell, worked on until after darkfall. They moved about the battalion aid post, doing what they could to help the wounded until the doctors could get to them. Townchurch lay groaning out in the open. He was asking for water. Costrell passed him many times, ignoring him, refusing to help him. Pecker Danson did the same. Tom fetched water and took it to him. He held the bottle while Townchurch drank. The man was in great agony. His face was contorted, his eyes glazed. He looked at Tom with slowly dawning recognition.

"Currying favour?" he whispered hoarsely. "You're wasting your time – I'm a dead man."

Late that night, Tom was sitting with Newers and Danson, drinking tea from a field-kitchen before going off to get some sleep. A young doctor came out to them.

"Your Sergeant Townchurch has just died."

"I'm not surprised," Danson said. "He was pretty far gone."

"He was saying some rather strange things."

"He was always like that, sir, even when he was in the pink."

"He wasn't delirious," the doctor said. "He knew what he was saying and he claimed he'd been shot from close behind."

"Well, we had Jerry on both our flanks, sir, and if the sergeant was turning round – "

"The hole in his body was definitely made by an

English bullet. I can guarantee that."

"Would you believe it!" Newers said. "He must've got in somebody's way. One of the accidents of war, sir. I've seen 'em often in the past year."

"I'll have to make a report of the matter. I can't just let it go at that."

"No, sir. Of course not, sir. Very sad thing to happen, sir."

The doctor looked at them each in turn, and went away without further comment. Newers took a drink of tea, breathing heavily into his mug. He was sitting between Tom and Danson.

"It wasn't me, chums, if that's what you're thinking."

"Nor me," Danson said.

"Nor me neither," Tom said.

"Accident of war, that's what it was. Lots of chaps've copped it that way, not all so deserving as Townchurch, of course, but there you are. Pity he never got his V.C."

Three months later, on a foggy night late in November, Tom and Newers, with Danson and Rush, were in an estaminet in Poperinghe.

It was much patronized by British and Colonial troops and the wall was covered with their scribblings. "Lost, stolen, or strayed: one Russian steamroller," someone had written, and another: "On August tenth, at the new St Wipers nursing home, to the B.E.F., 12 baby elephants, all doing well." There were other jokes, too, less pure, that Danson said made him blush.

Newers ordered four glasses of wine. Neither he nor the others would touch Belgian beer. They had drunk better stuff from shell-holes, they said.

"Have you seen the Americans yet?"

"I dunno. What colour are they?"

"Much the same as Canadians, really, but maybe more so," Danson said.

"Watch it, Limey!" a Canadian said from the next table.

"Sure, sure!" Danson answered, through his nose. "Whaddya know! Ontario!"

"Here, Toss," said Dave Rush. "There's two chaps looking in at the window, making ugly mugs at you. I reckon they're trying to get your goat."

Tom turned in his chair and saw two faces pressed against the glass.

"It's William and Roger! My foster-brothers! Glory be, can you beat that?"

He went to the door and yanked it open. William and Roger sauntered in.

"Catched you, ent we, drinking as usual?"

"We heard your outfit was up here somewhere so we took a chance of tracking you down."

"Ent that a masterpiece?" Tom said. He could not get over it even now. "Come over and meet my mates."

The two Izzard boys were now big men. Even Roger had grown thickset. But they were as fresh-faced and snub-nosed as ever, bright fair hair brushed sleekly down, eyes very blue under colourless eyebrows, wide awake, missing nothing. William was now a bombardier but pretended to think it nothing much when Tom, amazed, touched the stripes on his sleeve.

"Picked 'em up cheap," he said, shrugging, "from a chap that didn't need 'em no more."

"You artillery chaps is full of swank," said Danson, rising to shake hands. "So you're Bet's brothers? Fancy that."

"You know my sister?" William said.

"We know her from snapshots," Newers said. "And her letters, of course, that she writes to Toss. She writes a good letter, your sister Bet. We always like it when Toss hears from her."

The six of them sat at a small table. William ordered a bottle of wine. It was brought to them by a fierce old woman with frizzled hair who glared at them, scowling, as she set the bottle on the table.

"Six francs," she said, one hand held out to William.

"Get away!" said Newers. "We've never paid more'n five before, and that's five too many, you old bundle, you!"

"Six francs," she said, and tapped her palm with an impatient finger.

"Don't pay it, mate," Pecker Danson said to William. "She's trying it on 'cos she thinks it's a party."

"Five francs," William said, and put the money on the table.

"Non-non-non-non! Six francs! I insist! I insist!"

"Five!" William said. "And bring two more glasses if you please. You don't expect us to drink from the bottle?"

"Six! Six! I must insist!"

"Bring two glasses, please, madame, and not so much of your ruddy nonsense."

"Toot sweet," Newers said, "and the tooter the sweeter."

"Non-non-non-non! Six francs. I insist! I insist!"

The argument was attracting attention. The Canadians were laying bets on the outcome, and a group of Gloucesters were shouting abuse at the old woman. She had grown purple in the face and was threatening to remove the bottle when a younger woman appeared on the scene. She came to the table, placed two glasses in front of William, and picked up the five francs.

"Drink up, Tommees, and kill a few Boches for me tomorrow."

"I'd sooner get rid of your old woman."

"Don't mind the old one. She is greedy for money to

ransom her son. He is a prisoner with the Boches. She thinks she'll be able to buy his freedom."

"Tell her from me it'll soon be over."

"Never! Never!" the old woman said, and there were tears in her eyes. "I do not believe it will ever end."

"That's cheerful, that is! Are there more like her around these parts?"

William poured out the wine and raised his glass to the old woman.

"Viva la victoree!" he said. "Viva the happy smiling faces!"

The old woman went, still grumbling, led away by the young girl. William and Roger grinned at Tom.

"If mother and dad could see us now!"

"How come you're here?" Tom asked. "I thought you was down in the south some place."

"That's right. Lafitte. But we had to come up to Armchairs on a course and we thought we'd take the long way back."

"How're things with you, Tom?" Roger asked.

"All right," Tom said, and could think of nothing more to say.

"Your lot's been copping it again lately, I heard. Have you been in the new push?"

"We was at Steenbeek," Tom said.

"And the Menin road," said Pecker Danson.

"And Passchendaele," said Dave Rush.

"What was it like?" Roger asked. "Was it as bad as people say?"

"People!" said Danson. "What people?"

He and Newers drank their wine.

"I'm going on leave directly," Tom said. "Any message for them at home?"

"Wish them all the best, Tom, and say you found us in

the pink. Rog and me ent going on leave. Not till we've finished this bloody war. It'd mean splitting up if we went on leave and I promised mother we'd stick like glue."

"The truth is," Roger said, "they can't fight the war without us gunners."

"Why, are you the only two they've got?" Newers asked, lighting his pipe. "No wonder it's quiet in Picardy lately."

"We're two of the best, that's all."

"You're all the same, you artillery blokes," said Pecker Danson, "but seeing how I'm drinking your vin I can't hardly tell you what that is."

When the party left the estaminet, they met two girls just coming in.

"You buy drinks for us, yes, Tommee? Plentee monee! Buy café rhum?"

"Après la guerre!" William said, walking on, and then, to Tom: "If mother and dad could see us now!"

Outside the town the group split up, William and Roger going to their train, Tom and the others going to scrounge a lift back to camp. Their voices echoed across the street.

"So long, Bill! So long, Rog! We'll be thinking of you when we hear them guns of yours lousing off down there at Lafitte."

"So long!" Tom said, watching the two boys walking away. "All the best!"

"So long!" they said. "Be seeing you, Tom."

Home for ten days' leave at Cobbs, Tom strolled about the carpenter's shop, kicking the shavings that littered the floor and sniffing the old familiar smells of timber, putty, paint and glue. The carpenters watched him with some curiosity.

"Well, young Tom? I suppose you find it pretty tame at

home here now? Quiet, like? Nothing much happening in the old place?"

"Ah. Quiet. Just like always, or very nearly."

"Have you been having a good time? Making the most of things? Getting a bit of experience, eh?"

"A good time?" Tom said.

"Well, you're only young once, that's what I say, and you might never get the chance again."

"The mademoiselles, that's what Sam means," said Bob Green.

"Oh, them!" Tom said, and stooped to pick up a knot of wood. "They're just after your money, that's all."

"Well," said Sam, "you don't expect to get it for nothing?"

"Get what?" Tom said, and went a dark red as their laughter sounded along the workshop.

"Laws, Tom, you ent as innocent as all that?"

"A chap like you, turned twenty, and a soldier in the Army, too! Don't they teach you nothing at all?"

"You ent your father's son, boy, if you're as green as all that."

"Tom is keeping hisself nice for Tilly Preston. *She's* the mademoiselle for him. Ent that so, Tom?"

Tom merely shrugged and walked away.

In the big kitchen, Beth Izzard sat at the table with writing-pad, pen, and a bottle of ink set out before her. Her husband, Jesse, stood behind her, smoking his pipe. Opposite her, a mug of tea in mittened hands, sat Mrs Clementina Rainbow, a handsome old gipsy from Puppet Hill, where the gipsies had always camped in winter ever since never, people said.

Mrs Rainbow could not read or write. She had therefore come to Cobbs for help. Her son, Alexander, was in the Army, serving somewhere on the western front, and a letter must be sent without delay to his commanding officer, requesting that Alexander be sent home at once, for his poor ma and da had received an enormous order for pegs and Alexander's help was needed.

Beth sat, somewhat self-conscious, aware of her husband standing behind her and the boy Tom sitting quiet in the chimney corner.

"My daughter Betony's the scholar by rights. If you wait till this evening, Mrs Rainbow, she will write your letter for you."

"You can do it, Mrs Izzard. I seen you writing oftentimes. You done that notice for Georgie's waggon."

"Very well," Beth said, and took up her pen. "What shall I say?"

"Well, about the pegs, Mrs Izzard, please. An immendous great order we've had, tell him, and can't manage without Alexander."

"They won't send him home," Jesse said, "just to make pegs, Mrs Rainbow."

"You think not, Mr Izzard?"

"I'm certain of it, Mrs Rainbow."

"Then put in we've had an order for baskets as well, Mrs Izzard, and must have'm ready in time for Christmas."

"Anything else, Mrs Rainbow?"

"Tell the gentleman-colonel, please, that I seen things last night in the smoke of the fire that mean he's coming into money."

Beth, straight-faced, finished the letter and wrote Mrs Rainbow's name at the bottom. She put it in an envelope and wrote the address.

"Silly fella!" the gipsy said. "Going to the Army and 'listing like that. He'll never be the same again, Mrs Izzard, getting mixed up in this old war."

"No one'll be quite the same, Mrs Rainbow."

When the gipsy had gone, Beth looked up and met Tom's eye.

"I'd like to be there," he said, smiling, "when Alexander's colonel gets that letter."

"How was William and Roger?" asked Jesse. "Was they keeping hale and hearty?" He had asked the question a dozen times.

"They was fine," Tom said. "They've growed pretty big, the pair of them. William is nearly as big as a house."

"Ah, well, he's a bombardier now, remember."

William and Roger had had their photograph taken in Rouen and had sent it home. Then, in December, an old soldier had come through Huntlip, walking on crutches, having lost his left leg in the fighting at Mons in 1914. He eked out his pension by painting portraits from photographs of absent soldiers. He travelled about, knocking on doors.

"Husbands, fathers, sons, lovers. – If you've got a photo I'll copy it for you, a proper portrait, done in oils."

Beth had given him the photograph of William and Roger, together with details of their colouring, and he had copied it, true to life. The portrait hung in the front parlour, on the wall above the fireplace, and the two boys looked out on all the family gatherings: sitting side by side, fair hair greased down, faces glowing, keen blue eyes looking straight ahead; proud to be sitting together in khaki, William with his two stripes, both with their buttons polished to perfection.

"You should get your photo took as well," Jesse told Tom, "and we'll get the artist to paint you too."

He thought perhaps Tom might feel left out, because Granna Tewke, always knitting for William and Roger, never knitted anything for Tom.

"Not that you miss much," he whispered once, " 'cos granna's knitting is none too gainly nowadays."

"What's wrong with my knitting?" granna demanded, sitting up and glaring at Jesse. Her sight might be poor, but her hearing was perfect. "What's wrong with my knitting I'd like to know?"

"Why, that glove you made last week had a finger too many, and there was a cap as I recall that was half purple."

"Young Dicky done that. Changed the wools when I warnt looking." Granna leant forward and touched Tom's arm. "I'll knit you something. What'd you like? Socks or gloves or a comforter?"

"Don't you bother. I'm all right."

"You never did seem to feel the cold."

"I'm all right," Tom said. "I've got plenty."

Beth and Betony sent him woollens. They saw that he was kept supplied.

"What's the *best* thing to send?" Betony asked him. "What would you find really useful?"

"A big Dundee cake, like your mother sent in a tin one time. It was packed with fruit and had almonds on it."

"Don't you know there's a sugar shortage? It's going on ration in the new year."

"I thought maybe Beth could spare some honey."

"My mother says she's never known so many people ask so kindly after her bees as they have done lately since sugar got scarce. But no doubt she's got some to spare for you."

The two of them were alone in the kitchen. Tom sat staring into the fire. Betony watched him.

"You never used to like fruit cake."

"We're glad of it, though, out there."

"What do you mean by 'we' exactly?"

"The chaps," he said. "They always like Dundee cake."

"And must I make cakes to feed the chaps?"

"Not just them – we share things," he said. "We always share what we get in our parcels. It's good stuff, you see, and we're pretty nearly always hungry."

"But why?" she exclaimed. "Why on earth don't they feed you properly?"

"A lot of the food gets flogged," he said. "There's chaps that sell it to the shops and cafés. Or so I've heard, anyway, and I reckon it's true."

"But that's terrible! It makes my blood boil to hear such things! There ought to be better supervision."

"There ought to be, but it ent easy, out there."

The fire collapsed in the open stove, and Tom leant forward to put on more logs. He looked at her for a while in silence.

"I was sorry," he said, awkwardly, "to hear the captain was a prisoner."

"Yes," she said. "I hope the Germans don't treat him badly. He says in his letters he's all right, but I can't help wondering all the same."

"I don't think the Germans is all bad. Some of them must be, but not all. He'll be all right, Bet, don't you worry."

"I wish you wouldn't keep calling me Bet! You never used to in the old days."

"Sorry," he said. "I've got the habit off the chaps." And he went on to explain to her about the letters. "We share *them* as well. We read each other's. Except when they're private, from wives and that. The chaps always like it when I hear from you. Your letters go round like hot buns. You cheer them up and make them laugh. They always say it's a real tonic."

"I shall have to be careful what I write."

"You don't mind, do you, Bet? I didn't think you'd mind about it."

"No," she said, "I don't mind."

In fact the knowledge gave her pleasure. She felt herself closer to the men out there, suffering, enduring as they were. It was little enough, in God's name, and she must try to write more often.

"Tell me about them, these mates of yours," she said, and, seeing him smile: "What's the joke exactly?" she asked.

"I was thinking about Big Glover. He was always talking about you. He said once to ask if you'd marry him."

"Tell him I'd have to see him first."

"Big Glover is dead now. He was killed last summer on the Somme. He came from outside Bromyard somewhere. So did Ritchie and Flyer Kyte. Kyte was clever with a jew's harp. Ritchie was always full of tales. They was both good chaps, Kyte and Ritchie, but they're dead now."

And so it went on: Tom's own roll of honour: Cuddy; Evans; Mustow; Braid; Verning; Reynolds; Privitt; Smith; all good men but dead now.

"Good God," Betony said, "are none of them left alive at all?"

"Not many," he said, "but there's new chaps coming up all the time."

"It's all wrong," she said, "that so many men should be sent out to die, cut down like cornstalks in a field."

"Yes," he said, "it's all wrong."

Looking at him, she thought him changed. He had always had a haunted look, but now he was old before his time. His eyes had seen things no eyes should see.

"Dicky'll be called up next spring," she said.

"Ah. I know. He was telling me."

"Where will it end, Tom? Where will it end?"

"I dunno, but it's bound to end somewhere, I suppose."

"Shall we beat the Germans, do you think?"

"I reckon we've got to," Tom said, "or all them lives will've gone for nothing."

"Take care of yourself," Betony said, "and tell your mates the cake will be coming."

"Don't let the war be over yet," said Dicky, " 'cos I want to be in it and have some fun."

"Dicky, be quiet!" Beth exclaimed. "You've got no notion what you're saying."

"Ah, you jus be quiet, son," Jesse said, "and give Tom a hand with that there kitbag."

"I'll be knitting you something," granna said, "just as soon as I find the time."

"I hope you ent losing your touch as a craftsman," said Great-grumpa Tewke, thumping Tom's back as he climbed up into the trap. "You should practise carving whenever you can, to keep your hand in for when you come home."

And Tilly Preston, waiting outside The Rose and Crown, watching for the pony and trap, ran out into the road and threw a knot of ribbons, red white and blue, into Tom's lap.

"Keep them, Tom, and they'll bring you luck."

Tom stuffed the ribbons into his pocket. Jesse, driving, glanced at his face.

"D'you like Tilly Preston, Tom?" he asked.

"She's all right," Tom said, shrugging.

The Sixth Battalion, having moved south into France again, was re-forming, absorbing men of the Tenth Battalion, disbanded after heavy losses, and being made up to strength again with new drafts just out from England. Tom and Newers were now old sweats. They felt entitled to give themselves airs. They were veterans. Men of experience. It was their duty, Newers said, to take the new recruits in hand especially when they got to the trenches.

"See as much as you can, hear as much as you can, and do sod-all about either," he said. "It won't be long now. We're dying of boredom on both sides. And what's left of the B.E.F. will all go home in the same boat."

The new men were teased without mercy.

"Have you brought your sugar card?"

"The sergeant likes you to call him dad."

"Six months as san-man and you get the D.S.O. Twelve months and you get the V.C. Two years, you retire on a pension."

One young lad, entering his dugout, was horrified at the number of rats scampering and fighting there.

"Ugh!" he said, drawing back. "I don't like rats."

"You'd better get to like 'em," Newers said, " 'cos they bloody well think the world of us!"

"Hey, Toss," said Danson. "There's a chap here asking to see Jack Johnson!"

"That's nothing," said Rush. "I've got one here complaining about his thigh-boots. He says he never takes nothing but number nines!"

The weather turned cold. There was deep snow. The men had been issued with leather jackets. They sat huddled close in the tiny dugouts, woollen comforters pulled down over their ears, sandbags tied like gaiters round their legs.

"I find myself thinking of featherbeds, and my missus beside me, warm as toast, tickling my back," said Chirpy Bird. "Pathetic, ent it?"

"I think of my furnace," said Bert Moore, an ironworker from Wolverhampton, "and the heat in my face as I push a load in on the jib."

"I think of summer days and cricket on Pitchcroft," said Bob Newers, who came from Worcester, "sitting in the sun in my white flannels, waiting my turn to go in and bat."

"I think of damn-all when I'm cold," said Baines, " 'cos my brainbox is froze and won't work."

It was very quiet along most of the front during the cold spell early that year. Too quiet, Newers said, and they feared the worst.

"Nip and see what Jerry's doing and tell him not to, will you, Cox?"

"D'you think it's true he's getting ready to give us hell?"

"Nasty rumours are always true. He'll have a go at smashing us before the Yanks get organized. It won't be much use his trying after."

The rumours became established fact. German prisoners, coming in, all spoke of a big offensive, and from the forward observation posts, German reinforcements could be seen massing behind their lines, just out of range of the British guns. The weather was improving. March winds were drying the ground. In the little salient near

Cambrai, British troops, working to strengthen the defences there, were caught unawares by a heavy bombardment of mustard gas. Two men in three were incapacitated.

Tom, delivering a message at Montevalle, saw a long string of these gassed men, blinded, voiceless, filing hand-in-hand along a zig-zag communication trench, making their way to the rear line. He counted a hundred and thirty-three.

"Will they recover?" he asked an ambulance man at Chesle.

"After a fashion," the man said.

On the night of the twenty-first, the Germans began an intense shelling of the British line, all the way from Croiselle to La Fère. It was heavier than anything known before, and in the forward defences the British garrisons crouched low under the storm, deafened, concussed, as the earth split around them on all sides.

"This is it," Newers said. "Once this stops they'll be all over us like flies on a cowpat, God rot their wicked souls."

From where they lay they could see British shells exploding in St Quentin. Gunflashes turned the night to day. Some distance away, on their right flank, a machine-gun post was blown sky high, and, further on still, three shells in a row fell into a trench sector.

"Poor bastards," Newers said. "That's Wilkie gone up with them emma gees. I liked old Wilkie. I'll miss him a lot. He owed me a shilling from a game of poker."

First light came, struggling through a thick fog, but the German bombardment continued all morning. Then at nine-thirty it moved over and the German infantry were seen advancing, grey-clad men coming out of the grey fog. The forward posts opened fire.

The fog was helping the enemy, and they came not in waves but in separate groups, working their way through the weakly manned British defences, then turning on them from flank and rear. The forward posts were soon overwhelmed. The few survivors were falling back.

In the main line, there was confusion. Officers strode up and down the trench, calling to the men to keep their heads. One young subaltern ran to and fro several times.

"Keep calm! Keep calm!" he shouted to the men on the firestep. "Keep quite calm and choose your target carefully."

"Hark at him," Newers muttered. "He's the one that's getting excited."

But Captain Highet, their company commander, watching over the parapet, was calm and quiet to a degree, ready to give the order to fire. A group of Germans emerged from the fog out in front, coming across at a steady pace. The order was given and there was a burst of rifle fire. The group of Germans disappeared, its place was taken by another, and other groups loomed up behind. Elsewhere, in many places, they had broken through the main line.

The Sixth Battalion, in Artichoke Trench, had the enemy strong on both sides and was in danger of being cut off. Bombers were posted in shell-holes at either flank, to cover withdrawal, and Tom was in the party on the right, with Newers, Danson, Grover and Coombes. The battalion fell back, fighting fiercely as it went, till it reached the safety of Sandboy Redoubt. The bombing parties were the last to leave. They stayed until all their grenades were thrown, and then made a dash for it, every man for himself.

On the way, Tom came under fire from a German machine-gun, and was hit in the calf of each leg. He crawled to a shell-hole and lay low. The machine-gun was firing from the rim of a crater fifty yards off. There came an explosion and the machine-gun stopped. A well-aimed bomb had found its mark.

His puttees and trousers were ripped from the back of each leg and hung in tatters, sticky with blood and fragments of flesh. He was trying to open his field-dressing when a voice spoke and there was Newers, coming towards him, crouched low, unlit pipe between his teeth.

"Bloody fool!" Tom said. "Coming back through all this!"

"I thought you might have a match," Newers said.

He knelt beside Tom and broke a phial of iodine over each wound. The dressings were soaked with blood instantly, so Newers took off his own puttees and used them as extra bandages. Tom then fainted and knew nothing more.

Newers gathered him up in his arms and set out across the stretch of open ground now overrun by enemy troops. His only cover was the fog, but he reached the rear lines unharmed and carried Tom to the medical aid post at Vraine St Marie, a distance of almost two miles. When Tom recovered consciousness, Newers had gone.

Tom spent three weeks in the field hospital at St Irac, and was then put on a long period of light duty, in the stores at Aubrille. He fretted, rather, away from his mates, for the news coming in was grave indeed. The Germans had broken through everywhere, and the Allies were falling back all the time, fighting desperately over every mile of ground yielded. The Commander-in-Chief had issued a message to all his troops. They had their backs to the wall, he said, and every man must fight to the end.

By the end of May, however, the German offensive was losing its force, and the British line began to hold. Hope was reviving, growing strong, and soon there was confidence in the air.

In the middle of June, Tom rejoined his own battalion, in reserve at Chantereine. Three months had passed and many friends had disappeared, killed or sent home badly wounded, but Bob Newers was still there, and Pecker Danson, and Dave Rush was back again.

"And we've still got Fritz with us, of course. That's him over there, across the way, but don't provoke him if you can help it 'cos he's lost his sense of humour lately."

"I thought you'd got a Blighty one," Pecker Danson said to Tom.

"Not Toss," said Newers. "He's a lot tougher than he looks."

Twice in June the Germans attacked nearby Bligny, but were beaten back. Afterwards, the attacks died down in that sector, and things were quiet for the Sixth Battalion. Away on their right, the besieged city of Reims still held, and away on their left, the enemy advance had been stopped in the woods on the banks of the Marne. In the middle of July the Germans attempted another thrust, but were checked by Foch and thrown back to the Vesle, and by the end of the month the German offensive had come to a halt everywhere.

In the lull that followed, the Allies had time to nurse themselves back to strength again. They counted their losses and re-formed. Soon they were ready to strike the blow that would end the war. The American forces were building up. The French spirit was on fire again. This time it really *would* be over by Christmas.

August and September saw the turning of the tide. The Allies were advancing, driving the enemy back across

France. By early October the Hindenburg Line was in Allied hands.

"What'll you do when you get to Berlin, Pecker?"

"Dance the Blue Danube with the Kaiser."

"And then what?"

"Catch the next train for Blighty, of course."

The Sixth Battalion was on the march. They had seen little action in the past six weeks, but now, after careful and strenuous training, they were on their way to the front line again.

At a small town called Vaillon St Jacques, the people turned out to watch them march through. Women ran forward with cups of coffee for the soldiers to drink; old men wanted to shake their hands; children waved small tricolour flags. At one house, plainly a brothel, a group of women stood on the iron balcony, blowing kisses and baring their breasts.

"Tommees, come in! We give you good time! Soldats anglais, we surrender to you!"

"On our way back!" the soldiers answered. "Mind you keep the offer open!"

And, marching on, they sang their own version of a popular song.

> "Keep the red lamp burning . . .
> We shall be returning . . .
> Though a soldier's pay is poor
> He can spare two francs . . ."

Outside Vaillon, as they marched through, they could hear the noise of guns some miles away towards the east, reminding them that the war was not quite over yet.

"Here we go!" Danson muttered. "Back to the bloody mincing-machine."

"Only one more river," Newers said in a comforting way.

In pouring wet weather in late September, they marched through Les Boeufs, Le Transloy, Rocquingny, Chenay. It was a district they knew all too well. Many friends were buried there. They knew the kind of weather too. Did it never stop raining in this country? It was worse than Manchester, Shuttleworth said. A few days later they passed through the ruins of La Bouleau, and, on another dark rainy night, went into trenches in the front line.

Their objective was called County Point, a strongpoint in the enemy line. C and D Companies were to attack together and press on to the sunken road known as Bull's Alley. A and B Companies were to follow up on their right flank and take the position called Cock's Spur. At five in the morning, first light, the British guns opened fire and the four attacking companies advanced behind the creeping barrage, over slippery ground that rose slightly.

In front hung a curtain of thick choking smoke as the barrage fell, moving forward, perfectly timed. The first wave of troops was now straggling, thrown out by the broken ground, unable to see because of the smoke drifting past in coils. Orders were shouted but were lost in the noise.

Coming out of the smoke, Tom found himself stumbling against a thicket of barbed wire surrounding a German machine-gun emplacement. The gun was in pieces behind the shattered breastwork and the gun-crew were lying dead. He swung to the right, going round the entanglement, and half a dozen men went with him. Two of them fell, hit by snipers hidden somewhere in no-man's-land, and the others went forward at a trot. But the rest of the line had disappeared, somewhere under the drifting smoke, and in front of the few lay a water-logged wasteland rising to an empty sky. Rain was falling heavily. Visibility was bad. It seemed to Tom they had gone past their mark. The little group stopped to confer.

"If this is the Cheltenham racecourse," said Bird, "it seems there's no meeting today, lads."

"Do we go back or go on?" asked Tom.

"On," said Brownlee, "and hope for the best."

They had gone perhaps three hundred yards when a shell exploded in front of them. The five lay low, then went on again, and now they could see the enemy line, in the dim distance away on their left, marked out by the flash of guns and the puffs of smoke hanging in the rain. They could also see their own men, like ants in a swarm, seething on the slopes there.

"Jesus wept!" Newers said. "We *have* gone astray and no mistake."

They changed direction and began to run, the rain now blowing in their faces, and as they stumbled through the mud a machine-gun rattled from a sandbagged emplacement on their right. Brownlee fell dead, and Bird doubled over, hit in the stomach. The three remaining men dived for the cover of a shell-crater and Newers got a bullet in the arm.

Tom and Thurrop looked over the rim, trying to locate the machine-gun post. A chance British shell located it, one of six fired from a battery of field-guns at Souane-la-Mare, and the watchers saw it go up in smoke. Tom and Thurrop went out to help Bird, but found him dead, his face contorted. They crawled back to Newers, who sat in the crater, blowing through his empty pipe.

"Don't tell me – I know – we're in a hole. We'll be mentioned in dispatches for this and asked to lecture to the rookies. 'How to lose your way in a direct charge.' Oh, well, I daresay the chaps'll manage without us."

"You all right, Bob?"

"No, half of me's left, Toss."

"Let's see that arm. I'll do you up."

"Go easy, then, 'cos that's the arm I shall use for bowling when I play for Worcestershire next year."

Tom dressed the badly torn arm and gave Newers his water-bottle. Thurrop was up at the edge of the crater, looking out, his rifle at the ready. There came a sharp crack and he fell back, dead, rolling over and over down the slope till he splashed into the pool at the bottom. Tom went quickly up to the rim and lay looking out. There was a movement in the next hole and he took aim. The sniper heaved and then lay still. Tom stayed where he was, watching.

"Did you get him?" Newers called.

"Yes, but I reckon there's more of 'em out here somewhere."

"Our own chaps've got it in for us as well. We'd better get to hell out of here as soon as we can find another hole."

The field-guns at Souane were firing again and the shells were falling very close.

"Stupid sods," Newers said. "You'd think they'd know a British-held crater when they saw it, wouldn't you?"

Tom was just turning when a shell exploded within the crater and he was knocked over by the blast. Debris covered him and he felt scorched. He got to his knees and shook off dirt that weighed a ton. Everything now seemed very quiet and when the smoke cleared away he saw that Newers had been blown to pieces. Nothing remained that could be called a man. Yet the pipe from his mouth was quite undamaged, lying in the mud some yards away. Tom crawled towards it and picked it up. He put it in his pocket and buttoned the flap. And then without warning a shell exploded in front of him, a fireworks show inside his head, followed by darkness.

When he became conscious again, he thought it was night-time, but after a while he realized he was blind. The darkness was in his own head. It was not lit by stars, or Very lights, or the distant flashes of guns. It was darkness thick and absolute, and he was at its mercy.

The upper part of his skull felt numb, yet inside it was full of pain. When he put up a hand, there were hard splinters embedded in his flesh, all over his face and scalp and neck. His uniform hung in ribbons in front, and his body felt small, as though it had first been scorched then crushed; and everywhere, when his fingers explored, he encountered sharp chips of metal and stone, driven into his skin by the hot blast. He had an open wound in his chest, sticky with blood, and he held his field-dressing pressed against it.

He crawled from the crater, out onto flat land. His eyes were hurting him, hot in their sockets, and whenever he blinked he could feel the gritty fragments in them. He crawled on his belly; he had no strength to raise himself up; and he pushed himself on with one arm. His mouth was shrivelled and he drank from puddles, water corrupt, evil, stinking, for dead men had rotted recently in this ground and cordite vapours had spread their poison everywhere.

He came to a trench and wriggled down into its bottom. It was an old German trench, long deserted, and in many places its sides had collapsed. He crawled along it for some way, and then sat still, listening. The sound of gunfire was very faint, and he thought his hearing had been affected. He felt very cold and knew he ought to keep on the move, but before he could make another effort he had passed into a deep faint.

He awoke to a small scrabbling sound, somewhere close at hand. A rat, perhaps, scavenging among the bones. But then he heard a human footfall and the click of a rifle bolt being drawn back.

"Who's there?" he called. He could see nothing.

"Stehen bleiben oder ich schiesse! Hände hoch, Du englischer Tommee, keine dummen Geschichten. Du bist mein Gefangener. Verstanden?"

God in heaven! He had crawled right into the enemy lines. How had he managed to travel so far? But the German, it seemed, was all alone: a man like himself, cut off from his comrades, seeking shelter where he could. He saw that Tom was hurt and unarmed, and there was a sound as he leant his rifle against the wall.

"Du lieber Himmel! Du siehst ja schlimm aus. Trink einen Schluck Wasser."

"Water," Tom said. "Yes. Thanks."

He felt the bottle at his lips and drank from it weakly, his head back. It was muddy stuff, tasting of petrol, but might have come from a clear mountain stream, so cool was it in his aching throat. He was too weak to move and lay where he was, shivering, while the German touched him, looking at his wounds.

"Blown-up? Stimmt's? Dich hat's da draussen irgendwo erwischt?"

"Blind," Tom said, and put up a hand to touch his eyes. "My eyesight's gone. Napoo! Kaput!"

"Tut mir leid! Armer Kerl! Sehr unangenehme Sache. Wenn mein Kameraden kommen, können wir uns vernünftig um Dich kümmern. Wir haben gute Ärzte, die Dir wieder auf die Beine helfen."

"Kamerad," Tom said. It was the only word he understood.

The German had opened his ragged tunic and was cleansing the open wound in his chest. The unseen hands were quick, sure, gentle, as they put on a dressing and tied it in place.

"Thanks," Tom said. "It feels a lot better, that's a fact."

"T'anks? Hast Du Dich etwa bedankt? Vielen Dank?"

"Ah, that's right, danke schön."

"Ich heisse Josef. Und Du?"

"I dunno. Search me!" But after a moment he understood. "Tom," he said, wearily.

"Tom? Tommee? Führst Du mich etwa an der Nase 'rum?" The German was chuckling, slapping his leg. "Fritz und Tommee! Tommee und Fritz! Merk' Dir – ich bin nicht Fritz, sondern Josef." Then, as Tom shivered again, he gave an exclamation and got to his feet. "Ich werd' Dir was zu essen holen, und veilleicht was zum Zudecken."

He was gone a long time. Tom thought he had gone for good. But he came back with a German greatcoat and helped Tom into it, wrapping it round him and turning the collar up to his ears. He also brought food and a stoneware bottle full of liquor.

"Käse," he said, and placed a small piece of cheese in Tom's hand. "Was heisst das auf englisch?"

"Cheese," Tom said, putting it whole into his mouth and sucking slowly. "Danke schön."

"Brot," Josef said, and this time he gave Tom a crust of bread. "Was heisst das?"

"Bread," Tom said. "I hope you've got some for yourself. Eh? Have you? Brot for Josef?"

"Richtig. Ordentlich was zu essen für uns beide und natürlich 'ne Menge Schnaps."

When Tom had eaten, Josef took his hands and placed them round the stoneware bottle, helping him raise it to his lips. The drink was warming and brought some life into Tom's veins.

"Schnaps. Was heisst das auf englisch?"

"I reckon that's brandy," Tom said. "It's good. Very good. It's made me feel a lot better."

"Schmeckt's Ja? Freut mich. Du solltest Dich jetzt aber mal ordentlich auspennen." Josef was making snoring noises.

"Ah," Tom said, his head aching. "Yes, you're right, I'm about done."

"Leg' Dich hin – so geht's gut. Ich halte Wache. Bisschen später kommen meine Kameraden und wir sehen zu, dass wir Dich zur Sanitäts-Station hinkriegen."

"Is it night-time?" Tom asked. "Nacht, is it?"

"Nacht? Ja, es ist zehn Uhr."

"That's just what it feels like," Tom said.

He lay on his back, staring upwards, but could see nothing of the night sky. Only a kind of throbbing blackness. His eyes were ruined and he was too numb to think about it. He fell asleep like a dead man.

He awoke to a smell of hot coffee and sat up, looking around him. Surely his eyes were not quite ruined after all, for when he looked downwards at the ground, the darkness was greater than when he looked upwards into the sky, and there was the hint of a shadow moving, where Josef was busy preparing breakfast. Only a blurred featureless shape, it was true, but it made his heart leap up with hope. Yesterday, blackness. Today, a grey fog. Tomorrow, perhaps, there would be light.

"Morgen!" said Josef. "Trocken, sogar."

"My eyes are better!" Tom exclaimed. "I can see! I can see!"

"Was war das? Ich versteh' Dich nicht. Kannst Du mich sehen? Kannst Du mein Gesicht erkennen?"

"Eyes," Tom said, and pointed to them. "They seem a lot better than they was."

"Dir geht's besser – Willst Du das sagen? Schön, gut. Gott sei Dank!"

He brought Tom a breakfast of black coffee, faintly sweetened, and a hunk of rye bread with a slice of stale cold sausage on it. They sat opposite each other, with the fire between them, and Tom peered at the German's outline, a darker shadow against the greyness. He wished he knew what the man looked like. He wished he could touch the unseen face. And he put out his hands in such a way that the man understood him, and, laughing a little, guided the hands towards his face, allowing Tom to feel his features.

"Bin ich nicht schön? Ich find' mich wunderschön! Bin ein Bild von Junge, findst Du nicht?"

He laughed again, deep in his throat, and Tom smiled, guessing the nature of the joke. He now had a picture of the German's face: square in shape and broad-browed, the flesh shrunken on the strong bones, the stubbled skin tightly stretched; and he let his hands fall into his lap.

"You ent been getting enough to eat. You shouldn't have shared your food with me."

"Na? Was war das wieder? Was sagst Du da?"

"Have you got a wife?" Tom asked. "Frau? Kinder? Family?"

"Ja, klar. Ich habe Bilder von ihnen. Ach, stimmt ja, Du kannst ja nicht sehen. Ich hab 'ne Frau, Margarete, und zwei Kinder, Peterlein und Lottchen. Ausserdem noch einee Hund Waldi." He made a noise like a dog barking. "Hund!" he said. "Was heisst das auf englisch?"

"Dog," Tom said.

"Dog. Waldi. Er kommt gut mit Schafen zurecht." He made a noise like a sheep bleating. "Schafen!" he said. "Was heisst das?"

"Sheep," Tom said.

"Ja. Ja. Gut-dog-mit-sheep. Dann werd' ich wohl bald prima englisch sprechen!"

So the man was a shepherd and lived on a farm. Why had he left it and come to fight? Were German shepherds under conscription? Tom had no way of asking these questions. He picked up his mug and drank his coffee.

Suddenly there was a noise. Voices talking not far away. Josef sprang up with an exclamation and went running off along the trench. Tom remained sitting, ears strained, trying to interpret the sounds that reached him. Then came the loud-bouncing crack of a rifle, followed by several cracks close together, and, after a pause, footsteps coming to the edge of the trench. An English voice spoke, and Tom answered.

"Good God, there's one of our own lads down here!" said the voice, plainly that of an officer. "And in pretty bad shape by the look of things. What's your name, man, and which lot are you from?"

"28233 Maddox, Sixth Battalion, Three Counties."

"I thought you were a German, wearing that coat. It's lucky you spoke up quickly like that or I might have shot you. Can you walk, Maddox?"

"I reckon I can. The only thing is, I can't see too well."

"Hang on a minute. We'll give you a hand. Cunningham! Dodds! Come and give this man a hand."

"Where's Josef?" Tom asked.

"What, that bloody German?" said one of the men who came to help him. "He's bloody well dead, with three or four bullets in his rotten carcass."

"But he was my friend! He saved my life! He gave me his coat and let me share his food and drink."

"Did he, by God?" the officer said. "Well, I'm sorry, Maddox, but he *did* open fire on us first, and he got my man Ross straight through the heart. That made me see red, I can tell you, because Ross was the best servant I ever had."

As they led Tom away they told him that the battle of La Bouleau had been successful. County Point had been taken, so had Cock's Spur, and eight hundred Germans had surrendered. The whole of that sector was in British hands.

In the crowded hospital at Rouen, a doctor came every morning and evening and examined his eyes, looking into them with a tiny torch.

"Will they get better?" Tom asked.

"Oh, yes, I think so. They're improving already, aren't they?"

"A bit. Not much. I still can't see nothing but shapes and shadows."

"It's early days yet. That shell must have been a pretty near thing. I'd say you were lucky to be alive."

The hospital was never quiet. There were over a hundred men in the ward with Tom, many of them in great pain, groaning, whimpering, crying out. The nurses were terribly overworked. Their voices were often loud and impatient, their hands ruthless, plucking dressings from torn flesh. Tom, still in darkness even by day, was often confused by the bustle around him. It hurt his head and made him feel dizzy. He had nothing to say to these brisk white presences talking across him. He was all alone at the centre of a world of noise and movement.

But one day, out of the commotion, a more restful presence, a gentler hand, and a girl's voice speaking in quiet tones beside him.

"Private Maddox? Somebody said you came from Chepsworth, where they blow on the mustard to make it cool."

Tom smiled. The girl's voice was a voice from home. Her accents were his, though not so broad, and she called the town "Cheps'orth" in the local manner.

"You must come from there yourself, knowing that saying."

"I come from Blagg, a tiny place four miles out. Do you know it?"

"I should just think I do, for I come from Huntlip, right next door. Why, we're practically neighbours, you and me."

"The people of Huntlip are either foxes or hounds, they say, so which are you?"

"And the people of Blagg all go in rags!" he answered back, enjoying himself.

"Not me," she said, "I get my uniform free of charge." And he could hear that she was smiling. "Whereabouts in Huntlip do you live?"

"Place called Cobbs, out towards Middening. There's a carpenter's shop – Tewke and Izzard's."

"Oh, yes, I've passed it often."

"What's your name?"

"Linn Mercybright."

"I don't remember you at school in Huntlip."

"We've only lived at Blagg these past five years. Before that we lived at Stamley and before that at Skinton Monks. My dad's a bit of a wanderer. He works at

Outlands Farm at present and has a cottage in Stoney Lane."

"I know Outlands. I've been there a lot. But I'd better not say what I was up to."

"Poaching?" she said. "You needn't worry. My father's only a labourer there. He'd very likely give you his blessing."

Tom leant forward a little way, but could see her only as a white shadow.

"I wish I could see you properly."

"You will be able to soon, I'm sure, but I must go now or Sister will have me on the carpet."

"Nurse," he said, anxiously. "Nurse! Are you there?"

"Yes?" she said. "What is it?"

"Will you come and see me again?"

"Yes, of course, every day."

She had been in service at Meynell Hall before volunteering as a nurse. She would go back there when the war was over.

"God willing, of course."

"It won't be long now, from what they're saying."

"God grant they're right."

"Linn?" he said. "How old are you?"

"Close on twenty-two."

"Six months older'n me, then."

"I see you've had a letter from home. And a parcel too."

"Trouble is, I can't write back. Not a proper letter. All I could do was get someone to fill in a card."

"I'll write a letter for you, when I get time. Tomorrow, perhaps. It's my easy day."

Next day when she came, he was sitting out on the terrace. There was bright sunlight and he could see it on her hair, which was reddish-gold and shone like copper, for now, off duty, she wore no cap.

"I can see you better today," he said. "You've got red hair."

"Mrs Winson at Meynell Hall always used to call it auburn."

"Auburn, that's right. I couldn't think of the right word."

"I was only teasing you," she said, laughing. "Of course it's red, and who cares? The main thing is that you can see it. Has Dr Young been to see you today?"

"Early this morning," Tom said, and, after a moment: "Strikes me he's bald."

Linn, delighted, laughed again. He had never heard laughter quite like hers. He could see her leaning back in the chair.

"You *are* improving, aren't you?" she said. "Soon you'll be able to see our warts."

"Warts?" he said. "What, you?"

"That was just another joke."

"Are you going to write my letter?"

"Just this once, yes, but soon you'll see to write your own."

At the end of the week he *could* see. His sight was almost back to normal. He could see that Collins, in the bed beside him, who had lost both his legs, was only a boy of eighteen, and that Beale, in the bed on the other side, was jerking with tetanus. He could see the many men poisoned by the fumes of gas, who lay with faces discoloured and burnt, breathing painfully, with a terrible noise, drowning with their lungs full of foul bubbling foam, whose dying was drawn out day by day.

He could see, too, that the wound in his chest had now

healed, leaving a dark empurpled scar; that his face and body were criss-crossed all over with smaller scars; that the dressing on his foot had concealed from him the loss of two toes.

"Seems I came off lightly," he said, "compared with most of the chaps here."

"You'll be going to hospital in England soon."

"Ah. I know. The doctor told me."

He could see now that Linn's eyes and eyebrows were dark brown; that her features were small and neatly made; that, suffering as she did with the mutilated men in her care, her cheerfulness often cost her dear.

When his transfer came, he was given only an hour's notice. He packed his few belongings quickly and hobbled off in search of Linn. He found her in the last ward, renewing the dressing on a man's neck.

"Seems I'm for off. Marching orders. They're putting me on the next train."

"I heard there was a contingent going. I wondered if you might be among them."

"They don't give much warning, do they?" he said. "I've been running round like a scalded cat."

"Hoi!" said the man whose wound she was dressing. "You go ahead, nurse, and say goodbye to your chap here. I shan't hurt for a minute or two."

"No," Linn said. "I mustn't leave you half done. Besides which, Sister's watching."

"I'll say goodbye, then," Tom said. He could see the ward sister, three rows away, frowning severely across at him. "Maybe I'll see you back at Blagg."

"Sure to," she said, and turned to smile at him, looking at him in a searching way. "You might go to Outlands and look up my dad. Tell him I'm well and looking forward to coming home."

She turned back to what she was doing, and her patient gave Tom a sympathetic wink.

"I'd let you take her back to Blighty, cock, only my need is greater than yourn, I reckon."

Tom nodded and walked away.

A month later, after treatment at the military hospital in Sawsford, he was home in Huntlip, discharged from the Army and wearing civilian clothes again.

It felt very strange, sleeping alone in a room of his own, after the crowded hospital ward, and the crowded billets. Often he lay wide awake, listening to the silence, till the small sounds of the household at rest came to him through the deafening stillness. He would look at the window and wonder at the steadiness of the sky outside: its unbroken darkness when there was mist; the constancy of moon and stars when the night was a clear one. He expected the lightning of gunflash and flare to whiten the sky and set it pulsing. It took a long time to get used to an earth so dark, so hushed, so perfectly still.

"Why've you been discharged?" Dicky asked. "If your eyes is all right again, why don't they want you back in the Army?"

"Seems I ent quite up to standard. My papers've got 'shell-shock' on 'em."

"Is that all that's wrong with you?"

"Leave Tom alone," Beth said to her son. "Just be thankful he's back safe."

"Ah, don't ask so many questions, boy," said great-grumpa. "Tom may've lost a few bits and pieces."

"I've lost the tops off two toes," Tom said.

"There!" said granna. "And I was going to make you some socks."

"He'll still need socks, granna," Betony said, impatiently.

"What gets me," Dicky said, "is Tom's being hurt by a British shell."

"Them things happen," Tom said.

Dicky himself was in khaki now. He was based at Capleton and had a weekend pass every month. He had lost all desire to go to the front. Such a muddle it all seemed. He wouldn't have minded dying a hero, but to get blown up by your own side! People said it would end soon, and he hoped they were right.

At The Rose and Crown, when Tom went in with Dicky one evening, Emery Preston was quite friendly.

"A drink on me for you two lads. I always believe in treating soldiers."

"I knew you'd come back, Tom," Tilly said. "I never doubted it. Not once. Have you brought me any souvenirs?"

"No," Tom said, "no souvenirs."

"Show her the scar on your chest," Dicky said. "That's a souvenir, ent it?"

"How long d'you think it'll be before it's over?" Emery asked.

"Not long now," Tom said.

One Monday morning, Tom and Jesse were up on the slopes of Lippy Hill, repairing a field-barn for Isaac Mapp. The day was a cold one, with drizzle blowing on the wind, grey and drenching. Jesse was sawing a new beam, inside the barn, where he was sheltered. He stopped work, thinking he could hear music, and went across to the door to listen.

Brass-bands on a weekday? There must be something

wrong with his ears! Yet somewhere down in the greyness below there was certainly a banging, clanging noise of some kind and, as the explanation came to him, a bright sunrise dawned in his face.

"It's the Armistice!" he shouted to Tom. "That's what it is! It's come at last! The war is over!"

He dropped his saw, snatched up his jacket, and went hurrying down the steep track, leaving Tom behind. He reached the road at the bottom of the hill and there, sure enough, the villagers were out from Otchetts and Peckstone and Dugwell and Blagg, and were marching on Huntlip, armed with pots and pans and biscuit-tins, – anything that would make a din – gathering more people as they went.

"The war is over!" they said to him. "The Armistice was signed at eleven o'clock. The Kaiser has skipped it and gone to Holland. Our boys'll soon be coming home!"

"Glory be!" Jesse said. "I knowed what it was the very minute I heard the rumpus! I've got two boys of my own, you know, William and Roger. They'll be coming home! They'll be coming home!"

He fell in with the noisy procession and danced along with it, clapping people on the back and telling them about William and Roger.

"My eldest boy, he's a bombardier, and my second, well, he's a gunner, see. But God bless my soul! To have them back again after such years!"

And, growing impatient to reach home, he took a short-cut across the fields, sending sheep and cattle in all directions.

In the kitchen at Cobbs, when he stumbled in, Beth sat at the table, a cabbage half shredded on the board before her. Great-grumpa Tewke stood at the window. Granna Tewke sat by the fire.

"Ent you heard the news?" Jesse demanded. "It's the Armistice! The war is over! Everyone's out in the roads, creating, and the din can be heard from here to Scarne. Ent you had word of it down here?"

"Yes, we've had word of it," Beth said.

"Well, you don't seem too bucked," he said, laughing. "I thought you'd all be over the moon."

Her stillness stopped him, brought him up short, and he saw the telegram on the table, lying open, under her hands. William and Roger had been killed in action. Sunday the tenth. Eleven A.M. Twenty-four hours before the signing of the Armistice.

Only two days before, there had been a letter, written by William: "We're in the pink, Rog and me, still washing behind the ears and sticking together like you told us to do."

They had died together, serving their gun, when an enemy shell had fallen directly into their gunpit.

The carpenter's shop stopped work that day. The men were sent home. Dicky, coming on special leave, entered a house of terrible silence. Betony was there and broke the news. He went at once to look for his father and was shocked to hear him weeping aloud in the empty workshop. He crept away, unable to face such open grief, and returned later. His father stood hunched against the workbench.

"Why should my sons've been took from me? Why? Why?"

"You've still got *me*, dad. You've still got me."

Jesse made no answer, and Dicky went away again, hurt and baffled.

A few days later, a small package came, containing the two dead boys' effects: cap-badges, passbooks, letters, snapshots. Jesse was angry at sight of these things. He wanted to hurl them into the fire.

"What use are they without the boys?"

"No use," Beth said, "except just to remember them by."

She put the badges up on their portrait, pinning them to the ledge of the frame. Jesse gave a groan and left the room, pushing Dicky aside in the doorway. Beth turned and saw the boy's eyes as he looked at the portrait of his brothers.

"You mustn't hate them for having died."

Dicky was ashamed. How did his mother know his feelings? His father knew nothing. He had shut them all out.

"My dad don't want me nowadays. I reckon he wishes me dead like them."

"Your father's not hisself at present. It's up to you to be patient with him."

Betony, seeking to comfort Dicky, went with him to Chepsworth Park, to the special ceremony held there. A part of the grounds, about fifteen acres, had been given to the public by Mr Champley to commemorate the signing of the Armistice. A plaque was unveiled on one of the gateposts; a drinking-fountain was switched on; doves were released from the old stone dovecote. It would be known as Polygon Park and would be a place of recreation for the people of Chepsworth. The house itself, with the rest of the grounds, was already a home for disabled soldiers. Mr Champley's only son had been killed in the battle of Polygon Wood.

"Is it wrong for us to be gadding about?" Dicky asked.

"No, of course not," Betony said.

"My dad seems to think so," Dicky said.

Huntlip itself had almost a week of celebrations, ending after dark on Saturday night with a torchlight procession through the village, up onto the open common. A straw-stuffed effigy of the Kaiser, with a realistic withered arm and wearing a genuine pickelhaube helmet, was carried up with a rope round its neck and hanged from the old gibbet. A fire was lit underneath it and fireworks secreted in the dummy's body went off with loud bangs as the dummy burned.

Tom, alone in the outer darkness, stood watching the yellow flames leaping and the rockets fizzing towards the sky. The Kaiser had dropped from his rope now, and the gibbet itself was burning fiercely, beginning to topple into the fire. The dancers and singers were cheering its fall.

Tom felt withdrawn, a living ghost. The merrymakers were strangers to him. The night was unreal. Though the fire burnt, it could never warm him. Though the voices shouted, the words meant nothing. And although a great many people were gathered there under the moon, reaching out to one another, there were no pale arms reaching out to him. He was wrapped in a caul of darkness and aloneness.

"Tom?" said a voice, and Tilly Preston stood beside him. "I've been looking for you everywhere. Dicky said you was here some place. Why ent you dancing like the others? Harry Yelland's arrived now and brought his accordian."

"I ent much good at dancing, Tilly. I'm none too steady on my pins. But you go ahead and dance if you want to. I'd just as soon stand by and be quiet."

"I don't care about dancing neither. Great lumping louts they are here. I'd just as soon go for a walk, away from the noise, wouldn't you?"

She slid her arm into his and leant against him, looking into his thin dark face, lit by the bonfire, now burning red. She wanted to touch him, tenderly. She wanted to kiss his poor scarred eyes.

"What're you thinking about, Tom?"

"I was thinking of William and Roger," he said, "and all the other chaps that're gone."

"Don't be unhappy, Tom. Don't look like that. They wouldn't want you to grieve for them, would they, specially not on a night like tonight?"

"I was only thinking, that's all." And he turned his head to look at her. "You sure you don't want to join in the dancing?"

Tilly was wearing a hand-crocheted cap of fluffy red wool with a pompon on it, and a long scarf to match, with a similar pompon at either end. She looked very small, in her long winter coat and buttoned boots, like a child going skating on an icy pond.

"Don't you want my company, Tom?"

"I never said that."

"Wouldn't you sooner go for a walk?"

"All right," he said, "let's go for a walk."

She took him to a barn at New Strakes, her uncle's farm on the edge of the common, and led him up into the hayloft. She undid her coat and was warm against him, taking his hands and guiding them slowly till they covered her breasts, as she drew him down with her into the loose-tumbled sweet-smelling hay. Her breath was quick and hot on his lips. She ached for him and knew she could easily make him love her.

The church bell at Eastery, cracked for more than thirty years, had been recast in honour of Eastery's war dead, and on the fourth Sunday in November, when people from neighbouring villages came for the rededication service, it rang out tunefully over their heads, in celebration of the new peace.

"When your mother and me was married here," Jesse said to Betony, "that there bell made sorry music, but now it's something to hear, ent it?"

Old memories had unlocked his tongue. He was almost himself again.

"That's a wonderful thing to hear the church bells ringing out, after being stopped for so long, and to know they're ringing all over England. Ah, and that's a wonderful thing to know the captain is coming home, too, ent it? Are you sure you don't want me to drive you to the station?"

"No, father. I'd sooner go alone."

Betony was nervous, meeting Michael after two and a half years. She felt she hardly knew him at all; hardly remembered what he looked like; and could not, however hard she tried, pin down exactly what she had felt for him before the enforced separation.

But when at last he stepped from the train, helped by his mother, and she saw his starved face, with its slow-twisting smile and burning gaze, she knew that even if he were a perfect stranger he would still have a claim upon her love. She had seen so many men like this, their faces sculpted by suffering, and she felt that love should be theirs for the asking, given freely, without meanness.

"Betony," he said. "I thought this journey would never end. The train stopped at every station."

"Michael. Darling. You look so ill."

"I've had this damned 'flu. It's left me feeling as weak as a kitten."

When he took her in his arms, she could feel the tension thrumming in him, as though he were wound up tight like a spring.

"Will you marry me, Betony?"

"Yes," she whispered. "Yes. Oh, yes."

"Thank God for that. I have wanted you so. I think I would die if you said no now."

"I haven't said no. I've said yes."

"It was the one thing that kept me going. Thinking of you. Knowing you loved me. I remembered the way you looked at me, that last time, on this very station, when you got here just as the train was leaving. Do you remember?"

"Yes," she said, "I remember."

"If you hadn't been here today," he said "looking at me in just the same way, I don't know what I would have done."

"Michael. Darling. I *am* here."

And she felt the tension easing a little, as he let her go and looked directly into her face.

"Come along, both of you," his mother said. "There's a car waiting."

Their engagement was soon made public, and Betony was often at King's Hill House. Mrs Andrews gave her blessing, but thought they ought to wait a while before marrying. Six months, perhaps, or even a year.

"Don't you think I've waited long enough?" Michael said.

"You're a sick man. Is it fair on Betony to marry her before you're quite well?"

"I shan't take that long, getting well."

Alone together, he and Betony talked it out.

"My mother says it's unfair on you. Am I such a wreck?"

"Your mother thinks we're not really suited. She thinks if we have to wait a while we shall change our minds."

"In that case we'll wait!" he said grimly. "If only to prove how wrong she is. I don't really mind, so long as I can see you often."

"I don't mind, either. With my brothers only recently

dead, it would be better not to have a wedding in the family just yet. Also, there's so much work crying out to be done."

Her work in the factories had come to an end. She was now at Chepsworth Park, helping at the home for sick and disabled ex-soldiers. There, under the direction of volunteer doctors, men were learning to use new artificial limbs; nervous cases were learning to talk again; husks of men with burnt-out lungs were coming to terms with the remnant of life that was left to them; and those who had nothing left at all were being nursed through their last days of pain.

Betony travelled about the three counties, raising funds, recruiting helpers, buying equipment. And often she worked with the men themselves: washing and feeding those who were helpless; giving her shoulder to a cripple hobbling on metal legs; wheeling men in bathchairs out to a sunny place in the orangery. There were men who stammered very badly and men who spoke only gibberish, and Betony would sit with them, trying to interpret their crazy, tortured utterances.

There was a boy named Johnny Clegg whose brain, it seemed, was tied in knots. He had no family or friends; received no visitors; and frightened everyone at the home by dashing at them, shouting unintelligibly at the top of his voice. He was very wild-looking and, failing to make himself understood, would hurl himself about in a frenzy.

He came to Betony one day, took hold of her arms, and shook her savagely to and fro. He dragged her towards the piano.

"Lanno!" he shouted. "Lanno! Lanno! Midder-orders-plidder-chewing!"

"Tune?" she said. "Your mother always played a tune?"

"Assit! Assit! Plidder-chewing-obesit-obing!"

Betony went and sat at the piano and played *Home Sweet Home.* Johnny, beside her, stood perfectly still, listening intently to the end. Then when she turned round on the stool, he threw himself onto his knees before her, hid his face in her lap, and burst into tears.

He was always calmer after that. He had managed, just once, to make himself understood, and Betony, becoming attuned, was able to teach him to speak more clearly.

Tom stood at the bend in Stoney Lane, looking at the small neat redbrick cottage. The door was open, held back by an iron dog, and a few bits of matting lay out on the path. Blue smoke rose from the chimney.

A cloud of dust appeared at the doorway, followed by a man with a long-handled broom. He looked a lot older than Tom had expected and his face was half covered by a crinkly grey beard. He swept the dust out to the garden and stood leaning on his broom, staring at Tom who stood, hands in pockets, outside the gate.

"I seen you before. What're you up to, hanging about round my cottage?"

"I was looking for Linn," Tom said. "I wondered if she was home yet."

"If Linn was home," Jack Mercybright said, "I wouldn't be doing my own sweeping."

He came out onto the path and picked up the mats. Tom saw that one leg was lame at the knee.

"How come you know my daughter?"

"I was in France. In the hospital at Rouen. I live in Huntlip and Linn said to call and say how-do."

"Then why hang about instead of coming straight to the door? Did you think I'd eat you?"

"No," Tom said, "I didn't think that."

"Well, if you've come to tell me how she is, you ent making a lot of headway."

"She's all right. She said to tell you not to worry."

"No message besides?"

"I don't remember nothing else."

"Well, it's soon delivered, I'll say that!"

Mercybright was turning indoors. He seemed about to shut Tom out. But he paused briefly and spoke again.

"I had a letter from her this morning. Seems she'll likely be home tomorrow. Who shall I say was asking for her?"

"Tom Maddox."

"Well, you call again," Mercybright said. "In a day or two, when she's got settled. I'll tell her you're coming."

He went inside and closed the door.

Three days later, when Tom was again loitering in the lane, Linn saw him from the cottage window and ran out to meet him. She wore a dress of dark green, with a collar standing up at the neck, and above it her hair was bright red-gold, neatly twisted into a coil, but with fine-spun strands curling down over her nape. Her dark eyes were shining. She laughed at him in the way he remembered.

"Why don't you come to the door and knock? You surely don't think you aren't welcome?"

She took him by the arm and led him into the cottage kitchen. Her father sat beside the hearth, smoking an old-fashioned clay pipe, the bowl of which was shaped like an acorn. He motioned Tom towards the settle, and Linn sat there, too, perched sideways, watching Tom's face.

"How're your eyes since you've been home?"

"Pretty good, considering."

"Not giving you any pain?"

"I wouldn't say pain. Not exactly. My head beats a bit now and then, but nothing special."

"And your foot?" she asked. "How's that?"

"Pretty good, considering."

"Seems to me," her father said, "you must've been through the mill, young fella."

"I came out alive, though, that's something."

"Only just, by the look of you."

"Take no notice of dad," Linn said. "I never do. It's bad for him."

"Ent there some beer we can give this boy?"

"How should I know?" she asked, laughing. "I've only been home five minutes."

But she went out to the back kitchen and returned with two mugs full of frothing beer.

"That's what I like!" her father said. "Being waited on and mollied after. I missed that a lot while you was away, girl, and I reckon I bore it pretty well."

He took a deep drink and wiped the froth from moustache and beard. He looked at Tom with keen eyes.

"That'll come hard on me," he said, "when my daughter leaves me to get married."

When Tom had gone, and Linn was left alone with her father, she sat with her hands folded in her lap, laughing at him. He looked back at her, straight-faced.

"I been making enquiries about Tom Maddox."

"There, now!" she said. "Fancy that!"

"Seems his parents warnt never married."

"You surely don't hold that against him?"

"No. Surely not. But it's always better to know these things. And there was worser stories than that."

"What stories?"

"His father was a drunkard and killed his mother in a fit of temper. Then he hanged hisself in a tree. Your Tom was a babe about twelve months old."

"Poor boy," Linn said.

"There was good things told me as well as bad. They say the lad's a clever craftsman. Does carving and such, at Tewke and Izzard's, as well as first-rate carpentry." Jack leant forward to light a paper spill at the fire. "So it's just as well his sight warnt ruined by that shell."

"D'you like him, dad?"

"It's early days to answer that. He ent got a lot to say for hisself, has he?"

"Not as much as some I could mention."

"You ent growed less cheeky, since being out in foreign parts."

"Puff, puff, puff," she said, watching him as he lit his pipe. "Old tobacco-face! Always smoking!"

"The real question is, whether *you* like him."

"I think I do."

"But you ent sure?"

"He's a strange boy. He reminds me, somehow, of a wild animal. Oh, I don't mean wild in a fierce way, but awkward and shy, like a deer in the forest."

"I bet they wasn't all shy, them soldiers you nursed over there."

"No," she said, "far from it."

"It makes me boil!" Jack exclaimed, striking his chair with the palm of his hand. "It makes me boil that a young girl like you should've had to nurse a lot of rough soldiers the way you been doing these past two years. I'm a man and I know what they're like. They don't deserve to be mollied for by nice young girls of your sort."

"Father, be quiet, you don't know what you're saying!" she said, and her eyes were suddenly full of tears. "You've no idea what these men had to go through."

"I was a soldier once, remember, for a short while back in the eighties – "

"You still don't know what *these* men went through in *this* war. Nobody knows, except those who've seen for themselves, and it's wrong to say they're undeserving. It's wrong, very wrong, and I won't have it! You know nothing at all about the matter."

"H'mm. It's a fine thing, I must say, when a man is told he knows nothing by his chit of a daughter who knows it all!"

"I saw so much courage . . . so much unselfishness . . . and so much love, among these men. The work I did was nothing at all, and I won't have you grudge it to them, father."

She leant across and touched his knee. She had thrown off her sadness and was laughing again, teasing him, the tears still glistening on her cheeks.

"Own up," she said. "You were only cross 'cos I went and left you to fend for yourself. Now isn't that so?"

"Things ent much improved now you're home, neither. – My mug's been empty this past half hour."

Often when Tom was at Lilac Cottage, he would fall into a kind of dream, watching Linn as she ironed clothes at the kitchen table or sat by the fire with her knitting or mending. Sometimes his gaze was so intense that she felt herself growing uncomfortable.

"How you do stare!" she said to him once. "You really oughtn't to stare at people so hard, Tom, especially saying nothing for hours on end."

"Sorry," he said, and looked away, frowning at the fire in the stove.

But at sight of the colour rising in his face, and the fraught expression in his eyes, Linn regretted her little outburst, humbling him in front of her father, and wanted to put the matter right.

"You can stare if you want to. You can stare at me as much as you like! I know what it is. It's my red hair. It's enough to make anyone stare, I'm sure."

Tom smiled. His glance rested briefly on her face, then flickered away again. He tried to think of something to say.

"Won't be long now. Christmas, I mean. I reckon it's just about eighteen days."

"You'll have to do better'n that," Jack said. "We thrashed that one out an hour ago. Not to mention the chances of snow."

"Father, please," Linn said.

"I know I don't talk much," Tom said. "The chaps used to say so in the Army. Betony always says so too."

"I met Betony at Chepsworth Park. I told her I knew you and she said, 'So that's where Tom's been spending all his evenings lately.'"

"Ah. Well. Now she knows."

"Is it such a secret, Tom, that you come out here to see us?"

"Not a secret exactly. I wouldn't say that."

"You haven't told anybody?"

"No. Maybe not."

"Then it must be a secret, mustn't it, unless Betony's told other people?"

"She wouldn't do that," Tom said.

"That's all right, then. – The secret is kept."

"I reckon you're teasing me again."

"Good gracious!" she said. "As though I would!"

Later that evening, when Tom had gone, Jack spoke to Linn in a serious manner.

"What's your feeling for that boy?"

"I don't rightly know. It's hard to say. I haven't known

him very long . . . yet I feel I've known him all my life."

"Do you care for him?" Jack asked.

"Oh, dear! What a catechism! Must I make up my mind tonight?"

She was looking at him with her head on one side, laughing into his bearded face, making fun of his fierce eyebrows. But Jack was not to be deflected.

"It's as well for you to know your mind, 'cos he cares for you a mighty lot, just as sure as God's in Gloucester."

"Yes," she said, becoming serious. "Perhaps he does."

"You must mind and not lead him on for nothing."

"D'you think I'd do that?"

"No, I don't, but I reckon you ought to consider the matter and sort out your feelings as they are so far."

"Yes," she said, "perhaps I should."

Every evening now, immediately after supper at Cobbs, Tom made himself tidy and left the house. And today, Saturday, he hurried off after midday lunch.

"Where's he get to?" Jesse asked. "Is he courting, Dicky, do you suppose?"

"I dunno, dad. He don't say nothing to me about it."

"It's none of our business, anyway," Betony said.

"Ent it?" said Dicky, and rose, grinning, from the table, a piece of bread pudding in his hand. "Supposing I think it is?" he said. "Supposing I go and try to find out?"

He left the house and followed Tom to Millery Bridge, taking care to keep out of sight. Just past the Malthouse, Tom turned off along the road to Blagg, and when Dicky got to the corner, he had already reached Shepherd's Cross. There, as he passed the old ruined cowsheds, a girl stepped out and ran to meet him, and Dicky, watching from the Malthouse doorway, saw that it was Tilly Preston.

He returned home in triumph and told his father what he had seen.

"Oh, well," Jesse said, "she was always sweet on him, warnt she, that girl?"

But Betony was extremely puzzled.

"Are you sure it was Tilly Preston?"

"Laws!" Dicky said. "I've seen her often enough, surely?"

Tilly had waited for Tom at the old cowsheds. She was shrammed with cold and shivering. Her face was pinched, red, miserable.

"Are you avoiding me, Tom Maddox?"

"No, not exactly," Tom said.

"I think you are!" she said, hugging herself and rubbing the upper parts of her arms. "Oh, yes! I'm certain of it!"

"You'll catch your death of cold, Tilly, hanging about in this weather without a proper coat on."

"Whose fault is it I'm hanging about? You've got no right, avoiding me, not after all that's happened between us, and I shouldn't have to come looking for you. *You* should ought to be calling on *me*."

"It was all a mistake," Tom said. "It shouldn't never've happened by rights."

"A mistake? Really? Well, that's nice, I must say! You've made my day for me now, ent you, telling me a thing like that?"

"It *was* a mistake, though, all the same."

"It's a bit late for saying that, and it don't get us no further forward, does it?"

"No. Maybe not. But I dunno what else to say."

"You was glad enough the night it happened. You was quite content and don't you deny it, taking advantage like you did. But now you've got other fish to fry, ent you, and don't care tuppence what happens to me?"

Tilly was crying, her eyes almost closed, the tears squeezing out between reddened lids. She was shivering violently, cold to the bone, and she cried with little gasping noises, holding both hands against her mouth.

"You ought to get home," Tom said, "or you'll get a chill as sure as fate."

He put out a hand to touch her gently and she took it eagerly in her own, holding it close against her chest.

"Why not come home with me and see my dad? Why not tell him we're going to be married? I'm sure he'd be pleased. – He's quite changed his mind towards you ever since you went as a soldier."

"No," Tom said, and drew back his hand.

"Why not?" she asked. "Why shouldn't we get married?"

"It wouldn't be right for us, that's why."

"Supposing we had to?" Tilly said. "Supposing I was having a baby?"

Tom was silent. He looked at her for a long time.

"You ent, though, are you? No. Surely not."

"I don't know. It's too soon to say. But I think about it all the time and it makes me so scared I could nearly throw myself into the Derrent."

"You can't be," Tom said. "No. Surely not."

"Why can't I, for goodness' sake? These things do happen, as well you should know, seeing it's how you come to be born your own self."

"I know it happens, but is it happening to you, that's the point?"

"I don't know. We'll just have to hope for the best, shan't we? It certainly won't work out that way if I can help it."

"Don't you go doing nothing foolish!"

"It's too late saying that."

"You know what I mean."

"No. I don't. What do you mean?"

"Well, if it should happen there is a baby, you won't do nothing to harm it, will you?"

"No," she said. "I won't do that, I promise, honest." And she looked at him from under her lashes. "You do care what happens to me, then, after all? I knew you did, deep down, underneath. I knew you couldn't be horrid to me."

"I reckon I'd better see you home."

"And speak to my father while you're there?"

"No!" he said. "I got nothing to say to him at all." And he thrust his fists into his pockets. "I've got to have time to think things out. I shall need to know about that baby."

"Meantime, perhaps, you'll be making up to that Mercybright girl who lives with her dad in Stoney Lane? Oh, yes, you may well look surprised, but *I* know what takes you out to Blagg every moment you got to spare!"

"I've got to go," Tom said, and walked away, making towards Puppet Hill.

"You'll be hearing from me!" she called shrilly. "You can't just drop me like an old glove. Not after all that's happened between us! I won't take it. I won't! I won't!"

One evening, a week or so later, Jack Mercybright was in The Rose and Crown, buying a pint of Chepsworth ale and four new clay pipes.

"Quiet this evening," he said to Tilly, for he was her only customer.

"Too many folk ill in bed with the 'flu, including my dad and two of my brothers."

"You ent sickening for it, I hope?"

"I hope not indeed. I've got troubles enough already."

"I'm sorry to hear it," Jack said.

"You might be sorrier," Tilly said, leaning her elbows

on the counter, "if you knew the other party concerned."

"What're you on about, girl?"

"I happen to know that Tom Maddox is a friend of yours, made welcome in your home."

"That's right. He's a friend of my daughter's."

"You ought to warn her," Tilly said, "or she might end up the same as me, carrying his baby."

Jack, smoking, looked into Tilly's watchful eyes. His own face was blank. She would read nothing there if he could help it.

"Does Tom know you're having his baby?"

"I wasn't too sure of it last time I saw him, and he ent been near me since I mentioned the matter."

"What about your father? Does he know?"

"Lord, no! My father would kill me. He would, honest. He don't think a lot of Tom Maddox. I dare not mention it till the wedding day is fixed between us."

"You're very free in airing your troubles, young woman."

"I wouldn't air them to no one else. But you've got a daughter to consider. You wouldn't want no harm to befall her."

"It ent likely to," Jack said. "My daughter is no slut."

He drank his beer and left without speaking another word.

He went straight home to Lilac Cottage, and there, when he entered the bright, warm, comfortable kitchen, Tom was helping to wind Linn's wool, holding the skein on outstretched hands while she wound it up in a soft ball.

"Gracious," she said, as Jack stood on the hearth between them, "you look like murder, dad, you do, really."

"I've got good reason," Jack said. "I've been talking to Tilly Preston and she says she's carrying this chap's baby."

Tom and Linn were facing each other, sitting close, their knees touching. Linn had stopped winding and was looking at him with unbelieving eyes. He could see the laughter dying in them; could see her face growing slowly cold; and inside himself there was a similar coldness and deadness, together with an immense shame.

"Well?" Jack demanded, angrily. "Is it true or false that you've been lovering with this girl?"

"What a word," Tom muttered. "Lovering!"

"Choose what word you better prefer. I'm only asking if it's true."

"Yes. It's true. That ent disputed."

"And you knew," Linn said, staring at him, "that Tilly was going to have a baby?"

"Not for sure, no. She was afraid of it, but she wasn't sure."

"You didn't go to her to find out?"

"No," he said, and looked away.

"How long is it since you saw her last?"

"A week. Ten days. I dunno."

"And said nothing at all about it? Came here every evening the same, behaving as always, knowing Tilly was in such trouble? What did you think would happen to her?"

"I reckon I put it out of my mind."

"How nice for you, having a mind so *very* convenient!"

Linn leant across and took the skein of wool from his hands. She held it loosely in her lap. Her face was pale, and she still looked at him as though she could scarcely believe what she heard.

"Well?" Jack said. "What d'you aim to do about it? Tilly expects you to marry her."

"I dunno why," Tom said. "I reckon she knows I don't love her."

"But you must do!" Linn exclaimed. "Surely? Surely? At least a little? Or are you the sort that takes every girl that comes along?"

"It was the night of the bonfire," he said. "A lot of folk was mad that night. But it don't mean I love her. Not enough to marry her. Nor she don't care tuppence for me neither. I'm pretty damn well sure of that."

"How d'you know? Have you ever asked her?"

"I don't need to. I just know."

"You haven't thought of her feelings at all. It's too inconvenient. It's something else you've put out of your mind!"

"The way you're talking to me," Tom said, "I reckon maybe I'd better go."

"Yes!" she said. "Go to this Tilly Preston of yours and do what you know is right by her!"

Tom got up and stood for a moment as though lost. Then he walked out and they heard his footsteps in the lane. Linn sat staring with hurt, angry eyes. Her father watched her, aching for her.

"And I thought I knew him!" she said with sudden self-scorn. "It was silly of me, after so short a time, but I thought I knew him through and through."

"I told you before, you're a lot too trusting where other people is concerned, and men ent altogether quite the way you see them."

"Then no doubt you're pleased, being right as usual!"

"No, I ent pleased. Far from it. In fact I feel sorry for that boy Tom."

"It's the girl I feel sorry for, poor soul."

"You needn't worry on that score. Tilly can look after herself pretty well."

"It's a good thing she can," Linn said.

*

Tom went to The Rose and Crown and found Tilly still alone in the taproom.

"You got my message, then?" she said.

"Yes, I got it. That's why I'm here."

"I've been so worried these past two weeks, I'm nearly going out of my mind."

"It's definite, then, about your having the baby?" he said. "Have you been to see the doctor?"

"What, and let the whole district know about it?"

"No," he said, "I suppose not."

"It's definite, you take my word. So what're you going to do about it?"

"Get married, what else? It's the only solution. I'll ask Jesse if we can have the old Pikehouse to live in and a few bits and pieces of furniture."

"A house of our own?" she said, glowing. "Oh, Tom, won't that be lovely? Won't that be grand?"

"I'll see the vicar in the morning. If we get a move on, we can be married just after Christmas."

"My word, you're in a hurry, ent you?" she said.

"There's no point in hanging about."

At Cobbs, later, when the news was known, only Betony felt surprise. She took Tom aside and asked him about it.

"What happened to Linn Mercybright?"

"Nothing happened. I'm marrying Tilly."

"But for God's sake why? I don't understand."

"We've got a baby coming," he said. "He's forced our hand, as you might say."

"Oh, you're such fools, you men!" she said. "Getting yourself into a mess like that with a little trollop like Tilly Preston! I thought you'd more sense."

"Tilly's all right," he said, shrugging. "It ent just her fault she's having a baby and it's him we got to think of now."

*

He had lived at the Pikehouse as a boy. It was strange to be back there again now, with some of the same furniture, given to them by Beth and Jesse, and some of the same old crockery hanging up in the tiny kitchen.

"I lived here with my Grannie Izzard. She wasn't my proper grannie, really, but she brung me up from about a year old. That old rocking-chair was hers, and the footstool there, and that little old Welsh dresser."

"I bet you never thought," Tilly said, sitting beside him on the settle, "that you'd be bringing your bride home here and setting up house the way you have."

"No," he said, "I never did."

"I reckon we're lucky, don't you, having a nice little home of our own, miles away by ourselves like we are, with no nosy neighbours poking in?"

"Yes," he said, "I reckon we are."

"I shall try my best to be a good wife to you, Tom."

"And I shall try to be a good husband."

"Oh, I know you will! I know. I know."

"I put some wood aside in the workshop yesterday, ready for making a cot," he said. "I shall start work on that when I've got a bit of time to spare."

Tilly moved closer and put her arm through the crook of his, squeezing it hard against his side. She rested her face against his shoulder.

"The men'll see it if you do that. You know what gossips they all are, specially Sam Lovage."

"They've got to know sooner or later. You can't keep a baby secret for ever."

"Tom," she said, twisting the button on his cuff, "I've got something to tell you about that."

"What is it?"

"I made a mistake about having a baby. I'm not going to have one after all."

"Mistake?" he said. "How could you have made a mistake when so many weeks is gone past by?"

"You know what I mean. I was frightened to death! I thought you was going to let me down."

"There wasn't no baby. It was all a lie. Is that what you're trying to say to me?"

"I really don't see it makes much difference. We have been lovers, after all, and men so often need a nudge before they come up to scratch, the wretches."

Tilly felt the change in him. She sat up straight and looked at his face, and what she saw there made her afraid.

"Tom?" she said, in a small voice. "Don't look at me like that, Tom. It gives me the creeps. It does, honest. It makes me go icy all down inside."

Gently, her fingers plucked at his sleeve.

"Surely it's better to be by ourselves for a bit? We're only young once and babies'll come soon enough I daresay. Why not make the most of things while there's a chance?"

Tom got up and reached for his cap. His shadow leapt, huge in the firelight. His face was that of a graven image.

"Tom, where are you going?" Tilly demanded. "You can't go out on our wedding evening! You can't go out and leave me alone!"

Tom made no answer. He was already on his way out. A blast of cold air blew into the room, the door rattled shut, and he was gone. Tilly put her face in her hands and rocked herself to and fro, giving vent to small choking sobs. Then she took out her handkerchief and wiped her eyes, aware that her tears were washing the face-

powder from her cheeks and would stain the front of her
wedding-gown.

The fire had burnt low. She threw on three logs and
wiped her hands on the rag-made hearth-rug. She was
feeling hungry and she thought of the joint of cold mutton lying on the platter in the pantry. Ought she to wait
till Tom returned or would his sulks keep him out past
midnight? If so, that was his own fault. It was no reason
for her to starve.

She got up and went to the pantry.

Sometimes, at night, Tom would slip quietly out of bed, put on his clothes, and creep downstairs, out of the house. He rarely slept more than three or four hours at a time, for his head ached and there was a splitting of coloured lights immediately behind his eyes. Even his breathing gave him trouble. He had to get out in the keen night air.

Tilly, luckily, was a sound sleeper. She never knew when he left her side. She was still in bed when he set off for work at seven. But one morning, while he was eating his breakfast, she came downstairs in nightdress and shawl.

"You been out poaching again?" she said. "Brevitting about in them old woods?"

"I went for a bit of a walk, that's all."

"In the dark?" she said. "On cold winter nights like they are now? You must want seeing to, really, you must."

"It wasn't dark last night. There was a big full moon about three o'clock, and a sky full of stars."

"Respectable folk are warm in their beds at three o'clock in the small hours."

She came behind him and put her arms around his neck, and her face, close to his, was soft and warm like a sleepy child's.

"Don't you love me no more, now, Tom? Aren't you

going to try to forget that I told you just that one little lie?"

"I shall get round to it, given time."

"And will you be nice to me again?"

"I ent aware that I been nasty."

"I could make you love me again if only you'd give me half a chance. I could make you my slave. I know I could. There was plenty of chaps who was always after me in the old days. Harry Yelland for one. I could twist them all round my little finger."

"Then why ent you married to one of *them*?"

"I chose you instead, didn't I? Though I sometimes wonder why I did!" She was holding him back against her body, her arms tightening across his throat. "Tom?" she said softly, into his ear. "I know I can make you love me again if you'll only let me. I'm your lawful wife. You've got no right being nasty to me."

"I've got to go. I'll be late at the workshop."

He rose from his chair and Tilly released him. He began getting ready and she studied him with growing anger.

"Don't forget to ask Jesse Izzard about that new stove. I can't cook on this open fire. I've never been used to it, all my life."

"My grannie cooked on that open fire. She never found it gave her trouble."

"Oh, your old grannie was a proper wonder! But I'm not cooking at that there fireplace all my days and you may as well make up your mind I mean it!"

"All right," Tom said. "I'll ask Jesse's advice about it."

One evening when he got home, he saw a new broom with a brown-painted handle standing in the corner of the kitchen, and a new metal dustpan, painted green.

"Where'd they come from, all new and shiny like that?" he asked.

"A man came selling them at the door. From Birmingham, he said he was. I can pay bit by bit for that broom and dustpan, and anything else I care to buy."

"From Birmingham? And comes all this way?"

"He's got a motor-car," Tilly said. She looked at Tom with a little smile. "He offered to take me for a ride round. That's 'cos I said there was no buses. But I told him no, my husband wouldn't like it."

"It's no odds to me," Tom said, "though it's maybe wiser to watch your step with chaps of that sort."

"Chaps of what sort, I'd like to know? Mr Trimble's a very nice man. He was in the Army the same as you. Out in Egypt with the engineers."

"All right. You go for a ride if that's what you want. I ent raising no objections."

"What fun do I get, stuck out here all by myself, miles away from other people? I see old Mould from the lodge sometimes and I see Mrs Awner going past, but otherwise not a single soul do I ever talk to from one day's end to the next."

"I reckon it is pretty lonely out here, after your being right in Huntlip, with all the folk at The Rose and Crown. Why not go in now and then and give your father a hand like you used to?"

"Oh, no!" Tilly said. "Why should I work in my father's taproom, now I'm married with a home of my own? What'd people say, seeing me back there, serving beer? What d'you think I got married *for*?"

"Look!" Tom said. "You do whatever it is you want to do and stop going on at me. All I want is peace and quiet."

"And nothing else matters!" Tilly said. "You don't never think of me at all!"

She turned away and began crying, great heaving sobs

that wrenched her body. She leant against the back of the settle and hid her face in her folded arms. She looked small and frail, and it seemed she would never be able to stop crying.

"I wish I was dead! I do really! You're always so horrid nowadays. I never thought it'd be like this! Hating me, hating me, all the time!"

"Ah, no," Tom said. "You mustn't say that 'cos it ent true. You must stop crying or you'll make yourself ill. I never meant to make you cry."

He put out a hand and touched her shoulder, and straight away she was in his arms, clutching at him and pressing her body against his. The shivering sobs ceased abruptly and when she looked up at him, into his face, he saw she was laughing.

"I knew I could do it!" she said, exultant. "I knew I could make you love me again if I put my mind to it properly. Men are as soft as dough, really, but they have to be kneaded to bring them round." She put up her hands and entwined her fingers in his hair, trying to make him bend towards her. "Your *face*!" she said. "When I turned just now! If you could've seen it! I had to laugh!"

Tom pulled away from her, jerking his head back, free of her grasp. She clutched at him and he pushed her aside.

"Now what's the matter, for goodness' sake? You're not going out without your supper?"

"Damn the supper and you too!"

The door slammed and she was left alone again, strands of his hair still entwined in her fingers.

"I get the feeling," said Sam Lovage, toasting his cheese at the workshop stove, "that marriage don't agree with our butty here."

"He's quieter than ever lately, ent he?" Albert Tunniman agreed. "And his work's gone off something terrible."

"What've you got for oneses, Tom? Don't Tilly feed you, the bad girl?"

"He's got bread and dripping, same as always," said Fred Lovage, winking at Sam.

"Oh no I ent!" Tom said. "It's fried bacon."

"You ent got a motor-car, have you, Tom? A smart little Austin with a hood? No, well, it ent hardly likely, I don't suppose. Yet my girl Lilian swears she seen one, outside the Pikehouse on Friday morning, when she was going to sew at Scoate."

"It's a traveller-chap, selling brushes. He calls every Friday for his money."

"I shouldn't like that," Tunniman said, "a stranger calling on my missus when I ent there to see what's what."

"I know about him," said Sam Lovage. "He's been through Huntlip, door to door, and tried to sell Queenie a new mop. She sent him packing and a good thing too. There's too many salesmen going about bothering people since the war. Somebody ought to up and stop it."

"Tom should ought to speak to Tilly. I wouldn't stick it if I was him."

"It's no odds to me," Tom said. "Tilly must do as she thinks best."

He finished his lunch and went back to the bench, where the screen he was carving lay half done. He selected a chisel from the rack.

"Don't you never rest?" Lovage shouted. "It wants twenty minutes to one o'clock."

"I've had all I want," Tom said. "I'd just as soon get on."

The next day, Saturday, Tom had work at Crayle in the morning and finished it by eleven o'clock. The workshop was closed in the afternoon so he went straight home, thus arriving early, perhaps an hour before his time. And, seeing a motor-car in the roadway, he went across to the woods opposite and stood among the trees, waiting for the visitor to depart.

At one o'clock, a fair-haired man came out of the Pikehouse, glancing at his watch, and Tilly followed him to the gate. They stood talking for a little while, and the man had his arm round Tilly's shoulders. Then he got into the motor-car and drove away towards Norton. Tilly turned and went back indoors, swinging the end of the silken cord which she wore tied about her waist. Her heels click-clicked along the path.

When Tom walked in, she was combing her hair before the mirror.

"You're early today, aren't you?"

"Ah. Well. Maybe I am."

"I've been busy this morning. You'll have to make do with bread and cheese."

"Suits me," Tom said.

It was true, as Albert Tunniman had said, that his work was not so good lately. Great-grumpa Tewke said the same.

"You've lost your touch, boy, that's your trouble. You've been too long with a rifle in your hands instead of the tools of your proper trade. You can't go off for three years without it showing in your work."

"I reckon that's right," Tom said . "I shall have to practise all the harder."

But however hard he tried, it would not come: there was not the old unity between hand and eye; there was not the mastery over the chisel; and often his judgment played him false.

The work he was doing was for Mr Talbot of Crayle
Court. A fire had occurred there in December and some
old oak furniture had been badly damaged. Tom's task
now was to make two replica doors for a cupboard, each
one carved with a Talbot hound, surrounded by oak-
apples, leaves, and acorns, the initials E.B.T. among
them. One of the old burnt doors lay before him and he
was copying it, using oak great-grumpa had given him,
taken from an old oak pew.

One day, while carving the second door, peering closely to follow the delicate pencil-lines, he had trouble in
keeping to the tiny detail. His gouge seemed too big, the
tracing too small, and the whole design seemed to swim
hazily before his eyes. He stood up straight and looked
out of the window. The workshop yard was covered in
frost; the cobnut bushes were white-fuzzed; a blackbird
quivered on a slim stem. When he looked back again at
his work, the tracery seemed smaller than ever, and he
suddenly threw down his gouge and hammer.

"I can't do it," he said to Jesse. "George Hopson'll have
to do it."

And, pulling his jacket on as he went, he walked out of
the workshop door.

"What's up with him?" asked Great-grumpa Tewke,
coming to Jesse.

"I don't rightly know," Jesse said, frowning. "I reckon
maybe he feels it, you know, your telling him he'd lost his
touch. It ent like Tom to leave a piece of work unfinished. I must speak to him about that in the morning."

But Tom was not at work the next morning, nor the
morning after, so early on Saturday afternoon, Jesse took
the pony and trap and drove to the Pikehouse. His knock
brought no answer. The door, amazingly, was locked, and
when he peeped in at the window, he could see no sign

of life whatever. He returned to Cobbs puzzled and worried and spoke to his wife and daughter about it.

"Nobody at all?" Beth said. "Not even Tilly?"

"Neither hide nor hair of either of 'em."

"If Tom's there alone and in one of his moods," Betony said, "he may have been lying low when you called, just to avoid talking to you."

"Why should he do that? To me of all people? Ent I as good as a father to him?"

"I was thinking of him as a little boy and how he always ran off to the woods whenever we called on Grannie Izzard."

"But he ent a little boy now," Jesse said. "He's a grown man. I should like to know what it is that's upset him."

"So should I," Betony said, "and I mean to find out."

She went that very afternoon, going on foot to give no warning, and arriving just as dusk was falling. The house was in darkness, silent as the grave, lonely beside the old turnpike road, with only a handful of Scoate House sheep grazing on the surrounding wasteland. She opened and closed the gate with care, walked on tiptoe along the path, and stood for a moment in the porch. The door when she tried it opened before her and she stepped straight into the unlit kitchen.

"Tom?" she said. "It's me. Betony. Are you there?"

"Yes, I'm here," Tom said, and got up from the rocking-chair. "How did you come? I never heard no sound of the trap."

He struck a match and lit the oil-lamp on the table. The room came to life and Betony closed the door behind her.

"What's wrong with you? Why haven't you been to work? Why didn't you answer when dad called earlier today?"

"I'm taking a bit of a holiday."

"Just look at the mess in this kitchen! It can't have been cleaned in a month of Sundays. Whatever does Tilly think she's doing?"

"Tilly ent here, she's gone," he said.

"Gone where, for God's sake?"

"I dunno where. She didn't say."

"Has she gone back to her father in Huntlip? No, surely not, or we should have heard."

"I reckon she's gone with another chap."

"Don't you *know* what's happened to her?"

"I came home from work one day and there was a note to say she'd gone. I dunno no more'n that."

"What makes you think there's another man?"

"I seen him," he said. "A traveller-chap, selling brushes. Once he was here when I got home. I saw them laughing and talking together. Then he went off in a little car."

"Well, that's a fine thing, I must say, after only a few weeks of marriage! Don't you care where she's gone? Aren't you going to try and find her?"

"No. Why should I? It's no odds to me."

"It's cold in here," Betony said, shivering. "Don't you think you should light the fire? There's plenty of sticks and logs there and I don't like freezing even if you do."

"All right," he said, and began at once pushing the wood-ashes back in the hearth. "Maybe it *is* time I boiled a kettle."

"What about the baby?" Betony asked.

"There wasn't no baby after all. Just a mistake, Tilly said."

"You mean she led you up the path?"

"That's about it, I suppose, yes."

When the fire was burning, piled high, and the kettle hung above the flames, Tom rose from his haunches and crossed the room to hang up his jacket. On the way he stumbled, sending the little footstool flying, and almost sweeping the lamp from the table. Betony gave an exclamation and set the lamp in its rightful place.

"You can't be drunk at this time of day! What's wrong with you for heaven's sake?"

Tom stood quite still, his hands in his pockets. He was looking past her, into the fire.

"Seems I'm going blind," he said.

After a while, when the kettle boiled, Betony made a pot of tea. There was no milk to be found anywhere; nor any sugar; only a jar of her mother's honey; so she stirred a spoonful into the mug of milkless tea and sat opposite, watching him drink it.

"How long is it since your sight began failing?"

"I dunno. It's hard to say. It comes and goes, like, and sometimes it seems better than others."

"Have you seen a doctor?"

"Not since leaving the hospital at Sawsford."

"Then you must!" she said. "Where's the point in losing time?"

"Will they be able to do something for me?"

"We won't know that till we get there," she said. "But it's no use burying yourself away out here, without a word to anyone. What did you hope to achieve by it?"

"I wanted time to sort things out."

"How did you think you were going to live, stuck out here and not working?"

"I hadn't got as far as that. I just wanted to be by myself and make the most of what sight is left me."

"And afterwards?"

"I dunno. I hadn't decided. End it, maybe, somehow or other."

"Do away with yourself, you mean, the same as your father did before you?"

"I'd just as soon die, as go through life in the dark," he said.

"What rubbish you're talking!" she said, with scorn. "This is something you've got to fight! You fought over there for nearly three years. You didn't give in so easily then and you certainly mustn't give in now. You must fight back like a proper soldier."

Tom sipped at his hot tea, and the steam rose, moistening his face. His dark skin was smooth and shining, but still white-flecked in many places, where the shell-blast had scarred him. His deep dark eyes were bright, steady, contemplative, and looked at her with childlike hope. It was hard to believe those eyes could fail him.

"All right," he said. "Tell me what I ought to do."

Her family, when she broke the news, could scarcely believe what she was saying. Tom's injury was four months old. They had thought his sufferings were over.

"Ah, no, not our Tom!" Jesse said. "After all this time? And what he's been through?"

"Did Tilly know he was going blind when she left him?" Beth asked.

"No, mother. He told no one until today."

"He shouldn't have married her," Dicky said. "I said all along she was nothing worth it."

"Damnable war!" great-grumpa said. "Is there no end to its consequences, even now?"

"No, there's no end," Betony said. "I see its evil every day when I visit the men at Chepworth Park."

"I'll go out and see him," Jesse said. "I'll knock this time till he lets me in."

"No, don't go yet," Betony said. "I think he's better left alone."

On Monday, early, she travelled with Tom by train to Sawsford. The military hospital stood on a hill and had a fine view out over the town. To Betony it seemed very busy but to Tom it was quiet compared with when he had been there last. He was seen by three doctors and spent half an hour with each in turn. They were strangers to him but had his medical details before them and asked him a great many questions. He was then given X rays and told he would have to wait some time before they could tell him the results.

"I suggest you have lunch," the surgeon, Major Kerrison, said, speaking to Tom and Betony together. "The Fleece round the corner is good. Tell the waiter I sent you."

After lunch at The Fleece and an hour spent walking over the hill, they returned to the hospital and sat waiting. The day was a mild one, with a premature hint of spring, and in the gardens outside the window, heliotrope flowered, pink and mauve.

A nurse came into the waiting-room, and Tom stood up. He was white to the lips and a pulse was throbbing in his cheek.

"The doctor would like to see Mrs Maddox."

"I'm not Mrs Maddox," Betony said. "I'm his foster-sister. My name is Miss Izzard."

"Oh. Well. Come this way, Miss Izzard, please."

So Tom had to wait again, sitting on the bench with his back against the wall, while nurses in white and patients in blue passed to and fro along the corridor. When Betony came back at last, he knew from her face that she brought bad news.

"What'd they say? You may as well tell me straight out."

"They say there's nothing they can do."

"No operation nor treatment nor nothing?"

"The optic nerves are too badly damaged. There's nothing they can do about it. They say it's only a question of time."

"Total blindness?" Tom asked.

"I'm afraid so."

"How long?"

"They don't know."

"Six months? A year? They must have some notion, I'd have thought."

"No. They're uncertain. It could happen soon . . . or it could be as much as two years."

"I knew it was going to be bad," he said, "when they asked for you."

"The doctor wants to see you too. He has some advice he wants to give you and a letter for Dr Dundas at home. He says you're eligible for a pension."

"A pension!" he said, hollowly, and went away down the corridor.

Betony sat with her hands on her handbag. She had not told him everything, even now, because she and the doctor had decided against it, and she closed her eyes for a brief moment, seeking in herself some untapped spring of strength and courage. By the time Tom returned, she thought she had found it. She rose and went to him with a calm face.

When they reached Chepsworth and were on their way to The Old Plough, where they had left the pony and trap, Tom stopped suddenly and said he would prefer to walk back home across the fields.

"It's a nice afternoon. You don't mind, do you, Bet?"

"Promise you won't do anything silly."

"It's all right," he said, and a rare smile just touched

his lips. "I'm taking it like a proper soldier."

"You may never lose your sight at all," she said briskly. "Doctors have been known to be wrong sometimes."

She drove home without him, and as she turned into the fold, Michael came out of the house to meet her.

"You're very late, Betony. We're due at my uncle's by half past five but I doubt if we'll get there much before six."

"I'm sorry, Michael, I'm not coming. There's something important I have to do."

"More important than keeping an engagement?"

"I hope you'll make my excuses to your uncle and explain that it just couldn't be avoided."

"I suppose it's something to do with Tom? Your mother said you'd both been down to Sawsford today."

"Yes, I went with him to the hospital there."

"How much longer, may I ask, are you going to play nursemaid to that young man?"

"Tom's going blind!" she said bluntly. "I suppose you'd admit he needs help?"

"Betony, I'm sorry, I'd no idea. Your mother and father should have said. But still, even so, I don't see why you should take the responsibility. Not now that he has a wife."

"Tilly's left him," Betony said.

"Good God! What a mess it all is!"

"The longer you wait here, the later you'll be getting to Ilton."

"Yes, yes, I'm going," he said, but continued to stand there, watching her as she fed the pony. "You don't seem able to get away from Tom, do you? He haunts you like some guilty dream. You're always trying to pay off a debt for something you did or did not do to him in childhood."

"Yes, well, perhaps I am."

"In my opinion, it can't be done. I feel you're only wasting your time."

"It isn't only my debt. Tom was hurt while fighting in France. I think we all owe a debt to men like him."

"That can't ever be paid either."

"No, I don't think it can," Betony said, "But I think we should try all the same."

An hour later she drove to Blagg and called on the Mercybrights at Lilac Cottage. Jack was sitting reading his paper. He put it aside as Linn showed Betony into the kitchen, but he made no attempt to stand up, and she saw that one leg lay resting across a stool.

"I wanted to talk to you both about Tom."

"You'd better sit down. I'm willing to hear what you got to say, and so is Linn, though I doubt if his business can interest us much."

"Tom's wife has left him. He's all alone. It wasn't true she was having a baby. She led him up the garden path."

"I ent too surprised," Jack said. "She struck me as a sly piece. But it don't alter the fact that he'd been monkeying with her in the first place."

"One fall from grace," Betony said, "and you'd hold it against him all his life?"

She turned from him to look at Linn, who sat on the edge of an upright chair, her hands still nursing a cup and a tea-cloth. The girl was beautiful, Betony thought: delicate features, neatly made; colouring vivid and unusual; dark brown eyes full of thought and feeling. There was a gentle warmth about her, yet plainly she had a resolute will.

"Would you hold it against him for ever?"

"I'm not his judge," Linn said.

"I'm hoping you might be his salvation."

"Look here," Jack said. "That young man made my daughter unhappy. He hurt her, Miss Izzard, and she done right to send him away."

"He must have meant something to you, then," Betony said, still looking at Linn, "if he had the power to make you unhappy."

"He chose someone else. It's not my fault if it didn't work out."

"He never cared tuppence for Tilly Preston."

"He told me that, but I didn't believe him."

"You ought to have done. Tom doesn't tell lies."

"Why have you come to us, Miss Izzard?"

"I've come because Tom is going blind."

"No," Linn said, and turned her face away, hiding her pain. "No! Oh, no!"

"Can't something be done for him?" Jack asked.

"No, nothing," Betony said. "He saw the doctors this afternoon. Now he's out at the Pikehouse, alone, facing up to it the best way he can. But there's something else – something Tom himself doesn't know – that nobody knows except myself – and I hope to God I do right to tell you."

Betony paused. She was trying to read the girl's face.

"He's only got a short time to live," she said. "Twelve months at the most, and that only if he takes things quietly. If he had an illness of any kind, or too much strain, death could come sooner, the doctor said."

Linn sat perfectly still. It was some time before she spoke.

"I remember. . . at the hospital in Rouen . . . they were afraid of brain-damage . . . but then it seemed as if everything was all right after all." She was perfectly calm, though white as ashes, and she drew a deep, controlled breath. "I wish I could have known . . . when I first came home and met him again . . ."

"Linn, do you love him?" her father asked, and when she turned to look at him, giving her answer silently, he said, "In that case, I reckon you'd better go to him, don't you?"

"Yes," she said. "I think so too."

"I'll take you there," Betony said. "I'll wait outside while you get ready. Don't be too long. I've already kept the pony standing and the evening is getting a lot colder."

She went out to the trap and sat waiting, and after a while Linn joined her, carrying a small canvas bag. It was dusk by the time they reached the Pikehouse, and a small rain was sprinkling down, out of a sky the colour of charcoal. The house was in darkness, and Betony sat waiting again while Linn found her way to the door. A few minutes passed, then the lamp was lit and shone through the window. Betony turned in the narrow roadway and drove home through the drizzling rain.

It was a Sunday, and the family at Cobbs were about to sit down to their midday dinner when the back door burst open and Emery Preston walked in, followed by his eldest son, Matthew.

"What's all this?" granna demanded, bringing a pile of plates to the table, and Great-grumpa Tewke, carving-knife poised against the steel, said, "This ent The Rose and Crown, by God, and I'll thank you to knock before lifting the sneck of decent folks' doors."

"Decent folks?" Emery shouted. "Decent folks, did you say?"

"What d'you want?" Beth asked. "You can see our dinner's on the table."

"My business is with your husband."

"Why me?" Jesse said. "Why me, I'd like to know?"

"You're the nearest thing Tom Maddox has got for a father, that's why, and I want to know what's happened to Tilly."

"Yes, well," Jesse said. "That ent nothing to do with me." And he busied himself about the stove, leaving the matter to his wife and daughter. They, it seemed, found nothing amiss with the way young Tom was carrying on. They, therefore, could answer all the awkward questions.

"Tilly's run off," Betony said to Emery Preston. "Hadn't you heard?"

"I've heard a lot of funny things lately, but nothing at all from Maddox hisself, so what's he playing at, you tell me that!"

"Seems they weren't happy, so Tilly left him."

"Then why ent we seen her?" Emery said. "A girl falling out with her husband like that would surely come home to her own father?"

"Not if she left with another man."

"I ent having *that*! Not my girl Tilly. She was always a good girl and she certainly wouldn't behave like that!"

"Rubbish!" Beth said. "Tilly's no better than she should be, and well you know it, Emery Preston."

"She deceived Tom," Betony said, "making believe she was having a baby."

"She never told me she was having a baby."

"She wouldn't, of course. She knew you'd take your belt to her."

"Who says I take my belt to my children? And why shouldn't I if they deserve it? I always warned her against that boy. I tried to stop her marrying him."

"It's a pity you didn't succeed, Mr Preston."

"What'd he do to her, the swine, to make her run off without a word?"

"*He* didn't take his belt to her, if that's what you mean."

"We don't know that! We know nothing at all. He's been acting queer for some time past and I ent the only one to say so neither."

"Is it surprising, since he's going blind?"

"I know! I know!" Emery said. "It ent that I don't feel nothing for him. He's been through a lot, I daresay, but it don't excuse his ill-using Tilly and I'm going out there to see him about it."

"No, don't do that," Betony said. "Leave him alone."

"You needn't worry about my feelings! I know damn

well he's got another woman living there with him. It's no good hoping to keep it quiet, even if he does live three miles out. All Huntlip knows about the way he's going on."

"Huntlip would!" Dicky muttered.

"He didn't waste much time, did he, finding someone to take Tilly's place?"

"She was the one who walked out."

"I don't know that! That's just his story! It's like this chap she's supposed to've run away with. I don't know he even existed."

"He existed all right," said great-grumpa. "He came to my workshop, trying to sell me foreign brushes."

"Well, *I've* never seen him," Emery said, "and I'm the one that keeps the pub!"

"I've seen him, though," Matthew said suddenly. "Chap about thirty, driving a motor, sounded as though he came from Brum. I was parked beside him in the road once and he gave me some lip about my motor-cycle."

"Oh? Is that so?"

"Come to think about it," Matthew said, "he ent been around these few weeks lately, though one or two people still owe him money."

"Why didn't you say so before?"

"It warnt till they mentioned his selling brushes – "

"And it still don't prove nothing, neither, does it?"

"What're you hoping to prove?" asked Beth.

"I dunno!" Emery said. "All I know is that I don't like it and I tell you straight so's you know how I stand. But I'll say this – if Tilly turns up with this salesman fella, they'll both rue the day, I promise you that!"

He turned towards the door, shoving the boy Matthew before him, and Great-grumpa Tewke looked up from carving the joint of beef.

"I'd ask you to stop to dinner," he said, his voice laden with sarcasm, "if it warnt all gone cold while you was so busy showing yourself up for the fool you are!"

When the Prestons had gone, Jesse returned to his place at the table, next to Betony.

"All this talk!" he said, shaking his head. "I'm disappointed in that boy Tom, causing all this scandal and gossip. Whatever will people think of us? What'll the *captain* think of us?"

"You don't need to call him the captain now, father. He's not in the Army any more."

"He'll always be the captain to me."

"Even when he and I are married?"

"H'mm," Jesse said, "and when'll that come to pass, I wonder?"

He longed to see her married to Michael. He could not understand why they should wait.

"You're always so busy," Michael said, looking over Betony's shoulder at the exercise-book she was correcting. "What with your work at Chepsworth Park and now the school – I hardly see you nowadays."

"It's only temporary," Betony said. "The school, that is. It's only while Miss Likeness is ill."

"I'm surprised you teach them geometry. I'd no idea village schools were so ambitious. I thought it was all hymn-singing and sewing fine seams on linen samplers."

"Huntlip's got a *good* village school. All others ought to be like it."

"I've half a mind, the moment we're married, to whisk you off to South Africa and hide you away on my uncle's farm."

"You're always talking about South Africa."

"I had a very happy year out there, when I was a care-free boy in my teens."

"The trouble is not so much that I'm busy," Betony said, "as that you are not busy enough."

"Would you believe it!" he exclaimed. "My mother says I need a long rest and you say I need to be active. What's a man to do, between two women offering such conflicting advice?"

"He should choose for himself, every time."

"I don't seem able to settle down, since coming home from the war," he said. "I'm bored stiff with the factory and it runs itself anyway under George Williams. I think what I'd really enjoy is having a farm of my own."

"Then why not buy one?"

"You make it all sound so simple."

"Well, isn't it simple, if you've got the money?"

"Would you like living on a farm?"

"Yes, I should, though not in South Africa," Betony said.

Michael went and stood at the window, looking out at the old orchard. The plum trees were stippled white with blossom; the evening sunlight lit their trunks; and a woodpecker flew from tree to tree. Nearby, in the garden, Jesse was splitting seed potatoes and Beth was planting them in the rows, her back bent in a perfect arch, her gloved hands working swiftly and surely, opening the soil with her sharp trowel and closing it again over the seed in a movement almost too quick for the eye to see.

"I suppose South Africa is too far away from your collection of lame dogs."

"What lame dogs?"

"Oh, come, now," he said. "There's your foster-brother for a start."

"Why do you always call him that? You know his name

so why not use it?" Betony closed one exercise-book, placed it on its pile, and took another. "Sometimes I feel you resent Tom."

"Perhaps I do," Michael said, turning towards her. "He does claim rather a lot of your attention."

"You can't be jealous of someone like Tom, knowing he's slowly going blind. It's too absurd."

"I didn't say I was jealous of him."

"Then what is all this about, exactly?"

"Oh, I don't know! It isn't very easy to talk to you these days, Betony. You're always thinking of other things."

"Very well," Betony said, and swung round to face him. "You now have my undivided attention, so what is it you're trying to say to me?"

"Yes, you're very good at putting me in the wrong and making me feel ridiculous," he said. "You're always much better than I am at any sort of argument."

"But I don't want to be better at it! I don't want to argue at all. All I want is to understand you." Looking at him she could see there was something seriously wrong; some awful uncertainty in his face; some fear that lurked and flickered in his eyes. "Michael," she said, "was it very bad in the prison-camp?"

"It wasn't what I would call a picnic."

"I wish you'd tell me about it."

"No," he said. "There's nothing to tell, and you're mistaken in thinking I want to talk about it. It's the last thing I want. I'm always trying to forget about it."

Betony rose and went to him. She touched his arm and found he was trembling.

"You'll have to make allowances for me, Michael, when I don't understand things. It was so hard for us at home here to imagine what it was really like. We tried and tried – or some of us did – but we couldn't really understand.

And I must admit I stopped worrying – indeed I was thankful in a way – once I heard you'd been taken prisoner."

"Thankful? Were you? Were you really?"

"Of course," she said. "Especially after the uncertainty while you were posted missing. All I could think of was that you were safe. Safe and alive and out of it all!"

"Yes," he said, in a dull voice, and took her in his arms so that his face should be hidden from her.

The night was unusually warm for May. There were too many blankets on his bed and he lay sweating, unable to sleep, listening to the cathedral clock striking. It was half past two. The room was full of white moonlight.

He rose and put on his dressing-gown. He opened the door quietly and went out across the landing. His mother heard him and called out. Her door was half open, and when he looked in she was sitting up in bed, groping for the light-switch.

"Don't put the light on. The moon is bright enough."

"What's the matter, Michael, are you ill?"

"No, no. I just couldn't sleep, that's all. I thought a drop of Scotch might do the trick."

"I'm worried about you, not sleeping. You've been like this for weeks now."

"My bed's too cushy, that's the trouble. Perhaps I should get a wire-netting bunk."

His mother patted a place on the bed. He went and sat there, and the two of them were close together, with the moon shining on them, bright as a searchlight. Her grey hair was set in symmetrical wavelets, as orderly as in the day-time, and had the sheen of polished pewter. Her face was pale and her lips in the moonlight looked almost purple.

"Have you got something on your mind?"

"Nothing more than usual."

"Is everything all right between you and Betony?"

"If it isn't, the fault is entirely on my side."

"You can't expect me to accept that."

"It's true all the same."

"You've been home for five months, yet you grow more nervy all the time. You're drinking a lot. You never used to."

"That's what it does to us . . . lies in wait and pounces on us . . ."

"Were you ill-treated at the camp?"

"Some of the guards were pretty brutal, but most of them were all right. Hunger was the worst thing we had to bear, and I almost welcomed that in a way, as an expiation."

"Expiation?"

"Because I felt guilty at being safe."

"My dear boy! What nonsense you're talking – '

"Don't interrupt me. I want to tell you what really happened. I gave myself up, you see, because I couldn't face any more fighting. I wasn't all that badly wounded. I could have got back to our lines if I'd tried. Minching and Darby wanted to help me, but I made some excuse and stayed behind, where the German patrol was sure to find me."

His mother was silent, sitting upright against her pillows, her hands lying motionless on the quilt. For once he could guess nothing of her thoughts.

"I liked it at first, being a soldier. I was even good at it, up to a point. Promotion came quickly, as you know. But it all went on so long, so long, and the more one did the more they expected. I began to wish, like everyone else, that I might be wounded and out of it, but I was wounded three times and every time they patched me up as good as new and sent me back again for more.

"It wouldn't have been so bad, I think, if I had been just a private soldier, but I was an officer giving orders . . . blowing a whistle and sending men over the parapet . . . and when we were in a tight spot, I'd see them all looking at me, expecting me to know the answer, expecting me to do the right thing and get them all out of the mess. Sometimes their faith nearly drove me mad. I *didn't* always know what to do. Often I knew no more than they did. And there were one or two among them who were better men than I'll ever be."

From being hot, he was now shivering. The sweat lay cold on his face and body, and sickness crept on him, reducing him to nothing.

"I forgot when I gave myself up," he said, "that I'd have to live with it ever after."

His mother's face was still impassive, and yet she was reaching out to him, leaning towards him with out-stretched arms. And when he yielded his shuddering body, she drew him fiercely into her bed, pressing him close, trying to give him strength and comfort, trying to protect him from the bitterness of self-recrimination. He was her child again, creeping into her warm bed, letting her wrap him round in the bedclothes, letting her press his head to her bosom. He was her child, crying after a bad dream, and her only duty in the world was to him.

"They asked too much of you. Yes, yes, they did! How could you go on for ever and ever? Nobody could. It's too much to ask. You mustn't feel guilty for the rest of your life. What good does it do? None whatever!" And a little later, as the shivering passed, she said to him: "Have you told Betony about this?"

"No," he said, "I'm afraid to tell her."

"There shouldn't be secrets between man and wife."

"I'm afraid I might lose her. I couldn't bear that."

"If she loves you, it won't make any difference. She will understand you that much better. She'll be able to help you. It's only right that she should know."

"Yes," he said. "It's only right, as you say. I'll tell her tomorrow."

But in the morning, when he thought of Betony, he knew he would never be able to tell her.

High above the woods of Scoate House Manor a kestrel hovered, taking its ease on the warm summer air, and Tom, returning with Linn along the old turnpike, a bundle of osiers on his shoulder, stood still to watch it, one hand raised against the sun.

"Can you see it?" Linn asked.

"Yes, just about, though I wouldn't have knowed it for a kestrel if it warnt for *knowing*, if you see what I mean."

"Supposing you tell me what you mean."

"Well, it's the way he's lazing about up there . . . the way he's concentrating on something below . . . ah, and now the way he's gliding around, before going off, away down the wind."

The kestrel circled three times and swooped away, racing its shadow over the treetops. Tom turned his attention to a soaring lark.

"I'm a lot luckier than folk that've had no sight at all. Take that there lark, now, up in the sky. That could be a gnat for all I can see to tell me different, but when I hear it singing, well, it means I can see it at the same time, just as plain as I ever did, rising up and up all the time into a sky as blue as blue."

They had been shopping in Norton village. Tom drew his pension from the post office there, and they rarely went to Huntlip now. He bought his osiers at Washpool Farm and sold his baskets to a dealer who called every other Friday.

The day was a hot one in late July and the sun was immediately overhead. Every few hundred yards or so, Tom dropped his bundle on the grass verge and the two of them sat on it, side by side, among the meadowsweet and sorrel. What wind there was came breathing hotly out of the east, and Linn tried to cool it by fanning herself with a bunch of ferns. Under the brim of her big straw hat, her face was shadowed, and he saw her only as a shape. Yet he knew the day had exhausted her.

"You'd have done better stopping at home. You shouldn't be walking so far in this heat."

"We spend more time resting than we do walking. It'll likely be dark by the time we get home."

"Dark or light, what does it matter? We ent catching no train, are we?"

"I left my washing on the line. It'll go too dry for ironing."

"You just rest," he said firmly. "You know what Mrs Gibbs told you. You've got to rest and take things easy."

When they reached home and were passing through the Pikehouse gate, Linn saw a man standing watching them from the edge of the woods, thirty yards off, across the road. He was half-hidden behind a tree and stood quite still, his hands in his pockets, his cap pulled low over his forehead.

"There's a man over there. Can you see him? He's standing at the edge of the wood."

"Perhaps it's a keeper," Tom said.

But then the man stepped out to the open; he crossed the grass verge and stood in the roadway: a short stocky man with a chest like a barrel.

"It's Emery Preston," Linn said.

"What's he doing hanging about here for?"

"It's not the first time I've seen him about. When I went up to Eastery last Friday, he was standing on the churchyard wall, looking down at the Pikehouse, and he stared hard at me as I went past."

"I'll go and have a word with him," Tom said.

Emery Preston stood like a post. Tom went up to him, squinting a little, for he could see better by looking out of the sides of his eyes.

"Did you want to speak to me, Mr Preston?"

"No, why should I?" Emery said.

"Then why are you out here, watching us the way you are?"

"Is there a law that says I mustn't?"

"No, there's no law," Tom said, "or none that I know of, anyway."

"There's laws about *some* things," Emery said. "There's a law against bigamy for a start."

"I ent no bigamist, Mr Preston."

"You're both a lot worser to my way of thinking, living together, the two of you, with no sign of shame in either of you. I'm a publican and a sinner but I wouldn't carry on like that."

"What d'you want of us?" Tom asked.

"I'd like to know what became of my daughter."

"Tilly went off with another chap. I dunno no more'n that."

"So you say, but I sometimes wonder!"

"What do you mean?"

"Never mind! Never mind! I was thinking out loud."

"You should try looking in Birmingham. That's where he lived, the chap she went off with."

"Have you tried looking for her your own-self?"

"No," Tom said, " 'cos I don't want her back."

"That's understandable, sure enough. A lawful wife is something of a hinderment to the likes of you. You better prefer a looser arrangement."

Linn still stood at the Pikehouse gate. Emery could see that she was with child. His glance roved over her, full of contempt.

"You yourself was begot in the hedge, Maddox, and it seems it's a thing that gets passed on!"

He turned and walked off towards Huntlip, kicking up a cloud of dust. Tom and Linn went indoors.

"Take no notice," she said to him. "Don't let it upset you."

"It don't worry me, except for your sake," Tom said, "and maybe the little 'un's, when he comes."

"You are not to worry. There's no need."

It was very strange, the way his sight varied from day to day. Some days, especially when the sun was shining, he could see the poppies red along the roadside, the apples ripening in the garden, the white clouds crossing the blue sky. But other days were bad, and once, out in the empty stretch of wasteland surrounding the Pikehouse, he came to a standstill, lost as though in a thick dark fog.

He was quite alone, and he felt that the rest of the earth had gone; he thought of it as a smoking ruin, crumbling away into a pit, leaving him on the edge of nothing; and he knew a moment of whirling terror. But after a while, putting out his hands, he felt the long feathery grasses that grew high everywhere around him, and their touch reassured him. The earth was still there, unchanged, unchanging, and he must find his way across it, through the gathering darkness. Home was in front of him. Not much more than a hundred yards. He could smell the woodsmoke, and could hear Linn beating a mat. It seemed a long way.

"You should've called to me," she said, coming to him as he groped along the hedgerow to the garden gate. "I'm sure I'd have heard you."

"I've got to get used to finding my way about," he said.

But Linn rarely left him alone after that. She watched over him and was always at hand when he needed her. Their lives were tight-linked. They shared every moment of the night and day.

Once, when she was rummaging in the cupboard, she said, "I didn't know you ever smoked."

"I did smoke, a bit, in the trenches," he said. "Why?"

" 'Cos I found this." And she put a tobacco-pipe into his hands.

"It belonged to Bob Newers, my mate in the army. I meant to send it home to his people, but what with my getting blown up and that, I never got round to it after all."

Until now, whenever he had remembered Newers, he had seen only the space left after the shell had burst in the crater; had seen only the hole in the ground, and the debris falling, bringing down bits of human remains. But now, as he held the pipe between his hands, he saw Newers as a whole man again; felt his solid bulk beside him; heard his voice; and remembered a day at Liere on the Somme, when the first tanks had been seen on the road, making towards Rilloy-sus-Coll.

Newers and he, in the reserve line, had been drumming up tea when a new chap named Worth had let out a shriek.

"God Almighty! Take a dekko at these monsters! What the hell are they, d'you suppose?"

"What, them?" said Newers, standing up to look at the tanks. "They've brought the buns."

Linn went and sat beside Tom on the settle. She saw he was smiling.

"Newers could always make us laugh," he said.

Every day now, while the summer weather lasted, Tom worked out of doors, close by the pump where his osiers lay soaking in the trough. He sat on a mat on the paving-stones with a wooden board on his lap, and often when Linn went out to the garden she would stop and watch the basket growing as his clever fingers worked the rods, or reached for the hammer to rap them home, or took up the knife to trim the ends. Human hands, when they worked and made things, always filled her with a kind of wonder.

"I know you're there," he said once. "I can see you plain. Well, plain enough. You've got your blue dress on, and the new pinny with the big pockets."

"And what am I holding in my hand?"

"I suppose it's that medicine again."

"You drink it up and no nonsense."

"All right," he said. "You're the nurse. But it won't bring my sight back, I don't suppose."

"It'll help your headaches, Dr Dundas said."

"It'd be a miracle if that was to give me back my sight. I'd drink a whole bottle every day." He emptied the glass and returned it to her. He looked up at her with his side-ways stare. "It ent very likely, is it?" he said. "Miracles ent all that common nowadays."

"No, Tom, you won't get your sight back, I'm afraid."

"No. Well. It's not to be expected, I know that. It's just wishful thinking, as they say."

One day when Linn went out to the garden, to pick the last of the kidney beans, she saw Emery Preston again, coming out of Scoate woods. He stood for a while, looking across as though hesitating, then walked off towards Huntlip. She decided not to tell Tom, but the next time her father came to call on them, she took him aside and told him in private.

"I don't know what he means by it. I suppose it's to make us feel uncomfortable. In which case he succeeds all too well, 'cos it worries me, somehow, seeing him prowling about like that."

"I'll have a word with him," Jack said. "I'll tell him to mind his own damned business."

"I don't think it's wise to quarrel with him."

"Who said anything about quarrelling?"

"I know what you are, father."

"It's no use wearing velvet gloves when dealing with men like Emery Preston. You've got to tell them out straight."

Jack went to The Rose and Crown the following evening after work. He spoke to Emery regardless of the crowd in the taproom listening.

"What're you always hanging around the Pikehouse for?"

"It's a free country. I do as I please."

"Then hear this!" Jack said. "If you cause any harm to my daughter, or to Tom Maddox, you'll have to answer to me for it, and I'm none too gentle when dealing with ruffians like you, Preston, so just you watch out!"

Jack walked out again. Emery turned to his customers.

"He thinks hisself somebody, that chap Mercybright, don't he, by God? And him just a labourer on Outlands Farm!"

"What's wrong with labourers?" Billy Ratchet said, offended. "Jack's all right. He's a good sort. I feel sorry for him, with that daughter of his turning out so unexpected, living like she do with Tom Maddox and carrying his bastard, bold as brass."

"You needn't tell me!" Emery said. "I know how they're carrying on. I been out there and seen for myself. But it's what they done, the two of them, to get rid of Tilly that bothers me, and one of these days I shall find out!"

"Why, your Tilly's as bad herself, ent she?" said Norman Rye, calling from one of the small tables. "Going off with that traveller like she done?"

"That's the story that's been put about! But I've got ideas of my own on that score, and I shan't rest till I know more about it."

"What do you mean, Emery?"

"You'll know soon enough, when the time comes."

Emery went and drew himself a pint of Chepsworth. He drank till the glass was three parts empty and froth had given him a white moustache. His three sons watched him. His customers eyed one another in stony silence.

On a warm Saturday in late September, a car drew up at The Rose and Crown, and a young man got out, red-faced and sweating. He locked the car door, made a face at the children gathering round, and glanced at his wrist-watch. It wanted five minutes to closing time. He was very thirsty.

Matthew, in the taproom, called his father to the window.

"It's him," he said. "That travelling salesman. You can see the brushes in the car."

"Are you sure it's the same one?"

"I'm positive," Matthew said.

When the young man came in, glancing round at the customers, and smoothing his hair with the flat of his hand, Emery stood behind the counter.

"Your name Trimble by any chance?"

"Upon my word! What memories you country folk have got – "

"Is it or ent it?" Emery demanded.

"Yes, indeed," the man said, and found himself half way across the counter, with Emery Preston's enormous hands twisted in the front of his jacket. "Good God! What's the matter? Are you drunk or mad or what?"

"Where's my daughter Tilly got to?"

"I don't know what you're talking about."

"The story is she went off with you, in that dinky motor you got out there, and if it's true, Mr Smarty Trimble, I'll break every bone in your soft greasy body!"

"Of course it's not true! I don't even know your daughter Tilly."

"You know her all right. You sold her brushes out at the Pikehouse."

"Did I? Did I? Good Lord, let me see! The Pikehouse, you said? Yes, it does ring a bell. It's that tiny tollhouse out towards Norton. The young lady's name was Mrs Maddox."

"And what else do you remember?"

"Nothing whatever, I do assure you. I called there three or four times, I agree, and sold Mrs Maddox a few little items, but what you're saying is simply monstrous and I insist you let go of me at once!"

"Monstrous, is it?" Emery said. "Does that mean you're saying it's a damned lie?"

"Indeed I am! And I'd like to know who's responsible for it! I'm a happily married man. I can show you snaps of my wife and kiddies. I can get people to speak for me – "

"Never mind that," Emery said. "Just answer me one more question. Why did you leave the district so sudden, with people owing you money on orders?"

"I was taken ill. I went down with 'flu and very nearly

died of it. If it hadn't been for my wife, God bless her, nursing me for weeks on end, I shouldn't be here at this moment."

"Oh, is that so?" Emery said. "And now you've come back to collect what's owing? Well, you're hopeful, I must say, after so many months gone by."

He loosened his hold on the man's jacket, but continued to look at him narrowly.

"You got a business card you can give me?"

"No, no, I haven't," Trimble said. "I've had some trouble getting them printed." He shrugged himself into his ruffled clothes and tucked his necktie into his jacket. He half glanced round at the few customers in the taproom. "But I'll write my address down if you want it and then you can verify all I've told you."

"Yes, you do that," Emery said, and watched as Trimble, with a shaking hand, wrote his address on a scrap of paper. "Seems I got the wrong man. I'm sorry I rumpled you up a bit but it ent my fault you've been blamed for something you ent done. It's my son-in-law you can thank for that."

"Is it indeed? I should like to meet him!"

"Don't you tangle with Tom Maddox. I shall be dealing with him myself."

"Right!" Trimble said. "All's well that ends well, that's what I say, and no hard feelings either way."

"Ent you having the drink you came for?"

"No, no, I think not. I'm behind-hand already and I've got an appointment at two-thirty." Trimble walked towards the door. "Let me know," he said, "if there's anything more I can do to help you."

He drove away from The Rose and Crown and chugged slowly along the Straight, but once out on the main road he opened the throttle and let her go, eager to put the village of Huntlip well behind him, together with its ugly-tempered, violent people.

At The Rose and Crown, the last customer had now left, and Emery Preston was locking up. He threw the keys to the boy Matthew.

"So now we know where we stand, by God, and it's what I been scared of all along. I warned our Tilly often-times against taking up with Tom Maddox, but she wouldn't listen, oh no, not she!"

"You reckon he's gone and harmed her, dad?"

"He's done away with her, that's what he's done, the same as his father done with his mother, only *he's* been smarter about it, the swine, and made sure she ent to be found!"

"What're you going to do, dad?"

"I'm going to the police," Emery said, "which I should've done at the very beginning."

"Detectives?" Linn said, staring at the men who stood in the porch.

"I'm Detective-Inspector Darns, madam, and this is Detective Constable Penfold. We'd like a word with Mr Maddox."

"You'd better come in."

They stepped in after her and the younger man closed the door. It was not yet six o'clock, but the lamp had been lit and Tom sat beside it on a stool, mending a boot on a last in his lap. Linn stood behind him and touched his shoulder.

"It's the police. They want to see you."

"Ah, I heard. I was wondering what it was all about." He sat up straight, trying to see them. "What am I supposed to've done?"

"May we sit down Mr Maddox?"

"You go ahead. Suit yourselves."

"We're enquiring into the disappearance of your wife, Mrs Tilly Maddox, formerly Preston. Her father has reported her missing."

"Has he?" Tom said. "Whatever for?"

"Is there anything you can tell us?"

"She went off with another chap. I couldn't tell you where she is."

"What date would that be, Mr Maddox?"

"Early in February," Tom said. "I can't say no nearer than that."

"Did she tell you she was going?"

"No. Not beforehand. Not in so many words exactly."

"Can you make that a little plainer?"

"She *did* say she wished she could live in a town. She didn't like it out here. She said it was lonely and drove her mad."

"I'd like you to tell us how she left."

"I came home and she was gone. There was a note on the table there. All her things had gone too."

"Did you keep the note?"

"No," Tom said, "I threw it away."

"Perhaps you can remember what it said."

"She wrote she was sick of being so lonely. She said she wouldn't be coming back."

"Did she say she was going with a man?"

Not in so many words exactly."

"What *were* her words, Mr Maddox?"

"Well, she said she was tired of the way I treated her, and Mr Trimble would treat her better. He would look after her, she said."

"So you assumed they'd gone off together?"

"I'm certain of it," Tom said. "They was thick together. He was here a lot. I saw them once, laughing and talking. He'd got his arm round her, squeezing her tight."

"Were you jealous, Mr Maddox?"

"No, not a jot, it was no odds to me."

"I gather you didn't get on all that well with your wife?"

"You couldn't gather nothing else, after what I just been saying."

"What was the cause of your disagreements?"

"Everything," Tom said. "It was all a mistake, our getting married in the first place. We shouldn't never ought to've done it."

The two men were sitting side by side, almost filling the small settle. Tom could see them as two dark shadows; their faces were nothing but paler blurs; but he sensed that the young one was making notes.

"You writing it down, what I'm saying?"

"My constable is writing it down."

Inspector Darns was a man of fifty, quiet-spoken, easygoing. He sat relaxed, his hands clasped on the hat in his lap. He was rather interested in the half-cobbled boot on Tom's last.

"I'm surprised you can see to mend boots. I'd heard you had trouble with your eyes."

"I can see if I feel," Tom said. "But it's true what they said about my eyes. I got blown up during the war."

"He's going blind," Linn said.

"Were you going blind when your wife was with you?"

"It had started," Tom said, "but she didn't know it."

"Were you resentful, Mr Maddox, when this misfortune came to you?"

"Wouldn't you have been resentful?"

"You haven't really answered my question."

"Haven't I? I thought I had."

"Were you upset, Mr Maddox?"

"I wasn't exactly over the moon."

"And did you take it out on your wife?"

"Maybe I did. I wasn't too nice to her sometimes."

"Did you hit her by any chance?"

"No, never."

"Not even once, in a temper, perhaps, when she was nagging as she probably did?"

"I never touched her," Tom said. "Is somebody trying to say I did?"

"Mr Preston is not quite satisfied that his daughter left you for another man. He thinks you killed her, Mr Maddox."

"He's off his hinges!" Tom said.

"I take it you deny the allegation?"

"I do deny it! It's a bloody lie!"

Tom sat rigid on his stool. He felt imprisoned; trapped by his blindness; and a great anger ran through his blood, threatening destruction. He felt it would break him; that he would go to pieces like a man driven mad; that the darkness would engulf his mind. But he felt Linn's hand on his shoulder again, and her touch steadied him. He wished he could see the two men's faces.

"Why now all of a sudden? Tilly's been gone for months and months. Why don't Emery look for her in Birmingham, together with that Trimble fellow?"

"The man Trimble's been seen in Huntlip. Mr Preston asked him about your wife and the man denies that she went with him."

"But she must've done! She took all her things. She couldn't have took 'em if she'd gone alone. She couldn't have took 'em if she didn't have a car to drive away in. It's three miles to the nearest bus. Supposing Trimble is telling lies?"

"If somebody's lying, it's up to us to find out, Mr Maddox, and that's what we are aiming to do."

The two men stood up. They were very tall and their heads touched the rafters. Tom could feel them towering above him.

"You ent arresting me nor nothing, then?"

"Your wife has been reported missing and a certain allegation has been made. We have no choice but to follow it up. That's all there is to the matter at present, Mr

Maddox, and I hope we'll succeed in tracing your wife in Birmingham as you suggest."

"What happens if you don't?"

"We'll cross that bridge when we come to it. But one last question if you don't mind. Do you know the name of the firm this man Trimble worked for?"

"The name," Tom repeated, and thought about it. "It was Bruno," he said. "Bruno Brushes of Birmingham. It was on the dustpan and broom Tilly bought. You can have a look at them if you like."

"No need for that," Darns said. "It merely confirms what we've already heard. Thank you for answering our questions, Mr Maddox. We'll let you know if we have any news."

The two men went. Tom and Linn listened as they drove away. He turned towards her.

"*You* don't think I murdered Tilly?"

"Don't be foolish," Linn said.

"I should like to know."

"No, Tom, I don't believe it."

"What about them? Did they look as though they believed me?"

"I think so, yes. In fact I'm sure."

"Seems like I bring you nothing but trouble. I make a mess of things all the time."

His hands were still clenched on his cobbling hammer. He was breathing hard, and trembling a little. Linn took the hammer and the boot on its last and put them aside. She knelt before him, taking his hands between her own.

"You must try not to worry about it," she said. "The police will soon find her, I'm sure of that. I know how you feel, having Emery Preston spreading this lie, but you mustn't let it poison you. You must try and put it out of your mind."

Tom made no answer, but drew her gently into his arms.

At The Rose and Crown, when the two detectives entered the taproom, the gathering of customers fell silent. Emery Preston, sitting at one of the crowded tables, got up at once.

"Well?" he said. "Have you arrested Tom Maddox?"

"Mr Preston," Darns said, "I'd like a word with you in private."

"No need for that. I don't mind my customers hearing. I ent got nothing I want to hide."

"I'd sooner we were private," Darns said, and Emery, shrugging, led them into the back room.

"I'll ask you again. – Have you arrested Tom Maddox?"

"No, Mr Preston, for there's no evidence as yet that a crime has been committed at all."

"Evidence? It's your job to find it! Though there won't be much, I don't suppose, 'cos he'll have made certain of that, you mark my words. Out there in that lonely place, he could've buried her in them woods and no one the wiser, and I'll stake my last penny that's just what happened."

"If there's anything to be found," Darns said, "we shall find it, be sure of that."

"How long'll it take?" Emery asked. "From now to Christmas?"

"The only fact so far is that your daughter has disappeared. Everything else is speculation and I would advise you to be more careful in what you say or Mr Maddox could take you to law on a charge of slander."

"I'd like to see it!" Emery said. "A murderer taking me to law because I tell the world what he is?"

"What reasons have you for your suspicions?"

"Where's my daughter if he ent killed her?"

"Apart from that, Mr Preston?"

"His father was a murderer, did you know that?"

"That's no reason," Darns said, but he was interested all the same.

"It is to *me*!" Emery said. "I know the stock Tom Maddox comes from. His father was a wrong 'un. Anyone will tell you that. He attacked my poor old mother once and she was over eighty years old. He had a murderous temper always. He turned on the woman he lived with in the end and hit her over the head with a poker. He went and hanged hisself afterwards and saved the hangman a lot of swither."

"Yes, I remember the case, now you mention it," Darns said, "but is the son as violent?"

"Sure to be. It runs in the blood."

"But he's never actually been in trouble?"

"Not that I know of. He's been away. But he'll have got used to killing, won't he, out there in the war, fighting the Germans?"

"That could be said of thousands. But what I came for, Mr Preston, was to ask for the address of Arthur Trimble."

"I've got it here," Emery said, and passed over a piece of paper.

"I'd also like a photograph of your daughter."

"What for?"

"To help us trace her, Mr Preston."

"Trace her! Trace her!" Emery muttered, beginning to search a sideboard drawer. "How'll they trace her if she's under the sod?" But he found a photograph and handed it over. "That was took on her wedding day and a bad day it turned out to be for her, too, poor girl."

"She looks very happy in the picture."

"She didn't know what she was in for, did she?"

Emery followed them out through the taproom and saw them off the premises. He returned to his customers with a scornful face.

"A lot of use *they* are, going about so dilladerry, as though they got all the time in the world. Tom Maddox could vanish while they play about."

"Have they seen him, Emery?"

"Seen him? Yes! They been passing the time of day with him, just as though they was all good pals, or so it seemed from what they said."

"That's the way they go about it," said Emery's cousin, Humphrey Bartley. "They let him feel he's pretty safe and then when he goes and gives hisself away they pounce on him like a cat on a mouse."

"If I had Tom Maddox alone in my yard," Emery said, hard-faced, "he'd be telling the truth in ten seconds!"

Betony was away in Wiltshire when the rumours started. She returned to find them in full spate.

"Who started all this? Emery Preston, I suppose! And no doubt the village is all agog!"

"No doubt it is," her mother said, "but the best thing is to take no notice."

"Has anyone been to see Tom and Linn?"

"Dicky and me went a day or two back but your father's busy all of a sudden and can't find the time."

"Yes, well," Jesse said, not quite meeting Betony's eye, "what good can I do, going to see them?"

"I always said it!" granna exclaimed. "I always said he'd end up badly. It's the bad blood in him. He can't rightly help it."

"So he's tried and condemned already, is he?" Betony said, fiercely angry. "By his own family too!"

"We ent his family by rights," said great-grumpa. "We

took him in as an act of kindness."

"Yes, and it's him that's cut hisself off," said Jesse, "living over the brush with the Mercybright girl and making us feel ashamed to know him."

"I'm not ashamed," Betony said.

"Don't mind your father," Beth said. "Go out and see them. They need to know they've got a few friends."

"Yes, mother, I'll go now."

Driving along the main road, she overtook Jack Mercybright, and he rode with her the rest of the way. When they got to the Pikehouse, Tom was sitting in the open doorway, watching the sun going down in splinters of crimson light behind the church on Eastery ridge.

"Can you see it?" Betony asked.

"I should think I can!" he said, smiling, and the sunset colours were bright on his face. "Such sunsets we been having lately! Almost as good as the winter time. But I don't see much, besides lights."

In the lamplit room beyond, Linn, big with child, moved slowly to and fro, setting supper on the table. Tom rose from his chair and carried it in. He set it by the table, feeling his way.

"You heard what they're saying about me in Huntlip?"

"I've heard it all right. This fairy tale!"

"You don't believe it, then, Bet?"

"Not a single word."

"There's plenty that will," Jack said, and stood lighting a broken clay pipe, watching Tom through the smoke he was making. "As for myself, well, if you *had* upped and murdered Tilly Preston, I dunno that I'd really blame you. Her sort of girl often asks for trouble."

"Father!" Linn said, rounding on him. "What are you saying?"

"I reckon he's trying me out," Tom said. "The policeman

did the same thing. But I ent going to be catched that way 'cos I never touched her, neither by accident nor on a purpose, though I'd hardly admit it if I had, would I?"

"You needn't worry," Jack said. "I'd sooner believe what you tell me than anything the Prestons is putting about."

"The police are trying to trace Tilly, but what'll happen if they don't? What'll they do if she don't come forward?"

"What can they do when there's nothing to go on except a rumour? If you're innocent you got nothing to fear."

"It's the waiting and wondering," Tom said, "and the fact that the rumour might never get scotched."

"Forget about it," Jack said. "Gossip of this sort is not worth fretting over. It's less than the smoke going up that chimney. Meantime, we must look on the bright side, and hope that wife of yours turns up."

"I don't think she will," Tom said.

"Oh? Why's that?"

"I dunno why. I just don't, that's all."

Jack said no more, and Linn at that moment called on him to put out his pipe, for the soup-bowls were filled and on the table. But Betony noticed how, during supper, his gaze often rested on Tom's face, and, driving home later that evening, she asked him if he had any doubts.

"Doubts? Yes. Ent you?"

"I've never known Tom tell a lie."

"Everybody tells lies, especially when they're in trouble."

"Then you think him guilty!"

"I never said that. I *don't* think it. I only said I'd got my doubts. I'll have them for ever, I daresay, if that Tilly ent found."

"They can't be very serious doubts or you'd be frightened for Linn's sake."

"No, I ent frightened, 'cos it's like I said – if Tom did kill Tilly she very likely drove him to it."

"I don't think he killed her. He wouldn't, I'm sure." And she cast her mind back to that day early in the year when she had called on Tom at the Pikehouse: the day he had told her Tilly was gone and that he was beginning to go blind. "I'd have *known,*" she said. "I'd have felt it, somehow, in my bones."

A few days later, Michael called for Betony at Chepsworth Park, and took her to lunch at The Old Plough.

"There's good news about Kingsmore Farm. I'm taking over the lease at Christmas, so by the time we come back from our honeymoon, there'll only be a month or two to wait before we move in. We'll live at King's Hill until then. D'you think you can bear it?"

"If your mother can, so can I."

"You don't look all that delighted," he said. "Aren't you pleased about Kingsmore?"

"Of course I'm pleased. It's just that I'm worried about Tom."

"Ah, yes, I might have known. So much for my little celebration!" He raised his glass, sardonically, and sipped his champagne. He tried to purge himself of his irritation. "Is there any truth in the allegations?"

"No, there isn't. None whatever."

"You seem very sure."

"It's just wicked gossip. Huntlip has bouts of it from time to time." And, after a pause, she said: "I'm afraid this is all very unpleasant for you, Michael. You're not only marrying beneath you – you're marrying into a family that's getting talked about in a hateful way."

"Huntlip gossip is nothing to me, though I agree it's a very unpleasant thing to happen. Still, I'll have you out of it quite soon, and you'll be able to put it behind you."

"You don't understand," Betony said. "I don't want to be out of it. Not while this thing is hanging over my family. I think we should wait a little longer."

"Haven't we waited long enough? Hell and damnation! Your vicar has started publishing the banns."

"It's the going away I don't like."

"Look," Michael said, and he was suddenly very angry. "I'm not giving up my honeymoon for anything or anyone, least of all that foster-brother of yours. He got himself into this God-awful mess and he's only got himself to blame."

"I don't agree. None of this is his own doing."

"How can you be sure of that?"

"How can we be sure of anything?"

Betony's anger was as fierce as his. They stared at each other across the table. But, aware that people were watching them, they ate for a while in complete silence, until they were in command of themselves and could speak calmly.

"If Tom is innocent, you don't need to worry."

"But he's a sick man. It's the strain and the worry that will do the harm."

"He's got other people looking after him."

"Yes. That's true."

"Can you do more for him than they can?"

"No," she said, "perhaps not."

For a moment she was tempted to tell him the truth: that Tom was now a dying man; but she could not. This secret she shared only with the Mercybrights and old Dr Dundas out at Norton. It was better that it should remain so.

"You're right, of course, there's nothing much I can do for him."

"Well, then?" Michael said, and reached across to refill her glass. "Perhaps now I can have a few minutes of your time in which to discuss our future lives? Just trivial things, you know, like the wedding arrangements and the honeymoon and making Kingsmore fit to live in."

Betony smiled.

"Dear Michael," she said. "You're very patient."

One morning, when Tom awoke, he could see nothing, not even outlines. When he stepped out into the garden and turned his face towards the sun, its light was concealed from him, as though in eclipse. It fell on dead eyes.

He sat on the old backless chair against the wall and yielded to the darkness. He felt it surrounding him, pressing in on all sides, as though it would squeeze him from the face of the earth. Nothing was left of him, only a central bubble of fear, and if that burst he would be destroyed.

Then suddenly the fear was gone. He could not have said why. But it was as though he had been away from his own body, lost in a no-man's-land of nothingness, and now he had come upon himself again, sitting on this seat in the autumn sun, with the overgrown garden all around him, smelling of mint and marigolds and apples eaten-out by wasps.

"What is it?" Linn asked, finding him sitting there so still.

"I was thinking of Grannie Izzard," he said, "and how she used to tend this garden."

"Are you coming in to breakfast?"

"Might as well, if you've got it ready."

He was reluctant to tell her that the last of his sight had gone completely. It would only grieve her. But Linn knew without being told, and she took his arm to lead him indoors.

Betony often called at the Pikehouse. She brought him a white-painted walking-stick and a whistle for him to hang round his neck. She brought things, too, ready for the baby.

"No more visits from the police?"

"No. Nothing."

"I was thinking," she said once. "It might be as well if you were to see a solicitor. Great-grumpa's man, perhaps, young Mr Hay. I would go with you if you like."

"But I ent done nothing," Tom said.

"Think about it all the same, if the police come pestering you again."

"I reckon it's all blowing over now," he said.

But a few days later, on the fifteenth, the two policemen came again.

"Is it news of Tilly?" Tom asked.

"I'm afraid not, Mr Maddox. There's been no response to our poster so far, nor to our enquiries. But I'd like to ask a few further questions. What, for instance, was Mrs Maddox wearing the day she left home?"

"I dunno. I wasn't here."

"But what about in the morning, early, before you went to work? Can you recall what she wore then?"

"She was in bed when I left the house."

"And you did say, I believe, that she left no clothes behind her?"

"Not a stitch," Tom said. "Is that all you wanted to know?"

"Unless there's something more you'd like to tell me."

"No, there's nothing," Tom said.

Darns turned to Linn.

"Were you acquainted with Mrs Maddox?"

"No," Linn said, "I never saw her in my life."

"Would you mind telling me your name, Mrs –?"

"Mercybright," Linn said, "but it's Miss, not Mrs."

"May I ask what relation you are to Mr Maddox?"

"It's none of your business!" Tom said.

"I don't mind answering," Linn said. "We live together as man and wife."

"Thank you," Darns said. "It's always a help when people are perfectly frank with us. Were you acquainted with Mr Maddox before his wife disappeared?"

"Yes. I was."

"How long after her departure did you come and take her place as it were?"

"About a week," Linn said, and met the man's gaze with only the slightest change of colour.

"I'm just wondering," Tom said, "if I ought to see a solicitor."

"And what do you think he would do for you, Mr Maddox?"

"I dunno," Tom said. "I dunno what they ever do. Somebody said it, that's all."

"I shouldn't worry, Mr Maddox. Not yet, anyway."

"What do you mean, not yet?"

But Darns and his constable left without another word.

Betony, hearing of this visit, became very angry.

"That settles it!" she said. "I'm going to Birmingham to look for Tilly."

"There's no point in that," Tom said. "If the police can't find her, what chance have you?"

"Perhaps they're not trying hard enough."

"They've got posters out, or so they told me."

"I'm going there all the same."

But although she spent two whole days in Birmingham, tramping all the busiest streets, asking at shops and boardinghouses, she learnt nothing. "We've been asked already," a shopkeeper told her. "The police've been round trying to find that same young woman." And she saw the posters everywhere, asking for Mrs Tilly Maddox, of the Pikehouse, Eastery, near Chepsworth, to present herself at the nearest police station, as her next of kin were anxious about her.

At the Bruno Brush Company in Hall Street, however, Betony discovered an interesting fact: that the travelling salesman, Arthur Trimble, had left their employ at a day's notice on September twenty-ninth and had talked of taking his family to London. His wife, is seemed, had relations there. Her uncle was offering him a job.

Betony returned home and went to the Pikehouse. She found Tom alone, for Linn had gone up to Eastery, to see the midwife, Mrs Gibbs.

"September twenty-ninth! Don't you see? It means Trimble left Brum immediately after Emery Preston had asked him questions about Tilly. So obviously he must have been mixed up with her, just as you said, and was frightened his wife might hear about it."

"We're still no nearer finding Tilly."

"No, she probably parted from Trimble quite soon, and she might be anywhere by now. But at least the police must know all this. They'll know he went off in a terrible hurry and they'll draw the same conclusions as I have done."

"I hope you're right," Tom said.

"Of course I'm right!" she exclaimed, and went on to talk of her wedding instead. "Will you be coming, you and Linn?"

"Better not," he said, undoing knots in a piece of string. "What with her being pretty near her time, and the things folk're saying in Huntlip at present, we'd only spoil it if we was there."

"You could come to Cobbs, though, afterwards. Dicky could fetch you in the trap."

"Better not," he said again. "We ent really wanted there, Linn and me."

"*I* want you," Betony said, "or I wouldn't be asking."

But she knew he was wise to keep away. Only Dicky and her mother accepted him now. To the rest of the the family he was an outcast.

"All right," she said. "I won't press you if you'd rather not come. But I hope my present is ready in time!"

"It will be," he said. "There ent a lot to do on it now." He was making her a wickerwork chair. "Jack comes out to watch me at it, so's I don't make janders of it, but that'll be ready in time, you'll see. Honest John! as William always used to say."

Often, when he was unable to sleep, he would lie on his back, utterly still, afraid of disturbing Linn beside him. He would think of things to make himself sleepy, such as counting the cost of his osier rods, and the profit remaining when he sold his baskets. Sometimes he was back at Etaples during inspection, going over in his mind all the items laid out before him. Respirator. Field-dressings. Iron rations. Mess-tin, water-bottle, Tommy's cooker. Rifle, ammunition, ground-sheet.

Then the names would start coming. Newers. Ritchie. Glover. Braid. Danson. Evans. Privitt. Rush. Until, in a state between waking and sleeping, he wandered alone in a vast empty space, over ground much cratered by shells and mines, looking for men he knew were lost, while a voice kept whispering in his ear: Where are they? Where are they? Where are they *gone?*

Often Linn herself was awake, because of the baby moving inside her, or because she sensed his wakefulness. She had nursed many men during the war; had heard them groaning, sobbing, swearing; had held them, writhing, in her arms while they screamed out the substance of their nightmares. But Tom never tossed about in bed; never moaned or screamed; he lay quite still and silent always, and if she turned her head on the pillow, she would find that his eyes were wide open, twitching a little now and then, intent, it seemed, though they saw nothing.

"Tom? Can't you sleep? Is your head hurting?"

"It's throbbing a bit, but nothing much."

"What were you thinking about?" she asked.

"Oh, this and that. Nothing special. It's harder to sleep, you know, now that day and night are the same."

But sleep when it did come was often pure and sweet and clean, and sometimes his dreams were happy ones.

"I was up on Lippy Hill and the sun was shining. The berries was red on the rowan trees, and there was dozens of thrushes there, mostly gathered on just one tree. I had a little lad with me. He brought me some berries that the thrushes had shook down onto the ground and he showed them to me in his two hands."

"What did he look like?" Linn asked. "Perhaps he was our son."

"I never properly saw his face. Just the berries in his hands. Then we was sitting on a little hummock and all the rabbits was out playing. It was evening time. Still and warm. And some of the rabbits came so close, they was eating right between our feet, mine and the boy's, as we sat on the hummock side by side."

Tom was lighting the fire for breakfast. He liked to be able to do these things, and Linn, though she watched, never interfered. He was always careful, handling the matches, and the fire was always beautifully laid.

"The berries was just as red as red, and the thrushes was yellow, with great fluffed-up chests speckled all over as smart as you please."

He put a match to the laid fire and it crackled up. He crouched before it, the light of it flickering in his eyes.

"It's a funny thing, but I ent never blind in my dreams," he said.

One morning, early, when Linn was shaving him and trimming his hair, she thought she heard a dog barking, somewhere in the woods across the road.

"It's probably MacNab's spaniel," Tom said. "Maybe he's out after rabbits."

At half-past-nine, Jimmy Winger's milk-float stopped at the gate, and Linn went out with the quart jug.

"I see you got company," Jimmy said, and pointed to a car drawn up on the grass at the edge of the woods. "The police are rooting about in there. I seen 'em as I came round past Tyson's. What're they up to, do you reckon?"

"Haven't you heard the gossip, Jimmy?"

"I might've done," Jimmy said. "But I wouldn't stand for it if I was you. There should be a law against policemen."

Jimmy had once been fined ten shillings for riding his bicycle without lights. Policemen were worse than game-keepers and needed something better to do.

"I'll lend you a loan of my shotgun if you like, so's you can send 'em packing," he said, "and if I should meet one of 'em on the road, I shall let old Twinkler ride him down!"

When Jimmy had gone, Linn stood looking towards the woods, but could see no sign of the searchers there. Only, once, she thought she heard the same dog barking, somewhere deep among the trees.

She said nothing to Tom about it, but later in the morning another car drew up behind the first, and four policemen in uniform got out. One of them sounded a blast on the horn and after a while the first party emerged from the wood. Detective-Inspector Darns was among them. There were seven men altogether, one of them with a wolfhound on a leash, and they all stood talking for about five minutes. Then the newcomers went to their car and each took a spade and a sack from the dicky. All seven vanished together among the trees.

"What's the commotion?" Tom asked.

"The police are searching the woods," she said.

His face became bleak. He stood as though turned to stone. Linn went to him and took hold of his arm.

At one o'clock, the searchers assembled at the edge of the wood and sat on the grass, eating sandwiches and drinking tea from vacuum flasks. Tom went across to them, using his white walking-stick and making towards the sound of their voices, but they stopped talking as he drew near, and he stood in the roadway, hesitating. Darns got up and went to him.

"Yes, Mr Maddox, did you want me?"

"What d'you hope to find in there?"

"What are you afraid we'll find?"

"You're wasting your time. You won't find nothing."

"Then there's no need for you to be worried."

"Who said I was worried?"

Tom turned and walked back home, very slowly, counting the paces. Darns went and sat on the running-board of the first car, and one of the uniformed constables offered him a cigarette.

"Is he as blind as he seems, that chap?"

"What a suspicious mind you've got, Ryelands. You're very nearly as bad as me."

"You got any intuitions, sir, one way or the other?"

"Not reliable ones," Darns said. "But if he has done his missus in, well, the sight of us turning the place upside down may well poke a chink or two in that armour of his."

Towards the end of the afternoon, when the searchers again mustered on the turnpike, they found they had an audience there: three women and a man, all elderly, who had wandered down from Eastery.

"Is it true," the old man asked, "that you've found a grave in them there woods?"

"No, it's not true," Darns said.

"What *have* you found?"

"I'm afraid I can't answer any questions."

"Then they ent found nothing," the old man said to the three women. "I knowed it was all a pack of lies."

"Who spread these rumours?" Darns asked.

"Not me, not me!" the old man said.

"Have you got permission to search them woods?" one of the women asked Darns. "Have you spoken to Mrs Lannam?"

"Yes, and we've got a warrant," Darns said.

"What, signed by the king and his chancellors?"

"Move away, please!" a constable said. "Can't you see we're trying to turn?"

As the first car moved off, back towards Huntlip, a tall figure came striding down the field-path from Eastery and stepped out into the road. It was the Reverend Peter Chance, vicar of Eastery-with-Scoate, a big man with a shock of white hair, and he stood waving the car to a standstill.

"What is the meaning of this?" he asked, stooping to speak to Darns through the window. "Why are you persecuting Tom Maddox? Has he done something wrong? Is there any truth in these wild rumours?"

"It's our job to find out, vicar."

"Have you questioned the boy? Does he admit harming his wife?"

"People don't generally admit such things, until they're obliged to," Darns said.

"If he denies it, I'm quite sure he's speaking the truth."

"But just supposing he isn't, vicar?"

"Then God will punish him, without a doubt."

"I'm afraid that won't satisfy the law."

"The law takes too much on itself in these matters. Revenge belongs to God alone. 'Thou shalt not kill,' the commandment says, and it makes no exception of any kind. The hanging of murderers is therefore wrong."

"It has one advantage," Darns said. "It stops them doing it again."

He motioned the constable to drive on.

The next day, Saturday the twenty-fifth, was cloudy and dull and rather cold. Tom stepped outside as always, first thing, and stood for a while sniffing the air. The wind was blowing from the northwest.

"Betony's wedding day," he said, "and it smells like rain."

"What time is the wedding?"

"Two o'clock this afternoon. If we listen carefully we may hear the bells, though it ent very likely with the wind as it is."

"It's certainly a dark old day," Linn said, "but perhaps it'll brighten by this afternoon."

At ten o'clock two cars turned into the old turnpike and parked as before on the wide grass verge. Linn went to the gate and saw the policemen go into the wood. There were five altogether, four in uniform, one in plain clothes. Inspector Darns was not among them.

Linn for once was filled with hatred. She wanted to rush out after the men and pummel them. She wanted to strike their cheerful faces and see them crumple. She wished she and Tom could run away.

"Is it them?" he asked, when she went indoors. "They're deadly determined, I'll say that, when they once get a notion in their heads."

"Why must they stop just opposite? They could just as well stop in Tyson's lane."

"They want me to know they're there," he said. "They want to scare me and whittle me down."

"You mustn't let them," Linn said.

"I shan't, don't worry. But I wish it was over all the same."

By eleven o'clock, there was a gathering on the turnpike road of people from Eastery, Huntlip, Middening, and Blagg. Two newspaper men drove over from Chepsworth and took a photograph of the Pikehouse. They talked to all the local people. Emery Preston came with his sons, the four of them packed onto Matthew's motor-cycle and sidecar, so that when Darns arrived at half-past-eleven he was appalled at the growing crowd. He turned to Penfold.

"Send these people about their business! What the hell do they think this is?"

"I'm taking no orders from you, young fella," an Eastery man said to Penfold. "You ent even wearing a uniform."

But the crowd moved off eventually. The newspaper men drove away. Only the Prestons lingered on.

"Mr Preston," Darns said. "I must ask you to take yourself off and your sons with you. You've got no business hanging about here like this."

"It's *my* daughter you're looking for, remember, and I aim to give you a helping hand."

"Enter those woods," Darns said, "and I'll have you placed under arrest."

"Why, what've you found, for God's sake?"

"Nothing whatever so far, Mr Preston, but I'm in charge of this investigation and I will not tolerate interference."

"You can't turn me off the road, however. I've got a right to stand here if I so choose and so've my boys."

"I thought you had a public house to manage."

"My cousin's looking after that. I've got more important business here."

"Was it you who summoned those reporters?"

"What if it was? People got a right to know what's happening."

"We don't even know if anything *has* happened, Mr Preston."

"No, nor you never will, neither," Emery said, "if you don't shift yourselves better than this!"

Darns and Penfold turned away. Their work was often distasteful to them.

"I reckon he'd *like* it," Penfold muttered, "if we *were* to dig up his daughter's body."

The day remained darkly overcast, and from midday onwards a small rain fell, light but drenching. Emery Preston and his three boys took shelter just inside the wood, staring across at the tiny Pikehouse, where firelight flickered at the window and smoke blew downwards from the chimney.

"Sitting comfortably by his fire! – The murdering bastard!" Emery said, and turned his collar up to his ears.

At one o'clock, when Darns thought of cancelling further search, Penfold came to him with a cotton scarf, found in the deeper part of the wood, among the oaks and beeches. It had lain in the undergrowth a long time; its printed pattern was almost gone; and it had a dark brown stain upon it that could have been blood.

Penfold had marked the place of its finding, and Darns went with him to look around. Many trees had been felled during the war. Their stumps were still pale and clean-looking, and heaps of brushwood still lay around. Darns gave orders for the search to continue. He wanted the heaps of brushwood moved. Then he and Penfold went to speak to Emery Preston. They showed him the scarf, carefully folded with the stain inside.

"Have you ever seen this before, Mr Preston?"

"Seen it? Yes. It belonged to Tilly."

"Are you sure of that?"

"How sure must I be? She had one like it. That's all I can say. I bought it myself at the Christmas bazaar last year." Emery looked from one to the other. He swallowed hard. "Did you find anything else besides?"

"Nothing else, Mr Preston, and the scarf of course means very little. Your daughter could have dropped it at any time, if she happened to take a walk in the woods."

"Tilly never walked if she could help it. Not by herself, at any rate."

"I think we'll have a word with Mr Maddox," Darns said to Penfold.

"About time too!" Emery said. "I'll come with you."

"No, Mr Preston. You'll return home."

"I ent budging till it damn well suits me, so you might as well get used to the fact."

"Please yourself," Darns said, "but you're not seeing Maddox."

When Linn let them in, Tom was sitting at the table, finishing a meal of bread and cheese. He pushed back his chair a little way and crossed his legs. Darns put the scarf into his hands.

"We found that in the woods, Mr Maddox. Can you tell us anything about it?"

"I dunno what it is, do I? I can't see it." Tom felt the scarf between his fingers. "Is it a handkerchief?" he asked.

"It's a cheap cotton scarf, Mr Maddox, printed red and white, with a stripe at the edge and spots in the middle. Did your wife have such a scarf?"

"I dunno. I don't remember."

"Mr Preston said she did."

"Maybe she did, then. He ought to know. Why ask me if he's already told you?"

"It appears to be stained with blood," Darns said. "Does that help you remember?"

"It ent Tilly's blood, if that's what you mean. It's the blood of a dog that got catched in a trap."

"So you do remember the scarf, after all?"

"Yes," Tom said. "It's coming back. Charley Bailey was out after rabbits and his dog, Shorty, got catched in a trap. Charley called on me to help and I took that scarf to tie the dog's leg with."

"But the scarf has just been found in the woods."

"Shorty must've shook it off."

"Laboratory tests will show whether the blood on that scarf came from a dog or a human being."

"If there's human blood on it," Tom said, "that'll be mine, not Tilly's, 'cos Shorty took a bite out of my hand when I was trying to get him free."

"Mr Maddox," Darns said, "I'd like you to come with us to the police station."

"Why?" Linn demanded, stepping between them. "Why does he have to come with you?"

"He's not obliged to," Darns said. "I'm asking for his co-operation."

"What if I don't?" Tom said. "What if I refuse to go?" He was very pale.

"It's only for questioning, Mr Maddox."

"Why can't you ask your questions here?"

"Yes! Why can't you?" Linn exclaimed. "He's blind and helpless. Why do you have to take him away?"

"It's customary procedure," Darns said. "A refusal could constitute an obstruction of the law."

"But you said he wasn't obliged to go!"

"It's like the Army," Tom said. "Our N.C.O.'s used to say to us, 'I want volunteers for a listening party – you five in front will suit me fine!' " He got up and went to the door. He felt for his jacket and put it on. "I'm ready," he said, and stood waiting.

"Can I come with him?" Linn asked.

"I don't advise it," Darns said.

"No more don't I!" Tom said. "That won't do no good at all." His hand rested on Linn's arm. "You stop at home and don't worry. You must think of the baby – you mustn't let yourself get upset. They'll bring me back. You'll see."

"But when? When? How long will it take, asking these questions?"

She was looking at Darns, and he found it difficult to meet her gaze.

"It all depends. But we'll let you know if any developments occur."

"What d'you mean, developments? What developments *could* there be?"

"Come along, Mr Maddox," Darns said.

"I asked you a question!" Linn said, following them out along the path. "What developments do you mean?"

"Please! Linn!" Tom said, in distress. "Don't fret yourself. You must take it easy."

"Tom, I'm afraid! I don't think you ought to be going with them."

"Don't be afraid. They can't hurt me. They're just hoping I'll let something slip. You go indoors out of the rain and don't worry. I promise you I'll be all right."

But Linn continued to stand in the garden, her hands clenched in the pockets of her apron, watching as they led him away.

Outside, when they got to the car, the Prestons were waiting.

"Are you arresting him?" Emery asked.

"No, we're not!" Darns said, snapping. "He's coming to the station of his own free will. He's agreed to answer some further questions."

"But you will be arresting him when you get there?"

"Out of the way, please, and let us pass."

They got into the car and drove off, and Emery was left swearing. He hurried over to the motor-cycle and sidecar.

"Come on, you three. There's no sense in waiting here. Matthew, you can drop us off at home first, then go on to Chepsworth, to the police station. I want to know what happens next."

"But I ent even had my dinner yet!"

"You can buy yourself a sandwich when you get to Chepsworth. But mind you remember what I said! – Don't come away till you know what they're doing with Tom Maddox!" And Emery, waiting while Matthew adjusted his goggles, looked back to where Linn still stood in the rain. "She should think herself lucky they've took him away, before he turned nasty and done for her like he done for our Tilly."

Matthew stepped hard on the starter and the engine roared. They drove off towards Huntlip. Behind them, in the woods of Scoate House Manor, the police search continued.

Linn, going back into the kitchen, was struck by its look of emptiness. Tom's chair set sideways at the table; his dinner plate with its few crumbs; his empty teacup askew in its saucer: these things cried out to her like ghosts, and she could scarcely bear to see them.

Sitting upright on the settle, she made herself breathe very deeply and slowly, till the tightness eased from around her heart. She wished with a kind of sick longing that her father were with her, for she felt, as she had always felt in childhood, that he would know just what to do. So intense was her longing that she sprang up and went to the window, convinced she had heard his step on the path. But she was mistaken. He was not there. She knew she would have to go to him.

She got up and put on her coat. She drew a shawl over her head. She stepped into her rubber galoshes. The clock on the mantelpiece said five to two. She went out into the rain.

At Cobbs, when the clock on the workshop roof struck the hour, a crow took off from the weathervane and left it swivelling against the wind. Jesse stood at the parlour window. He watched the crow flying off towards Anster.

"That's two o'clock striking. We're going to be desperate late, ent we?"

"A bride is expected to arrive late. Granna said so. It's the done thing."

Betony smiled at him, seeing him frowning at his watch. She went forward and took it from him, and slipped it into his waistcoat pocket, where it belonged. She held his hands between her own, to keep them from fidgeting with his collar and tie.

"Just look at that rain!" he said to her. "That vexes me so's I could bost! Why did you have to choose October?"

"Today is my birthday. I'm twenty-four. It seemed as good a day as any. What does a drop of rain matter?"

"It'll spoil your dress. That's why it matters. Now where's that cloak you're going to put on?"

"It's here, handy, on the back of the chair."

"Do I look all right in this new suit? Is my parting properly straight? Have I shaved myself nicely, would you say?"

He got his hands free and touched his hair, which was well greased down and shone like straw. He touched his chin, feeling critically for traces of stubble.

"You look very handsome," Betony said, "and far too young to be my father."

"The church'll be crowded. D'you realize that? Folk have been going up forever. I seen 'em as early as twelve noon."

"I hope there's room for them all to sit."

"There won't be," he said. "No lections of that! A lot'll be standing about outside. The rain won't stop them. You mark my words."

He turned from her to the dining-table, extended as far as it would go, caparisoned in a white damask cloth, and already spread with the wedding breakfast.

"There's cold roast venison. Have you seen it? Mrs Andrews sent it yesterday." He took up a spoon and polished it on his jacket sleeve. "Of course," he said, "the men'll be eating in the kitchen."

"The men from the workshop, do you mean?"

"The table in the kitchen's more fuller than this one. Your mother and granna have worked very hard, and your sister, too."

"I suppose *you'll* be eating in the kitchen, then, seeing you're a carpenter just like them? Dicky, too, and great-grumpa."

"Not us! Laws, no! Not the bride's own family!" And,

turning away from her teasing glance, he said: "The men'll be happier, keeping theirselves to theirselves out there. They wouldn't be properly come-for-double, mixing with the captain and his mother and all the guests on *their* side."

"Michael will see that they mix," she said, "and so shall I."

"Glory be, just look at the time! Where d'you think that boy can've got to?"

"It's only five minutes past, father. Try and relax and stop fussing."

"That's all very well," Jesse muttered. "We should've hired another carriage. Ent I been saying so all along?"

Michael and his mother, with his uncle and aunt from Ilton Lye, and his best man, Major Peter Thomas, had gone to the church in the King's Hill carriage, with a King's Hill servant in livery driving. The Cobbs family had gone in the trap, and Dicky was returning for the bride and her father.

"What's the betting Duffer's cast a shoe?" Jesse said. "Or gone lame, even. It's always at times like this, ent it?"

A door slammed at the back of the house, and Jesse snatched up Betony's cloak.

"Here he is! Here he is! Better late than never, I suppose." And as Dicky burst into the room: "Good heavens, boy, how's it you've been so long a-coming?"

"It's Tom!" Dicky said. "The police've took him away to Chepsworth."

"Who told you that?" Betony asked.

"I seen it my own-self. They drove past me as I came from the church. They'd got Tom sitting in the back of the motor."

"Didn't you stop them and ask why?"

"There wasn't no chance," Dicky said. "By the time I

realized what was happening, the motor-car had gone right past. I did draw up straight away and while I was stuck there, wondering what I ought to do, the Prestons came up on that motor-cycle. Seems they was out at the Pikehouse all morning and saw our Tom get took away."

"Did they say he'd been arrested?"

"No, they didn't say that, or not exactly."

"What *did* they say, for God's sake?"

"They said he'd got what was coming to him. They said we'd be reading it in the papers."

"What about Linn?" Betony asked.

"Left at home," Dicky said.

"Laws!" Jesse said, looking anxiously at Betony. "That this should happen on your wedding day! Was ever anything so unlucky?" He felt he could scarcely look at Dicky. If only the boy had had the sense to keep the news until after the wedding! "Never mind, my blossom. Try not to let it spoil your day." He moved towards her with the cloak.

Betony was staring at the clock in the middle of the mantelpiece. Her mind worked with great clarity. The wedding ceremony would take perhaps an hour and a half. It would all be over by four o'clock. Not very long, she told herself, if she went from the church immediately afterwards. And yet it was *too* long. Some part of her said so. Some part of her had already settled all the questions.

In fancy now she saw Michael's face as he waited for her inside the church. He seemed to know what she was thinking; his grey eyes were worried, intent on hers; he was asking her to come to him. Then she saw Tom's face, his eyes deep and dark and hollow-looking, staring past her, asking nothing.

"Come on, my blossom," Jesse said. "We're late enough as it is already."

"No, dad, I'm not going. The wedding will have to be postponed."

"Postponed? Are you mad? You surely can't mean it! It's out of all reason!"

"You'll have to go to the church and tell them. I'll drop you there on my way to Chepsworth. But first I must go and change my dress."

"Betony, no!" he said, outraged, and stepped in front of her, barring the way. "You can't go and do a thing like that! Think of all the people waiting! Think of the captain and Mrs Andrews! What in God's name are they going to say?"

"Don't you care what happens to Tom?"

"I care all right. A whole lot more'n he deserves. But what can you do to help matters?"

"There must be something I can do."

"Well, afterwards, then, when it's all over. We can go and see about it then."

"No, father, I'm going now."

"I don't understand you!" Jesse said, following her out across the hall. "I don't know how you can do such a thing! I'd never've believed it! You of all people – my favourite daughter!" He continued to shout at her as she hurried upstairs. "What if the captain don't forgive you? I'm sure I shouldn't, in his place! I shan't forgive you anyway! – You're making us a byword in this village, you and Tom between you."

When Betony descended again, having changed into an ordinary dress, her father sat on the bottom stair and Dicky stood over him, arguing with him. Jesse's face was averted from her. He had never been angry in his life till today. She could see he was sick with disappointment.

"I ent going to the church to tell them. You needn't think it."

"Then Dicky must go instead," she said.

"That's up to him. I can't stop him. My children take no account of me."

"If you won't go to the church, will you go to the Pikehouse and see Linn? She must be worried out of her mind."

"Not me. Oh, no! That young woman is nothing to me. I'm just stopping where I am."

"Come on, Dicky," Betony said, and Dicky followed her out to the trap.

Driving briskly through Huntlip, they passed little knots of villagers, who turned and stared as the trap went past them. Further on, when they got to the green, she could see the people gathered in the churchyard, standing under the yews and birches, sheltering from the rain. The bells were ringing out loud, and the rooks, disturbed, were floating in circles round the tower. Betony stopped to let Dicky down, then she drove on towards Chepsworth.

Linn walked as fast as her heavily burdened body would allow. She tried to keep fear from clawing at her mind. It was three miles by road from the Pikehouse to Huntlip, and another two and a half from Huntlip to Blagg, but by taking the footpath to Millery Bridge and the old drove road over Puppet Hill, she was able to cut off a mile.

The rain was now a steady downpour, and she felt glad of it, soaked though she was, for it meant her father would surely be at home, sitting with his leg up, beside the fire. He hated wet days, for his bad knee became swollen and caused him much pain, and only the heat of a good fire brought him any measure of relief.

So strong was her faith that he would be there, reading his paper and smoking his pipe, that when she found the

cottage empty she stood for a moment in shocked disbe-
lief. A terrible weakness flooded through her, and a great
anger. Why couldn't he be there when he was needed?
What business had taken him out of his home on a wet
Saturday in October? A boy scaring birds in the field
below came to the hedge and gave her the answer.

"Mr Mercybright's gone to Upham. The master sent
him to look at a boar."

"How long'll he be, Godwin, do you know?"

"He said he'd be home by six o'clock. He said for me
to light his fire and he'd give me tea when he got in. He
generally does on Saturdays."

"Then I'll write him a message," Linn said.

She went into the cottage and sat for a while, shivering
in her wet clothes. She felt sick and giddy, hot and cold
at the same time, and pain burnt in the small of her
back, as though her spine were splitting and breaking.
She thought of putting a match to the fire; of resting
and warming herself for an hour; even waiting for her
father; but she was afraid the police might return with
Tom to the Pikehouse and that he would be worried at
finding her gone. Or, she thought, they might call to say
he had been arrested. So she got up, found paper and
pencil and wrote her message, and went out again into
the rain.

Just past the farm, at a bend in the lane, where it was
narrow, she had to stand aside for a herd of bullocks.
They had just come down from Puppet Hill, and the man
in charge of them, Frank Kendrick, was driving them too
fast down the steep track. Linn, though she pressed herself close into the hedge, was bumped and buffeted several times and had to hold tight to a hawthorn branch to
avoid being spun out into the lane and trampled under
the cloven hooves. But the last bullock lumbered by, and

Frank Kendrick came panting behind, his stick on his shoulder, his dog at his heels.

"Bloody cattle!" he said as he passed. "I could shoot them sometimes. I could. Honest."

Linn walked on, up the steep track and through the wicket, out onto the open hill. At the top of the rise she stopped to rest, leaning with her back against a tree, her hands on her stomach, seeking to still the throbbing there; seeking assurance that all was well within her womb. Then, having felt her child moving vigorously under her hand, she walked on over the hill.

All the way along Cricketers Lane, where the horse-chestnut trees hung over the hedge, the ground was strewn with the fallen chestnuts, bursting out of their spiky shells. Passing that way earlier she had met not a soul, but now a ragged figure crouched there, shuffling along low on his haunches, the skirts of his overcoat trailing in the mud. Although a man of forty or more, Jumper Lane had the face of a schoolboy, smooth-skinned and pink, with little arched brows over eyes a brilliant china blue. He looked at Linn with a gap-toothed smile and sprang upright, showing her the chestnuts crammed to the tops of his overcoat pockets.

"Yes, Jumper, they're beautiful. You're going to be busy, collecting all these."

"Look at this one!" he said, and snatched up a chestnut still in its skin, pressing it open to show her the dark-shining nut inside. "Look at *this* one and *this* one and *this* one and *this*!"

He was shuffling after her, stooping repeatedly to snatch up the chestnuts, then jumping up to thrust them at her.

"Yes, they're lovely," Linn said. "But I must hurry. I've got to get home."

"No need to hurry. The clocks are slow. Stop and help me collect the conkers."

"Not now, Jumper, I'm in a hurry."

"You always used to play with me."

"Not today, however. There's no time."

"I shall tell on you if you don't stop. I know what you done. You're just as bad as Alice Quinton."

And, blocking her way, he made his arms into a cradle, rocking slowly from side to side and uttering croodling noises in his throat. Then, his whole body squirming suddenly, he leapt high into the air, his knees going up like the blades of a jack-knife.

"Can't be helped! Can't be helped! What's done is done and can't be undone!"

"Please let me pass, Jumper," Linn said. "I'm tired and wet and I want to get home."

"Not till you let me have my way. I ent so simple as you seem to think."

"If you don't let me pass I shall speak to your auntie, Mrs Tupper, and tell her you were behaving badly. You won't like that, now, will you, Jumper?"

"Play conkers, then. I'll thread one for you."

"I told you before. I haven't got time."

She had never been frightened of Jumper Lane. There was no harm in him beyond a boisterous playfulness and the lewdness he learnt at The Rose and Crown. She was not frightened even now but she couldn't get past him and tiredness was bringing her close to tears. She made a great effort to keep her composure.

"Look here, Jumper, what about seeing me half way home? I'm passing not far from your Auntie Tupper's. We can walk together as far as the bridge."

"All right," he said. "But people will talk, you know. People will say I'm to blame for the babby."

"Never mind. Talk never hurts us, does it, Jumper?"

"They was asking me at the public once if I was to blame for getting Alice into trouble. But I ent saying. Oh, no, not me! I ent so green as I'm cabbage-looking."

Walking beside her along the lane, he kept kicking the chestnuts and leaves on the ground, but now and then he would turn towards her, putting both hands on her right arm and giving it a hard squeeze. He was plainly enjoying his walk with her.

"My auntie's got a mangle. She lets me turn the handle for her. She gives me a penny if I don't turn it backwards."

"You're always very good to your auntie. I've heard people say so oftentimes."

"I want watching, though. I'm a dark horse. Joe Wilkes says I'm as sly as the devil. He wouldn't leave his missus with me for five minutes . He said it hisself. So did she."

"People talk a lot of rubbish."

"They do, they do, they want sewing up!" Jumper said. "They want their gobs stopped, that's what I say."

On reaching the stile at the playing-field, he vaulted over in a single bound, slithering a little in the mud. Linn followed, slowly and awkwardly, and Jumper watched her in some concern.

"The trouble is, you've gone too fat. You're as fat as a landlady, that's what you are. Now, easy does it, that's the ticket. Easy and over and down and round."

He reached for her hand to help her down, but the moment his fingers closed on hers, he was seized by a sudden spasm of mischief.

"Statues!" he said, and pulled her headlong off the stile, so that she fell with great force, face forward onto the ground.

The pain was worse than anything she had ever

experienced. The scream of it echoed on and on, in her mind and her body, shrilling along every nerve. She thought she was going to lose her senses, but she lay on her side in the long wet grass and fixed her gaze on a marguerite that hung, drenched with rain, about eighteen inches from her face. She made herself think of it, concentrating with all her will, focusing on it until she could see every clean white petal sprouting from the yellow middle. And after a moment the faintness passed. But the whole of her body shrieked with pain. It was spreading out from the core of her being, where her child lay coiled like a spring in her womb. It made her powerless to move.

Jumper was bending over her, trying to look into her face. His big clumsy hands were locked together.

"I never done it! Oh, no, not me! She was climbing the stile and she tumbled off. It's not Jumper's fault she went such a whomper. He warnt nowhere near the playing-field."

He ran off, whimpering, back along Cricketers Lane, plunging his hands into his pockets and scattering the chestnuts as he went.

When Linn got up, raising herself little by little, he had vanished completely. It was useless calling him back to help her. He would be at the marlpits by now, or even at Outlands, hiding in one of the farm buildings. She stood for a time holding on to the bar of the stile, waiting while the sickness ebbed and flowed; waiting till her sight no longer rippled. Then she went on her way, across the playing-field and out at the gate by Millery Bridge.

Every step she took was a step homewards. Pain must not be allowed to matter. The sensible thing, as she well knew, was to turn into Huntlip and ask for help. Fifty yards off, if she turned left, there was a row of cottages, but she shrank from the thought of appealing to strangers. In half a mile, if she turned right, she would come to Cobbs where she was known, but there, she thought, the wedding party would be under way and her arrival would spoil it all. So she crossed the main street of the village and took the path up through Millery Wood.

But now a new kind of pain took hold of her, and she stood still, as though listening to it, as though her stillness would smooth it away. It was different from the pain she was already suffering: it was one sort of pain underlying another: the sudden clenching of a savage fist and then the slow, reluctant unclenching, leaving nausea in its wake. There was also a terrible liquid warmth and she knew that the waters protecting her child in the womb were breaking and moving.

But if animals could hold back their young without any harm coming to them, then so could she, for her will was surely as strong as theirs? And she went on steadily as before, up the steep slopes of Millery Wood, over the open fields at Peckstone, out onto the Norton road. When the pains came she stood quite still, gripping the fence with both hands, breathing great deep measured breaths. Fear and pain were working together. They would pluck her down if her strength failed, and she would be like a hare in its form or a vixen creeping into its hole.

"Please, God," she whispered, "don't let my baby be born at the roadside."

The Pikehouse was as empty as when she had left it, the fire dying on the hearth. She took a white sheet from a drawer, went out to the garden, and pegged it securely on the line. It was a signal to the midwife, Mrs Gibbs, who lived in a cottage near Eastery church. The cottage could not be seen from the Pikehouse because it was hidden among the trees; nor could the Pikehouse be seen from the cottage; but if Mrs Gibbs stepped out to the churchyard and looked down between the two elms as she had promised to do every morning and evening, she would see the signal very plainly.

Linn went in and closed the door. She reached for the bellows to revive the fire. But then, since darkness was not very far away, she lit the lamp with the pink-frosted shade, took it upstairs into the bedroom and placed it in the window facing towards Eastery church.

"Please, God," she said, as she turned up the flame, "make Mrs Gibbs step out to the churchyard."

She went downstairs again into the kitchen, to rebuild the fire and shed her wet clothes. The pains were coming more frequently now. Fear could no longer be shut out.

When Betony arrived at the Chepsworth police station, she found Matthew Preston sitting on a form in the main hall.

"What are you doing here?"

"My father sent me. He said to wait and see what's happening."

"Isn't your father satisfied with the trouble he's caused already?"

"It ent my dad that's caused the trouble. It's him in there – Tom Maddox."

"Tom never hurt anyone in his life."

"The police don't think that. Or why've they got him in there?"

"Why indeed!" Betony said.

At the desk in the hall sat a uniformed sergeant, writing in a ledger and drinking a cup of tea at the same time. He stopped writing and looked at Betony over his cup.

"Yes, miss?"

"I want to know why Mr Thomas Maddox is being held here."

"Ah," he said slowly, and put down his cup, looking at her with sharper interest. "Are you some relation to the man Maddox?"

"*Mister* Maddox is my foster-brother."

"And your name is?"

"Miss Betony Izzard."

"Well, Miss Izzard, Mr Maddox is here to answer questions concerning the disappearance of his wife. Inspector Darns is in charge of the matter, and Constable Penfold is helping him."

"I would like to see Inspector Darns."

"I'm afraid that's impossible at the moment. The inspector is with Mr Maddox now and he won't relish being disturbed."

"That's nothing to me. I insist that you tell the inspector I'm here. It's very important."

"Very well, Miss Izzard, I'll send in a message as soon as I can."

"When will that be? After you've had another cup of tea?"

"If you will kindly take a seat – "

"No, no. I'd sooner stand."

She walked about the hall, reading the notices on the boards. The station was a big one, newly built. A corridor ran from the back of the hall, with five doors at either side. She watched people coming and going for a while, and, with growing impatience, returned to the desk.

"I've got a pony and trap outside. If I'm going to be kept waiting – "

"I'll get someone to see to it for you," the sergeant said, and beckoned to a constable who was crossing from one door to another. "There's a pony and trap outside, Simmonds. Drive it round to the stables, will you?"

"I'm obliged to you," Betony said.

"All part of the service, miss."

"Is it part of the service to keep a man in custody when he's done nothing at all to deserve it?"

"Mr Maddox is not in custody, miss. He came along of his own free will."

"Did you send in my message to Inspector Darns?"

"Yes, miss, but I doubt if he'll see you for a while yet."

"Which room are they in, out of all those?"

"Third on the left," the sergeant said, and eyed Betony with some suspicion. "You weren't thinking of just walking in, were you, miss?"

"I might," she said, "if I don't soon get satisfaction."

"I wouldn't advise doing that, miss. It'll only draw things out that much longer. Why not sit down and wait patiently?"

"It's very important that I see Inspector Darns."

But she went and sat on one of the forms, watched by Matthew Preston, sitting nearby.

The clock on the wall said ten past three. She thought it was probably rather slow but five minutes later the cathedral clock was striking the quarter. At twenty past four a man in plain clothes emerged from a door in the corridor and stood talking to the desk sergeant. Betony rose and went to him.

"Miss Izzard?" he said. "I'm Detective-Constable Penfold. I gather you're enquiring for Mr Maddox."

"How much longer do you intend keeping him here?"

"That depends on what he tells us."

"And what has he told you so far?"

"Nothing much," Penfold said, "but it's often surprising what a man will tell us when he's been here for a few hours, and we've had time to wear him down."

"Perhaps if you wear them down enough, they may even confess to things they've never done!" she said.

"That's hardly likely, Miss Izzard. We don't employ the thumbscrew, you know."

"Tilly went off with a man named Trimble. Why don't you try finding him?"

"Arthur Trimble is proving elusive."

"Exactly!" she said. "Because he had an affair with Tilly and doesn't want his wife to know."

"Not necessarily. People often take fright for nothing at all. But, of course, it may be that Trimble was indeed having an affair with Mrs Maddox and Mr Maddox took exception to it. In which case, if jealousy was the motive, and provocation could be proved, the charge would be manslaughter, not murder."

"Aren't you being a little previous?"

"I was theorizing. Nothing more."

"Mr Penfold," she said. "I want to see Inspector Darns. There's something important I want to tell him."

"Is it directly concerned with the case?"

"It's directly concerned with my foster-brother. That's all that matters to me. But it *is* important."

"All right, Miss Izzard, I'll see what I can do."

Penfold went along the corridor and back into the room on the left. He emerged again with an older man and they stood talking in quiet voices, glancing often in Betony's direction. Then they went off down the corridor and into a room at the far end. Betony took a few steps forward but the desk sergeant stood in her way. She returned in great anger to her seat against the wall.

"Take their time, don't they?" Matthew Preston said to her.

Betony glanced at him but made no answer. He was, with his dark curly hair and thick stocky body, the very image of his father, and she hated him for it.

"Wasn't you getting married today? I thought the wedding was two o'clock. Did you leave the chap standing on account of Tom Maddox?"

"Don't speak to me!" Betony said. "There's nothing I want to say to you!"

She would not allow herself to think of Michael. Not yet, anyway. Such thoughts would have to wait.

Tom sat in a room that smelt of hot water pipes and floor-polish. It was stuffy and airless, and he wished they would open the window wider, but he couldn't bring himself to ask. The silence, ever since Darns had gone out, was too sweet to break, and he sat quite still in the chair at the table, his ankles crossed, his hands in his lap, his head turned in such a way that the current of air coming in, teasing though it was, blew directly into his face, bringing with it the smell of rain.

He knew he was not alone in the room. He knew that a constable sat in the corner and watched him. But so long as the man remained silent, Tom could pretend he was not there; could pretend the room was utterly empty; could picture the walls receding, receding, until they were gone altogether, giving way to open country where the rain blew like smoke on the wind and the clouds rode low on the backs of the distant hills.

Some little way off he could see the Pikehouse, lonely beside the old turnpike road. He was walking towards it, down the slope from Eastery, across the wasteland known as the Chacks, with the long tawny grasses brushing against him, leaving him dusty with their pollen. He had been on an errand to Mrs Hurst's shop. He carried flour, yeast, sugar, matches, candles, soap, rock salt, in a sack slung on his shoulder, and a can of paraffin in his left hand. Linn would be waiting for the yeast. It being Saturday, she was going to make bread.

Now, in fancy, he saw the tiny Pikehouse kitchen, with its scrubbed deal table and two varnished chairs, its oak

settle and corner-cupboard and brass-topped fender
round the hearth. And yet there was something that worried him. He could not picture what Linn was doing. The
fire was burning brightly enough. The kettle, on its hook,
was puffing steam up the chimney. The whole place was
neat and trim and spoke of Linn's recent attention, yet
she herself was somehow absent, and he heard his own
voice calling, "Linn? Where are you? Are you upstairs?"
But although he listened carefully, inside his mind, there
was no answer.

"What time is it?" he asked sharply.

"Half-past-five," the policeman said. "Would you like a
cup of tea?"

"No, I'd like to go home," Tom said, and when
Inspector Darns came into the room, he sat up straight
and turned his head. "I reckon you've kept me long
enough. I've answered your questions. It's time I went
home."

"We'd all like to go home, Mr Maddox, but there are
just a few more questions I'd like to ask you before we
finally call it a day."

"A few more? Or the same ones all over again?"

"You saw your wife with Arthur Trimble. You walked in
and found them, in your own home, in something of a
compromising situation. That's what you said, I think,
when I first questioned you some weeks ago?"

"Oh no it ent!" Tom said. "I never said nothing of the
kind!"

"What *did* you say, Mr Maddox?"

"I said I saw them. I never said I walked in. I didn't
walk in. I went away."

"You mean you spied on them, without their knowing?"

"Not on purpose. It just happened."

"What were they doing when you saw them?"

"She was seeing him off at the gate. He had his arm around her neck. It looked like they was pretty friendly."

"That must have made you very angry."

"Not me," Tom said. "I was past being angry by that time."

"But you had been angry in the beginning?"

"When I found out she'd lied about having a baby, that made me angry, right enough. I could've struck her."

"Quite natural, I'm sure. Any man would have felt the same. But when you struck your wife, Mr Maddox, what exactly did you use? A stick? A hammer? A fire-iron snatched from the hearth?"

"I didn't use nothing!" Tom said.

"Just your bare hands, is that what you mean?"

"No. It ent. I never touched her."

"Perhaps you only meant to slap her. Just a light blow with the flat of your hand. Or a bit of a push that sent her reeling, so that she fell and hit her head."

"Seems to me you're getting muddled. You been listening to tales about my father."

"Did it happen at home or did you persuade her to walk in the woods?"

"No more questions!" Tom said. "We been over and over it time and again. You won't get me saying nothing different, not if you try from now to domesday."

"You certainly had plenty of time," Darns said, "to decide what story you would tell."

He drew a chair from under the table and sat down opposite Tom. He opened a folder and turned over a few of the papers.

"About this court martial when you were in the Army."

"Yes? What about it?" Tom said.

"You were charged with refusing to obey an order. You were found guilty and given five days' F.P."

"You should know. You're the one that's looked it up."

"What was the order you refused to obey?"

"Don't it tell you in my record?"

"The details are sparse. Even at the court martial itself they don't seem to have asked what the order was."

"No. That's right. It didn't suit them."

"What was the order, Mr Maddox?"

"I was told off as one of a firing-party."

"What made you refuse? A delicate stomach?"

"I didn't hold with killing my mates. They'd no right to ask me. They knew that."

"What about sergeants, Mr Maddox? Did you hold with killing them? Or one sergeant in particular, say, by the name of Townchurch? A man you fell foul of, I understand."

"Me and a few score others, yes."

"A man who was mortally wounded in the back, although he was facing the enemy, and who died making certain accusations. Or so I was told at Capleton barracks."

"I never killed him, if that's what you're saying. It was more than likely an accident."

"An accident! That takes some believing."

"Them things happened," Tom said. "I was blinded by an English shell but nobody says it was done on purpose."

"You look a bit groggy," Darns said. "Are you feeling ill?"

"I'm all right," Tom said. "I'm just wondering what else you're going to try and blame me for."

"You do look groggy all the same. Perhaps you'd like a cup of tea."

"I'd like to go home," Tom said. "That's all I want. I just want to be took back home."

Outside the room there was a sudden loud commo-

tion; a scuffling at the door and voices upraised; then a
woman's voice ringing out above the rest. Darns got up
and went out quickly. The policeman in the corner
moved to the door. Tom sat listening as the voices outside slowly died away. His head felt hollow, like an empty
shell, and the usual pins-and-needles feeling was spreading out from the back of his skull. Perhaps he was having
strange fancies, but he could have sworn it was Betony's
voice he had heard outside in the corridor.

Betony and Darns stood facing each other in a small
room with barred windows. They were quite alone.

"Well, Miss Izzard, now you've got your way, what is it
you have to say to me that's so important?"

"My foster-brother is a sick man. It's very wrong that
you should keep him here like this, and I have come to
take him home."

"A sick man? Are you referring to his blindness?"

"It's not only that. Tom was badly blown up in the war
and there was some damage to the brain. The doctors
who saw him last February gave him a year at the outside. Too much strain could be very harmful and perhaps shorten his life still more."

"I see," Darns said. "And he himself doesn't know this?"

"No, nor mustn't, ever!" Betony said, with great passion.

"Don't worry, Miss Izzard," Darns said. "We aren't
monsters here, you know."

"You can check what I've told you by telephoning Dr
Dundas at Norton."

"I may do that, but at present I'm willing to accept
your word."

"Then I can take him home?" she said.

Before Darns could answer, Penfold knocked and

looked into the room, waving a piece of paper. Darns excused himself to Betony and stepped outside.

"It's Waring's report on that scarf at last," Penfold said. "The blood is animal's blood, sure enough, so we're left with precious little to hammer Maddox with, aren't we?"

"I'm losing the desire to try," Darns said.

"Feel he's innocent, do you, sir?"

"I don't know. I've got no feelings either way. He certainly isn't easy to rattle."

"One other thing," Penfold said. "Blackmore's back from searching Scoate. He says it's getting too dark to see. But he reckons he'd bet his last penny that there's nothing to be found in those woods."

"That settles it, then. I'll tell his sister she can take him home."

A few minutes later, Betony and Tom walked out through the hall. Matthew Preston rose from his seat. He looked past them at Inspector Darns.

"You letting him go? My dad won't like that! I thought you was going to arrest him for murder."

"There is no evidence whatever against your brother-in-law," Darns said, "and you can tell your father I said so."

"I'll tell him all right, but he ent going to like it! I reckon he'll just about raise the roof!"

Matthew ran out, leaving the glass door swinging, and they heard him ride away on his motor-cycle. When Betony followed, guiding Tom down the steps, the pony and trap stood in the roadway with a caped policeman in attendance, and the two lamps had been lit ready. The sky was very dark now, but the rain was little more than a drizzle.

"Smells good," Tom said, as they drove off. "I thought I should likely smother in there." And, after a while, he said: "I don't understand about your wedding. I don't, that's a fact."

"It's perfectly simple," Betony said. "It's been postponed till another day. Such things do happen sometimes, you know. There's nothing extraordinary about it."

As they journeyed homeward dusk became night, although it was not much later than six o'clock. Tom was silent, sitting hunched behind her, and whenever she turned to look at him, his face in the glow of the lamps looked worn, his eyes anxious.

"Are you all right?" she asked once.

"Right as rain," he said promptly.

"I thought you looked tired."

"I was thinking of Linn, left alone all this time. She'll be worried sick."

"We won't be long now. We're almost in Huntlip. We've just passed Steadworth Mill."

At Carter's Bridge, where the road crossed a bend in the Derrent Brook, a light was glimmering through the drizzle, and as she got nearer Betony saw that a man stood in the middle of the bridge, swinging a lantern.

"What is it?" Tom asked, as the pony slowed to a hesitant walk.

"Someone with a lantern. I don't know who."

Betony halted and was at once sorry, for out of the darkness stepped four more men, and now she realized who they were. The man with the lantern was Harry Yelland, who had once been "engaged" to Tilly Preston. The others were Emery and his three boys. They had chosen a good place for their ambush. The nearest house was half a mile.

"It's Yelland and the Prestons," she said to Tom. "We're at Carter's Bridge and they're blocking the way."

"Can't you drive through them?"

"No. I've left it too late."

She drove forward a little way, up the incline onto the bridge, hoping the Prestons would give ground before her, but Emery caught at the pony's bridle and jerked him to a standstill. Betony took the whip from its socket.

"Step aside and let us pass or you'll be sorry, I promise you."

"*He's* the one that's going to be sorry. Him there behind you, who murdered my Tilly."

"The police have sent him home because there isn't a shred of evidence against him. If they're satisfied, why aren't you?"

" 'Cos I know Tom Maddox better'n they do. I know what sort of stock he growed from. His father was a murderer and everyone knows it and the old saying speaks the truth – like father, like son, every time."

"If that were true, we'd all be murderers," Betony said, "seeing we're all descended from Cain."

"I'm not wasting time in arguments. Just hand that man over and you can get home."

"Do you set yourself above the law?"

"He may be able to fool the police, but he'll soon tell the truth when I get hold of him, you may be sure of that, by God!"

"I've already told the truth!" Tom said. "I've told it and told it and it ent going to change!"

"Supposing you step down from there!" Yelland shouted. "Instead of hiding behind a woman!"

"This man is blind!" Betony said. "Have you lost all sense of pity?"

"We know he's blind," Emery answered, "but it don't mean he's going to get away with murder."

"You will not set hands on my foster-brother unless you deal with me first!"

"We mean you no harm, being a woman, but if you

choose to hinder us, it's your own fault if you get hurt."

Emery let go of the bridle and came alongside the trap. He tried to step up onto the wheel. Betony struck at him with the whip-stock and he fell back, swearing, one hand covering his eyes. She flicked the reins and tried to drive on, but Matthew had taken his father's place and was pulling hard on the pony's bridle. The pony reared up and danced a little, the white sparks flying as his shoes scrabbled the smooth-worn cobbles. Alfie Preston got kicked on the knee, and his twin, Victor, was squeezed between the wheel of the trap and the low stone parapet of the bridge.

Harry Yelland set down his lantern and took a stone from the heap he had ready between his feet. His arm went back and the stone flew close past Betony's face. Tom, behind her, gave a cry of pain, and when she turned to look at him, the blood was dark on his left temple. At the same moment, Emery Preston came forward again, but this time when Betony lashed at him with the whip, he caught hold of the thong and wrenched it clean out of her hands.

"Now, then!" he bellowed. "I've had about enough of this! Come down from that trap, Tom Maddox, or it'll be worse for you in the end 'cos I'm just about running out of patience!"

Approaching the trap, he was trying the whip in his right hand. He looked as though he would use it on Tom. But now, suddenly, there came the sharp crack of a shotgun, which set the pony dancing again but brought the five men to a standstill. The skitter of shot went into the boughs of a willow overhead, and in the little silence that followed, a few spent pellets fell among them, pattering down like extra heavy drops of rain. Then a voice spoke and Jack Mercybright came up onto the bridge, into the light shed by the lantern. His shotgun lay in the crook of his arm, smoke curling from one barrel, and he turned it full on Harry Yelland.

"Come away from that trap, all you others, or he gets the next lot in his guts. Make haste about it! No dilladerrying or trying tricks. The sort of day I've had today, I'm in the right mood to murder someone, and I'd just as soon it was one of you as anyone else I can think of offhand."

"This is none of your business!" Emery shouted. "We've got a score to settle with Maddox and it's no concern of yours whatever!"

"It is now," Jack said. "Move out of the way or Yelland gets it."

His wet bearded face was grim and ferocious. They decided he meant every word he said. Emery twisted the whip in its thong and threw it onto Betony's knees. He motioned his sons away from the trap, and led them back over the bridge, picking up the lantern as he went. Yelland followed, and the five of them stood at the side of the road, watching as Jack climbed into the trap.

Betony gave a flip of the reins and the pony pulled off over the bridge. As the trap passed him, Emery took a step forward, but at sight of the shotgun pointing towards him, he thought better of it and vented his feelings by pounding the panelwork with his fists.

"We'll get you, Tom Maddox, even if we do have to bide our time! No murderer yet ever went unpunished. Your crime will catch up with you, mark my words!"

"Take no notice," Jack said, and, peering closer into Tom's face: "Are you all right, boy? It looks like you've had a crack on the head."

"I'm all right," Tom said. "I just want to get back to Linn."

"We shan't be long now," Jack said.

"How did you happen to come by just then?" Betony asked, over her shoulder.

"I got a message from Linn, that's how, saying Tom'd been took away, so I set out to go to Chepsworth to see the police like she asked me to."

"Armed with a shotgun?" Betony said.

"I saw the Prestons come jumbling out of The Rose and Crown and I judged they was up to some sort of mischief. So I went along to the haywarden's office and borrowed this gun from Billy Ratchet."

Tom, sitting hunched against the rain, could feel the blood from the wound on his forehead trickling down the side of his face. He wiped it away with his handkerchief. The wound was not hurting overmuch, but his whole head ached in a dense way, especially the back of his skull.

"How did Linn manage to send you a message?"

"She brought it herself," Jack said. "Godwin saw her."

"What, walked all that way?" Tom exclaimed, and gave a groan, pressing the knuckles of his fists together and squeezing them hard between his knees. "But I *told* her not to go out of doors! She had no right to go walking so far! Supposing she was took ill going back? Supposing she was to lose the baby?" And then suddenly, from the depths of his darkness and helplessness, he cried out in a great trembling voice, "For God's sake, Betony, get me home!"

Betony whipped up the little pony and they drove fast through the stinging rain.

"It's all right," she said, when they came at last within sound of the Pikehouse. "It's all right, Tom, there's a light in the window so she must be there."

*

In the Pikehouse kitchen, Mrs Gibbs removed her soiled apron, wrapped it in newspaper, and stowed it away in her leather bag. She heard the sound of the trap approaching and stood listening for it to stop. She went to the door and opened it wide.

"My dear life!" she said, seeing the blood on Tom's forehead. "The policemen never done that to you, surely?"

"Mrs Gibbs! How come you're here? Where's Linn?"

"Linn's all right. So's your little baby son. They're both pretty fine, all things considered, and now they're having a well-earnt rest. Here, sit down, young fella, you look as though you're about all in."

"No, no," Tom said. "I want to see her."

"Well, you can't go up dripping wet, can you? Nor with your head all bloody neither."

"Of course he can't," Betony said. She drew him towards the blazing fire. "A minute or two won't make much difference. You must shed a few of these wet clothes."

He took off his cap, jacket, and bloodstained shirt, and Mrs Gibbs received them from him. She hung a towel round his shoulders.

"Are you sure she's all right?" he asked. "You ent keeping nothing from me?"

"I give you my word," Mrs Gibbs said, and touched his arm.

"How long ago did the baby come?"

"Half an hour or thereabouts, and if he'd come sooner he'd have stood a chance of getting hisself born between here and Blagg."

"You sure she ent done herself no harm?"

"She's used up every ounce of strength for the time being, but she'll be all right, I promise you."

"Oughtn't we to get the doctor?"

"Yes," Jack said, "I'll go and fetch him."

"It might be as well, to be on the safe side," said Mrs Gibbs. "It's Dr Dundas down in Norton. Second house past the post office."

"Tell him it's urgent," Tom said.

"I'll bring him, don't worry," Jack said, and the door closed behind him.

Mrs Gibbs was warming a shirt at the fire. She gave it to Tom and he put it on. He was trembling all over and his fingers could scarcely fasten the buttons. She had to help him. Betony brought a bowl of water and cleaned the blood from the cut on his temple. He bore it in silence, only dimly aware of what she was doing. He tucked his shirt into his trousers and ran a hand through his hair.

"Am I tidy enough? Can I go up to her now?" he asked.

"Go, you," Mrs Gibbs said, "and I'll come in a minute to show you your baby."

In the tiny bedroom, Linn lay in bed feeling she would never move again. Close beside her, her baby lay in its wickerwork cot, a doll-like shape under the blankets, a smudge of dark hair just showing above. She could hear the voices in the kitchen below, and when Tom came up the steep stairs into the bedroom, she turned towards him, putting out a hand.

"You've hurt your head," she said, in a weak voice.

"It was an accident," Tom said. He did not want to tell her about the Prestons. "I hit myself on a low rafter."

"You look pale and tired. They had no right to keep you so long."

"I wish I could see how *you* are looking, after all you been through today."

"I'm not too bad. Mrs Gibbs was wonderful. Did she tell you we've got a son?"

"Oh, I've heard about *him*. Is he there beside you? Does he like the cot I made for him?"

"Come round," she said. "Seems to me he's heard your voice and he's listening to it. He's turning his head this way and that."

"Is he?" Tom said, and felt his way round to the cot. "Does he know I'm his father, d'you suppose?"

When he touched the blankets covering his son, and felt the warm body moving, small, under his hands, something leapt at his throat and took his breath away completely. Until this moment the baby had merely been part of Linn's body; a part of the life they had together; something that made him fearful for her. But now as it stirred beneath the blankets, and he felt the warmth of it throbbing against the palms of his hands; felt the shape of it, and the way it squirmed, trying the strength of its small limbs; he knew it had a life all its own, its own heart and soul and obstinate will, its own place under the sun.

"Pick him up," Linn said. "He's your own son."

"I'm afraid to," he said. "I might hurt him, being blind."

The stairs creaked and Mrs Gibbs came into the room. She took the baby out of his cot and placed him, in his blankets, in Tom's arms. And now, with the small warm face nuzzling with such surprising strength against his own, the small hands pushing against him, Tom stood for a while feeling that he and this baby son of his were alone together in the dark. Alone together as one flesh. But, right at the heart of this shared darkness, there was a sunny picture forming.

"I can see you," he whispered. "I can see you, little boy, one summer's day, after rain, reaching up with both hands to touch a wild pink rose in the hedgerow, and you're laughing the way your mother laughs, 'cos one or two raindrops is splashing down into your face."

Mrs Gibbs took the baby and laid it back again in its cot. Tom returned to Linn's bedside and sat with her hand between his own.

"Your father was here. Did you hear him? He's gone to fetch Dr Dundas."

"Yes, I heard him."

"You went against me, didn't you? You left the house and went all them miles to Outlands Farm. That frightens me to think of, your going all that way."

"Did father come and fetch you home?"

"It was Betony that done that. She put off her wedding, would you believe it? I dunno what she said to the policeman, but they let me go, whatever it was. Then we picked up your father on the way home."

Tom felt Mrs Gibbs beside him. She was touching his shoulder.

"We should ought to let her rest. The doctor'll be here before long. You can come up again in an hour or two. I'll sit up here while she has a sleep."

"I reckon that's right," Tom said. "I'm gabbling on like an old goose."

He rose from the stool and leant over to kiss Linn's forehead. He felt her fingers touching his face. He turned and went down into the kitchen.

"How is she?" Betony asked.

"She says she's all right. And Mrs Gibbs don't seem too worried about her, does she? Anyway, Dr Dundas will be here directly."

"How's the baby?"

"Oh, he's a masterpiece, he is! I daresay they'll let you see him later."

"Sit down here," Betony said. "I'm going to clean that forehead properly."

"All right," he said, and sat on the edge of the rocking-chair, his back quite straight, his hands folded between his knees. He was thinking about his baby son. "Maybe he'll be a carpenter, the same as me. Maybe they'll take him on at Cobbs." And after a while he said, "D'you think he'll mind overmuch, having a father that's stone blind?"

"No, he won't mind, I'm sure of that."

Betony was swabbing the deep cut, wiping away the dried blood.

"I don't like the look of this at all. It's very ugly."

"It's a funny thing, but I can't feel it. I felt it all right when the stone hit me. I thought I was going to fly to bits. But I don't feel nothing any more." He put up a hand and touched the wound with the tips of his fingers. "No, not a thing," he said, pressing. "My head just feels numb, that's all."

"Numb all over, do you mean?"

"Pretty well all over. I ent sure. It's like pins-and-needles inside my skull."

"I wish the doctor would come!" she said. "Surely he ought to be here by now?"

"Maybe he was out some place else. Maybe Jack has had to wait. Are you worried about Linn?"

"I'm more worried about this cut."

"I told you, that's nothing, I don't hardly know it's there at all. I'm a bit muzzy, but I'm used to that."

"I think you ought to try and rest."

"Can a man rest when he's just this minute become a father?"

"They haven't all spent such hours as you have, under police questioning."

"No," he said, and, after a pause: "I never murdered Tilly, Bet, and that's the truth as God's my witness."

"I never thought you did for one moment."

"I wish she'd come forward and put an end to all this talk. I don't want my son growing up in the world with people saying his dad's a murderer."

"Lean back and rest," Betony said. She was worried and frightened by the colourless, leached-out look of his skin. "Lean back in the chair and take it easy."

"All right," he said, and leant his head against the flat cushion that hung on tapes from the back of the chair. "I am a bit tired, now that I think of it, I suppose."

Betony lifted his booted feet and put the stool underneath them. She fetched a blanket and spread it over him, up to the chin.

"Sleep if you can. You'll be better for it. Linn and your baby are in good hands."

"We're going to call him Robert, you know, after Bob Newers, my mate in the Army. We was going to ask if you'd be his godmother."

"I'd be cross if you asked anyone else!"

Betony went about the kitchen; turned the napkins airing on a string above the fire; eased the kettle out on its bracket; set the teapot on the hob to warm. The lamp on the table was burning crooked. She went and turned the wick down low. Then she took up scissors and an old newspaper and sat down with them in her lap. She began making spills, cutting and folding carefully, making hardly any noise.

"I know what you're doing," Tom said. "You're making spills."

"Yes," she said, "I noticed the jar was almost empty."

"That was always a favourite job of yours, even when you was a little girl. You wouldn't let nobody else make them. Nobody else done a proper job."

He could picture her plainly at her childhood task and somehow the thought of it made him smile. Sitting back in his chair, wrapped in his blanket, he had the heat of the fire in his face, could hear the small sounds it made, and could smell the sweet smell of old mossy applewood burning on it. But slowly the world was slipping away. The picture inside his mind was fading. His blind eyes were closing of their own accord. And because he was really very tired, death came to him disguised as sleep, so that when he gave himself up to it he was still smiling.

"Michael's not here," Mrs Andrews said. "He motored up to London this morning and is staying the night with Major Thomas. Tomorrow he sails for South Africa."

"How long for?" Betony asked.

"He may decide to stay for good. If he does I shall probably go out and join him there. But should he decide to return to England he would prefer not to see you again. That was the message he asked me to give you."

"Yes. I see. In that case I think I'd better leave this with you." Betony took the ring from her finger and placed it on the hall table. "I came as soon as I could," she said, "but it seems I'm too late."

"It wouldn't have made a scrap of difference however soon you had come. He wouldn't have seen you."

"I'm sorry he feels so bitterly."

"*Are* you sorry? – I very much doubt it, Betony. You never really loved Michael. I always thought that, from the very first." Mrs Andrews was unyielding. "You could never have done such a thing," she said, "if you'd really loved him."

Armistice Day was cold and sunless. A bitter wind blew in the churchyard yews and birches, and a few dry snowflakes fell on the people below. The war memorial, cut from a piece of Springs Hill granite, was a tall Celtic cross surmounting a rough-hewn pedestal, and stood inside the main gateway. Huntlip had given thirty-six lives. The names were cut on three sides of the stone. Some were repeated twice or three times. Hayward. Izzard. Mustoe. Wilkes.

"Thirty-six young men," the vicar said, at the end of his address, "whose courage and sacrifice will live forever."

People stood very still, during the two minutes' silence, and their heads were bowed. The silence would last in many hearts. But heads were raised again during the singing of the hymn, and the frail human voices rose defiantly round the cross, strong because they sang together. The people, singing, all looked up, and the cold wind dried the tears on their faces.

Afterwards, walking home through the village, Dicky said: "Tom's name should be on that stone by rights, along with the others."

"Yes, perhaps so," Betony said.

She and Dicky walked with their father. The rest of the family came behind. Jesse was staring straight ahead. He found it difficult to speak.

"No 'perhaps' about it. Dicky's right. Tom gave his life for King and Country, just the same as William and Roger."

Betony took her father's arm.

The following day, she spent three hours at Chepsworth Park, where all the invalid veterans wore sprigs of greenery in their coats, remembering their dead comrades. There were many "helpers" there that day: every wheelchair case had been taken for an outing through the park, all the bedridden men had someone to talk to, and several ladies had banded together to put on a concert in the evening.

"Oh, we've got floods of helpers at the moment!" the superintendant said dryly to Betony. "Armistice Day has made them remember, certainly. But it'll fall off by the end of the week and then we'll be left short-handed as always."

"Perhaps it would help," Betony said, "if I came more often."

Afterwards, on her way through Chepsworth, she stopped to look at the new memorial standing in the cathedral grounds. It was the figure of a private soldier, bareheaded save for a bandage, and he stood with his rifle in front of him, the butt on the ground, the barrel clasped between his hands, staring at the ground as though bowed down with weariness. All around the monument, the steps were strewn with laurel wreaths.

As Betony left the cathedral precincts, a column of unemployed men passed by, each with a placard on his chest and back. "Hundreds more where we come from!" "We take charity but what we want is work." "Old soldiers never die, they only fade away – from starvation!" And one man, seeing Betony coming away from the war memorial, called out to her: "The dead are remembered all right! It's us live ones that get forgotten!"

Sipping a glass of Madeira wine in the vicarage drawing-room, Betony could easily guess why the vicar, Mr Wisdom, had summoned her there. Miss Emily Likeness, headmistress of Huntlip school for forty-three and a half years, was retiring at Christmas, reluctantly, due to a general decline in health.

"Am I correct," the vicar asked, "in thinking you will not be marrying Captain Andrews after all?"

"Quite correct," Betony said.

"I am very sorry, Betony, that it has worked out so sadly for you."

"Thank you, vicar. You're very kind."

"I was wondering whether, in view of your changed circumstances, you'd consider taking over from Miss Likeness as headmistress of the village school. I can think of no one more suitable. Miss Likeness herself hopes you'll agree. But, of course, you needn't give your answer tonight. You will probably wish to think it over."

"Yes, I will," Betony said, "but I think the answer will probably be yes."

As she was leaving, the vicar said: "There's a rumour in the village that Tilly Preston's been seen in Warwick. Is it true, d'you suppose?"

"Yes. It's true. Jeremy Rye saw her there, serving in the bar of a public house. She's been living there for some time as the wife of the landlord."

"Why did she never come forward, then? Surely she must have seen the posters?"

"Jeremy Rye asked her that. She claimed she knew nothing at all about it."

"I never doubted that your foster-brother was innocent."

"Neither did I," Betony said.

Her sister Janie had been ill with 'flu. She was now recovering, sitting up in bed, eating the grapes Betony had brought her.

"Have you heard from Michael?"

"No, not a word."

"Mother tells me there'll be no wedding but surely – "

"Yes. That's right. Michael's gone abroad. He doesn't want to see me again."

"Oh, Betony! Are you sure?"

"Don't be upset. I'm not. I feel, somehow, that it wasn't really meant to happen."

"But what will you *do*?" Janie asked. She could not imagine her own life without her husband and her three children. She could not imagine such emptiness. "Whatever will you *do*?"

Betony smiled. She thought of the school, where she would soon be mistress-in-charge, with over a hundred small children in her care. She thought of the invalid veteran soldiers needing help at Chepsworth Park, and she thought of the grey-faced men she had seen walking the streets because they had no work to go to. She thought, too, of Linn Mercybright and her fatherless baby.

"There's always plenty to do, Janie. It's only a question of where to begin."